"NO, JORDAN. IT WOULD BE HELL FOR BOTH OF US."

To be the wife of Jordan di Mario, to work beside him, watching each new masterpiece take shape under his gifted fingers, to sleep in his arms each night.... It would be sheer bliss, for as long as Gemma did what he wanted.

"I left Colorado for many reasons," Gemma said, "but mainly it was to get away from a man who, although he loved me, thought he knew how to run my life. I know damn well you don't love me, and you're a hundred times more ruthless than Dave could ever be. If you force me to marry you, I'll hate it. I'll hate you."

Jordan's hands framed her face. "What you really hate," he said, "is being a woman. And I'll have to see if I can change that...."

LYNDA WARD

**is also the author of
SUPERROMANCE #3**

THE MUSIC OF PASSION

Marriage had left Megan emotionally shattered—her faith in men destroyed as her husband, Erich, had destroyed himself.

Now, years after Erich's death, his aristocratic brother, Kurt summoned her to Austria. Two shocks awaited here there: a valuable inheritance, and a man to rekindle flames and feelings she'd thought were buried with her husband.

Overwhelmed by Kurt's seductive, destructive charm, Megan fell in love with him. But his love brought a heritage of hatred and deceit—a heritage that threatened her happiness and her life.

LYNDA WARD

THE TOUCH OF PASSION

A SUPERROMANCE FROM
WORLDWIDE

TORONTO · NEW YORK · LOS ANGELES · LONDON

For Larry, for always.

Published September 1982

First printing July 1982

ISBN 0-373-70033-4

CHAPTER ONE

THE DUST LAY OVER EVERYTHING, pervasive, perpetual, giving a patina of great age even to the bright new needles of the pine trees and the shiny blue Fiat parked beneath. Idly Gemma etched delicate designs on the hood of the car with her fingernails, observing with pleasure the contrast between the gleam of revealed paint and the mat gray powder surrounding it. She trailed one finger through the gritty dust and rubbed it against her thumb, lifting her hand to her face to sniff the dust, taste it. Marble dust. *Pietra santa*, holy stone. Detritus of the very rocks over which Michelangelo himself walked centuries before, picking his way carefully in the hot Tuscan light as he searched for the one slab of marble whose color and texture revealed to his artist's eye the masterpiece concealed within.

Gemma dipped her fingers into the dust again and with great sweeping strokes scrawled, "ALL MEN ARE BASTARDS!" on the hood of the Fiat.

She stared at the crude words and winced, disgusted with herself. She was being incredibly infantile, as childish as those students who had sneaked into her classroom to scribble obscenities across the blackboard, mindless epithets gouged into the slate so hard that crumbs of chalk adhered to the board even after she erased it. With her palm she quickly rubbed the offensive declaration off the car.

From a few yards away Caroline called irritably, "Gemma, are you going to fetch the basket, or aren't you? We're waiting!"

"Sorry," Gemma murmured, blinking behind her large round-lensed sunglasses. She wiped her hands on her jeans and brushed back the short silver gilt tendril that had worked loose over her forehead, poking it securely beneath the dark blue bandanna covering her smooth boyish hair. She opened the car door and fished in the space behind the seat for the large wicker hamper Signora Ricci had packed that morning. As she hefted the basket, she wondered if the *signora* had thoughtfully included a few chunks of marble along with the rest of the lunch, sort of a unique antipasto for her mad American guest who seemed so obsessed with the rocks. If not, then the good woman had provided what felt like food enough to feed an entire crew of quarrymen, let alone two female tourists and the *signora*'s teenage son.

Without warning, Franco appeared at Gemma's side, crowding her against the Fiat. *"Permesso,"* he breathed insinuatingly, twitching his spotty mustache as he reached for the picnic basket.

Gemma said stiffly, *"Grazie,"* and she tried not to flinch when Franco's hands fumbled a little more than absolutely necessary in shifting the weight from her arm to his. As she recoiled quickly, a puzzled expression flickered in the boy's liquid black eyes. After a brief hesitation he shrugged lightly and lugged the hamper over to the blanket Caroline had spread beneath the sheltering branches of the ancient pine trees.

"We'd better eat in a hurry before that cruddy dust gets into the food," Caroline grumbled. Gemma noted with wry amusement that the girl had installed herself firmly in the center of the blanket to insure that Franco had no choice but to sit next to her. She had been pouting ever since the trio had left the *pensione* that morning. Franco had insisted on Gemma's taking the passenger seat in the Fiat, leaving Caroline to squeeze her plump body into the third seat of what was essentially a two-seater automobile. Gemma was sure that her young friend was upset less about her discomfort than she was about eighteen-year-old Franco's mystifying preference for Gemma, a woman six years his senior. And when Gemma showed more interest in the hunks of stone lying along the roadside, dropped off by the lumbering quarry trucks, than she did in the melting glances being cast her way by her young guide, poor Caroline's already fragile self-esteem had taken another nose dive.

Gemma observed the way the boy hovered impatiently, waiting for her to settle so that he could position himself as close to her as possible. Behind him the girl on the blanket looked up at Gemma with mute appeal, and Gemma made a quick decision. Trying to sound as firm as her naturally husky alto voice would permit, she said briskly, "Franco, you sit down and help Caroline unpack the lunch. I want to move around a bit after being in the car so long."

"But Signorina Culver—"

"Franco, I said *sit*!" As the boy slowly sank down

beside Caroline, Gemma thought dryly, *my school-teacher voice, it never fails... well, hardly ever.* She spun on her heel and stalked past the car, her sandaled feet crushing the thick mat of pine needles scattered on the ground, spreading their pungent perfume on the somnolent breeze. For just a second she closed her eyes and imagined she was home in the Rockies, breathing the thin bright evergreen-scented air of the mountains. But no, even with her eyes closed, it was impossible to maintain the illusion. The air of Colorado had never had that winy, almost viscous quality that made breathing in Italy so intoxicating; nor, of course, was there ever the underlying salt tang of the sea only a few kilometers away. Once again the thought occurred to her that she was being melodramatic, running off like this. "Overreacting in typical female fashion," her father had phrased it. She looked at her naked left hand, at the slight strip of telltale white on her ring finger. It wouldn't take much to return Dave's discreet diamond solitaire to the place where it had rested for the past year. Hah, she thought, that wouldn't take anything more than an admission that she was wrong, the men were right, that she should have let them handle things their way....

Gemma pulled off her sunglasses and rubbed the bridge of her nose, dislodging flecks of dust that had settled onto her long dark lashes. In the far distance she could hear a piercing whistle echo on the foothills, then seconds later a rumble so low it was almost subliminal started and grew like the accelerating roar of a locomotive, as dynamite loosened a sixty-ton chunk of gleaming white crystalline marble from the mountain that had held it captive for aeons. A few more seconds and the countryside was quiet again. Gemma lifted her gray eyes to the trees and wondered how soon it would be before those pines and evergreen oaks were sprinkled with the airborne debris of this latest upheaval. Funny, but when she picked up her plane tickets, the travel agent had carefully neglected to mention that whenever there was blasting in the quarries, marble dust coated the vicinity for miles around.

Not that she would have paid much heed if he had told her, for just at that moment Italy had beckoned her like a siren, a mystic and welcoming land, where for a few fleeting weeks she would be safe, and among her own kind: people of different nationalities and backgrounds, of course, but still, people who would understand her desire for freedom, her artistic spirit; people whose eyes would not glaze with that bored disinterest, familiar to her since childhood, if she mentioned the names of sculptors like Moore or Noguchi or di Mario. When Marsha Somerville, the mother of one of Gemma's students, asked Gemma if she would accompany seventeen-year-old Caroline on her graduation trip to Europe, she had no doubt thought that she was offering a chance to escape the gossips and rumormongers momentarily. She could not have understood the deeper significance this trip held for Gemma.

Even Dave hadn't understood. Dave, who supposedly knew Gemma better than anyone. "Italy?" he had echoed with the same bemused intonation he might have given to "Borneo" or "Nepal." When he came to her apartment two nights before her depar-

ture, he had run his hand through his sandy hair as he
stared at her pristine new passport with the photo
that delineated brutally Gemma's pale heart-shaped
face, the wide cheekbones and small mouth drooping
with a malaise far deeper than anyone suspected.
"Why the sudden interest in Italy? You aren't still
sulking, are you?"

"No, Dave," Gemma had said quietly, running a
pencil down the checklist she had made of things to
do before leaving. "I'm not sulking. I just have to get
away for a while."

Dave said, "Poor baby, you should have listened
to me. I told you how it would be. If you had let your
father and brothers and me handle things, we could
have made sure that little creep never bothered you
again. But no, you had to file assault charges; he is
the son of the director of the school, Gemma. So
much unpleasantness, and for what? He gets his
wrists slapped, and you lose your job."

"I did what I thought was right, Dave. I've told
you that before. Women have to fight against that
sort of harassment. I was lucky. I got away from him
with a few bruises, but what if someone else isn't so
lucky?"

Dave shook his head indulgently. "Oh, Gemma,
Gemma, you're so impetuous. I guess that's why I
love you. Look, honey, now that you've had time to
cool off, I want you to reconsider about breaking
our engagement. I know I said a lot of things I
shouldn't, and I'm sorry. But you have to understand, it was damned embarrassing having police
and reporters pry into the intimate details of our
relationship."

"They did it to me, too, you know," Gemma pointed out.

Dave nodded, his face shadowed. "Yeah. I guess it's been rough on everyone." After a moment he brightened. "Tell you what, love, let's get married right away, by whatever justice of the peace is handy. I don't think a big wedding would be a good idea now, anyway. After that, if you really want to see Italy, we'll go there for our honeymoon. Venice, maybe. How would you like that? Think of it, darling, just you and me in a gondola. . . ."

He pulled her into his arms and began kissing her hotly, his hands slipping under her shirt. Before she could stop him, he began fondling her. Then with a tremor of distaste she managed to squirm away.

"Stop it," she said shakily, fumbling as she straightened her shirt, "I don't want to marry you. It wouldn't work. I thought it would, but now— I just have to be alone for a while, don't you see?"

He snorted, "Alone? With that chubby Somerville brat in tow? Some vacation that'll be."

Gemma said, "You're wrong about Caroline. She's a sweet girl once you get to know her. It's going to be fun."

Dave regarded her grimly. Taking a deep breath, he squared his stocky shoulders and declared, "Gemma, I'm not going to take no for an answer. There's been too much between you and me for us to break up now. I'll let you run off to Italy for a few weeks and get your head together, but when you come back, you and I are going to be married. By then everyone will have forgotten about the incident at the school, anyway. We should have married years ago, when we first met. I know your father wanted us to. He told me I was just the kind of man to keep you in line...."

Gemma winced. "Goodbye, Dave," she'd said flatly, turning away. After a few seconds she'd heard the front door slam.

Now, as Gemma glanced over her shoulder at Caroline, who was grumpily setting out the picnic provisions while she tried vainly to attract Franco's attention, she wondered if she hadn't been overly optimistic when she'd said the trip would be fun. In the three short days since their plane had landed in Genoa, Gemma had already discovered that Caroline was apparently determined to oppose every suggestion Gemma might make. No, the girl didn't want to look at musty old cathedrals and churches, not even Santo Stefano where Columbus was baptized. She'd had enough history in school to last a lifetime. No, she didn't want to take time to check out the artists' colony at Portofino when she could instead be baking like thousands of other well-oiled tourists jammed onto the beaches of the Italian Riviera. And most of all, no, she didn't want to waste her vacation in some dusty jerkwater town no one ever heard of, vegetating while Gemma beat on rocks with a mallet and chisel.

Gemma sighed. She had already been thinking about leaving Golden, her hometown fifteen miles west of Denver, when Marsha Somerville asked if she would consider chaperoning Caroline's trip to Italy. An aunt was supposed to go, but unfortunately she had broken her ankle at the last minute, and Marsha was desperate for someone to accompany her daughter. Gemma agreed, but only on the condition that she be allowed to spend most of her time in Pietrasanta, a small town in the Apennine foothills that was Mecca for sculptors from all over the world. Marsha, who greatly admired the clay statuettes Gemma sometimes sold on consignment in her pottery shop, accepted the change of plans—and so, presumably, had Caroline. But the drive southward from Genoa in the rented Fiat, while not far in miles, had seemed endless to Gemma. She had to cope not only with bewildering Italian traffic—donkey carts on the highway, for God's sake—but also with her young companion's constant griping. Caroline had grumbled continually, hating everything, until at long last they reached the boardinghouse on the outskirts of Pietrasanta, and she met Franco Ricci, the landlady's son.

Replacing her sunglasses, Gemma watched the teenagers with an ironic smile. It would have been asking too much of a fickle Providence, she supposed, to hope that the *signora*'s adolescent lothario might be attracted to Caroline's well-rounded charms. The girl was really rather pretty with her masses of curly light brown hair, and she could be very sweet when she wasn't hiding her lack of self-confidence behind a mask of brash aggression. But no, from the moment the car shuddered to a halt in the courtyard of the Ricci's three-story stucco house with the red tile roof, young Franco had pursued Gemma with a determination she found as bewildering as it was embarrassing.

Gemma had never understood what men saw in her. Dave—well, Dave loved her. But other men, and that horrible boy at the school with his groping hands and vile insinuations... it seemed incomprehensible that they could be aroused by her slight boyish figure, her narrow hips and small breasts. She didn't find her face particularly beautiful—the nose was too short, the mouth too small—and she had always regarded her features as rather colorless. Her very straight blond hair was so light it was almost silver, a lingering reminder of her north European heritage, and she kept it cropped in a short no-nonsense cut as deliberately sexless as the jeans and chambray work shirts she usually wore. Her complexion was also very fair, but fortunately her creamy skin had always been remarkably resistant to the sun, even in the rarefied atmosphere of the Rockies. Gemma thought that her eyes were her best feature, wide and long lashed, deep gray with flecks of blue like the sky peeping through storm clouds. Whenever possible she kept them obscured behind dark sunglasses.

Or perhaps it was Gemma's voice that some men found appealing. During the final difficult weeks of the semester, while she tried to conduct her classes as usual until her contract expired, she had overheard some students mimicking her, and she had been shocked at how provocative and sensual the teenagers perceived her voice to be. When she was nine, not long after her mother's death, Gemma had fallen victim to streptococci and nervous strain, contracting a throat infection so severe it left her mute for two months. When her voice finally returned, it retained a low, permanently husky timbre ill-suited to her bony elfin body. Her big brothers promptly dubbed her ''Frog,'' but their affectionate teasing changed to uneasy concern when they realized that what had sounded merely piquant in a child might seem something else entirely in a young woman. They advised her to be quiet in the presence of strange men.

Now, of course, she had no choice but to speak. Her Italian, while strictly Berlitz quality, was far superior to Caroline's. Maybe, Gemma decided with a grimace, Franco had misinterpreted her throaty request for a tour guide as some kind of come-on.

Reluctant to join the others, Gemma slowly wandered along the side of the road, away from the clearing. Here the ground was littered with scraps of marble dropped by the trucks, some in chunks of five and ten pounds. Gemma marveled that the stone that would have been so precious and expensive in Colorado was here available for the taking. She stooped to pick up one piece that caught her eye, an irregular rectangle that suggested to her the figure of a reclining woman, and she wondered whether she dared ask Franco to put it in the trunk of the Fiat, along with all the other pieces she had already collected that day. The back springs of the little blue car were sagging dangerously. God alone knew how she was going to get them back home.

Gemma chuckled as it occurred to her that the two teenagers probably thought she was *pazza*, crazy. She knew that she could never make them understand the lure of the stone, the way the shapes inside it called to her to free them. When Gemma ran her fingers over the smooth planes of the marble, she felt the way she had felt when she was eleven, and her brother Bob's wife, who was expecting her first baby, had invited Gemma to lay her hand on her rounded belly and feel the movement of the child within. When the tiny limbs pressed against her fingers, Gemma jerked away as if burned, stunned by the miracle of creation and at the same time wondering if the child resented being imprisoned that way.

She had another memory, even farther back, that haunted her, of a time when her father had put a wedge-shaped piece of ore into her hands and said with a smile, "Now, sweetheart, see if you can tell daddy what this is."

Under the intent gaze of her mother and those godlike creatures, her three older brothers, Gemma had carefully considered the crumbly black rock with its streak of pink quartz and the flakes of mica that shone silver gold like her mother's hair. Finally she returned the ore to her father and said triumphantly, "Pirates."

There was a murmur of approval from her brothers, and her father hugged her and crowed with delight, "Very good, Gemma, I knew you could do it!" Then he added, "But sweetheart, the word is 'pyrites,' not 'pirates.' "

Gemma had shaken her fair head and insisted, "No, daddy, it's 'pirates.' The rock looks like a pirate ship. See, here's the bow, and that's the deck where the captain stands, and these sparkles are the treasure."

Gemma could still remember the embarrassed silence that fell over her family following her pronouncement. Her mother patted her gently on the head as one of her brothers drawled, "Well, after all, dad, she's just a girl...."

"*Signorina*," Franco called, "don't wander away. The lunch is ready!"

Reluctantly Gemma retraced her footsteps to the blanket under the pine. When Caroline spotted the piece of marble in Gemma's hand, she groaned, "Oh, good grief, not another one!" Franco didn't say anything, but his expression echoed Caroline's.

Gemma said, "Give me the car keys, please, Franco, and I'll put this in the trunk."

The boy fished the keys from the pocket of his tight flashy trousers and handed them to Gemma. "*Signorina*," he ventured hesitantly, obviously hating to contradict the woman he was pursuing, "I do not think it would be wise to put any more weight in the car. A Fiat is a small automobile, unsuited for such a load. Already it is difficult to handle."

"Just this last one," Gemma said, "I promise. And if it bothers you, I'll be happy to drive for the rest of the day. I can—"

"No!" Franco protested indignantly, his olive skin flushing under the tan. "I did not mean that I couldn't control the car, only that I...."

Gemma turned away, chuckling. That morning she had learned that no self-respecting Italian male would even consider being chauffeured by a woman. The very idea was an affront to his machismo. Thus Gemma, who had been competent enough to rent the Fiat in Genoa and drive all the way down the Ligurian coast to Pietrasanta, found herself riding as passenger in her own car, driven by an eighteen-year-old boy who apparently had sworn an oath never to relinquish the right-of-way, even to huge stone-laden trucks on narrow twisting mountain roads. Gradually she had relaxed as she realized that while Franco did seem to drive with excessive panache, her car nevertheless remained unscathed. Perhaps, Gemma decided judiciously, Italians just had a different concept of driving.

After easing the rock into the last available space in the trunk, Gemma closed the lid and made her way back to the blanket, where Caroline had spread out olives and pickled mushrooms, long sausages, their casings black and shriveled, and round loaves of crisp Italian bread. Franco was using a knife to extract from a large wicker-covered bottle of Chianti the cork that had apparently crumbled when he tried to pull it out. Gemma dropped gracefully to the edge of the blanket farthest from him, an action that earned a swift smile of gratitude from Caroline. Gemma wasn't hungry, and she sat with her knees drawn up under her chin, gazing at the landscape and nibbling on a piece of pepperoni, while the two teenagers demolished the rest of the food with youthful enthusiasm. When the spicy meat made Gemma thirsty, she declined the Chianti in favor of *acqua minerale*. Immediately Franco protested. He apologized volubly for the bits of cork floating on the surface of the bright red wine, he castigated himself for polluting it, making it unfit for the *signorina*'s pleasure, and he assured her that he could pour her another glass free of debris, as pure as any mountain stream. Gemma interrupted his oration. No, it wasn't the cork, she said, she wasn't that fastidious. She simply didn't want any wine. In this heat it would give her a headache.

Beside her, Caroline scowled at the speckled surface of the liquid in her own glass, and with a defiant toss of her head she gulped it all down. "Take it easy, Caro," Gemma murmured, but the girl ignored her and held out her glass for more. With an indifferent shrug Franco refilled it.

Gemma watched uncomfortably. She could feel the frustration and tension building between her companions as they chased around in tantalizing pursuit like figures on a Greek vase: Caroline pursuing Franco pursuing Gemma pursuing...whom? There had to be at least one more person to give symmetry to the design, someone Gemma chased after. Automatically she looked for the ring gracing her left hand, but it wasn't there anymore. She had ripped it off her finger and flung it at Dave.

Dave. Was Dave the fourth figure on the Greek vase she visualized, the unknown image she pursued? Even as her mind framed the question, Gemma slowly shook her head in silent denial. All the running had been on his side. He was a friend of her brother Tom—they were both instructors at the Colorado School of Mines—and he had spotted Gemma the summer she returned to Golden from her three years of exile on the plains of Kansas. He told her later that she had seemed a pale slip of a girl, cool and quiet, as delicate and wary as a luna moth. When she shied from his first advances, he noticed her reaction with surprise, finally attributing it to her age, seventeen, and those years she had spent in the convent school. He changed his strategy and began to treat her simply as Tom's little sister. Under the watchful eyes of Gemma's father and brothers, Dave began escorting

her to church functions or football games at the
University of Colorado, where Gemma enrolled as a
freshman art major. Gemma liked Dave, and almost
unconsciously she started to use him as a shield
against other men. She knew that he dated other
women, and she assumed that he slept with some of
them—after all, he was in his twenties—but to Gemma he was always friendly and undemanding, a surrogate big brother to fill the void left when her other
brothers married and made lives of their own. When,
after years of this restrained relationship, Dave asked
her to marry him, Gemma hesitated only briefly
before accepting his proposal. She knew she wasn't
in love with him, but they got along well, her family
liked him, and someday there'd be the shared joy of
children. And despite Gemma's trepidations, she
decided that that ought to be enough.

When it became clear that that would *not* be
enough for Dave, she tried to make herself fall in
love with him. . .but that was something she didn't
want to think about.

Cold liquid sloshed onto Gemma's slim denim-clad
legs, and she looked up to see that the hand holding
her almost full glass of mineral water was trembling.
Quickly she gulped down the rest of it, grimacing at
the faintly bitter metallic taste. She hated mineral
water, but in this heat it was still preferable to wine.
She glanced at the Chianti bottle. To her dismay she
saw that it now lay on its side amid the remains of the
picnic, completely empty. She looked at Caroline and
Franco, who both seemed unnaturally still. The girl
was staring with glassy-eyed hunger at the boy beside
her, her gaze riveted to the gold religious medal that

glinted in the tangle of dark hair revealed by his open shirt. Franco in turn was ignoring her as he watched Gemma sullenly through half-closed eyes. Gemma gritted her teeth and swore silently. Her jolly little tour of the countryside had turned into a disaster, and now it was up to her to get two drunken teen-agers safely back to the *pensione* before something regrettable happened.

With outward calm she began to gather up the crumbs and scraps of food, replacing them neatly into Signora Ricci's picnic hamper along with the dirty plates and the empty wine bottle. In her firmest schoolteacher voice she ordered the others to help her. She hoped that they were both still so fresh from the classroom that they would react instinctively to that tone of command, and after a moment when Gemma held her breath, Caroline, who of course had been one of her students, did begin to move slug-gishly. The girl rose on unsteady legs and smiled weakly, brushing her thick brown hair out of her eyes as she picked up the basket. She trudged off to the Fiat, and Gemma glanced at Franco, who still re-clined on the blanket. She said gently, "Franco, would you please fold the blanket and put it away?"

He blinked. "You are ready to leave so soon?"

"No," Gemma said, "I thought we might all walk around a bit. If we climb to the top of this hill, will we be able to see the sea?"

He shrugged. "Maybe. But it is too hot now to do much walking. You should relax, *fare la siesta*."

"No," Gemma said firmly. "I want to move around."

"But, *signorina*...."

Caroline returned from the car. She said thickly, "Oh, leave her alone, Franco. Gemma always wants to go on walks, look at things. You and I can stay here and...and enjoy the shade while she tries to get sunstroke."

Gemma caught a hint of desperation in Caroline's slurred words. What the hell, she thought, it would probably be easier just to let them sleep it off. She said, "That's a good idea, Caro. There's no need for you two to come if you don't want to. I won't go far away." Before Franco could protest again, Gemma ducked beneath the trees and into the underbrush, plunging across a shallow gully to reach the hill that rose smoothly on the other side.

She began her ascent fiercely, loping along the shallow incline through the trees and the *macchia* until she slipped on a disintegrating pinecone, and her aching ankle reminded her forcibly that her flimsy sandals were not hiking boots. After that she proceeded more slowly, picking her way with care. She wasn't sure why she had been in a hurry, anyway.

At the top of the hill the vegetation died back until there was only one old pine tree like a gnarled sentinel, its branches bent by the prevailing winds from the sea. Gemma heaped up feathery brown needles into a soft cushion at the base of the trunk and sat down, her hands clasped around her legs. Before her the coastal hills receded in an undulating blanket of variegated green until at last they ended at the shore of the vivid blue Ligurian Sea. Southwest on the horizon, shining in the midday glare, lay the great island of Corsica, Napoleon's birthplace, and almost due south, about halfway between Corsica and the

Italian mainland, Gemma could just make out Elba, the much smaller island where the onetime emperor of France went into temporary exile after his abdication.

Gemma sighed. Napoleon's sojourn on Elba had lasted only a few months. She had been in exile in Kansas for three years.

It was unfair, she supposed, to think of those days as a kind of exile, for everyone at the school had been more than kind to her. Gemma had gone there as if to prison, a bewildered fourteen-year-old unsure of the crime she was supposed to have committed. All during the two-day journey to the convent, Gemma had ridden in silence beside her taciturn father, still too cowed by the memory of that horrible scene to question him further. She'd stared out the car window with red-rimmed eyes, certain that at her destination she would find twelve-foot walls and barred windows, pale-faced women in medieval habits who glided soundlessly through grim corridors and never smiled. Instead she had discovered a bright, thoroughly modern school with an excellent curriculum. The teaching staff was composed of eager young nuns, distinguishable from their secular counterparts only by the short scarflike veils some of them wore. Of the several hundred girls in the student body, only a handful actually boarded. Gemma became well acquainted with most of the teachers, but she remained aloof from the other live-in students. With a little effort she might have been reasonably happy there, but she would not make the effort. She hated Kansas; the flat monotonous plains made her agoraphobic. She hated being surrounded by women all the time; she was used to the company of men. She wanted to go back to the Rockies, she wanted to go back to her family, and she couldn't understand why her father wouldn't let her. In every letter she wrote to him she promised to be good.

Once when no one was aware that she was nearby, Gemma eavesdropped as Sister Katharine declared angrily to one of the other teachers that it was criminal the way John Culver had abdicated his responsibilities to his daughter, that in her opinion he had deliberately overreacted to a trivial incident in order to have an excuse to abandon the girl.

Gemma had crept away feeling sick. Abandoned? No, no, her father would never do that. Even now Gemma felt the teacher had judged him too harshly. It was not that he didn't want to raise his daughter; it was simply that he didn't know how. He came from a long line of males, one of five brothers, and he produced three strapping sons of his own. They would follow the proud Culver tradition and work alongside him in the mining industry, no longer with pick and shovel, but as geologists or engineers. He was stunned when, almost ten years after the birth of his youngest son, his delicate blond wife presented him with a daughter as fair and fragile as she was. Once his initial shock passed, John Culver decided that a daughter might be a pleasant novelty, an adoring audience for the men of the family. And she wouldn't be all that much trouble. Her mother would initiate her into the secret rituals of womanhood, and he would buy her frilly party dresses.

But Gemma's beloved mother died when she was nine, and her father was left with the bewildering task of rearing the girl himself. His sons were fully grown by then: Bob was married; Tom was working on his graduate degree in chemistry; and Chris was a sophomore at Denver State and was well on his way to becoming captain of the soccer team. Because the boys had all turned out so well, a credit to the family, John Culver decided to rear Gemma the same way he had his sons. He knew nothing about feminine things, so instead he would teach her all about sports and camping. That way at least she wouldn't feel out of place when he took her brothers on trips into the mountains. They'd worry about the dainty stuff later. If Gemma grew into a tomboy, so what? Jeans were sturdier than dresses, and besides, everyone knew that at about age eighteen, tomboys blossomed into lovely young women who promptly married the boy next door.

It never occurred to him—or perhaps he simply refused to admit it—that long before eighteen most girls reach puberty, develop busts and begin to think about boys in a decidedly womanly way.

In the shade of the pine tree Gemma pulled off the cotton scarf that covered her silvery hair, and she wiped her moist brow with it. She massaged her nape, running her fingers through the short tendrils that curled damply against her neck. When she went to the convent, her hair had been so long that she could sit on it, a flowing mane with the sheen and texture of silk floss. It was drudgery to care for, of course, but she loved her hair. It reminded her of her mother's. Most of the time she had kept it piled high on her head, looped through a leather barrette secured with a wooden pick. Everyone admired it, even the other girls at the school who considered Gemma standoffish and unfriendly. She could still recall the way her roommates had screamed in shock for Sister Katharine the day they walked into the dormitory and discovered Gemma hacking at her hair with a pair of nail scissors. By the time the nun rushed into the room, the deed was done. Gemma sat at the dressing table pale and defiant, and her shorn tresses lay on the floor like shards of sunlight.

On the hillside Gemma stood up, stretching languorously in the sultry perfumed air. She turned her back on the sea and gazed at the green hills that rose in ridges progressively higher until they formed the Apennines, the chain of rugged peaks that ran like a spine down the Italian peninsula. She loved mountains, their majesty and grandeur. At moments of stress her impulse was to flee to high places, searching for peace. She thought sometimes that she might have enjoyed the convent school more if only Kansas hadn't been so *flat*. But Gemma was a child of the Rockies, and almost every day, when from her dormitory window she stared forlornly at the plains sweeping uninterrupted for hundreds of miles, she had found herself quoting that familiar line from Burns: "My heart's in the Highlands, my heart is not here...." When, after graduating with honors, she finally returned to Golden, she vowed she would never leave home again. One day when her father was at work, she even hiked across Lookout Mountain to the shrine of Saint Frances Cabrini, the nineteenth-century Italian woman who became the first American citizen canonized. There, under the benign gaze of the saint, Gemma prayed that she might be always surrounded by mountains and—please, dear Lord—people who loved her. Later, when she thought about Mother Cabrini and considered the way she had devoted her entire life to the poor and suffering, Gemma wondered if her prayers weren't trivial, even selfish. But now as she surveyed the terrain of that good woman's homeland, she thought at last that she might have understood.

For Italy abounded with mountains, from the Matterhorn on the Swiss border—Monte Cervino, the Alitalia stewardess called it when the jet flew by—to Mount Etna on Sicily, with its eternal plume of volcanic smoke. And after all, it was mountains that had summoned Gemma to Italy, those very special mountains between Carrara and Pisa, from whose bosom men had gouged out the holy stone, marble, since before the birth of Christ.

With an eager smile Gemma thought about the chunks of marble waiting for her in the trunk of the Fiat. Somehow she would get them shipped back to Colorado, where she could work on them at her leisure. When the new semester started, if she found any students who showed great promise, she would share the stone with them. But, no, she was forgetting, she no longer had a job; the new semester would begin without her. It was a pity, really. She would have loved to work with marble when she was a student. In college she had modeled with clay, and she had even done some bronze casting on a very small scale, but marble—that was the ultimate, the medium of Michelangelo and Bernini, of Praxiteles and the unknown Greek who'd carved *Winged Victory*.

Somewhere Gemma once read a quote about the

materials sculptors use: "Clay is life, plaster is death, and marble is resurrection." Certainly the desire to work in stone had resurrected her interest in art at a time when she had resigned herself to teaching drawing to reluctant high-school students like Caroline. Not that teaching was an unworthy career, of course, but Gemma had been more or less pushed into it, and she was worried by the thought that she might never know what it was like to be a "real artist." Well, now she had all the time in the world to pursue that ambition, although she had no hopes of supporting herself as a sculptor. At the end of this trip, however long it lasted, she would return to Colorado and find another teaching position. But at least then she would be able to guide her pupils with some authority. She might even be able to tell them, "When I was in Italy, I saw Henry Moore at work," or "I spoke to Jordan di Mario."

Gemma made her way carefully down the hillside. She stepped cautiously to avoid slipping on the mat of leaves and pine needles. As she walked, she laughed ironically at her fantasies. In the summer Pietrasanta was overrun with tourists like herself, aspiring sculptors, all drawn to the marble mountains, and all longing for one chance to see or speak to the masters, as if somehow their greatness might rub off. Probably most of them wouldn't recognize a great artist if they fell over him, although Gemma admitted it would be interesting to see what Jordan di Mario looked like, to find out for herself if his appearance matched the frankly sensual style of his work. When Gemma was a senior at the girls' school, Sister Katharine took her and three other promising art students to Chicago one weekend to see *Privilege*, the new di Mario statue that was upsetting the art world. Some critics dismissed it as "unabashed romanticism," while others compared it to Rodin's *The Kiss*. But whatever the critics said, Gemma had been stunned by the force of her response as she gazed at the representation of a very beautiful, obviously rich and aristocratic woman undressing under the appraising eyes of a handsome but rough peasant in shabby clothes. The female figure was a superb piece of work, but it was the male figure that riveted her, that air of cool confidence transcending social barriers. Somehow the artist had imparted to cold stone a sexual aura that aroused Gemma as she had never yet been aroused by a living man, not even Dave.

When Gemma reached the clearing beside the road, she found Caroline alone on the blanket, asleep. The shade had lifted, and in the bright sun her thick brown hair swirled in a corona around her head, glinting with auburn highlights. In repose she looked very young and vulnerable. Gemma sighed. Caroline was a pretty girl, but she seemed to suffer from a massive inferiority complex, probably because she was always comparing herself with her mother. Marsha Somerville was a tall willowy redhead, the kind of woman who managed to look elegant even in clay-stained smocks. After her divorce she had opened a pottery shop in Heritage Square, the replica of an 1880 frontier town that was located just off the highway between Denver and Golden, and Gemma had worked for her part-time while she attended college. After seven years she knew both the Somervilles rather well. She knew that Caroline thought her mother was the most beautiful woman in the world, and she seemed to resent the fact that in looks she resembled instead her short stocky father. In the vain hope of achieving her ideal, Caroline was forever embarking on dangerous starvation diets that made her jumpy and hollow eyed. Then, each time when the loss of ten pounds failed to alter the color of her hair or increase her height by six inches, Caroline would shift to the other extreme and binge on food until she regained all her weight, plus a few more pounds. Right now she was in one of her "chubby" cycles. If only some nice young man would notice her, Gemma thought sadly, the girl might finally learn that she didn't have to compete with her mother, that she was pretty and desirable as she was. If only Franco would....

But where was Franco now? There was no sign of him in the clearing. He had to be somewhere near. The blue Fiat still waited in dusty splendor on the shoulder of the road, and the keys lay on the blanket where she had dropped them earlier. Gemma started to call Franco's name, but she didn't want to disturb Caroline, who was liable to wake with a hangover.

As Gemma puzzled about what to do, she suddenly heard Franco. She glanced up. The boy was beckoning eagerly from the shade of the trees edging the clearing. "Signorina Culver, *avanti*! There is something I want to show you."

Gemma stared at him. "What is it?" she asked, moving closer.

He grinned. "A surprise. *Per favore, signorina*, please come." His crooked teeth gleamed very white against his swarthy face as he held out his hand.

Gemma hesitated momentarily, impatient with herself. She was becoming paranoid, that was the problem. She had to overcome this lingering fear that any male above the age of twelve was just waiting to leap on her.

Franco seemed to sense her unease. He smiled at her reassuringly. "It's a very beautiful day," he said. "I promise you'll like it."

Slowly Gemma smiled back. Franco was a nice boy. "Okay," she said. She avoided his outstretched hand by tucking her sunglasses into her hip pocket as he led her back into the cool darkness under the trees. She pushed her way through the underbrush where he indicated, and as they walked, she studied his features, trying to see what it was that Caroline found so appealing. He wasn't Gemma's ideal—was anyone, she sometimes wondered—but he was attractive enough. She was struck by the eternalness of the classic Italian face. In one of her art classes in college she had seen a Roman portrait dating back to the time of the Caesars, and the boy in that picture could have been Franco's cousin. They shared the same olive complexion, the same black curls and wide dark eyes, the same incipient aquiline nose. Only the Roman youth's toga distinguished him from his modern-day counterpart. Dressed in tight trousers and a gaudy open-necked shirt, he would have been quite at home riding a motor scooter on the Via Veneto.

Franco halted abruptly. "Here we are," he announced.

Gemma glanced around. The trees were thick, and only occasional splashes of sunlight dappled the ground. "Here we are where?" she asked.

He pointed toward the patch of sky showing between the crowns of two stately pines. "Look," he said, "in that space and just to the right. Can you see it? We had to come here to get the correct angle. The other hilltops block the view from the road."

Gemma stood on tiptoes and craned her neck. When she saw the vista before her, she caught her breath. In the far distance she could just make out the slope of a mountain, rugged and barren except for a few skeletal trees. Beneath those trees gleamed great patches of white, brilliant and blinding in the hot summer sunshine. She turned back to Franco. "Snow?" she asked in bewilderment.

He shook his head. "No, *signorina*, not snow. Marble chips. Men have mined these mountains since before the time of Gesu Cristo, and the tailings cover the ground as far as the eye can see."

Gemma stared again, marveling. "To think that men have come here for thousands of years to find materials for their buildings and statues...."

"I knew you would understand," Franco said with satisfaction, but as he gazed at the mountain, his face twisted into a grimace of frustrated longing that imparted an unexpected maturity to his young features. He continued, "Of course, you look at that hillside and think of artists, but I remember instead the men who cut the marble from the earth. My family has labored here for generations. We have a proud tradition in the industry. My father cut stone, as did his father before him. Someday I shall follow them."

Gemma looked at him curiously. "You say that as if there were some difficulty. You're young and strong. Why can't you work in the quarries now, if that's what you want?"

"It is because I am young that I must wait. New jobs are rare. In my grandfather's day thousands of men processed the marble by hand, but now with modern machinery a few dozen can do the work of hundreds. The men who remain are all old, but they can be replaced only when they retire, and many of them say they will stay in the quarries until they die." He frowned. "That is what my father did. An explosion misfired, and...." He shrugged expressively.

After a long pause Gemma asked, "So, what do you do now?"

"I help my mother run the *pensione* in the summer when the tourists are here, then in the winter I look for odd jobs. It is not always easy to find work."

Gemma said, "Don't many young Italians go to other Common Market countries these days to work in the factories?"

Franco nodded. "*Si.* I went to West Germany a few months myself. I built automobiles. The pay was good, but my mother did not like me to be so far away, so after a while I came home again. Now I do whatever I can to occupy my time while I wait for a job. The money isn't important. Working in the quarries is all that matters."

Gemma smiled faintly, thinking of her own family's devotion to mining. She gazed again at the mountain that reflected the sunlight like summer snow. Franco and her father would have been soul mates. Neither of them would see the mountain's in-

trinsic beauty; they would think of it only as tons
of raw material to be moved and processed. She
sighed, "It's so very lovely."

"Like you," Franco said huskily.

Gemma jerked her head around. "What?" she demanded, alert to his abrupt change of mood.

He said fervently, "You are beautiful, *bellissima*."
He reached out eager fingers to stroke her face. "So
slim, so fair, with hair like spun silver."

Gemma blinked, suddenly aware of how alone
they were. "Really, Franco," she laughed as she
backed away slightly, "don't you think you ought to
save that Latin charm for Caroline?"

Franco snorted dismissively, "Caroline is a child."

Gemma pointed out reasonably, "She's not much
younger than you are."

Even in the deep shade she could see Franco's dark
eyes flare as he stepped toward her. "I am not a
child," he declared, reaching for her again. "When I
was in Germany, I—"

Gemma jerked out of his range, and as she did, she
slipped on the decaying vegetation underfoot. One of
her ankles twisted painfully when a flimsy sandal
strap broke, and her temper flamed. As she dropped
onto one knee to survey the damage, her voice shook
with irritation. She snapped, "How dare you! Just
because you cut a swath through the Fräuleins, it
doesn't mean that I—"

The boy stared at her, abashed and confused, and
his obvious embarrassment made him look so incredibly young that Gemma's expression softened
despite her still-simmering anger. She stood up again,
making her tone deliberately maternal as she said, "I

have no interest at all in a summer romance, Franco. If you want to continue as tour guide for Caroline and me, I'd be delighted. You're a very good guide, and you know the area well. But we'll only get along if you never touch me again, do you understand?''

After a moment Franco said, "I understand." He regarded Gemma uneasily, all signs of incipient passion vanished from his youthful features. "Signorina Culver," he ventured hesitantly after another pause, "you...you won't tell my mother about what I said about—when I was in Germany, will you? *Mamma*, she thinks I am still...."

Suddenly Gemma knew she was safe with the boy. As she relaxed, she smiled kindly. "No, Franco, I won't tell her."

"Grazie, signorina."

They made their way back to the clearing slowly on account of Gemma's sandal, and by the time they broke out of the trees and crossed the shallow ditch, they were laughing easily, like old friends.

Gemma's laughter died when she saw Caroline standing slumped against the Fiat. The girl clutched the car keys nervously in one fist while she scrubbed at her tearstained face with the other. When she heard the other two, she jerked upright and cried, "Gemma, where have you been? I've been so worried! I thought...I thought...." Her voice trailed off in a strangled sob.

"Calm down, Caro," Gemma soothed, trying to stride toward her and stumbling. Grumbling irritably, she bent down to readjust her shoe. "We just went for a walk. You were asleep and...."

Caroline scowled, noticing the boy for the first

time. Her eyes widened at the way he caught Gemma's arm when she faltered. "You were in the woods—you and Franco—together?" Her words slurred, and Gemma wondered if she was still feeling the effects of the wine.

"I told you," Gemma insisted brightly, "we just went for a walk. There was something Franco wanted to show me."

Caroline sneered, "Oh, I'll just bet there was!"

"*Signorina*—" Franco interposed.

"Oh, shut up, Franco!" Caroline wailed, her voice rising hysterically. "You couldn't wait to get her alone. All day long you've been making eyes at her. I'll bet the two of you planned this. You deliberately got me to drink that—"

Gemma snapped, "Don't be an idiot, Caroline. I'm not interested in Franco!"

"That's just it: you don't have to be interested! You're just like my mother. Men fall for you the moment they see you, and you don't even *care*!" She flung open the car door and jumped into the driver's seat. "Well, I'm not going to waste my summer watching you steal guys from me. I'll go somewhere on my own, somewhere I can—" She switched on the ignition.

"Caroline!" Gemma shrieked, but her words were drowned by the cough of the little car's engine as it sputtered to life. Gemma jumped for the Fiat, but her sandal came completely loose and she tripped, sprawling headlong in the dust. She watched helplessly as Caroline revved the motor. The back wheels spun for a second on the soft dirt of the shoulder, then the weight of the rocks in the trunk gave the added traction necessary, and the little blue car skidded erratically into the center of the roadway.

"Franco, stop her!" Gemma yelled as she picked herself up off the ground. "Don't let her...."

But Franco didn't hear Gemma. He was deaf to everything but a new sound, the high-pitched roar of a powerful engine approaching rapidly. He stood transfixed, his sallow face ashen, as he watched a flame-colored Ferrari crest the hill with breathtaking speed. Now Gemma saw it, too, and she gasped in impotent terror as the sports car rocketed around the long blind curve, heading straight for Caroline.

CHAPTER TWO

GEMMA SCREAMED, but her cries were drowned out by the squeal of brakes and the double impact as the Ferrari first crashed against the Fiat and then skidded into a tree. Weighted by the rocks in its trunk, the small blue car whipped around like a slingshot before it slid sideways off the road, upending in the ditch that ran along the edge of the clearing.

Gemma stood mesmerized, stunned. The acrid tang of burned rubber bit at her nostrils, wafting up from the wide strips of black that arced across the pavement, and shattered glass sparkled in cruel array, glittering like coins flung by some Oriental despot. Gemma tried to breathe, but no air would enter her paralyzed lungs.

"Madonna!" Franco whispered fervently at her side, and the sound of his young frightened voice broke Gemma's trance. She kicked off her hobbling sandals and sprinted to the Fiat, heedless of the glass cutting her bare feet. As she ran, she shouted for Franco to help the other driver.

When Gemma reached the smaller car, tilted crazily in the ditch, she found Caroline slumped unconscious across the seat, half lying on the passenger door, which was buried in soft dirt. Gemma could not see any signs of blood on the girl, but already a vicious bruise purpled deeply across her forehead, and the windshield was a telltale spiderweb of cracks radiating from the point where she must have struck it. "Caroline!" Gemma yelled so hoarsely that she hurt her throat. The girl did not stir. Gemma yanked on the door handle, but the bent door was jammed into its frame and would not budge. Gemma thrust her head and shoulders through the open window and cried again, "Caroline, can you hear me?" As silence stretched ominously, she felt herself grow weak with terror. She extended frightened fingers to poke her friend's limp body. "Caroline!" At last she was rewarded with a faint moan. The girl's lashes fluttered briefly, then stilled again.

Gemma felt the car shift slightly while she balanced across the windowsill, and she extracted herself from her awkward position. She stared at Caroline intently. Her brown curls looked almost black against the unnatural pallor of her cheek, but at least that cheek did twitch perceptibly now and then. She was alive. Gemma's worst fear subsided, and she trembled with relief.

As she leaned against the crushed side of the Fiat, she took deep delicate breaths until her heartbeat slowed its galloping pace. Then she glanced around at the Ferrari, which had skidded to a halt on the other side of the clearing. The front end of the low sleek automobile was smashed almost beyond recognition. Above the pile of twisted metal a gash of raw wood showed pale yellow in the dark bark of the massive pine, and red paint streaked it like smears of blood. Gemma feared for the driver, but as she watched, Franco jerked open the door to assist him, and the man unbuckled his shoulder harness and unfolded his long frame from its almost reclining position behind the steering wheel. When he stood upright, he swayed slightly as he towered over Franco. He shook his dark leonine head to clear it, then he ran his hands down his lean frame, checking for injury. With a muttered oath he touched his right forearm experimentally. He shoved the sleeve of his drab work shirt back up over his elbow and flexed his long fingers.

Gemma gazed at him raptly, biting her lip in bewilderment as she studied his long narrow face with the high forehead and pronounced cheekbones. She knew that face, those sculptured features. Somewhere she had seen him before.... Gemma rubbed her aching eyes. Tension and anxiety were melding into the start of a ferocious headache, and she needed to relax, remain calm. Otherwise she would be no help at all to Caroline. She had no time to puzzle over handsome strangers who drove like maniacs. Besides, unless he was an actor in one of the spaghetti Westerns she used to see with her brothers, there was no way she could have encountered him before. In her three days in Italy Gemma had met only Franco and his mother. All other Italians were a blur to her, dark and beautiful but individually anonymous. But this man she would have remembered.

Gemma heard Caroline stir, and at once she returned her attention to the Fiat, forgetting the other driver in her concern for her friend. She tried to analyze the situation dispassionately. Now that she knew the girl still breathed, she felt less panic-stricken, more able to direct her energy efficiently.

She rattled the door once again. When it would not budge, she reached inside to the interior handle, but it, too, was inoperable.

Before she could plot her next move, her shoulders were grasped from behind, and she was pushed aside unceremoniously. The tall man stooped to peer inside the little car, and Gemma could see his dark face blanch as he stared at Caroline. *"Dio!"* he gritted. When he tried the door, automatically using his right hand, he winced fiercely. He turned to Gemma and growled something in harsh idiomatic Italian too rapid for her to follow, upset as she was.

"M-mi dispiace," she replied, enunciating with great care as she tried to recall her Berlitz lessons. "I'm sorry, but I don't know what *leva di ferro* means."

Behind the man, Franco said in English, "Signorina Culver, he asked—"

The man interrupted in the same language, his accent excellent, his deep voice impatient and cold, *"Leva di ferro* means 'crowbar.' Do you have one, or a tire iron or any other kind of tool that might serve the purpose?"

Gemma said helplessly, "I don't know. The car's rented."

He swore irritably and pivoted, elbowing Franco out of the way as he took one long stride back to the rear of the Fiat. The impact had popped the trunk lid loose, and he flung it up with an angry jerk.

"But there's only..." Gemma tried to protest. Her words died out when the man halted abruptly, frozen with astonishment as he stared at the marble chunks secreted in the trunk.

He lifted his head, and his dark eyes bored into Gemma's gray ones for endless seconds. She felt herself blush under his intense scrutiny. With carefully controlled movements the man slowly closed the lid over the load of rocks. "No tool kit, I see," he observed.

Gemma fought an impulse to giggle nervously. This was hardly the time for explanations. With difficulty she tore her eyes away again. She lost track of time as she crooned softly to her friend, praying that her low soothing tones would somehow comfort the girl in her semiconscious state. Intent on what she was doing, Gemma was startled when the man caught her by the waist once more and moved her aside.

"Hey, quit pushing me around!" she squawked indignantly, but he ignored her. She watched as he squatted down to unroll on the ground a leather case emblazoned with the Ferrari emblem. Inside was an array of shining, obviously unused screwdrivers, wrenches, pliers and—Gemma noted with relief—a short crowbar. But as he hefted the tool in his right hand, she heard him hiss, *"Maledizione!"*

Gemma asked, "Can I help you?"

He shook his head firmly and shifted the lever to his other hand. "No. Just stay out of the way." He fitted the bar into the crack between the jammed door and its frame, and with a powerful shove he popped the door loose so that the handle could once more be operated. As soon as the door swung wide, Gemma plunged into the opening, but the man stopped her. "Don't try to move her," he ordered. "There are no signs that gasoline has spilled, so it might be better to leave her where she is until the ambulance arrives."

Gemma frowned. "But how—"

"I've sent your boyfriend for help. It's only half a kilometer to the main road, and if he's lucky, he'll soon be able to catch a ride to the nearest telephone. The automobile club will send someone. But we had better be prepared to wait for a couple of hours."

Gemma stared at Caroline, and she wanted to sob with frustration at her own impotence. She exclaimed, "What I wouldn't give for a C.B. right now!"

"A what?"

"A citizens-band radio. I don't know if you have them in Europe, but at home they're quite common. My father carries one in his pickup truck, and if he ever gets into trouble in the mountains or spots an accident, he can radio for assistance at once."

The man regarded her with impersonal curiosity as he packed up the tool kit. "Home, I gather, is the United States?"

"Colorado. Have you been there?"

"No. The farthest west I ever traveled was Chicago."

When Caroline began to whimper, Gemma slid carefully into the car beside her. She fished in back for the picnic basket and found the bottle of mineral water, which had miraculously survived the crash. Wetting her blue bandanna, she bathed Caroline's wan face gently and prayed that Franco would return soon.

Caroline relaxed beneath Gemma's tranquilizing hands. When she was quiet again, Gemma tried to settle comfortably beside her, but the acute angle of the car in the trench made it impossible. Moving with great care to avoid stirring the girl, Gemma pulled herself out and leaned weakly against the fender. She noted absently that the shining metal scraped bare in the crash was already acquiring a dulling film of dust.

She looked across the clearing to the Ferrari, where the man had returned. She watched as he circled the car slowly, kicking at tires and rattling strips of twisted metal. He seemed to regard the wreck with a mixture of impatience and ironic disgust. Gemma wondered at his calm acceptance of the incident. She had always heard that Italians were volatile in the extreme, greeting adversity with wild gesticulations and imaginative oaths as they vented their emotions. Always severely restrained in her own feelings, Gemma had dreaded the thought of being exposed to outbursts of Latin temperament while she traveled in Italy, and she had wondered how she would cope if faced with such embarrassing histrionics. Now she was confronted with a man who had every right to be emotional, perhaps even violent, and astonishingly his reactions seemed more controlled than her own. He must feel something about the loss of his beautiful automobile. Anyone would. Gemma's knowledge of racing cars was limited, acquired by osmosis during her years in a male-dominated household, but she did know that in the States a Ferrari like the one just destroyed would cost more than the house she and Dave had been planning to buy after....

But was she correct in her assumption that the car belonged to the man driving it? Now that she thought about it, she wasn't so sure. The car was almost sinfully expensive, a rich-man's toy, but the man who drove it was dressed not shabbily but cheaply, in faded denim work pants and a rough cotton shirt with the sleeves rolled up over his elbows. His thick, rather curly hair, not blue black like Franco's but with surprisingly ruddy highlights, was brushed back from a widow's peak on his high forehead, and it needed trimming. He was very tall, unusually tall for an Italian, but he moved with a lithe grace that belied his size.

Who was he? Gemma was more certain than ever that she had seen him before. In a movie somewhere, she wondered again. She couldn't think of any other likely place. She bit her lip in confusion. While he was certainly handsome enough to be in films, she didn't think he was an actor. When he unrolled the tool kit, she had noticed that his long narrow hands were callused and scarred, as if he used them for some harsh demanding labor. From his hands and his clothing she might have concluded that he worked in one of the quarries in the area, but somehow she doubted that, too. He had apparently traveled far in his thirty-five or so years, and he moved and spoke with an air of sophistication that seemed unlikely in a man whose life had been spent in the confined world of the marble pits.

Just as Gemma wondered if he might be a mechanic test-driving a client's car, he strode back across the clearing. He glanced at Caroline, whose condition appeared unchanged, then at the blue Fiat. His expression was grim as he asked, "I presume your friend is insured?"

"Of course I—" Gemma began indignantly. She stopped suddenly, shivering as the implications of the accident seeped into her. In Gemma's wallet was an international driver's license and the green card that indicated that she had automobile insurance. But it was Caroline who'd been behind the wheel, and she carried no such documents. At Marsha Somerville's insistence, they had planned that Gemma would do all the driving on the trip. Gemma wasn't even sure if her friend was legally old enough to handle a car in Italy. And now, unlicensed, uninsured, the girl had become involved in a serious collision, with injuries and two vehicles demolished. Even worse, she had been drinking. Gemma knew that Italy's penalties for drunk driving, like those of most European countries, were severe, with a possibility of as much as six months in prison. Gemma felt sick. Oh, God, Caroline was hurt and in grave trouble, and it was all Gemma's fault. She had promised Marsha she would take care of her daughter....

"From your expression I gather she doesn't have insurance," the man observed shortly. "We'll have to contact whoever is responsible for her while she is in Italy."

"I am," Gemma said.

He stared at her. "You?" he roared and swore violently. "What kind of parents do you have, permitting two teenage girls to run wild in a strange country—"

"I am not a teenager," Gemma gritted. "I am twenty-four years old, and I'm quite capable of taking care of both of us."

"Oh, really? And this little incident is an example of your so excellent guardianship, I suppose?"

Gemma blushed furiously, but she refused to react

to his sarcasm. The man was an arrogant beast, but after all, he was only echoing her own thoughts. She had failed. Again. She had failed as a teacher; she had failed as a woman. Only in her art did she have any confidence. . . . She shook off the mood. She surveyed the remains of the Fiat and in an effort to lighten the atmosphere smiled ironically. "I guess I'd better not count on getting my rental deposit back when we return to Genoa."

But the man refused to be placated. "You'd better not count on returning to Genoa soon," he snapped, his eyes cold as he gazed at the unconscious girl.

Stung by the brutal truth of his statement, Gemma lashed out, "Why does it matter if she has insurance? Why should it be all her fault? You were the one driving like a madman, speeding around blind curves—"

"I was quite within the legal limits for an automobile with the size of engine mine has. And I had no reason whatsoever to assume I would encounter some idiot tourist stalled across the center of the road with a carload of rocks!" He glanced at the trunk of the Fiat. "What's the marble for?"

"To carve, of course."

"Madonna," he snorted as one dark brow arched into a sardonic circumflex punctuating his impatience. "Don't tell me that child is another one of the so-called artists who flock here every summer like starlings, every bit as noisy and twice as dirty?"

Gemma took a deep angry breath. "No," she said through clenched teeth, "I am."

He turned and studied her more carefully then. From his superior height his dark eyes raked down over her slight figure from her tousled silver white hair and pale face to her bare dusty feet. Gemma lowered her lashes over her stormy eyes and ordered herself not to color, not to be intimidated by his disdain, even though she was acutely aware of her appearance, the dirt encrusting her T-shirt and jeans where she had fallen.

"You're a sculptor?" he asked dubiously, pointedly appraising her thin frame. "You'd make a good model, but you don't look as if you have the strength to work in stone."

Gemma bristled at his patronizing tone. "With modern pneumatic equipment, stone carving is no longer a matter of brute strength," she said huffily. "There is no reason I can't do as well as a man." Then honesty forced her to add, "Actually I've never worked with marble before. I've always used clay. That's why I'm here, to learn the technique."

His mouth thinned. "You've come to the right place, of course. The region abounds with workshops and people willing—for a price—to teach you how to become another Michelangelo in three easy lessons. But to find a good studio, a qualified instructor, and more important, one willing to take you on as a student—"

"But I have letters of introduction," Gemma said eagerly. "One is from the professor who directed my postgraduate work at university, and the other is from the curator of the Jefferson County Museum of Art." When she noticed the amused glint in his eyes, her enthusiasm faded. She was sure he was silently laughing at her. She said huskily, her voice thick with hurt, "I suppose my . . . my credentials seem very provincial to you. But I was touched and honored that people thought enough of my talent to give me good references.'' She lifted her head defiantly. "Anyway, what's it to you? Are you an artist?''

He stared at her blankly for a second, then he looked away. "Sometimes I wonder,'' he murmured.

She might have asked him what he meant by that enigmatic remark, but just then the sultry air of the clearing was pierced by a weird ululating siren fast approaching, and with an aching sigh of relief Gemma knew that help was on the way.

PERCHED ON THE NARROW RIM of an algae-stained marble fountain in the center of a piazza, Gemma wept. She gazed blindly toward the point on the skyline where the dome of the beautiful old fourteenth-century cathedral gleamed gently golden in the westering sunlight. When she felt the first betraying trickle of moisture on her cheek, she brushed it aside impatiently. Tears were futile, a sign of feminine weakness. They would do no one any good now, not Gemma, and certainly not Caroline, lying helpless in the hospital across the square. Gemma stared at the anonymous facade of the grim old building, its rows of small windows characterless, the plaster ornamented only with rivulets of green that had leaked from the copper rain gutters. Inside, the hospital was immaculate, but to Gemma, used to white-on-white medical buildings in the United States, it seemed antique and forbidding, relict from some less enlightened era. Every moment she expected to be confronted by a doctor with side-whiskers and sleeve garters, who smelled of chloroform and carbolic acid.

Gemma rubbed her aching eyes, dislodging more tears. She scrubbed the offending wetness from her cheeks. She was tired, that was the problem, she was exhausted and upset. She needed to return to the *pensione* and rest. There was nothing she could do here now. The nun in her long white nursing habit with the crucifix dangling from her waist had told Gemma that Caroline might not regain consciousness before morning, and that she would serve her friend best by getting some sleep herself. Prayers would be welcome, of course; but there was no need for an all-night vigil; the girl was in no real danger. Yes, her injuries were serious—a concussion and three broken ribs—but she was young and healthy and would soon mend.

And, the nurse had added with a reassuring smile as she led Gemma toward the exit, she need not trouble herself about the *burocrazia*, the paperwork and red tape generated when the accident was reported to the authorities. Signore Giordano had taken care of everything.

Gemma sighed. Well, at least she knew the tall stranger's name now. She had been dazed by the way he took command of the situation, barking out orders to the ambulance attendants, later addressing the nurses in the hospital in a voice only slightly modified out of deference to their habit. Franco had accompanied the medical team back to the accident site, and he jumped to the man's bidding as quickly as anyone. In the hospital corridor when Gemma questioned the boy about his instant obedience, he shrugged fatalistically, "No, *signorina*, I do not know his name. But he is obviously a *uomo*

rispettato, a respected man, someone with much...
influence, and it is better not to anger him.''

As Gemma sat on the edge of the fountain, she
pondered the nuances of the Italian language that she
had failed to learn during her six-week course in
Denver. It was that shrug of Franco's, more than his
tone of voice, that told Gemma that a *uomo rispettato* was not somebody to take lightly. Dear God,
had she and Caroline inadvertently become involved
with a Mafia chieftain? No, of course not, she was
being absurd. This was the industrialized north, not
the wilds of Sicily. Whoever the puzzling Signore
Giordano was, whatever power he wielded—and remembering the man's arrogant self-confidence,
Gemma admitted that he acted like someone who
might have a great deal of power—he probably
operated within the law.

Gemma looked around the piazza. Earlier, traffic
had been heavy, the air in the narrow streets blue
with exhaust fumes, as people hurried home from
work. She could still hear automobiles on the main
thoroughfare several blocks away, but now the
square in front of the hospital was quiet except for
the occasional put-put of a Vespa or a rackety Fiat
circling the fountain. One old car had made the circuit four times while the driver honked, and his companions called out effusive compliments to the *bella
signorina*, offering to escort her personally to all the
spots in Pietrasanta where the great and venerable
Michelangelo once stayed. Gemma ignored them
resolutely, and after a few minutes they drove away,
leaving her alone once more. She assumed that most
of the townspeople were settling down to hearty sup-

pers after their long day in the quarries or the art studios. Gemma's growling stomach reminded her that she had eaten almost nothing all day. She wondered what delights Signora Ricci had prepared for this night's meal. During her brief sojourn at the *pensione*, Gemma had already learned that the signora was a remarkable cook. Last night she had served *cacciucco*, a rich fish soup similar to bouillabaisse, and the whole house had been redolent with garlic and herbs. Gemma had loved it, although Caroline hissed behind her napkin that she would rather have pizza.

As she remembered Caroline, Gemma's smile faded. Franco had returned home to help his mother with dinner, and he could not come back for Gemma for some time yet. He would see if perhaps one of the other tenants could pick her up at the hospital. There was a young German sculptor who drove into town almost every evening to visit his Italian girl friend; probably he could give Gemma a lift. Gemma sighed heavily, hunching her thin shoulders against the velvety warm air. It was going to be a glorious night; already stars were peeping through the twilight; and Gemma was sure that if she listened hard enough, she would hear someone tuning up a mandolin somewhere in the distance. But while she waited for her ride, instead of enjoying the delicious romantic aura that seemed to waft from the ancient stones of Pietrasanta, she had an unpleasant duty to perform; she must find a telephone and call Colorado to tell Caroline's mother what had happened.

Gemma did not look forward to making that call, to admitting to Marsha that she had proved incapable of protecting her daughter from harm. No matter that Caroline had caused the accident: Gemma had been in charge and should have maintained better supervision. For half a moment she debated not calling Marsha at all, then just as quickly she rejected the idea as cowardly and insensitive. If she had a child, and that child was hurt, she would never forgive anyone who tried to keep the news from her.

In addition to the obvious difficulties of what she would say to Marsha, and how she could relay the message without panicking the woman, Gemma had another problem: from where was she going to place the call? Signora Ricci's boardinghouse did not have a telephone. That meant that Gemma was going to have to make an overseas call from a pay phone, a prospect she found daunting in the extreme. She glanced around the piazza. The shops facing the hospital were all closed for the day, and besides, none of the doors bore the yellow telephone-dial sign indicating a public phone inside. Gemma would have to look for a bar or café still open on one of the busier streets, and she knew that the instant she stepped inside, disheveled, and more to the point, alone, she was going to become the object of advances she neither welcomed nor enjoyed.

"Think of it as penance," she told herself irritably as she slipped down from her perch, "the price you pay for being incompetent and female." She ran her fingers through her tousled hair, slicking it back from her face.

Suddenly a rough callused hand touched her shoulder from behind, and a deep voice said, "Miss Culver."

Startled, Gemma jerked around, her heart pounding. When she recognized the man, she gasped, "Oh, it's you!"

Towering over her, he smiled reassuringly. "Forgive me," he murmured, his voice dark and silky. "I didn't mean to frighten you. In the hospital they told me I might find you out here."

She struggled to regain her composure. Drawing herself up to her full five feet six, she averred, "You didn't frighten me. I...I just didn't notice you coming, that's...that's all."

"Yes," he agreed smoothly, "you did seem rather absorbed in your thoughts."

Gemma had to tip back her head to study him in the waning light. He was very tall, taller even than her father and brothers, and they were hulking six-footers, every one of them. They had always made Gemma feel a little like Gulliver in the land of the Brobdingnagians. Her gray eyes traveled uneasily over the Italian's broad powerful shoulders, the strong column of his neck. He was not massive, as were the Culver men. Instead, his body was lean, finely honed, without an ounce of surplus flesh anywhere, and Gemma had the feeling he would be more than a match for any of her family.

When she realized she was staring, her pale cheeks flushed. She hoped he would think the color came from the reddening sunlight. Quickly she said, "Signore Giordano...." He frowned, puzzlement flickering in his dark eyes, and she paused. "I beg your pardon, isn't that your name? One of the nurses called you that, and I assumed—"

His features relaxed as he chuckled, "Oh, of

course, you must have been talking to Suora Letizia; she's an old friend of my family. Certainly you may call me Giordano if you wish. And am I correct, your name is...Gemma Culver?" His baritone voice lingered over the two short syllables of her first name, giving it a foreign intonation she found unusual and strangely pleasant. When she nodded, he continued curiously, "Gemma is an Italian name. I know you said you come from the United States, but are you perhaps of Italian ancestry?"

"No. I'm mostly German, with a touch of Danish, the usual American hybrid."

He nodded. "Of course, I should have known. You have the look of a Scandinavian, that...moonlight quality. Italian blondes are children of the sun."

Gemma caught her breath. His tone was quite matter-of-fact, but his words stirred her oddly, poetic words uttered so prosaically that she didn't know whether he meant them for a compliment or not. She said, "My father chose my name. It's a pun on the word 'gem,' and he thought it would be a good one for a miner's daughter. I've just always been grateful he didn't decide to call me something like Opal or Goldie."

"You're right," the man said softly. "Goldie would be most inappropriate. Silver, perhaps, with that glorious hair of yours." He frowned. "Why do you wear your hair so short? It's almost a crime to cut it; it was meant to be long and flowing so that it can reflect the light." He reached his hand out as if to stroke her hair.

Gemma jerked back. Her reaction seemed to puzzle him. She noticed for the first time that below the rolled-up sleeve of his tan cotton shirt his right wrist was taped tightly. "Oh, you're hurt!" she exclaimed, grateful for a reason to distract him. "Is it very bad?"

He shook his head. "No, just a slight sprain. It will be better in a couple of days, *grazie a Dio.*"

Gemma frowned at the bandage that contrasted sharply with the bronzed skin of his arm. Little black hairs curled over the edge of the gauze, emphasizing his dark masculinity. A thought occurred to her that she hated to ask, yet knew she must. "Until your injury heals, will it interfere with your work?"

He shrugged. "Perhaps. However, lately everything seems to have been interfering with my work."

Gemma listened with dismay, her worst fears confirmed. She said, "I'm sorry about that. I promise that somehow you'll be compensated for any...any wages you may lose while your wrist is...."

Although he did not move away from her, suddenly he seemed very distant. "That will not be necessary," he said flatly.

Gemma shivered at the sting of ice in his deep voice. As she had suspected it might, her offer had hurt his tetchy Latin pride. "I beg your pardon," she said humbly, "I didn't mean to offend you. I only wanted to make sure you would suffer no more inconvenience than you had to. There are so many things I'll have to take care of: the damage to the cars, the medical bills. At this point I'm not sure just how I'm going to handle it all, but I intend to."

His tone warmed slightly. "Didn't they tell you in the hospital? Everything has been arranged. You need not worry about any of it."

"But how? Since I wasn't driving, I'm almost sure my insurance won't cover this."

Impatiently he said, "But mine will. And I am assuming responsibility for the accident."

Gemma stared at him. "I don't understand. Out on the highway you said—"

He smiled at her, the kind of smile he might use to calm a fractious child. "I said too many things, and I apologize. I was shaken and furious, and I took my anger out on you, rather than on myself as I should have done. You told me I drove like a maniac, and you were right. Rather than concentrating on my driving, I was fuming over an incident that happened this morning...." He paused, muttering wryly, "Yes, it was just this morning, wasn't it? *Madonna*, it's been quite a day!" The corners of his hard mouth turned upward, and this time for some reason Gemma couldn't define, she felt the warmth of his smile so deep inside her that her bare toes curled. She looked away hastily. He said, "Had I not collided with your unfortunate friend, I might as easily have hit something else—a hay wagon, perhaps a child on a bicycle. I should thank God I didn't kill someone."

He paused once more, and Gemma, disturbed by her physical reaction to this overwhelming man, wondered irritably if he was waiting for her to contradict his admission of guilt. It was a favorite male ploy, she had learned over the years: they made these disarming little confessions and then expected the woman to reassure them that, oh, no, of course they weren't really to blame....

When she did not speak, he continued calmly, "I shall see that any medical expenses are met, and if you'll give me the address of your car-rental agency in Genoa, I'll take care of that, too. Once they send down an automobile to replace the one that was destroyed, there's no reason you cannot go on about your vacation as planned."

His mention of the Fiat reminded Gemma forcibly of Caroline, the way she lay in her bed as helpless and pathetic as a broken doll. Guilt welled up in Gemma, and she stared at the man, her gray eyes stormy and accusing. "Go on with my vacation?" she gasped. "My God, what kind of monster are you? Have you forgotten there's a seventeen-year-old girl unconscious in that hospital, a child who is not only my responsibility but my *friend*, as well? And now you say...." She covered her face with her hands and twisted away from him, trembling.

For a long moment he was so quiet that the evening sounds of the town began to filter through Gemma's distress. Someone in the next street exclaimed indignantly over the day's soccer scores, and a woman yelled, "*Zitto!*"—"Shut up!"—to a whining child. When at last he did speak, he stood so close that Gemma could feel his warm breath on the back of her neck. His voice was low and rigidly restrained. "I think you know, Miss Culver, that I did not mean you must not be concerned for your friend, nor, for that matter, should you infer that I am not worried about her. I will excuse your outburst because I think you are suffering a delayed reaction to the accident. You obviously need rest, and you probably haven't eaten in hours, am I right?"

Gemma was shaking with shock and weakness, but she said tightly, "I'll eat when Franco takes me back to the *pensione*."

"Ah, yes, Franco, the young boyfriend." The man's voice was carefully neutral, but Gemma suspected he was laughing at her. "Where did he disappear to?"

"Once he saw there was nothing more he could do at the hospital, he went home to help his mother. And he is *not* my boyfriend!"

"*Non è vero?* Isn't he?" the man murmured silkily, suggestively. "I'm surprised. He's obviously interested in you. But perhaps you are bothered by the fact that he is so young. You needn't be. Italian men mature very early. I'm sure you'll find him a satisfactory lover."

Enraged, Gemma spun around. She glared up into his mocking face as she hissed, "Damn you, how dare you talk to me like that? I told you, I've come to Pietrasanta to study sculpture, and I've done nothing—*nothing*—to give you or Franco or anyone else reason to think I'd be interested in some kind of summer affair. My God, why won't you men just leave me alone?"

He had been watching her as if she were a spitting kitten or a fussy child, his eyes alight with indulgent amusement, but when that last cry was wrenched from her, the light dimmed and he scowled. Gemma did not ponder his lowering expression. Instead she turned away and stared into the murky green depths of the mossy fountain. Stars reflected clearly on the smooth surface of the water, then their images distorted and wavered when a goldfish stirred up ripples as it snapped at a night-flying insect. At the edge of the fountain she could see her own reflection peering back at her, shadowy except for her shining hair. Then the man's face appeared beside her own, ob-

scure and ominous, threatening to engulf her. Gemma
sighed. She had come to Italy, of all places, to escape
overpowering males, and suddenly the thought struck
her as so outrageously ironic that her sigh changed
into a hysterical sob, humorless and racking. One
large hand closed over her quivering shoulder reassuringly, and she heard him murmur, "Steady now...."

As she labored to retain her composure, she tried
to deny his touch, tried to deny the comfort that
seemed to radiate from those strong rough fingers.
She fought the impulse to lean her face against his
hand, feel those crisp black hairs tickling her smooth
cheek.

When at last she could speak, her husky voice
sounded reasonably cool and firm. "Signore Giordano, while I...I appreciate all you've done for
Caroline and...and me, I must ask you to let me
handle things my own way. So I'll say thank you now
and good-night." He did not move. She lifted
pleading eyes to his. "Please, won't you just go
away?"

"You don't know when to give up, do you?" he
observed quietly. "I'm sorry you find my presence so
distasteful, but I insist on remaining with you until
you have eaten and are safely back at your lodg-
ings."

Gemma colored faintly. "I told you, I'll eat after I
return to the Riccis' house. Right now I don't have
time. I must call Caroline's mother. Can you direct
me to a telephone?"

His brows lifted slightly. "A telephone," he repeated. "You intend to call—where was it, Colorado—from a pay phone?"

Gemma shrugged. "I have to. The Riccis don't have one."

"I see." He sighed, "*Allora*, I just hope you know what you're taking on."

"What do you mean?"

His smile was rather condescending as he explained, "I'm afraid you may have been spoiled by the excellent telephone system in America. Here things operate a little differently. Once you find a bar or café with a pay phone, first you'll have to purchase a great many *gettoni* from the cashier." When Gemma looked blank, he fished a couple of metal discs from the hip pocket of his denim pants. "*Gettoni*—tokens. You don't put coins directly into an Italian telephone." He puzzled aloud, "Let's see, each *gettone* is fifty lire, and the last time I called the United States, it cost about seven thousand lire for three minutes." He chuckled, "Are you certain you want to do this?"

Gemma said doggedly, "I have to let Caroline's mother know what happened."

He nodded and slipped the tokens back into his pocket, the action momentarily drawing Gemma's attention to the powerful lines of his lean body. He said, "Of course you must call her. I meant, are you sure you want to do so from a public telephone? You'd be much better off to find a private one somewhere and worry about the bill later."

"But I don't know anyone here with a telephone."

He made a gesture as if waving away her protest. "I have one. In fact, I don't know why I didn't think of it earlier. After we've eaten somewhere, I'll have a taxi take us up to my place, where you can make your call in comfort and privacy. When you're finished,

I'll drive you back to your *pensione* in my mother's car."

At the mention of "his place," Gemma was instantly wary. "Your mother?" she asked suspiciously.

"Yes, my mother," he echoed, obviously annoyed. "My father is dead now, but I do have a mother. I also have a sister who lives in Connecticut." He regarded Gemma with exasperation. "Are you always so ungracious when someone tries to do you a favor?"

Gemma drooped her head, her cheeks burning. "I...I'm sorry," she stammered hoarsely. "As you said, I'm tired and hungry and...and it's been a rotten day."

He caught her chin in his strong fingers and lifted her face to his. "Yes, it has," he murmured. His eyes moved lightly over her pale heart-shaped face, resting for a second on her quivering mouth. She had the astonishing notion that he was thinking about kissing her. Then he said vigorously, "Poor Gemma, you'll feel better after you eat something. Come now, there's a restaurant a few blocks from here where you can get incredible *pappardelle con la lepre.*"

Gemma's lashes lifted uncertainly. "*Lepre?* That's...that's hare, isn't it?" She grimaced.

"I expect if you insist, you could have spaghetti instead." His smile was gently mocking.

Gemma looked up at him, her gaze drawn irresistibly to the planes of his face shadowed in the yellow light from the streetlamps. She was teased once again by the tantalizing familiarity of his features, and yet she did not know where she might have seen him before, unless it was in some forgotten dream. She ventured shyly, "I...I think I would like some spaghetti, after all."

"Good," he said.

Then she shook her head fiercely as if coming out of a trance. "Oh, damn, I can't go anywhere, not looking the way I do." She regarded her soiled T-shirt and jeans with disgust. "I'm a mess, my clothes are filthy, and my shoes are lying back beside the highway somewhere. I'm sorry, but I just can't—"

He lifted a hand to silence her. "You look fine," he soothed. "Perhaps a little casual for most towns, but not here. In Pietrasanta work clothes are almost *de rigueur* for tourists. I have actually seen people sprinkle marble dust over their overalls so that everyone will think they just spent a long busy day in one of the art studios."

Gemma stared, then the corners of her mouth twitched. The picture he described struck her as so incredibly ludicrous that suddenly she threw back her head and laughed. Her eyes sparkled as her voice rang out merrily across the piazza. Her companion watched with approval. When her laughter had subsided to an occasional chuckle, he said, "You ought to do that more often. You're far too young to be so somber all the time."

Gemma blinked in surprise. "I guess," she said wistfully after a moment's pause, "that it's just been a long time since anything seemed very funny to me."

Before he could comment, he was interrupted by the sound of a small car entering the square. Gemma glanced around and saw a black Volkswagen with West German plates trundling toward her. "Oh, there's my ride," she exclaimed as she recognized the couple inside. "They came much sooner than I thought they would."

The Volkswagen pulled to a halt beside the fountain, and the driver rolled down his window and leaned his blond head out. "Fräulein Culver," he said in heavily accented English, "Franco told us of your misfortune with your automobile. You are well?"

"Yes, I'm fine, but poor Caroline is hurt badly, I'm afraid. She's unconscious right now. In the hospital they told me to go home and rest and then come back in the morning. Do you think you could give me a lift back to the *pensione*?"

"Of course, *Fräulein*, if you'll—"

Abruptly the man standing beside Gemma cut in. "That won't be necessary," he told the driver, and he laid a large hand on Gemma's arm to emphasize his point. "I shall see that Miss Culver gets safely back to the house."

Gemma frowned at him, bewildered by his proprietary air, and his grip tightened. She protested, "But, *signore*, there's no need for you to go to all that trouble now, surely."

His heavy brows came together sharply. "No need?" he repeated in a low voice, moving still closer. "Have you forgotten your telephone call?"

The young German scowled as he listened to this exchange, and after a moment he got out of his car and confronted the pair by the fountain. He asked quietly, "*Fräulein*, do you know this man?"

The pressure on Gemma's arm increased, and she said quickly, "Oh, forgive me, I should have introduced you." She waited as the girl who had also been in the Volkswagen left the car and sidled up to the driver. "I'd like you to meet Dieter Stahl," Gemma said. "He's a guest at the Riccis' *pensione*, just as Caroline and I are." The German nodded stiffly, losing his frozen look only when his girl friend slipped her arm through his. Gemma continued, "And with him is Claretta...Claretta—I'm sorry. I don't think I know your last name."

"Claretta Fiore," the girl giggled. "I work at the post office."

Gemma smiled at the couple. The vivacious girl seemed such an unlikely companion for the dour young man that she wondered how they had ever got together. When they stared expectantly at the tall man beside her, Gemma said, "Claretta, Herr Stahl, I'd like you to meet Signore...." Again she hesitated, realizing that she did not know his full name, either.

"Oh, I know you," Claretta said easily, giving the man a long appreciative look. "You're always coming to the post office to pick up packages. You're the sculptor, Giordano di Mario."

CHAPTER THREE

IN THE SILENCE THAT FOLLOWED, Gemma thought she might just possibly die of embarrassment. Hot color stained her face with such intensity that she felt sure it must tint the roots of her silvery hair. She hung her head and screwed her eyes shut, biting her lip to keep from groaning. The tall stranger was Jordan di Mario, one of the greatest sculptors of the twentieth century, and she had actually dared to ask him, "Are you an artist?" as outrageously insolent in her ignorance as a novice fiddler inquiring of Heifetz, "Are you a musician?" She prayed she would wake to find this scene only a nightmare brought on by a surfeit of Signora Ricci's marvelous cooking, a reaction to an overdose of garlic and olive oil.

But hard fingers dug into the soft flesh of her arm, convincing her painfully that this was no dream, and reluctantly she lifted her lashes and looked up at the man who touched her. He gazed down at her, his dark eyes unreadable, and one corner of his thin mouth quirked with what she hoped was amusement. Before he could speak, the couple standing in front of them stirred, and Dieter choked in awestruck tones, *"Sie sind di Mario?"* When Jordan nodded curtly, his eyes still trained on Gemma's flushed face, the German gushed, *"Mein Herr,* you have no idea what a great honor and a privilege it is to meet you. Long have I admired your—''

Jordan dismissed him with a wave of his free hand. ''Yes, yes, thank you,'' he muttered. He frowned at the woman whose arm he still held, and he inquired softly, ''Gemma?''

She shook her head miserably. ''You should have told me,'' she mumbled. ''You shouldn't have let me make such a fool of myself.''

''It wasn't intentional, I assure you,'' he said, and he smiled gently, the harsh planes of his face softening, becoming cajoling.

Her pride still smarted too painfully for her to respond to his overture, and when she felt his grip loosen slightly, she jerked her arm out of his grasp and turned deliberately to the other couple, lifting her chin in a defiant gesture as she did. ''Herr Stahl, Claretta,'' she said brightly, ''if your offer still holds, I would really appreciate a ride back to the *pensione*. It's been a very long day, and I am—''

Jordan interposed smoothly, ''There's no need to trouble your friends now, Gemma. I'm sure after a hard day in the studio Herr Stahl must have better things to do than ferry you about.'' He glanced at Dieter. ''I'm correct, am I not? You, too, are a sculptor?'' The German nodded in surprise, and Jordan smiled coolly. ''I thought as much. I'd be interested in seeing some of your work sometime.''

Gemma said desperately, ''But Herr Stahl—''

Dieter stared uneasily at Gemma, then at the man towering over her. ''*Fräulein*,'' he said in a condemning voice when his pale eyes flitted back to her,

"Herr di Mario has already said he would take you wherever you needed to go."

"The only place I need to go now is back to the boardinghouse," Gemma insisted, but even as she spoke, she knew the words were futile. The look on Dieter's face told her clearly and bluntly that he was not about to contradict the express wish of an eminent influential artist, especially not one who had indicated a desire to see his work.

As if to reinforce her hesitation, Claretta now joined in the conversation, snuggling closer to Dieter and saying, "It's not that we don't want to take you, Gemma, but we did have plans for this evening." She leaned her head on her lover's shoulder, and he glanced down at her long enough to smile warmly before returning his rapt gaze to Jordan.

Gemma sighed with resignation. "Of course. Forgive me for delaying you." She turned to Jordan and tried not to glare resentfully. "It seems I shall be going with you, after all."

"I told you you didn't know when to give up," he murmured dryly. He addressed the other couple in tones that clearly meant dismissal. "Thank you for checking on Gemma, but as you can see, she's quite all right. We won't keep you any longer. I shall look forward to meeting you again later." Dieter and Claretta quickly took their leave.

Gemma flopped down on the edge of the fountain and watched the haste with which the black Volkswagen rolled out of the piazza, rattling over the worn cobbles. When it had vanished into one of the dark narrow streets, she became aware again of how lonely the little square was, deserted except for her and the man she found so disturbing. She had dreamed of one day meeting a great sculptor, and now that she had, she did not know what to say to him. Rather than risk humiliating herself further, she began with great concentration to brush the dust from her bare bruised feet, cringing as she accidentally rubbed one of the many small cuts inflicted by the broken glass at the crash site. Pointedly avoiding Jordan's gaze, she rolled the cuffs of her jeans up over her slim calves and swiveled around on the smooth marble so that she could dip her aching feet into the mossy depths of the fountain. She winced as the cool water stung her raw skin.

Jordan studied her expressionlessly, his dark eyes stroking the shapely line of her legs, and he observed, "While you were at the hospital, you really ought to have had someone take a look at those cuts. You might need a tetanus injection or something."

His paternal tone irritated Gemma, and she muttered waspishly, "I had all my boosters before I came to this benighted country. Rest assured, Signore di Mario, I won't try to collect from your insurance company for my few scrapes and scratches." She scooped up a handful of water and dribbled it over her toes.

His eyes narrowed at her emphasis on his name, but he only said mildly, "Don't use that water. God knows what the fountain is polluted with. If you won't see a doctor, at least wait until we get to my house, where you can clean your feet with some antiseptic."

Gemma jerked her head up, her gray eyes blinking with surprise. "Then you really meant it about going to your house?"

He sighed impatiently. "Of course. I told you I'd take you there. Why should you think I wouldn't?"

She stammered in confusion, "But that was before I knew...I knew...."

"Before you knew who I was. And now that you do know who I am, just what do you think I have in mind, if not to help you with your telephone call and tend your injuries as I had said?"

"I don't know. I suppose I thought...." Her voice trailed off in embarrassment.

"My God, the workings of the female mind!" he snorted. He shook his head in exasperation and muttered something that her Berlitz lessons had not equipped her to translate. Reverting to English, he exclaimed, "Are you sure you're twenty-four? You're behaving more like a repressed fifteen-year-old."

Blushing once more, Gemma covered her face with her wet hands, wrinkling her nose at the foul odor of the water. "Do we have to go over all that again?" she asked plaintively through her fingers. "I told you I'm exhausted, and I'm not thinking clearly. If I've offended you somehow, I'm very sorry, but you must understand, I'm not used to dealing with international celebrities."

"I'm not a celebrity," he said tersely. "My work has some renown, but personally I have always deliberately kept a very low profile. However, that is something we can discuss at some later date." He extended a hand to her, and cautiously she looked at him, smiling with an effort. When she noticed the bandage on his wrist, she gasped with renewed horror as she stared at the white gauze. "Oh, Lord," she groaned, "I forgot you're hurt, too. You won't be able to work, and it's all my fault! What if there is some permanent injury, and you—''

Instead of taking her hand, he laid his fingers lightly over her trembling parted lips to silence her, and in her surprise the tip of her tongue flicked across his skin. The pads of his fingers were rough and slightly salty.

His expression deepened at that inadvertent caress, and she felt him tense, but his hand did not move. His voice was silky as he murmured soothingly, ''Don't say another word, Gemma. You're too tired to be coherent. Be quiet and just listen to me. I'm going to go ahead and find a taxi to take us to my home in the foothills because it is clear you are not up to dining in a restaurant. My mother can fix you something to eat, or if she is busy, I can make rather good pasta. When you are feeling more yourself, we will place the telephone call to your friend's mother so that you can reassure her that the girl is being well cared for. After all of that is done, I shall drive you back to your *pensione*, where you can get the rest you so desperately need. Is that agreeable to you?''

She nodded mutely, lulled into submission by the dark honey of his voice, and he smiled benignly. ''*Bene*,'' he said, ''I knew you'd see reason.'' His long fingers moved away from her lips and brushed lightly over her smooth skin, tracing the line of her wide cheekbones. It wasn't until much later that Gemma wondered why she had been so uncharacteristically acquiescent, why she had let him touch her.

THE LITTLE TAXI sped through the night, its numerous rattles punctuated by the teeth-shivering grinding of gears as the driver downshifted on the blind curves that wound through massive pine trees and skirted the rims of sharp cliffs. He joked blithely in Italian with Jordan, waving his hands to punctuate each point, and he was oblivious to the agitation of his other passenger. Gemma was used to traveling in mountains, but in the dark the twisting roads into the forested Apuan foothills, alarming even by day, seemed to her to assume a threatening, almost sinister aspect, as if the car were following the body of some giant snake that would devour them the instant they reached the head. She chuckled grimly at her fanciful image. She was in worse shape than she had suspected if her mind could conjure up a picture like that.

The taxi swung sharply on another bend, tires squealing, and Gemma was thrown against Jordan. His hard arms came around her automatically, and for a moment she was acutely aware of the tangy masculine scent of his body radiating through the rough fabric of his cotton work shirt. When she eased herself away from him, he asked with concern, "Are you all right?"

She smiled sickly and shrugged. "I'm fine, except I was wondering if there is some law that says Italians have to drive like madmen."

He laughed a rich deep sound, and when the man behind the wheel cocked his head inquiringly in their direction, Jordan repeated Gemma's question in Italian. The driver joined in the laughter and threw back a ribald response that Gemma translated with difficulty. Watching her puzzled expression, Jordan asked, "Did you understand what he said?"

She frowned. "Some of it. My Italian is improving, but you all still speak much too rapidly for me to follow with any precision."

"You'll learn," Jordan said, nodding. After a pause he drawled, "Essentially the driver's remark was that speed satisfies a need as basic as that for good wine or...feminine companionship."

Gemma looked at him suspiciously. "Why do I have the feeling you've censored that translation?"

"Probably because I have." His eyes glinted. "Somehow I didn't think you'd appreciate being compared to a Maserati: tricky to handle but very rewarding to a driver with sufficient skill."

Gemma stiffened, her momentary affinity for the sculptor vanishing. She turned away from him with a deliberate gesture of rejection and peered out the grimy window of the taxi. In the dark she could see little, but the sight of the quarter moon hanging low in the sky made her realize that they had come out of the forest and were now traveling through what appeared to be cultivated fields, long rows of staked vines that stretched into the night. She inhaled deeply, picking up the sharp sweet scent of ripening grapes heavy on the warm breeze. "How delicious the air is," she murmured. "It smells as if you could get drunk just breathing.... Is much wine made around here?"

"Some," Jordan said, "but most of it is for local consumption, very little for export. The largest commercial vineyards are farther inland. I lease out these fields because I don't have time to supervise the operation myself."

Gemma glanced quizzically at him. "All this land belongs to you?"

"There isn't really all that much acreage," he said. "In the daytime you can see the outcroppings of rock that make cultivation difficult if not impossible. Those rocks were the bane of my father's existence. He used to say that he ought to have been running a quarry instead of a farm, except that then the grapes would have sprung up like weeds just to spite him."

"Your father was a farmer?"

Jordan shrugged. "He was many things, few of them successful, but mostly he was a loving husband to my mother and a wonderful father to Sylvia and me."

"Sylvia?"

"My sister, the one who lives in Connecticut. I took her to New York with me for my first international exhibit, and while she was there, she met a young lawyer, and they eloped after a whirlwind courtship. She has three small children now."

Thinking of how aggressively maternal Italian women seemed to be, Gemma commented, "Your mother must enjoy her grandchildren."

"She's never seen them," Jordan said, scowling. "Sylvia feels her babies are still too small to travel overseas, and mother refuses to go back to the United States." For a moment Gemma thought he was about to say something else, but just then the driver asked for directions, and Jordan's attention was diverted. The taxi turned onto a steeply graded incline, and when Gemma looked out the window, she could see house lights halfway up the side of the hill. In a few moments the car ground to a halt on a leveled parking area, and Jordan dug into the pocket of his denim trousers to fish out his wallet. As he handed the driver a wad of thousand-lire notes, Gemma got out of the cab on her side and gazed at the house.

With only the porch light and the sliver of moon providing illumination, Gemma could not make out details of architecture, but the villa appeared to be constructed of the cream-colored stucco traditional in Latin countries, with a gently sloping roof of red ceramic tiles that would insulate it against the fierce heat of the Mediterranean sun. However, instead of rising several stories, as did most of the homes in the area, with perhaps an encircling balcony high up under the eaves, this house spread low and wide, stepping up the slope of the vine-covered hillside in graduated levels.

As Gemma studied the clean lines of the shuttered windows, appreciating the blend of old and decidedly modern styles, in the back of her mind she became aware of the receding rattle of the taxi as it wended its way down the long driveway, and she could feel Jordan's presence, intimidating and oddly disturbing, just behind her. She did not look at him. After a moment he asked, ''Well, what do you think of Villa Sogno Dolce?''

She translated slowly, ''The house of sweet dreams? It's very beautiful.''

''The name or the building?'' he asked. She could hear the amusement in his voice.

Gemma pondered. ''Both, I suppose. The name seems pretty—perhaps a little flowery, but then, I'm not used to houses with names, only street addresses. But I've always liked architecture with uncluttered lines.''

''*Grazie,*'' he said dryly. ''I'm glad at least something of mine meets with your approval.'' After a pause he explained, ''My mother named the house when she was a bride, hence the faintly honeymoon flavor.''

Gemma frowned. "The building doesn't seem nearly old enough for that. I would have guessed it was built no more than three or four years ago.''

"Six, actually. The original house was of wood, and much smaller. It caught fire during an electrical storm. We were able to save most of the contents, but the structure itself was gutted, and I built this one to replace it.''

Gemma surveyed the villa again and then looked up at Jordan. "Did you design this one yourself?''

He shrugged. "I used an architect, but I knew exactly what I wanted. My mother designed the kitchen.''

"It's very nice," she said inadequately.

He smiled down at her, the lines of his narrow face limned in the yellow porch light. "I hope you like the interior, as well,'' he murmured, his deep voice caressing, almost seductive. Gemma blinked uneasily, and his expression changed, became carefully neutral again. "I'm being a very poor host, I'm afraid," he said. "You must be faint with hunger. Come on inside. I'll introduce you to my mother, and then we'll see what we can find for you to eat.'' He strode across the driveway to the front door, where he tried the heavy bronze knob, scowling when it would not turn. He took out his keys and unlocked the door, flinging it open as he called in Italian, "Mother, we're home!''

When there was no answer, his frown deepened. His long legs carried him into the center of the cavernous living room, and he signed for Gemma to follow him.

Hesitantly she complied. The air beneath the high-beamed ceiling was surprisingly cool after the heat outside, and under her bare aching feet the shining marble terrazzo floor felt almost cold, soothing and silky smooth. As Gemma glanced about with pleasure, Jordan said, "I'll go try to find my mother," and he stalked out of the room, mounting a short flight of steps to disappear into the passageway to one of the upper levels. Gemma scarcely noticed his departure, enrapt as she was with her survey of the house. This part, she could see, was one large open room, divided into living areas by strategically placed furniture and shag rugs and—she realized with surprise—several life-size statues. Quickly her eyes flitted from one piece to the next, and she noted the framed sketches hung on the off-white textured stucco and the smaller bronzes that were displayed in irregular niches in the walls. Even at a distance she could tell that the quality of the work was exceptional. Gemma caught her breath as gradually her brain acknowledged that what she was looking at was the private collection of Jordan di Mario, the works admired personally by one of the masters of contemporary Western art.

She had never seen art of this caliber anywhere except in a museum, and she moved slowly about the room, trying to imagine what it would be like to live surrounded by such treasures. She gazed with reverential awe at a red crayon drawing of a beggar that bore the unmistakable imprint of Rembrandt, evidently a study for some painting she was unfamiliar with; in the margins were several quick sketches where the artist had worked out the placement of the hands. In a depression in the wall alongside the Rembrandt she found an exquisitely detailed statuette of a young girl in Renaissance dress, her long skirts lifted to reveal tiny feet in beribboned dancing slippers. The piece was breathtakingly beautiful. Gemma raised a fingertip to stroke the floating bronze ruffles, almost expecting them to feel soft and lacy, but instead she let her hand fall back to her side, fearful that the oils in her skin would tarnish the burnished metal. Hard steps caught her attention, and she glanced up just as Jordan returned, glowering, from the upper level. Before he could speak, she asked, "This couldn't really be a Cellini, could it?"

When he noticed what she was looking at, he smiled. "I see you found the gem of my collection, or at any rate, my favorite piece." Striding to Gemma's side, he laid one arm casually over her shoulder as he admired the figurine of the dancing girl. "No," he said, "for all its grace of detail, this lovely thing is not a Cellini, although you're close. The official provenance reads, 'By a student of Cellini.'" He chuckled, but there was no humor in his deep voice. "Nearly five hundred years ago some poor sod poured his heart into the creation of a statuette that by any standards ought to be called a masterpiece, and his accomplishment has been ignored because he was only 'a student of Cellini.' I discovered it in the back room of an antique shop in Pisa, black with tarnish and utterly forgotten. God alone knows what would have become of it if I had not happened upon it."

Gemma gazed down at the statuette and winced at the prospect of such beauty lost or destroyed. She pursed her small mouth and said thoughtfully, "The artist might have been a woman, you know. That could be why the piece was ignored. For centuries women artists have been deliberately dismissed as merely 'the student of' somebody else, when their works weren't disparaged or appropriated by some better-known male artist."

Jordan nodded. "Yes, unfortunately you are correct." He gave Gemma's shoulder a reassuring squeeze. "Thank God those days are over."

"Are they?" she asked belligerently, gray eyes flashing as she suddenly remembered her many grievances against the male sex. His arm weighed heavily on her. The embrace seemed casual enough, but his closeness disturbed her, his hard masculine body evoking an unwelcome harmonic response in her own. Great sculptor or not, she was altogether too conscious of him. She pulled away from him sharply, her thin shoulder tingling where his long fingers dug into her flesh, and she demanded, "Did you find your mother?"

He shook his head, regarding her coolly. "No," he said after a moment's hesitation. "Apparently she has gone out for the evening. It appears you and I have the house to ourselves now."

Gemma's eyes widened. "You mean we're alone?" she exclaimed, suddenly remembering the long road that had brought them to the villa, winding through the hillside for miles without passing another house. As if in answer, her voice echoed mockingly back to her, reverberating from the polished floor, the high ceiling. She closed her eyes to the sight of the numerous couches that served as room dividers, all long and seductively wide. She peeked apprehensively through her lashes at the tall powerful man standing before her, and she felt perspiration break out on her pale forehead. She tried not to think of Franco, or her attacker at the school in Golden. She tried to remember that this man was Jordan di Mario, a respected figure in the world of art, not some teenager fueled by an overabundance of hormones. But all she could think was that he was a man, a stranger, and blinded by his talent, like an idiot she had allowed herself to be brought to this deserted house where she was completely at his mercy.

He watched the emotions playing over her expressive features, reading them with ease. His lips thinned and he grated, *"Dio!* Did I call you a repressed fifteen-year-old? Better make that twelve!" And before Gemma could realize what he was doing, his hands caught her shoulders, pulling her against him with muscles as hard as the stone he carved, as his mouth closed hotly over hers.

She was too stunned at first to react, surprised and bewildered by the pressure that brought her lips to his. One of his arms encircled her waist and pinioned her against him, making her acutely aware of the urgent compelling strength of his lean body. Then, after the first dazed seconds, all her fears and angers reasserted themselves, and she tried to twist away from him, thrashing wildly. His grip tightened relentlessly. She wanted to cry out in protest, but his swift movement had robbed her of breath, making her gasp futilely. Then his hand traced up her spine to her nape, holding her head immobile while his tongue parted her lips and delved the inner sweetness of her mouth with dizzying purpose.

As quickly as it had begun, the kiss was over. He flung her away from him, and she stumbled backward. He snorted, "There, now that I've done what you're afraid of, you can quit acting like a hysterical virgin."

"I'm...I'm not!" Gemma stammered indignantly as she fell clumsily against the wall, her bare feet slipping on the terrazzo. She righted herself awkwardly. Disgusted at the quaver in her husky voice, she glared at him balefully, gray eyes stormy. She knew that he had found no more pleasure in that travesty of an embrace than she had. His assault had been an act of pure domination, the kind she loathed. Her fear began to ebb. She knew instinctively that, having proved his point, he would not repeat his action. But as her alarm faded, it was replaced by blind rage. She felt shaken and subdued, and he appeared totally unaffected by what he had done. In fact, he seemed amused.

She wanted to lash out at him and dared not; he would only laugh at her. Her impotent fury increased when he asked outrageously, "You're not what—not hysterical or not a virgin?" She turned away without answering, her hunched shoulders quivering with temper.

The room was filled with a charged silence until at last behind her she heard him say grudgingly, biting off the words, "All right, I'm sorry. But you must admit you were asking for that."

Seething, she spun around to confront him. "Isn't that just like a man? I admit nothing of the sort! You were the one who—"

He held up his bandaged hand to silence her, but whatever he had intended to say was choked off as he barked, *"Maledizione!"* He flexed his wrist, scowling. He muttered darkly, "I must have aggravated the sprain when I grabbed you."

"Good," Gemma snapped coldly.

He stared down at her, and Gemma stared back. For a moment they glowered at each other, the tall man and the much smaller woman, and then almost at the same time they seemed to become aware of the absurdity of their posture. In unison they began to chuckle. Jordan suggested gently, "Perhaps we could call a truce?"

Slowly Gemma relaxed. "I think that would be an excellent idea," she agreed.

With a coaxing smile he nodded toward the lowest level of the house. "Come on," he said, his deep voice smooth. "There's a telephone in the kitchen. You make your call while I see what I can produce for our dinner. I don't know about you, but I'm starved."

The kitchen of the villa was a tribute to a different kind of art, the art of haute cuisine, or at least of the appliance manufacturer. The bright spacious room was shiny with stainless steel and Formica, and it seemed to be equipped with every modern cooking gadget imaginable. Gemma could not help comparing it with the cramped smoke-stained kitchen at the *pensione* where her landlady prepared her culinary masterpieces. She wondered if food cooked here would taste as plastic as the counter tops.

Jordan looked up from rummaging through the massive freezer to incline his leonine head toward the telephone hanging on the wall. "Go ahead and place your call," he said. "To reach the long-distance operator, dial 1-7-0."

"Shall I reverse the charges?" Gemma asked, and when he frowned at the suggestion, she sighed and picked up the receiver. "I suppose I'd better call the pottery," she muttered. "It's only about noon in Golden right now, and Marsha will be at work." She lifted the earpiece, wrinkling her brow when she heard only silence. "Nothing's happening," she said. "Are you sure your telephone is in order?"

Jordan laughed. "I told you you were spoiled by American phones. Just wait. The dial tone will come eventually. It's a sort of dash-dash-dash sound. If you get a dot-dot-dot instead, it means the central computer is overloaded, and you'll have to try again later."

"Good heavens," Gemma murmured, "I'll never complain about my bill again," and she returned her attention to the telephone.

SOMETIME LATER Gemma replaced the receiver and stared blindly at the gleaming copper pans and utensils dangling from the high-beamed ceiling, focusing on her image distorted and reflected ruddily on their rounded surfaces, yet not really seeing anything. Jordan glanced up from setting the table to inquire with concern, "What's wrong? You seemed to have reached Colorado with surprising ease. Has something happened there?"

Gemma smiled mechanically. "No, I...I guess everything is all right. It's just that I can't get hold of Caroline's mother. That was her assistant I talked to, and she says that Marsha suddenly decided to take a short vacation of her own and won't be back for several days."

"I see. Did you give the assistant the message?"

Gemma shook her head. "No. I don't know the woman very well, and I'm afraid she might get it mixed-up. It will be awkward enough telling Marsha her daughter has been hurt without relaying the news fourth hand." She bit her lip, wincing at the tenderness caused by Jordan's abrasive kiss, and she murmured, "But I really must let Marsha know what has happened."

Jordan pulled out a chair and motioned for Gemma to be seated. "Here. You can eat while we decide what to do."

With a grateful smile Gemma plopped down at the table, and she gazed with wonder at the steaming platter before her, piled high with fragrant little pillows of pasta, redolent with spinach and Parmesan cheese and a whiff of nutmeg. As Jordan filled her wineglass with crystalline liquid from a dusty green bottle, he said, "You are about to have an authentic Tuscan treat, one that can never be ordered in a restaurant: *ravioli nudi*—naked ravioli. The only place this is served is in the home."

Gemma dug her fork into one of the patties, admiring the colorful mixture of green vegetable and white cheese that oozed out. "Don't try to convince me that this is something you just whipped up," she commented as she took a bite. "It's delicious."

Jordan said, "No, my mother made it; I simply defrosted it. It's a complicated recipe, and it makes far too much for only two people, so we freeze a lot. Hardly traditional, but convenient."

"Then there's just your mother and you?" Gemma asked, thinking of the echoing expanses of the villa, which was big enough to accommodate a very large family.

"I'm not married, if that's what you're wondering," Jordan said dryly.

Irritated by his bland assumption that she was interested in his marital status, Gemma shrugged elaborately and stabbed another ravioli with her fork. "Actually I wasn't," she said distantly. "It didn't occur to me to be concerned one way or the other. I was merely thinking in terms of all this wasted space."

Jordan's mouth twitched. "I like privacy," he said. "There is an apartment for a housekeeper, but at the moment it's vacant, since the women who do the cleaning prefer to live in their own homes. Because the house is so remote, we entertain rarely, although there is, of course, room for quite a house party, should we ever desire to do so."

Gemma chewed thoughtfully. "Don't you ever find it lonely?"

Jordan shook his head. "It suits us. Mother likes to live with her memories, and I found out long ago that the social whirl is not conducive to getting much work done."

"You work here?"

He sipped his wine. "That depends on what you mean by work. All my carving is done in Pietrasanta. I usually send my bronzes to Germany for casting, but here I have a studio where I sketch and model and experiment." His fingers toyed with the stem of the goblet, as if he were appreciating the feel of it.

Gemma watched him fondle the glass. As she gazed at his long narrow hands, the olive skin sprinkled with fine black hairs and crisscrossed with faded scars that she knew now must have been inflicted by ill-aimed chisels, she thought with awe of the magic in those hands, the incredible talent that allowed him to touch a lump of clay or a hunk of rock with the same heightened sensitivity that ordinary men would use when touching a lover; that gave him the power to mold inanimate material into something so beautiful that it seemed to acquire a life of its own. She tried to envision the images inside that head, knowing with the insight of a fellow artist that for every idea that eventually took shape in wood or bronze or marble, a thousand more proved elusive, intangible. She thought of the richness of his work, and she longed wistfully for an opportunity to see just a little more, approach just a little closer to the center of his perception than could the ordinary viewer in a museum. She wondered if she dared ask. Sharing a meal in the intimacy of his family kitchen, the idea did not seem too outrageously presumptuous, so when he smiled across the table at her, Gemma ventured huskily, "I would dearly love to see your studio."

His smile faded instantly, and with it the easy camaraderie between them. "No one sees my studio," he said in tones as cold as the chilled white wine in his glass, "not even my mother."

Gemma blanched at his obvious scorn, and when she tried to stammer her apologies, tension made her low-pitched voice even throatier than usual. "I...I beg your pardon, I d-didn't mean to pry."

He gazed at her thoughtfully, his expression altering subtly as his eyes moved over her slowly with insinuating purpose. He set down his fork, and his right hand snaked over the table to capture her left. "Perhaps I should be the one to apologize," he murmured, stroking her palm with his callused thumb. Gemma stared apprehensively at their joined hands, and suddenly it occurred to her that the combination of good food, wine and their enforced proximity had begun to have an effect on him, as well, the effect he had denied earlier. He said smoothly, "I must be more tired than I realized not to understand that you were asking not to invade my privacy but to...see my etchings." His voice rose suggestively on the last syllable, and Gemma's heart began to race.

"That's not what I meant at all," she insisted, trying to pull her hand away.

His grip tightened. "Come, my dear, you needn't be coy. I assure you I'm experienced enough to recognize that husky note in a woman's voice, that breathless little—"

"Damn it," Gemma snapped, "I am not being coy! I can't help the way I talk." She struggled hard to retain her temper, knowing full well that if she did not, Jordan would not hesitate to take advantage of her loss of control. Somewhere between the collision on the highway and that shared meal in the villa on the hillside, the sculptor had become aware of her as a woman—although in her disheveled state she couldn't imagine why—and because he was obviously a man the female half of the population would never ignore, her resistance both irritated and amused him. No doubt he thought Gemma should feel honored by his notice.

Thinking quickly, she said urgently, "Please, I've

just thought of someone I can call in Colorado who will make sure the message gets to Marsha.''

"Who?''

Gemma stammered, "My...my fiancé.''

Jordan's expression was thunderous. "Your what?'' he demanded.

Gemma said with studied casualness, "My fiancé. The man I'm going to marry.'' Automatically she tried to flash her engagement ring—remembering too late that it was not there.

Jordan stared pointedly at the betraying stripe of white at the base of her finger. "You've forgotten your ring,'' he observed silkily.

Gemma shook her head. "No, I haven't. I...I just decided not to wear it on the trip, that's all.''

"Why not? Was the diamond so large that you were afraid that in a—benighted, I think you called it—country like Italy some brigand might try to relieve you of it?'' His fingertips traced her knuckles, shaping the fine bones that gleamed palely through her translucent skin, mapping the network of veins, then suddenly he flung her hand away from him. He growled, "Or did you prefer not to let a symbol of another man's ownership interfere with any summer romances you might choose to enjoy?''

His sarcasm stung and bewildered her. Her gray eyes widened until the blue flecks were clearly visible. "No one owns me,'' she persisted, confused. "You're being deliberately hateful. I don't understand why you are acting like this.''

He snorted and shrugged. "Forget it,'' he muttered. "Go make your damned phone call.''

Still staring at him, she scraped her chair back

from the table and went to the telephone. This time
the wait was longer before the dial tone sounded, but
eventually she made contact with the long-distance
operator, and after that it was only a matter of
minutes before she heard Dave answer gruffly,
"Hello?"

Leaning her forehead against the wall, she wanted
to sob with relief at the comforting familiarity of his
voice, and her emotions made her speak more warmly than she had intended. She said, "Dave, darling,
this is Gemma."

He squawked in disbelief, "For God's sake, Gemma, why are you calling all the way from Europe?
Are you all right? You are in Italy, aren't you?"

"Yes, yes," she interrupted, conscious of the man
at the table listening intently to every word she spoke.
"I'm fine, but please, Dave, I need your help."
Quickly she outlined Caroline's accident and the ex-
tent of her injuries.

She heard him swear roughly. "I knew that kid
would be too much for you to handle. I never should
have let you leave without me." He paused for a second and then said firmly, "Look, sweetheart, don't
worry about a thing. If I hustle over to Denver, I can
be on a plane to New York within hours, and then
from there it'll just be a matter of—"

Gemma cried in dismay, "No, Dave, I don't want
you to come to Italy! I just want you to find Marsha
and tell her that—"

"Gemma," Dave said firmly in his most patronizing tones, "don't argue with me. This is one time
when you obviously need a man to—"

"But, Dave—"

The receiver was ripped out of Gemma's hand, and she staggered backward, gasping in amazement as Jordan, who had come up silently behind her, barked into the mouthpiece, "Blanchard, listen to me and pay attention. It is entirely unnecessary for you to make the journey to Italy. I assure you that I have everything well in hand, and Gemma and her little friend are being properly cared for. You need not worry about them." Even several feet from the telephone Gemma could hear Dave's indignant protest, and she watched Jordan's mouth curl up mirthlessly as the other man argued. She tried to figure out how Jordan could have known Dave's surname, then she realized that she had given the name when she placed the call with the operator. After a moment he interjected smoothly, but with the hard ring of authority in his voice, "I am di Mario. If you know Gemma well at all, you may have heard of me." There was another outburst from Dave, and Jordan said, "No, you will help most by finding Mrs. Somerville for Gemma. She'll be in touch with you later. *Ciao!*" He replaced the receiver in its cradle.

Gemma gaped at him, speechless. "Who the hell do you think you are?" she rasped when she could find her voice again. "And just what did you mean by that crack about if he knew me well, he might have heard of you? I've never met you before today."

"No," Jordan agreed, waving away her protest with a very Latin gesture, "but if your fiancé has tried to share or at least keep abreast of your interest in sculpture, as any attentive lover should, then I flatter myself that my name might be vaguely familiar."

"I see," Gemma said weakly, turning away. She wondered what Jordan would say if she told him that Dave, like the rest of her family, had never shown any desire at all to learn about the art that was so important to her. He had thought nothing of expecting her to read chemical abstracts in obscure trade journals, but on the rare occasions when she had managed to drag him to the magnificent Denver Art Museum, he had tagged along after her with the pained air of an adult indulging a willful child.

Jordan studied Gemma's shoulders drooping glumly, and he commented, "Your fiancé seems fairly hostile. When's the wedding?" Gemma didn't answer. After a pause Jordan said hardly, "There isn't going to be a wedding, is there?"

Gemma looked up at him, startled. She thought about lying, then said only, "How did you know?"

Jordan shrugged. "If you were still engaged, he'd be here with you now." His eyes ran easily over her slight figure and lingered on her silver white hair. "No man in his right mind would let you out of his sight."

Leave it to a man to bring up sex, Gemma thought acidly. "Thanks for the compliment," she said, biting off the words. "If it was a compliment."

"Oh, it was, I assure you." His voice was light, but she wondered if he had noticed her instinctive recoil. "Who broke the engagement," he asked curiously, "you or him?"

Gemma took a deep breath. "Not that it's any of your business, but I did."

Jordan nodded. "I thought so. Do you mind telling me why?"

She stared at him incredulously. "Yes, I mind!" she snapped. "For God's sake, who do you—"

Her words were cut off by a commotion coming from the direction of the front door, and she heard light footsteps on the terrazzo in the entryway. "Giordano!" a feminine voice called out in Italian. "Where are you?"

Jordan's face lighted up at the sound, his thin mouth and hard dark eyes crinkling into a pleased smile of such devastating charm that Gemma almost gasped at the sheer masculine beauty of him. In the few hours since she had met the sculptor, Gemma's emotions had been so volatile and so overwrought that she had lost sight of the fact that he was exceptionally attractive even for an Italian, and Italians were by and large a handsome race. Moreover, she was troubled once again by the niggling certainty that she had seen him at some time in the past—and not, as might be expected, in a photograph. When he told her he avoided publicity, she was sure that he had meant that literally.

Jordan's smile altered to a mocking grin as he glanced at Gemma. "At last," he drawled, "my mother has returned. I know you were beginning to believe she was just a figment of my imagination. Either that or a clever ploy to lure unsuspecting girls into my lair." Before she could say anything, he lifted his head and sang out in the peculiarly musical intonation Italians use for calling someone, *"Mamma, alla cucina!"*

The footsteps approached rapidly, and Gemma, once again made aware of her raddled appearance, tried to slick back her tangled hair with her hands.

She scuffed her bare toes together in the self-conscious gesture of a child. When Jordan's hands suddenly reached for her breast, she yelped and tried to pull away, and he said impatiently, "Be still. Your blouse is unbuttoned."

She looked down and saw with dismay that the lapels of her cotton shirt were indeed gaping open, exposing a considerable amount of bare skin. Blushing hotly, she groaned, "Oh, heavens, how long has it been like that?"

Jordan shrugged. "A while. You shouldn't flail around so much when someone tries to kiss you." He began with methodical precision to refasten her buttons, and she shivered as his fingers stroked against her smooth flesh.

In a shaking voice she demanded, "Why didn't you just tell me that—?" But her indignant question was interrupted by a stunned voice gasping from the doorway.

Jordan's hands continued their task without pause, and Gemma turned her head reluctantly in the direction of that voice. A very tall rawboned woman with silver-frosted brown hair stared at them, pale blue eyes wide in her plain face. "Giordano!" she choked, staring pointedly at her son's hands apparently caressing the younger woman, and she launched into harsh vituperative Italian of which only one word was intelligible to Gemma, a word, which, oddly, she had always assumed was an American colloquialism.

Calmly Jordan looped the last button into place and then, digging his hands deep into his pockets, he turned to confront his mother. Although Signora di

Mario was very tall, he still towered over her by at least six inches, and he was obviously master of the situation. He said quietly but firmly in English, "Yes, mother, I do have better taste than to get involved with groupies, and since Gemma is not one, I think you owe her an apology." The woman bristled, running her eyes contemptuously over Gemma, and Jordan added sternly, "In English, mother."

At last, sullenly and with an effort the woman muttered, "It seems I must beg your pardon, Miss...Miss...."

"Culver. Gemma Culver," Gemma said automatically, disconcerted not by Signora di Mario's obvious hostility so much as by her accent. When the woman spoke English, she did so in a voice that even in anger was redolent of magnolias and honeysuckles, banjo music floating on sultry evening breezes—a languid Southern drawl that would have done credit to Scarlett O'Hara. Gemma cast a startled glance in Jordan's direction. She had had no idea his mother was an American.

Satisfied with her apology, Jordan relaxed and kissed his mother's thin cheek warmly for all the world as if he had not been giving her stern orders only seconds before, then he turned to Gemma. He said, "Gemma, I'd like you to meet my mother, Beatrice di Mario." Gemma noted that he pronounced the name in the Italian fashion, Bay-ah-*tree*-chay. He continued with a grin, "I expect you've figured out already that my mother is a *compaesana* of yours, although anyone who heard her haggling with the fishmonger over the price of squid would be hard pressed to believe that she was born in Memphis, Tennessee.''

Signora di Mario smiled lovingly at her son, but there was something at the back of her pale eyes that made Gemma certain that the woman was not thrilled to have her personal history aired for a stranger. Timidly Gemma extended her hand and said, "I'm delighted to meet you."

Jordan's mother touched her fingers briefly and looked at her son again. "Giordano, where is the Ferrari?" she asked, frowning. "We didn't see it in the garage when we drove up. And what have you done to your arm?"

Jordan looked puzzled. "We?"

"Yes, Francesca is here. But, Giordano, your arm—"

When she was interrupted once more by the sound of the front door opening, followed by yet another woman's voice calling out their names, Jordan glanced sharply at his mother, his expression inscrutable, and he said impatiently, "I'll explain later." Again they heard footsteps on the terrazzo, this time the staccato clicking sound of high heels hurrying across the floor, striking the tiles with such force that Gemma wondered if they made sparks. Suddenly, with a trill of silvery laughter, and as if wafted on a cloud of Joy perfume, a stunning brunette burst into the room.

She halted at the doorway, one hand with its long cyclamen nails resting fetchingly on the jamb. Watching that gesture, Gemma knew in a flash of insight that the woman was posing deliberately to give her audience—or at any rate, Jordan—a moment to appreciate the effect of her voluptuous body in its stylish rose-colored sun dress of clinging silk. And, Gemma acknowledged with the eye of an artist, the effect was outstanding. She appeared to be about thirty, of medium height, with lustrous blue black curls that fell in artful disarray to her shoulders, framing a face of remarkable beauty. She had the pure unsullied features of a Renaissance Madonna— or she would have had, had not her fine black eyes flashed petulantly as they glanced at the two women watching her, her own sex obviously holding little interest for her. That momentary expression vanished as she smiled up at Jordan, and when he did not respond, she sidled across the kitchen, the provocative sway of her hips emphasized by the unnatural gait caused by the stiltlike spike heels she wore, and launched herself at him.

His arms caught her automatically, but he did not pull her to him. He murmured coolly, "Francesca, what a . . . surprise. Just what are you doing here?"

Signora di Mario reproved, "Giordano, that's no way to speak to a guest!" and Francesca flashed a grateful smile at her. Her gaze passed over Gemma as if she were invisible.

Francesca sighed elaborately, "Don't blame him, Beatrice, it is all my fault. Obviously Giordano is still angry with me." She looked back up at Jordan again, her lips widening sensually. "Please, *caro*," she wheedled, "you must forgive me. It was such a stupid argument. I'm sorry." He still did not react. She pressed her body invitingly against his. "I'll make it up to you, I promise," she said, her voice low and seductive, and reaching up to draw his head down to hers, she began to kiss him fervently.

Jordan's mother watched that embrace benignly, but Gemma felt embarrassed and uncomfortable. She trained her gaze on the artsy-craftsy lobster-shaped gelatin mold decorating one wall, and she tried to ignore the peculiar wrenching sensation that curled deep inside her as the kiss went on and on. When at last Francesca released Jordan, her beautiful features were flushed, that Madonnalike purity that Gemma had first noticed now masked by a look of knowing triumph.

As Gemma reluctantly glanced at the woman again, she realized with a start that she had seen that face, that expression before—not living, but carved in stone. Francesca was the model for the female figure of *Privilege*, the subtly erotic statue that was Jordan di Mario's masterpiece.

And Jordan—now she knew why he had seemed so elusively familiar to her, why all day long she had been certain that she had seen him somewhere before, and the implications of her newfound knowledge disturbed her greatly. Yes, she had seen Jordan, not in person and not in anything so mundane as a photograph, but, like Francesca, shaped in marble. The male figure in *Privilege* had been a self-portrait...and that statue had haunted and aroused Gemma ever since she first saw it when she was seventeen years old.

CHAPTER FOUR

"YOU'RE BEING VERY QUIET," Jordan observed as he drove his mother's small sedan toward the *pensione* on the outskirts of Pietrasanta. "I hope you didn't let my mother and Francesca upset you."

"Of course not," Gemma said sarcastically. "I just love being treated like something that crawled out of the sewer." She screwed her eyes closed, trying to shut out the memory of Francesca's disdainful sniff when she was introduced to Gemma, or the wary contempt that marked Signora di Mario's carefully impassive features whenever Jordan was not looking at her. Gemma glanced down at her dingy jeans and shirt, her bare dirty feet. She considered the immaculate grooming of the other two women, and she shrugged ruefully. "Oh, hell," she sighed, "I guess I do look like—like hell."

"Nonsense," Jordan said imperturbably. "You're beautiful."

Gemma snorted, "Yeah. Sure." She made an elaborate show of brushing the grime from her scuffed knees.

His hard mouth curved upward into an arresting indulgent grin. "I wasn't being facetious, Gemma. Of course, now you are tired and dirty and depressed, but those are merely temporary conditions.

Basically you are a very beautiful woman with remarkable bone structure. When you are elderly, you
will still be beautiful.''

Gemma blinked in astonishment. "Th-thank you.
I . . . I hardly know what to say."

"Why not say you'll model for me? I should like
very much to sketch you."

Gemma swallowed hard, uncertain that she had
heard him correctly. When she found her voice, it
came out as a croaky whisper. "You'd like to sketch
me?" The idea was unbelievable, incomprehensible.
There were people in the world willing to pay fabu-
lous prices for the privilege of posing for Jordan di
Mario; he could have his pick of beautiful models,
women like Francesca.

He smiled down at her again, and she looked away
quickly, unable to meet his dark gaze. Unbidden, an
image flickered in her mind: the two of them clois-
tered in the secret confines of his private studio, her
half-naked body draped in some provocative pose
while his eyes moved slowly and caressingly over her,
those long strong hands setting aside his sketchbook
and reaching out to. . . .

Gemma shivered, disturbed by the direction of her
thoughts. From beneath lowered lashes she glanced
sidelong at Jordan, at that lean and powerful frame
folded behind the steering wheel. He was downright
dangerous, she admitted with a wry grimace, a
menace to any woman's peace of mind. That sexual
aura that emanated from his stone self-portrait was
doubly potent around the living man. She bit her lip
to keep from giggling shakily.

When Jordan shot a puzzled look in her direction,

he noticed her shudder and asked, "Is something wrong?" She did not answer right away. He frowned as he returned his attention to the road.

Gemma offered up a quick fervent prayer of thanks that he seemed ignorant of the devastating effect he was having on her senses. She improvised, "I...I was just trying to imagine myself posing in...in Francesca's place for a statue like *Privilege*. The idea is absurd."

He said sternly, "Of course it is. There is no comparison at all between the two of you."

Although Gemma knew that she could never compete with the lovely Francesca, still she felt stung. But while she struggled not to betray her hurt, Jordan remarked, "You have a very discerning eye, to recognize Francesca as the model for *Privilege*. Most people have difficulty equating a statue with a living human being, even when they are told of the connection."

"I recognized you, too," Gemma said quietly.

Jordan chuckled dryly. "You mean my...self-portrait? That's one bit of schoolboy vanity I've often regretted, especially in light of the ridiculous furor the statue aroused. I excuse myself on the grounds that I was still young and rather cocky, but it could have been embarrassing had it become generally known what I had done. Fortunately few people are as observant as you."

"It's still a marvelous piece of work."

Jordan inclined his head. "*Grazie*. Are you very familiar with *Privilege*?"

Gemma's eyes shone. *I might even be able to say that I talked to Jordan di Mario about sculpture,* she had dreamed, and now that fantasy was coming true. She enthused, "I saw the statue years ago when I was in high school, about the time it first went on display in the United States. One of the nuns took several of us to Chicago during the semester break, the first really major exhibition I ever saw. I was stunned! I'll never forget that moment when I—"

Jordan turned his head again to stare at her, interrupting curiously, "You attended a convent school? I didn't think Americans went in for that sort of thing anymore. Even in Europe the practice is dying out."

The eager light in Gemma's face dimmed, and she turned to gaze resolutely out the window. They were traveling through the center of town now. The narrow streets were deserted except for one sidewalk café where a few dilatory customers clustered about a curbside table, conversing noisily, drinking cheap potent grappa and passing around a suspicious-looking cigarette butt. As the sedan drove by, one young woman with stringy hair and dusty blue denim overalls glanced up. Her eyes widened, losing their glazed look, and she pointed wildly at Jordan. He noticed the gesture, scowling, and before the woman's companions could rise from their seats, he had pressed down on the accelerator, speeding away in a haze of exhaust fumes. When the café was several blocks behind them, he asked Gemma again, as if the little incident had not happened, "Why did you go to a convent school? Did your family cherish hopes that you might find a vocation there?"

Gemma shook her head without looking at him. "My mother died when I was nine," she said tightly.

"My father...thought I...needed some female influence in my life."

Noting the rigid set of her shoulders, Jordan said quietly, "I see." They continued in silence until he asked further directions to the *pensione*. Gemma pointed the way, and he turned where she indicated. As the car approached the outskirts of town, he continued blandly, "You never really gave me an answer, so I'll inquire again. Will you pose for me?"

She turned to stare up at him, her eyes wide and oddly vulnerable in her heart-shaped face. "No," she said, quietly insistent. "Thank you for asking, but I've come to Pietrasanta to study sculpture, not to model."

Jordan nodded. "Yes, I thought you'd say that. Of course, I understand, but...*che peccato*—what a pity!"

When Jordan pulled the car to a halt in front of the boardinghouse, Gemma was surprised to see lights still burning in Signora Ricci's little *salotto*. Franco's mother usually retired early after her busy day attending to her tenants and ordering her son to do likewise, and while the guests were free to roam at will, the parlor on the ground floor, with its stiff and uncomfortable horsehair suite, pride of the *signora*'s heart since her days as a bride, was commonly accepted as out-of-bounds once she went to her own room for the night. Gemma noted the fringed and flowered lamp that glowed through the open window, illuminating the graveled courtyard, and she said, "I...I guess someone waited up to see how Caroline is doing." Reaching for the car door handle, she turned to Jordan and smiled awkwardly.

"I must thank you once again for all your help. It was—" Her words were cut off when abruptly he got out of the sedan and came around to open her door for her.

As she stepped out onto the driveway, wincing as the sharp pebbles hurt her scratched bruised feet, she looked at Jordan in puzzlement, and he smiled benignly. "I thought you might invite me in for coffee," he suggested in that honey-dark voice of his.

Gemma nodded uncertainly. "Of...course. I'm sure the *signora* wouldn't—" She took one step and stumbled, hissing with pain.

Instantly Jordan's scarred hands grabbed her, and she gave a startled cry as he swung her up into his arms and carried her across the gravel to the porch of the *pensione*. Instinctively Gemma clung to him, her thin arms around his neck, and she was uncomfortably aware of the hard muscles under his warm brown skin, the tight ringlets of black body hair just visible through the open collar of his shirt. When he set her down with care, she trembled with relief. In the yellow light he studied her face. "I told you you should have had a doctor look at your feet," he said harshly. "Now we'll have to attend to your cuts here. Do you feel up to—?"

"I am perfectly capable of dressing my own scratches," Gemma snapped. "There is no need for you to concern yourself with—"

The front door to the *pensione* flew open, and Dieter Stahl's voice gushed with an excitement utterly foreign to his usual grim demeanor, "Herr di Mario, how glad I am to see you again! Oh, and of course, Gemma, too. I was hoping for a chance to show you...that is, Claretta and I waited for you because we wondered how poor Fräulein Somerville is faring.''

Jordan stiffened visibly, but when he turned to address the young German and the Italian girl who hovered behind him, her clothes somewhat askew, his manner was politely cordial. ''It was kind of you to be so concerned,'' he said, ''but Gemma and I will not have further news on Caroline's condition until morning.'' He glanced at Gemma, his eyes raking down her slim figure to her feet. ''You'd better dress those cuts now,'' he muttered. ''Will you need help?'' Without waiting for Gemma to speak, he nudged her through the door into the house.

Extremely conscious of the other couple's intrigued appraisal, Gemma shook her head quickly. ''If I do need help, I'm sure Claretta can assist me. There's no need for you to delay further. Thank you again for bringing me home and for—''

''Gemma, I won't leave until I am assured you are all right,'' Jordan said, his dark eyes glittering infuriatingly. ''You really don't—''

Gemma glared balefully at Jordan and sighed. ''I know, I don't know when to give up. You've mentioned that before.''

He mocked with a grin, ''Then it's too bad you can't seem to learn the lesson.'' His teeth were very white against his olive skin.

Gemma clenched her fists in impotent fury, staring up at him with turbulent gray eyes. She wondered how an artist of such sensitivity could also be such a sarcastic beast. Silently she vowed, *someday... someday I'll wipe that arrogant smirk off your face.*

Their glances locked, ebony and moonstone. She had the uncanny feeling that he knew exactly what she was thinking, and that he did not find the knowledge particularly alarming.

While Gemma fumed, Dieter exchanged an unctuously man-to-man look with Jordan and called back over his shoulder, "Claretta, go help Fräulein Culver while I talk to Herr di Mario."

"Si, caro," the girl said blithely, unperturbed by his curt order, and she caught Gemma's arm and led her away toward the stairs. As they mounted the steps, moving slowly because of Gemma's aching feet, Claretta looked down at the two men standing on the landing. She smiled indulgently. "They are very much men, *non è vero?*"

"Yes," Gemma murmured waspishly as she hobbled after the girl, "they're both very typical." But as she followed Claretta's gaze, noting the way the tall Italian dominated the stocky blond figure of the German even at this foreshortened angle, Gemma acknowledged reluctantly that her statement was only half-true. Dieter Stahl might be a typical overbearing male, but even after only a few hours' acquaintance she knew with absolute certainty that there could never be anyone else like Jordan di Mario.

WHEN GEMMA AND CLARETTA RETURNED to the *salotto* a little later, Gemma heard Jordan say to Dieter, ". . . and I'll telephone his studio in the morning so that he'll be expecting you."

Dieter's stolid face was twitching and flustered. "Herr di Mario," he said hoarsely, "I can't begin to thank you enough, to tell you what this means to me." As the women stepped into the salon, he leaped up from the settee and cried, "Claretta, *Liebling*, he's arranging for Carcione himself to look at my work!" He grabbed his girl friend by the waist and waltzed her heavily out of the room, crowing in exultant German. Briefly Gemma wondered if Claretta could understand him, but when the couple stumbled to a halt in the hallway and began to kiss passionately, she smiled and turned away. Obviously they had means of communicating that required no translation.

Jordan stood up the instant he saw Gemma, towering over her, and he did not sit down again until he had settled her on the sofa beside him. He peered intently at her small feet, several Band-Aids just visible over the soft bedroom slippers she had donned. "How are you feeling?" he asked.

Gemma shrugged. "Much better, thank you. None of the cuts was very deep; it was mostly a matter of getting the grit out of them. I'll be fine tomorrow."

"I insist that you see a doctor tomorrow to make certain there is no infection."

"Oh, that won't be...." Her voice died away at the glint in his dark eyes, and after a moment she sighed with resignation, "All right, in the morning when I go to visit Caroline, I'll ask someone to take a look at my feet."

Jordan nodded his approval, smiling at the disgust evident in her husky voice. "You're learning," he murmured.

Their attention was distracted by the bang of the front door as Dieter and Claretta wandered out into the night, by now too enrapt in each other to say goodbye to the people in the parlor. Gemma assumed they would search out someplace in the warm inviting darkness where they could be alone and undisturbed, perhaps deep in the forest on a mat of fragrant pine needles. Signora Ricci's hospitality did not extend to permitting unmarried couples to share her bedrooms.

When Dieter's rattly Volkswagen had trundled off into the distance, Gemma looked at Jordan. She said, "It was kind of you to offer to help him. I've only known him a short time, but I can tell already that Dieter is very serious about his art."

Jordan picked up a portfolio of sketches that lay on the coffee table. Gemma had already seen Dieter's work. His ideas all seemed to be very massive and monumental, rigid in a way that appeared to Gemma to cry out for rendering in granite rather than Italian marble, but with a definite strength and promise. Jordan lifted the portfolio in one hand and said, "The man has talent, I can see that, but unfortunately the so-called instructor he has been studying with is worse than useless, one of those leeches who are out only for the money. I am putting Dieter in touch with Sergio Carcione, a friend of mine, head of the best studio in Pietrasanta. Sergio is expensive and a hard taskmaster, but Dieter will learn more from him in five minutes than he would in a year with that *imbroglione* he's working with now."

"I'm sure Dieter appreciates what you're doing for him," Gemma said, and she smiled ironically at the inadequacy of her words.

"I'm sure he does," Jordan agreed. Suddenly his dark eyes bored into her, and he said, "There's something else I want to talk to you about, Gemma," and he pushed Dieter's portfolio aside to expose a small battered canvas-bound folder that Gemma recognized instantly.

She blanched alarmingly, paling under her creamy tan, then hot embarrassed color flooded back into her face. "Oh, please," she stammered hoarsely, "you don't want to...to waste your time with those." She tried to reach for the folder, but Jordan held it out of her reach.

Jordan demanded, "Then Dieter was correct: these are your sketches?"

She nodded in confusion. "Y-yes. I...I got them out to show Signora Ricci last night. I thought I had taken the portfolio back to my room but I...."

He selected one drawing, a portrait she had done from memory of an elderly nun at the convent. "What about this one?" Jordan asked intensely. "No one helped you with it?"

Taken aback, she said, "No. Of course not. One night I just began thinking about her, how her wrinkled careworn face had always seemed to transcend earthly beauty—"

"And after you had finished your sketch, you tried to sculpt it?"

For the first time Gemma noticed the silk scarf that draped some mysterious object on the coffee table, and she pulled it back to find the maquette she had made from her study of the nun, the small preliminary model of clay that she had hoped someone might like well enough to scale up into a full-size stone bust. She had been so proud of that model, but now, after all the wonderful pieces she had seen in Jordan's home, *real* art, her work seemed clumsy, ugly. "Oh, God," she groaned, "don't *look* at it!"

But Jordan was looking at Gemma. The long narrow hands that clutched the canvas folder seemed to tremble, and in Jordan's face Gemma glimpsed a strange agitation, a passion that, oddly, made her think suddenly of Dave and the way he had looked whenever he touched her. She wasn't sure she liked that look. Involuntarily she scooted backward across the slick upholstery of the settee, but she was brought up short by the armrest, and before she could slip away, Jordan caught her wrist.

She could feel the tremor that passed through him like electric current. He demanded, "Have you shown your work to anyone in town yet?"

Gemma shook her head. "No, only the people here at the *pensione*. There hasn't been time. I was going to—"

He took a deep breath, relaxing. "Thank God," he sighed. He squeezed her arm for emphasis, and she winced at his strength. He said urgently, "Gemma, it is very important that you do not show these things to anyone but me or possibly Sergio Carcione. I don't want to take a chance on someone less than reputable finding out what you have here and trying to exploit you."

She stared blankly at him. "Exploit me? I don't understand."

In the dim light of the parlor the planes of his face were shadowed, mysterious, giving his expression a compelling urgency that frightened her. He declared hoarsely, "Gemma, in all my years as a sculptor I don't think I've ever seen a young artist whose work showed more promise, more sheer talent, than yours does.''

His words fell between them like pebbles in a pond, and the sense of them rippled over Gemma in ever expanding waves of shock. He liked her work. Jordan di Mario thought she had promise. One of the most influential figures in contemporary Western art thought she was very, very talented. Gemma choked, "You can't mean that. How can you, when compared to yours it's so...so....You're joking."

"I never joke about art," he said, and the quiet force of his words was more convincing than ringing declarations would have been. "Of course, you need training, experience; you're just a beginner! But in time, Gemma, in time...."

Gemma shook her head in wonder. "Dear God," she murmured. "I had no idea...."

His dark brows came together. "You didn't know how good you were?"

She shrugged nervously. "Oh, I knew I was *good*. In my heart I've always known that, even when my family said—but you're not talking about just being good, are you?"

Slowly he shook his head, and even in the dim light of the *salotto* his eyes seemed to glow. "I want to tutor you, Gemma. Tomorrow I'll introduce you to Sergio Carcione, and he and I will decide the best way to begin developing—probably for the first few weeks you should just observe him and his crew...."
Jordan's deep voice faded into a low sensual drone, and although his fingers still grasped Gemma's thin arms, she knew that he was unaware of touching her. His mind was far away on some higher plane where

her physical presence had ceased to have meaning, where only her precious talent was real.

To bring him back to earth, Gemma interrupted bluntly, "*Signore*, I doubt very much whether I can afford to study with your friend. And even if I could, I can't stay here for weeks on end. My time is as limited as my funds. Soon I'll have to go home and look for a job."

He stared blankly at her. "A job? What do you mean?"

Gemma said, "I'm a schoolteacher, and if I want to find a new position by the time the fall semester starts, before long I'll have to return to Colorado." Briefly she visualized facing a classroom of sullen unruly teenagers, wistfully contrasting that uninviting prospect with a chance to work with Jordan di Mario, then sternly she put her thoughts behind her. She knew what she had to do, and pining accomplished nothing.

Jordan's lips thinned into a hard line of disapproval. "Isn't summer a little late to be looking for a fall teaching job?"

Gemma laughed uncomfortably, picking words she prayed would mask the hurt and humiliation she still felt whenever she thought of her dismissal and the events leading up to it. "Well...yes, but I...didn't—I hadn't planned to...quit my last job. It...it—"

He interrupted brusquely, "It seems clear to me that you are not terribly enthusiastic about returning to teaching, and little wonder, since obviously you are not a teacher but a born artist!"

Gemma snapped, "Even artists have to eat!"

Astonishingly her words seemed to amuse him. He relaxed and remarked languidly, "Do they? I take it you don't subscribe to the idea of starving in a garret for the sake of one's art?" His fingers began to move caressingly over her arms, his thumbs shaping the fragile bones. With a dry chuckle he noted, "It would appear that schoolteachers don't eat too well, either."

She snorted, "They eat better than sculptors do—or at any rate, female sculptors."

"What's that supposed to mean?"

Gemma shrugged. "Everyone knows that the world of fine art is one of the last, strongest bastions of male chauvinism. What's the point of trying to succeed when my sex is against me?"

Jordan stared at her. "That's the most self-defeating attitude I've ever heard of," he stated coldly, "and even if there is a grain of truth in what you say, you must realize that a woman with sufficient courage and dedication can make it anywhere. If Barbara Hepworth and Georgia O'Keefe can succeed, why can't Gemma Culver? Or is it that you're simply too great a coward to try?"

Gemma's temper flared, but before she could protest indignantly, his hands moved upward to capture her small face, and his callused thumbs closed with amazing gentleness over her parted lips. "Hush, Gemma," he whispered, his irritation and blatant amusement altering, transforming into something more disturbing, more subtly threatening. "You're just feeling confused right now, and a little afraid. You don't need to worry, *piccola*, I'll see that you have everything you need." He gazed down at her, his eyes obsidian, unreadable in the dim light of the parlor. When she tried to squirm away, his grip tightened, a velvet snare, and her silver gilt hair spilled over his splayed fingers. The bandage on his sprained wrist rubbed roughly against her cheek, and she realized suddenly that she might escape his hold by putting pressure on his injury. But she also knew that she would not do so, that the artist in her could not take a chance on hurting him permanently.

Thus she lay helpless in his grasp, imprisoned as much by her own sensibilities as by his powerful hands, and she waited for him to kiss her. In the silence of the little parlor her heart was pounding wildly, so loud she was sure he must hear it, driven by her apprehension at what to expect. She could feel his excitement mounting. His breath was warm on her face, and his body was hardening and tensing in the time-honored fashion of the dominant male, and yet she was certain that he was acting out an emotion that had nothing to do with her as a woman. He was saluting not her but her talent, and she might have been mortally offended had she not been equally curious about what would happen when his mouth touched hers. She knew it would be different from that bruising embrace he had inflicted on her earlier, as different as roses were from thorns, marble from limestone. . . Jordan from Dave. *What am I doing,* her mind demanded with momentary clarity, but there was no time for an answer. Her gray eyes widened endlessly as his lips lowered to hers.

"*Bella donna,*" he murmured.

The spell shattered and Gemma tittered.

Jordan jerked back, his black curls ruffling with

the force of his recoil. His hands dropped away from her face, and the haze of passion burned instantly from his eyes. He regarded her with cold impatience. "Do you always giggle when someone calls you a beautiful woman?" he demanded.

She shook her head helplessly, and her relief at being released from that seductive tension he had created was so great that she felt giddy, her breast shaking with stifled mirth. "I...I'm sorry," she snickered, "I didn't giggle on...on purpose. It's just that when you...when you—in English 'belladonna' is a poison!" Jordan stared at her in amazement, and Gemma wished suddenly that she had kept quiet. She knew he would not find the joke nearly as amusing as it had seemed to her. She continued awkwardly, "'Belladonna' is an old-fashioned word for atropine; I read about it in a murder mystery once. Renaissance ladies employed it as an eye drop—when they weren't using it to dispose of rivals. It's supposed to make the pupils large and beautiful, hence the name."

Jordan snorted in disgust. "Just my luck that you read murder mysteries." He stood up abruptly. "Maybe the name is appropriate. There's nothing quite so deadly to a man's ardor as being laughed at."

Gemma slowly rose to her feet. She said, "I'm sorry, truly. I didn't mean to offend you."

He shrugged. "Don't apologize. It was bad timing on my part. I should have realized that after the day you've had, you'd be far too overwrought to—" He bit off his words and quickly strode out of the *salotto*, calling back over his shoulder, "I'll pick you up in the morning, and we'll go to the hospital to see your little friend." And before Gemma could answer, he had gone, slamming the front door of the *pensione* behind him.

CAROLINE SQUINTED PAINFULLY as she peered past Gemma's shoulder to the tall man standing next to her beside the bed. "Who's he?" she asked her friend bluntly, her voice a weak imitation of its habitual whine.

Before Gemma could answer, Jordan said, "My name is Jordan di Mario, Miss Somerville."

"You speak English," she exclaimed with relief, lifting her head away from the pillow. "I was going out of my skull not being able to understand anyone around here." She collapsed limply into her supine position again, exhausted by her effort to sit upright.

Jordan caught one of the girl's small hands in his own, stroking the plump fingers with their bitten nails. "You mustn't tire yourself," he murmured, radiating suave charm as he smiled caressingly at Caroline. "We all want you to get better as quickly as possible."

Gemma glanced sharply at Jordan. He was dressed slightly more formally than he had been the day before, in buff trousers and a dark red knit shirt that emphasized his broad shoulders, and Caroline stared up at him as if she had been poleaxed. "Should I know you?" she asked hesitantly.

He shook his head. "Perhaps not. It was my Ferrari that you—encountered yesterday. I've come to beg your forgiveness for my carelessness."

Caroline's pallid bruised face flushed with becoming color, and she stammered, "I'm...I'm sorry, I don't really recall very.... I remember seeing this *super* car, and then—" She winced fiercely.

Jordan patted her hand and said, "Hush, child, don't think about that. Forget about everything but getting better. Promise me."

His low soothing tones seemed to calm her, and she nodded uncertainly. "I promise." When Jordan straightened up as if to leave, Caroline's eyes flew to Gemma, and she pleaded, "Gemma, can't you stay with me?"

Jordan shook his dark head firmly. "I'm afraid Gemma has an important appointment this morning that—"

Seeing the anguished expression in the girl's eyes, Gemma interrupted, "But surely, *signore*, I can see your friend some other time?"

"No," he said flatly. "It is imperative that you meet Sergio today, now." He glanced down at Caroline. "I'm very sorry, Miss Somerville. I hate to deprive you of Gemma's company, but it is vital that she keep this appointment. I'm sure you'll understand when I tell you it could be very important to her career as an artist. But I'll bring Gemma back to you just as soon as possible." Suddenly he leaned over and brushed his lips across the girl's fingers. "That is my promise," he murmured.

Caroline lifted her hand to her bemused face and gazed at her fingers as if they tingled. "I...understand," she echoed. "It's just that it gets kind of...scary...not being able to understand what anyone is saying."

"Of course it does," Jordan agreed. "You're being very brave." Listening to this exchange, Gemma marveled at the ease with which he could make the girl accept Gemma's interest in art. If Gemma had tried to mention anything about sculpture, Caroline's response would have been peevish and sarcastic. Just then they heard a noise and looked up to see Franco hovering in the doorway with a basket in his hands. Caroline's face lighted up again, and Jordan observed with a smile, "See, there is no need for you to worry about being lonely. Already you have a visitor, one who speaks excellent English."

Franco stepped into the room, nodding briefly at Gemma and Jordan, then to the beaming girl in the bed. *"Buon giorno, signorina,"* he said. "How are you feeling this morning?"

Gemma grinned to herself when she noticed the way Caroline surreptitiously patted her thick brown hair into place and tugged at the neckline of her unbecoming hospital gown. With an effort she raised herself into a half-sitting position and said, "Oh, I'm much better, Franco. It was kind of you to come."

He shrugged bashfully and held out the basket. "It was nothing. My mother sent some freshly baked *panfrutto*, and I picked some peaches from. . . ."

Jordan touched Gemma's arm. "Come," he muttered. "They don't need us around anymore." When the two adults were out in the corridor, Gemma trying without much success to match Jordan's long strides, he noted dryly, "Franco will do her far more good than either of us ever could. That boy can be quite a charmer when he chooses."

Gemma snorted, "You weren't doing so badly

yourself. That gallant Latin routine of yours was quite impressive, but don't you think Caroline is a little young for it?''

Jordan jerked to a halt, almost causing a nun pushing a gurney to collide with him. He murmured an apology and then turned to confront Gemma, his black eyes stabbing her. "What is that remark supposed to mean?" he demanded. "The child was obviously feeling rotten and needed cheering up, and if a little masculine attention was what it took to raise her spirits, I was happy to provide it." His expression altered, and he asked softly, insinuatingly, "What's the matter, Gemma? Jealous?"

Bright flags of color formed in her cheeks, and she hung her head, abashed and ashamed. She couldn't understand what had prompted that outburst in the first place, only that something had twisted painfully inside her when she watched him kiss the girl. She mumbled miserably, "No, of course I'm not jealous of poor Caroline. I just—I'm sorry. It was a bitchy thing to say, and I can only assume I'm on edge at the prospect of meeting your friend who runs the studio."

As she had suspected it might, the mention of Sergio Carcione instantly distracted Jordan, and he smiled reassuringly at her again. "You needn't worry, Gemma. He's going to love you."

THE DOCTOR WHO SAW GEMMA had dismissed the scratches on her feet as very minor and healing nicely, and after she and Jordan left the hospital, she asked him if they might walk the few blocks to the Carcione studio so that she could see more of the antique town. They strolled through narrow winding streets, some little more than corridors shaded by buildings that had overhung the pavement for more than half a millenium, and in the medieval atmosphere of Pietrasanta, Gemma at last began to really believe that Michelangelo had once lived and practiced his art there. Briefly she wondered what the master would have thought about the work being done in the town now. Every door seemed to open onto some kind of a studio, and although she was amazed at the number of people engaged in carving, she was appalled at much of the items on display: kitschy reproductions of ancient Greek statues, hackneyed religious groupings, busts of the Pope or the American president. Jordan watched her reactions without comment, and when he at last directed her through a low archway into a crowded and dusty workroom, at first glance she thought it was no different from the dozens of other little studios they had passed. Then she saw the quality of the work being produced there.

When Jordan introduced Gemma to Sergio Carcione, the wizened little man surveyed her skeptically, then glanced up at Jordan, his monkeylike face dubious. Gemma was sure that Jordan's prediction of the illustrious instructor's reaction to meeting her had been hopelessly optimistic. She had to strain to hear his voice over the machine-gun clatter of the pneumatic hammers his crew were operating. His bright intelligent eyes flickered between Jordan and Gemma again, noting the arm the sculptor had flung possessively around Gemma's shoulders, and he asked derisively in Italian, "Another one?"

Jordan frowned. "What do you mean?"

Carcione grimaced. "I didn't really mind the German boy camping on my doorstep, but that model of yours, the one who fancies herself a great Florentine lady, was here yesterday afternoon, disrupting the workmen, poking her dainty nose everywhere, demanding to know where you had disappeared. I tell you, Giordano, how you run your private life is your business, but I will not have your women cluttering up my studio!"

Gemma followed this exchange with such ease that she suspected the older man had deliberately slowed his speech to ensure that she could translate. As the sense of his words pounded into her brain, she felt herself go cold with frustration and rage. So she was one of Jordan's "women," was she, condemned by her sex? She had deep and pervasive doubts about whether her talent was in truth as great as Jordan seemed to think it was, but the idea that now, without even looking at her work, the other man could dismiss her as of no account as an artist.... She quivered at the sheer injustice of it all. When Jordan sensed the temblor of emotion that passed through her, he drew her close to his side as if sheltering her from Carcione's scorn. Automatically she tried to pull away. His long fingers dug into her soft skin, and she knew she could not escape without an undignified tussle, something she refused to do under the observant eyes of the other man. Besides, there was something strangely comforting about Jordan's protection.

"Sergio," Jordan said quietly, "Gemma is something very special."

Carcione sniffed eloquently. "Every woman is special until you've...." The rest of his sentence was too idiomatic for Gemma to translate, but the meaning was clear. She felt Jordan tense.

With the blunt impatience of long-standing friendship, but with a hard note in his deep voice, he said, "Sergio, you'd better watch what you say, or else you're going to feel like a fool when you've seen Gemma's work."

Carcione stared at Jordan for a long moment, disbelief twisting his wrinkled face, then he sighed with resignation. "All right, *amico*, if you insist. Let's see what your girl friend can do. But I tell you now, I haven't much time to waste. Those worthless *imbecilli* I am forced to employ—" he gestured to some men armed with calipers and grease pencils, gravely marking lines on an amorphous block of mottled Iranian travertine "—are already so far behind on the scale-up of that piece for the convention center in Oslo that it may not be ready for the dedication."

"Che disgraziato!" Jordan exclaimed, his laugh belying his words. "Sergio, you know perfectly well that you have the best crew in the world, and that the Norwegians will gladly wait upon your convenience for their celebration." He grinned down at Gemma. "Don't let his moans fool you; there's no studio anywhere that can match the output of Sergio's, but he thinks it's bad luck to say so. Why don't you show him your portfolio now?"

Gemma glanced around, puzzled. "I don't seem to have it with me. I was sure I...." Her gray blue eyes clouded as in her mind she retraced her steps that morning. "I guess I must have set it down when we were at the hospital," she said at last, shrugging helplessly at Jordan.

"Damn," he muttered. "I really wanted him to see.... Look, Gemma," he said, "I'll go back and get the folder, and you stay here and talk to Sergio. I'll go much faster without you, and I'll bring the car back with me. In the meantime, you two get acquainted." Before either of the others could protest, he strode away.

The noise of the studio rushed in to fill the vacuum left by Jordan's abrupt departure. Air compressors made the cramped room throb explosively and handheld hammers rang out as pieces were crated for shipping. Gemma rubbed her temples and, aware that Carcione was watching her intently, resisted the impulse to cover her ears with her hands. She looked warily at him, meeting the gaze of his bright buttonlike eyes, and after a moment he demanded bluntly, "What have you come here for?"

She decided to be as straightforward as he was. "I'm here because Jordan brought me."

"I suppose he told you you could become a great sculptor?"

Gemma hunched her shoulders, hurt by the man's obvious doubt. "Something like that," she mumbled.

Carcione's expression was eloquent. "I didn't know Giordano used that kind of line," he observed curiously. He added after a second, "Naturally you believed him."

Gemma shook her head. "Not really. I'm...I'm gratified that he likes my work, but all I am interested in is learning as much as I possibly can in the short time I can stay in Pietrasanta.''

She had thought her candor would please Carcione, but instead his scowl deepened, and he growled out something she was glad she couldn't translate. "Tourists," he spat. "I've worked in this studio for over forty years, and you people think you can come and learn all there is to know in a few weeks! Look, *signorina*, why don't you just go back to California or wherever the hell it was and make your plaster figurines for the craft shows and leave Pietrasanta to the people who really care about art?''

"But I do care about art!" Gemma cried.

Carcione's eyes bored into her. "Very well," he said, "we shall see." He turned and barked a command to a youth who had been sweeping up marble chips, and the boy disappeared through a partition into another section of the workroom. Seconds later he returned lugging a chunk of white Carrara marble the size of a soccer ball, which he set on an upended wooden crate. Carcione nodded, and the boy went back to his broom. Picking up a chisel and a heavy wooden mallet, Carcione handed the tools to Gemma with a flourish. "All right," he said, "if you're serious about working in stone, the first thing you must do is learn the ways of marble. And the best way to do that is by carving.''

"Carve what?" Gemma asked, sure he was mocking her. She hefted the steel chisel and noted its very sharp edge. "You can't just say to someone, 'Go carve something.' "

"But that is exactly what I am saying, *signorina*. I

want you to cut up that stone until there is nothing left but gravel. By the time you have done that, you will have learned almost all there is to know about marble and the way it behaves under the blade.''

Gemma stared at the hunk of stone. Even in its rough form it was beautiful, the flat planes of each tiny crystal catching the light and glittering like ice; she knew it would polish to mirror brightness once it had been shaped and smoothed. She trailed her fingers over the surface, noting the surprisingly soapy texture. After a moment she looked up at Carcione and said, ''There's enough material here for a small piece. Are you sure you want to waste it?''

The artisan laughed humorlessly. ''It won't be wasted. Giordano has already paid for it. This is scrap from his latest project. Besides, the marble is flawed.'' He rolled it over, revealing a seam of crumbly brown dirt that ate into the purity of the white stone like a worm in a peach. He noted grimly, ''Giordano was fortunate that the flaw proved to be only a minor one. If it had continued farther into the body of the marble, he might have had to start this statue all over again.'' He clicked his tongue at the vagaries of fate and then said briskly, ''Very well, *signorina*, you'd better begin.''

Through the veil of her silky lashes Gemma glanced around. Sergio Carcione was not the only one watching her with interest. His workmen eyed her, as well, their dark weather-beaten faces alight with amusement. She picked up the chisel with her left hand and positioned it against the stone. With a sigh of resignation she lifted the heavy mallet and tapped it against the end of the chisel. Nothing happened. She blinked. The marble beneath the edge of the blade seemed untouched. Raising the mallet again, she hit the chisel harder, and this time instead of cutting the stone the end of the blade skittered over the surface and almost fell out of her hand, twisting her wrist painfully in the process. Perspiration began to bead on her forehead. Grasping both the mallet and the chisel so tightly that her knuckles blanched, she struck the marble once more, and this time a chip of stone broke loose and flew up to hit her in the chin.

Someone laughed.

Gemma lifted her head. She realized with surprise that the noisy workroom had grown silent. The men had all laid aside their own tools and were frankly staring at her, grinning widely. She looked at Carcione, and he murmured, "Had enough?"

Rage swept over Gemma, fiery, blinding rage at these overbearing men with their hateful sneering smiles, every one of them just waiting for the moment when she would admit defeat. "Never!" she choked, and she turned once more to the marble. No longer was the white stone an object of beauty and respect; it had transmogrified into the vile masculine smirks that distorted those swarthy faces, and with renewed strength she began to pound on it, cutting and gouging the innocent marble as if she were wreaking revenge for every wrong the male sex had ever inflicted on her.

She beat at the stone mindlessly, heedless of the increasing ache in her arms as she wielded the heavy tools, the burning blisters that began to puff up on her palms. She was deaf to her labored breathing, blind to the faint red streaks that appeared on the growing pile of white chips whenever the chisel slipped. She was unaware of anything happening around her until suddenly the unnatural silence in the studio was broken by a deep enraged voice bellowing, *"What the hell is going on here!"*

Gemma froze, her hands poised in midair. Slowly, slowly she turned in the direction of that voice. Against the bright afternoon light Jordan stood silhouetted in the doorway, his tall lean body vibrant with tension. At the sight of him all strength seemed to ebb from Gemma, and her arms went limp. The mallet and chisel slipped out of her flaccid bloodied fingers and fell to the floor with a loud clatter.

Jordan gaped at her, his dark eyes raking her comprehensively, noting her sweat-streaked face, the way she shook with fatigue. *"Dio!"* he choked. Grimly he confronted Carcione. "What have you done to her, Sergio?"

All at once the din in the studio welled up again as the workmen quickly resumed their various tasks, carefully avoiding Jordan's gaze. The expression on his face obviously shook Carcione as much as it did his crew, but he faced the taller man squarely. "I was just letting the *ragazza* prove she wants to be an artist."

Jordan's fists clenched around the canvas portfolio he carried. He snapped, "Gemma doesn't have to prove anything: she *is* an artist!" and he flung the folder at Carcione. Startled, the man grabbed for it, but as he did, the narrow ribbons fastening it came untied, and the portfolio fell open, littering Gemma's drawings over the floor like withered rose petals.

"No!" she wailed at the sight of her precious sketches strewn on the dirty floor, and she lunged for them, but her reserves of strength had already been exhausted, and she would have fallen had not Jordan caught her. "My drawings," she cried again, struggling to escape him.

He cradled her against his chest. "Hush, *cara*, hush. No one will hurt your drawings, I promise."

She relaxed against him, too overwrought to fight anymore. She could feel Jordan's long fingers stroke her sleek silvery hair, then move gently over her slight shoulders and down the length of her arms, at last capturing her hand in his. When he eased her fingers apart so that he could survey the cuts and blisters, he caught his breath with a hiss, and she felt a tremor of emotion pass through him. He lifted his head and stared bleakly at Carcione. He said sternly, "Sergio, there was no need for this."

Carcione was gathering up Gemma's scattered sketches, handling them carefully, almost reverently. He stared at them as if awestruck, and when he met his friend's gaze, his eyes seemed shadowed with remorse. He shrugged fatalistically as he replied, "I'm sorry, Giordano. But how was I to know she was different from the usual tourists who come here in the summer?"

Jordan shook his head impatiently. "You know me. That should have been enough."

Gemma pulled back slightly and muttered, irritation evident in her tired voice, "I wish you two wouldn't talk about me as if I weren't here."

"Sorry, *piccola*," Jordan said with a faint smile. He looked at Carcione again. "I'm going to take

Gemma home now. After she is rested, we'll discuss things further.''

"Yes, of course," Carcione replied, and he handed the portfolio to Gemma. "My apologies, *signorina*. I didn't understand."

Gemma nodded mutely, and clutching the folder to her breast, she followed Jordan out into the sunlight.

In the little sedan he leaned over to switch on the ignition. Then, instead, he reached across the seat and caught Gemma's fingers in his own. He almost had to pry her hands away from the battered portfolio, she clung to it so fiercely, but her frail strength was no match for his. "Please, Gemma. I just want to see whether I think you ought to go back to the doctor once more." Gently he uncurled her clenched fingers, and when he saw the bruises and cuts, the flesh that glared pink and raw from beneath popped blisters, he winced, sickened. As he pulled a large immaculate handkerchief out of his pocket and with great care wrapped it loosely around the more seriously wounded of her hands, he exclaimed, "But why Gemma? This was so unnecessary."

She tried to smile wryly. "I guess. . . I guess I just got carried away," she said uneasily. "I'm not usually so. . . passionate."

Leaning nearer, he stared at her, his dark gaze searching her heart-shaped face intently, looking for—something. He was so close that she could see the narrow line of gold that rimmed the almost black irises of his fine eyes. His unblinking stare held her captive, and she could not turn away, even when she saw out of the corner of her eye that passersby in the street where they were parked had begun to notice them, even when Jordan whispered softly, "You're lying, Gemma."

Her mouth felt dry, and she flicked her tongue over her lips. "What do you mean?" she asked huskily.

He said, "You say you are not passionate, and for some reason you try to act as if that were so, but I know the truth about you, Gemma. You are a woman of very deep feelings, of great fire and...and passion. It shows in your work."

When he spoke, his warm breath stroked her face seductively, and she shook her head back and forth in denial, trying to break loose from the spell he was weaving around her. "You can't tell anything about me from those sketches of mine," she averred. "They're just...just pictures of people who I thought...looked interesting. If there is any emotion in them, it comes from the people themselves, not from me."

He inclined his head mockingly, his dark curls showing fiery highlights in the bright sunlight. "Nice try, *cara*, but it's no good. Don't you know what Oscar Wilde once said? 'Every portrait that is painted with feeling is a portrait of the artist, not of the sitter.'" And before she could think of a suitably scathing retort, he kissed her.

His lips brushed across hers in a fleeting caress, gentle, almost tentative, tasting and teasing, so unlike what she had expected that she blinked at him in surprise, gray eyes wide and questioning. He pulled back slightly and surveyed her startled features assessingly. With a complacent smile he lowered his head again. This time his mouth touched hers more firmly, kissing her with authority, and she could feel his tongue stroking her lips, urging them to part. When she hesitated, chary and uncertain, leery of surrender, his urgency turned to demand. "Kiss me back, Gemma," he growled against her mouth as one arm tightened around her slender waist, dragging her closer. When his free hand trailed downward, closing over the soft swell of her small breast, she shivered, and the harsh aggressive note in his voice jarred her. Instinctively she recoiled, brushing his fingers aside, working her wounded palms into the nonexistent space between their bodies, but even in her panic she noted the soothing warmth that radiated through the thin knit fabric of his shirt, generated by their closeness. Shaking off that momentary distraction, she pushed her fists against the hard muscles of his chest, and with an effort she shoved him away from her.

"Gemma, for God's sake—" he exclaimed irritably as he rocked backward, cutting off his words when he glanced past her to the car window on the passenger side. Gemma twisted so that she, too, could look over her shoulder, and to her dismay she saw two grubby little boys of about six or seven with their noses pressed to the glass, staring raptly into the car. One grinned broadly, revealing a gap where his front teeth should have been, and he lisped, *"Bacio, bacio!"* With a wry chuckle Jordan shook his head and waved them away impatiently, and they scampered off down the sidewalk.

The two adults watched the children disappear into the crowd, then Jordan looked at Gemma's carefully expressionless face and said lightly, "I'm sorry. I should have waited until we didn't have an audience."

Gemma stared down at her hands, fingering the sharp edge on one of her broken nails. "It wouldn't have made any difference where we were," she said quietly. "I've told you several times: I'm very grateful for all you've done, but I am not interested in a summer romance, not with you, not with anyone. That's not the reason I came to Italy."

"Does that mean you are still pining for your ex-fiancé? If so, it's obvious he would take you back in a second."

"No!" Gemma snapped, furious at Jordan's arrogant assumption that she would reject him only if she were already interested in someone else. "Dave has nothing at all to do with this!" Then, recalling that her temper seemed to arouse him, she deliberately smoothed her voice, forcing it into a bland monotone. She said, "I've already told you why I'm here. And even if I were... on the prowl, I would never become involved with someone after only one day's acquaintance."

"I see," Jordan replied in a voice equally neutral. "Does that mean I would stand higher in your favor if we had known each other longer?"

Gemma shrugged faintly. "The question is academic, *signore*. I will be returning to Colorado in a matter of weeks, as soon as Caroline is fit to travel. It's unlikely that you and I will see much of each other in the interim." She turned to gaze wistfully through the window at the motley crowds bustling through the narrow streets of Pietrasanta. Everyone seemed so vibrant and vital, not just the Italians, but also the foreign tourists who had flocked to the siren call of the marble mountains; even in their outlandish pseudoartistic work clothes they seemed charged with a real dedication, a love of their art. Gemma longed to be among them, part of the throng, but she knew she could not. She was different; even Sergio Carcione had said so. She had always been different, and it had taken her a lifetime to realize that she would rather be alone than have to face the compromises necessary to blend in with the crowd. Compromise meant surrender, especially for a woman. She had broken up with Dave because he wanted her to fit his ideal of the submissive wife, incapable of directing her own life, and now Jordan di Mario, despite his astonishing regard for her talent, seemed to think that he ought to be the one to tell her how to use that talent, and he apparently had no scruples about trying to seduce her to his point of view, overriding her fears and doubts with the force of his sexual magnetism. Without looking at him she said, *"Signore—"*

Behind her, Jordan drawled lazily, "Don't you think it's time you began calling me by my given name? After all, I've already kissed you twice—not, I will concede, with much success. The third time—"

"There won't be a third time," Gemma snapped indignantly. "I told you, we won't be seeing much of each other from now on."

"Oh, but that's where you're wrong." His voice was cool and mocking. "You're most definitely mistaken, Gemma. You and I shall be seeing a great deal of each other in the near future. You see, when I went back to the hospital for your portfolio, I talked to Caroline's doctor, and he told me that there is no reason for the girl to remain there while she convalesces. In fact, he said, since she finds the alien atmosphere of the hospital so alarming, her recovery would probably be speeded up if she could go someplace quiet where she could be among familiar faces, or at least other Americans. So...." His voice trailed off suggestively, as if he expected Gemma to anticipate what he was about to say. She tensed, afraid to look at him, afraid of the outrageous idea taking shape in her mind. When she did not speak, Jordan continued matter-of-factly, "So, Gemma, with the doctor's permission I have made arrangements for you and Caroline to move into Villa Sogno Dolce, to live with me."

CHAPTER FIVE

GEMMA STARED AT HIM and gasped, "Live with you? You must be out of your mind."

With a mocking grin Jordan shook his head. "No, my dear, I'm just being logical. The *pensione* where the two of you have been staying is pleasant enough, but you know, as well as I, that the Riccis have neither the time nor the facilities to care for a sick girl. At my home Caroline can recuperate in comfort, with my mother to supervise—"

"How can you be sure your mother will want to look after Caroline?" Gemma interrupted. "She's never even met her. Aren't you making rather a lot of assumptions?"

Jordan said imperturbably, "My mother will do what I ask her to. Besides, since she is a nurse, her professional pride would never allow her to neglect the girl."

Gemma sank back into her seat. "I didn't know your mother was a nurse," she said in surprise.

Jordan smiled. "Oh, yes, for many years. That's how she met my father. She came to Italy with the American occupation forces after the Second World War. My father had been one of the *partigiani* fighting the Fascists, and during the war he had received a bad wound that had never been properly treated, so afterward his comrades brought him to the American hospital for corrective surgery. When he and my mother met...." As Jordan gazed through the windshield of the small car, his expression grew tender. Gemma could tell that he was fondly recalling stories he had been told as a small child. He chuckled, "Papa always claimed that he fell in love with my mother's accent, that the first time she ordered him to roll over on his stomach so that she could give him an injection, he knew he was going to marry her. I don't know how much truth there is to that particular tale, but—well, they were both very young, and I guess whatever happened between them was pretty explosive. When the army left, *mamma* stayed behind."

Gemma thought with wonder about the grim and rather homely Signora di Mario, a woman who, she was sure, had never been pretty, even as a girl. It was difficult enough to accept her as mother of someone so astonishingly handsome as Jordan, but to envision her as the young heroine of a drama of "explosive" passion.... Gemma thought wryly, *well, it just goes to show, you never can tell.* Aloud she asked, "Does your mother still work as a nurse?"

Jordan turned to Gemma again, his dark eyes blinking in the bright sunlight. "She is retired now," he said, "but she has always made a point of keeping abreast of developments in her field, and several times she has volunteered her services when they were needed. She worked for weeks in the Naples area following the 1980 earthquakes."

His voice was filled with quiet pride, and Gemma realized that despite her own negative first impressions of Jordan's mother, the woman was obviously a deep and complex character, whom her son loved and respected very much. She commented, "She sounds like a remarkable person."

"I think she is," Jordan agreed with a smile. "And while you are living with us, I hope the two of you become good friends."

"Living with *us*" sounded much less ominous than "living with *me*," but still Gemma hesitated. "*Signore—*" she protested. At his hard look she hastily amended, "I mean, Jordan. Although I realize, of course, that your villa is much roomier and more comfortable than the *pensione*, I still think you are presuming too much when you expect your mother to drop everything to look after Caroline. After all, if Caro really can't bear to remain in the hospital, I can always take care of her. She's my responsibility. And besides, we are committed to staying with the Riccis. Franco's mother depends on her tenants for her income. We can't just walk out."

Jordan gestured impatiently. "Leave the Riccis to me. I'm sure they'll agree once I explain the situation to them."

Gemma's gray eyes narrowed. "Of course. No one argues with a *uomo rispettato*."

Jordan glanced at her sharply. "What did you say?"

She shrugged elaborately. "Oh, just something someone called you."

Jordan frowned. "Considering the usual implications of the term, I'm not sure I'm flattered."

"I don't think you were supposed to be. But, my God, the way you charge in and start issuing orders, expecting instant obedience—and for what? A child you don't even know! Is it any wonder that someone thinks you're a Mafia type?''

He regarded her quizzically, his leonine head tilted to one side. "No, probably not," he conceded after a pause. "But, Gemma, you are mistaken if you think I am going to all this trouble for Caroline. Of course, I feel some obligation toward the girl because the accident was as much my fault as hers, but I assure you I do not usually invite strangers into my home, no matter what the circumstances."

"Then why?" Gemma asked, bewildered. "Why are you doing these things?"

He sighed, chagrined by her obvious puzzlement. "What an appalling self-image you must have! I suppose it never occurred to you that I might be doing this for *you*, that my regard for your talent is so great that I am willing to sacrifice some of my privacy in order to help you to develop that talent? Despite my offers of assistance you persist in saying you can only remain in Pietrasanta a few short weeks, that you must return to your home to find a 'real' job." The snort he made showed Gemma exactly what he thought of that idea. "The decision is yours, and I will abide by it. . . for now. But I know that as long as you are worried about Caroline, you will be unable to make proper use of even the limited time you do have in Italy. So to ease your mind, I am offering a way for you to be assured that the girl has good care, a way that still allows you opportunity for concentrated study with Sergio Carcione and me. Is your pride so inflexible that it will not bend enough to let you accept even these terms?"

Gemma looked up at him, then turned away quick-

ly, gazing instead at her injured hands. Despite the
pain the blisters and scratches were mostly superficial,
and she doubted they would leave scars when they
healed. Out of the corner of her eye she glanced at Jordan's strong thin fingers, at the moment lightly drum-
ming a tattoo on the fabric stretched tautly over his
powerful thighs. Over the years his olive skin had
become scored with a network of pale lines that contrasted sharply with the fine black hair curling across
the back of his hands, and the pads of his fingertips
were rough and callused. Ironically she recalled the
popular stereotype of the effete artist, her family's
scornful dismissal of anyone not a "working man" as
some kind of limp-wristed dilettante. Flexing her own
aching fingers, Gemma thought with awe of the sheer
physical pain Jordan must have endured to acquire
those scars, and she fought down a sudden astonishing
urge to press her lips to his hands in homage for what
he had been willing to suffer for his art.

Her agile and very visual imagination began
sketching a scene not unlike the David painting of the
coronation of Napoleon and Josephine, only in this
one it was she who knelt humbly in obeisance at the
foot of her lord, ermine cloak spreading wide behind
her, and instead of Napoleon, Jordan stood tall and
proud at the top of the dais, exalting her with his
notice.

Jordan interrupted her fanciful ruminations by
saying sternly, "Gemma, I've invited you to stay at
my home, be my guest for the remainder of your time
in Italy. The least you can do is give me an answer."

Blinking in confusion, she broke out of her fugue
and slowly looked up at his face. He was scowling at

her, obviously puzzled. Hot color began to creep into Gemma's cheeks as she remembered the outrageous fantasy she had been weaving. Napoleon and Josephine, indeed! She shook her head to clear it. She had to watch out, she had to be wary—not necessarily of Jordan, but of her own vivid imagination. Her respect for his work was making her see him as some superhero, some figure larger than life, when in fact he was just a man, an extraordinarily handsome and intelligent man, true, but still, a man who would not hesitate to take advantage of any feminine weakness she showed him. She took a deep breath and stammered, "If...if I do decide I—we should stay at your home, you...you must understand it's only because of Caroline, because it seems the best thing for...for her."

Jordan smiled enigmatically. "Of course, *cara*, if that's the way you want it," he drawled, his bass voice silky and caressing. "We're doing it for Caroline. What other reason could there be?"

BUT SEVERAL DAYS LATER, Beatrice di Mario was very definite about what she thought Gemma's reasons were. The woman stood menacingly in the doorway of the bathroom connecting the two bedrooms Gemma and Caroline were to occupy, watching with pale angry eyes as Gemma transferred her clothes from her suitcase to the hand-rubbed walnut dresser, and she spat, "Don't get the idea that just because you've somehow inveigled your way into Giordano's home, you mean anything special to him. There have been many women in my son's life, and in the end he always goes back to Francesca."

Gemma stiffened at Signora di Mario's uncalled-for outburst. The words grated, somehow doubly irritating because of the soft Southern drawl in which they were uttered. Gemma gritted her teeth and decided it would be prudent not to respond, lest she give the woman ammunition to fling at her. Despite Jordan's insistence that his home could easily accommodate an entire house party, Gemma had doubted that his mother would be thrilled to have two unexpected guests dumped on her, but she had not been prepared for the open hostility Signora di Mario displayed the instant Jordan's back was turned. Had the decision involved only Gemma, she would gladly have repacked her bags and, if necessary, walked back to Pietrasanta and the cozy hospitality of the Riccis. Unfortunately there was also Caroline to be considered. Jordan's devastating charm had made an easy conquest of the girl, and when he asked her if she would like to stay at his house while she convalesced, she had agreed eagerly. Not even Franco's increasing attentions—something about Caroline's frailty seemed to appeal to the boy's protective instincts—could dissuade her. Now Jordan had gone to pick her up at the hospital, and Gemma was left to cope with an irate woman who made it clear she considered the two Americans interlopers and opportunists.

Silently and methodically Gemma continued stacking her jeans and T-shirts in neat piles, and when she had finished doing that, she pointedly glanced around for someplace to hang the one dress she had brought with her, a plain blue cotton she had thought would be appropriate if she wanted to attend Mass in one of the beautiful little chapels that were so abundant in Italy. The starkly simple furnishings of the bedroom did not include a wardrobe, and Gemma looked questioningly at Jordan's mother. When the woman did not speak, Gemma was forced to ask, "Is there someplace I can hang this? I don't want to get it wrinkled."

The disdainful look in Signora di Mario's light eyes told Gemma eloquently that the woman didn't see how a few creases could make the garment any less presentable than it already was, but after a second she motioned behind her to the spacious bathroom, and she said grudgingly, "There is a dressing area in here. You will find a closet and plenty of hangers."

"Thank you," Gemma muttered. She edged past the *signora* and stepped into the dressing room. After she had put the dress away, she took the opportunity to lay out her few toilet articles in the bathroom. She washed her hands and rubbed glycerine lotion into the fading abrasions on her palms. When she set the bottle down again, she could not help noting the bathroom's very modern plumbing, comparing it wryly with the Victorian fixtures in the *pensione* that gurgled rustily despite Signora Ricci's continual care. Here all was streamlined and quiet, a symphony of cream-colored porcelain and stainless steel, obviously of the highest quality.

But then, everything she had seen in the villa was of the highest quality. The furnishings were sparse, their lines simple—clean and functional, rather like Shaker furniture—but the woods and the workmanship were excellent. Gemma knew instinctively that Jordan had decorated the house, and she suspected he had chosen each beautifully understated piece deliberately so that nothing would detract from his art collection. Even in her guest room, which contained only a double bed draped with a handwoven coverlet, and dresser and a small but comfortable chair for reading, the dresser was ornamented with a tall Ming vase, and on the wall opposite the dresser hung a large framed lithograph by Picasso.

When Gemma emerged from the bathroom, Signora di Mario was still waiting for her, but her scowl had been replaced by a more amiable expression, one that did not quite reach her eyes. With the air of a concerned hostess she gushed, "Did you find what you needed? We usually have to limit these rooms to people who will be staying only a short time, a day or two, since I'm afraid the closets are not very large. When Giordano was designing the house, I told him these rooms were too small, but he would not listen to me, and now we must be very careful about whom we put here. They would never do for, say, Francesca. When she comes, she always brings a huge assortment of clothes, beautiful clothes, the latest designer creations. But then, I suppose that is to be expected, since she is a model...."

Thinking of *Privilege*, Gemma said quietly, "Yes, I know."

The woman flashed another saccharine smile at Gemma, and Gemma wondered edgily just what she was leading up to. That there was some purpose to this sudden effusiveness, she had no doubt; she had refused to react to an overt attack, so now Beatrice was trying a different tactic. She asked coyly, "Perhaps you recognized Francesca from the fashion magazines?"

Gemma shook her head, a little surprised. Compared to the rather emaciated mannequins usually employed in the world of haute couture, Francesca seemed voluptuous, almost overblown. But, Gemma conceded, her face was so incredibly lovely that those few extra pounds probably didn't matter. She said, "I don't know her from the fashion magazines, no. I never read them."

"I didn't think so," Signora di Mario said sweetly. After a moment she continued, "For years now, Francesca has been one of the most sought after fashion models in Europe. She's had a glorious career—there was even talk of her going into films— and she has loved every moment of it. The only unfortunate thing about her career is that it has delayed her marriage to Giordano far beyond what either of them had intended."

Gemma wondered why her throat suddenly felt tight. "Then Jordan and Francesca are engaged?" she asked huskily.

"Not officially," Beatrice said coolly, aware of Gemma's tension. "Formal betrothals are fine and well for teenagers in the throes of first love, and Francesca and Giordano had such an arrangement when they were very young, but they broke it off by mutual consent when she went to Paris to pursue her career. Now she has returned to Italy because her father has been ill, and she and my son have an. . . arrangement, an understanding, much more suitable to adults of their age, who have achieved a certain. . . place in life. I expect they will get around to marrying once Giordano has finished the new statue of Francesca that he is carving."

Uninvited, Gemma's vivid imagination took fire

again. She saw *Privilege* as she had seen it as a girl, but while she watched, the cool white marble warmed, colored and became the sculptor and his mistress living, and Jordan's long fingers reached out to stroke the curve of Francesca's voluptuous breast.... Rather than dwell on that unwelcome image, Gemma puzzled aloud, "Jordan is doing a new statue of Francesca? In Sergio's studio?" When his mother nodded, Gemma murmured, "That must be what's in the back room that Dieter and I never get to go into. I thought it was a storage area or something. I had no idea...."

Signora di Mario's smile broadened at Gemma's obvious bewilderment. "Clearly," she suggested smugly, "you are not as privy to Giordano's secrets as you flatter yourself you are."

"I've never pretended I—" Gemma's angry retort was interrupted by the bustle of feet and voices suddenly invading the front entryway. The only disadvantage Gemma had noticed about the beautiful villa was that its shining terrazzo floors and sparsely furnished rooms tended to amplify sounds and make them echo throughout the different levels. She was sure that if someone dropped a pan in the kitchen, Jordan would be able to hear it in his private studio at the opposite end of the building.

At the sounds of arrival, Gemma and Beatrice left off their bickering and hurried into the corridor just in time to see Jordan mounting the short flight of steps, carrying Caroline, who was wrapped in a long yellow dressing gown and fuzzy slippers, in his arms as easily as if the chunky girl were no heavier than a doll. Franco tagged along behind them, panting while he lugged her suitcases and another of Signora Ricci's ubiquitous baskets of goodies.

"Gemma!" the girl cried out in delight when she spotted her friend. Gemma noticed at once that Caroline sounded much better than she had the last time she had seen her. Her face was still pale, except for the bruise on her forehead, which had reached the garish rainbow stage of healing, but her voice was stronger, and she seemed in far better spirits. Obviously all that masculine attention was agreeing with her.

"Hi, Caro," Gemma said with a grin, moving aside so that Jordan could carry the girl into her room. Everyone else trooped in after them. Jordan laid her down on the bed with amazing gentleness, then he relieved Franco of some of his load. Gemma sat down on the edge of the mattress and observed to her friend, "I see you've acquired quite a retinue."

Caroline looked momentarily blank, but after a second she laughed, "Oh, you mean Franco and Jordan. They've both been so nice, it's hard to believe."

Behind Gemma, Beatrice di Mario said stiffly, "Italians are noted for their hospitality."

Caroline glanced past Gemma's shoulder to the tall woman standing there, and Jordan quickly made introductions. To Gemma's surprise, the girl extended a shaky hand and said politely, "Mrs. di Mario, I want you to know how much I...I appreciate what you're doing. I know it must be hard for you, taking two strangers into your home, but I can't begin to tell you how good it feels to get out of the—what it's like to be with people who...." As unexpectedly as she had begun that little speech, Caroline's voice trailed away, and Gemma realized with a pang that although the girl's spirits were improving rapidly, physically she was still very weak. Her hand drooped, and Signora di Mario caught it quickly. She shooed Gemma off the bed, and pushing back the sleeve of Caroline's yellow robe and pressing her fingers over the wrist with a practiced professional movement, she checked for the pulse. Caroline lifted her eyelids with an effort and stared up at Beatrice helplessly.

She felt Caroline's forehead and crooned soothingly, her Southern accent especially pronounced, "Don't worry, honey, you're welcome to stay as long as you like. You don't concern your pretty little head with anything but getting better, y'hear?"

Caroline's head dropped back wearily, her thick brown hair spreading richly over the pillow. "Yes, mama," she mumbled, "I mean, ma'am...." Heavily her lids closed over her hazel eyes.

Watching this, Gemma asked in concern, "What's wrong with her? She shouldn't just doze off like that, should she?"

Signora di Mario looked up impatiently. "No, there's nothing wrong, except that the journey by car has tired her. Falling asleep so abruptly is just a lingering side effect of her head injury, one that will soon pass." She eased the girl out of her dressing gown and pulled the sheets up over her. Then she turned to Jordan and asked in Italian, "Did the doctor give you instructions regarding her care?"

Jordan shook his head. "No. He said he had the utmost confidence in your skill. I told him you would telephone him as soon as you get the child settled."

"Bene," Beatrice said. Her attention concentrated

on Caroline, she waved absently toward the door. "Now, all of you get out of here and let me take care of my patient. *Andate!*"

In the living room Jordan seemed absorbed in his own thoughts, but Gemma and Franco stared at each other uncomfortably with the jittery hopeless agitation of people waiting in a hospital corridor. The boy jammed his hands deep into the pockets of his tight trousers and shuffled about, staring blankly at Jordan's art collection. Gemma watched him pause before a small bust carved from black Yugoslavian marble, and when he reached out tentative fingers to stroke the profile, she knew that he was admiring not the skill of the sculptor, but the stone itself.

She looked back at Jordan, and she was surprised to find him now gazing at her fixedly, his eyes unreadable. She ventured nervously, "Is something wrong? Was...was the doctor uncertain about letting Caro leave the hospital?"

Jordan shook his head. "No. As I said, he has complete confidence in my mother, and from this point on, the girl's recovery is simply a matter of letting nature take its course. You must not worry."

Gemma sighed. "Of course you are right, but...." She grimaced with frustration. "It really bothers me that Caroline's mother doesn't know what has happened. Even though there's nothing Marsha can do, she has a right to know."

"You still have not been able to reach Mrs. Somerville?"

"I tried again this morning, but no luck. I think her assistant is getting tired of my calls."

Jordan asked quietly, "What about your ex-fiancé? Have you spoken to him lately?"

Gemma had the impression that Jordan was inquiring about more than a simple telephone call, but she wasn't sure what. "No," she admitted uncertainly. "He seems to have vanished, too." She laughed unconvincingly. "Maybe he's looking for Marsha."

"Would it bother you if he were?"

Gemma stared at him in confusion. "Bother me? No, of course not. I wish him luck in his search. Why should it upset me?"

"I thought you might be regretting his departure from your life," Jordan suggested lightly. "You know, the one that got away."

Gemma snapped, "Believe me, my only regret is that I waited seven years to—" She choked off her words and regarded Jordan with silent exasperation. As always, her temper had exploded at his baiting, but she was aware that Franco, standing in apparent absorption in front of the bronze dancing girl, had begun to monitor their conversation; every line of his unnaturally tense posture betrayed his interest. With forced lightness she chuckled, "You know, Jordan, I always have the most peculiar feeling that you and I talk on completely different levels. I don't understand you at all."

His eyes narrowed, glinting like jet, and he took a step toward her. "Would you like to understand me?" he murmured deeply.

Gemma caught her breath. She wondered why it was that whenever he approached her, she became acutely conscious of his height, his sheer physical magnetism. No other man had ever had that effect on her. She supposed it had something to do with his image having been imprinted on her mind at an early age; she had become infatuated with his self-portrait the way most teenage girls developed crushes on film stars. She could feel her pulse begin to race in unwelcome response to his nearness, and she despised herself for her ridiculous weakness; she was a grown woman, not an adolescent. She turned away quickly.

Behind her she heard Jordan growl in an undertone, "Damn it, Gemma, I am *tired* of you backing off every time I come near you!" One large hand closed over her thin shoulder, holding her so that she could not escape. When he touched her, the effect was electric. She could feel his thumb shaping her shoulder blade through the flimsy fabric of her shirt, scorching her with his presence. Everything about him was warm: his hands, his voice, his breath on her nape, ruffling tendrils of her silvery hair.

She screwed her eyes shut and fought off the shaming impulse to move closer, lean her cheek against that caressing hand. It wasn't *fair*! How could she maintain her emotional independence, her sovereignty over her spirit, if a man could have this effect on her simply by being near? Again she tried to squirm away from him.

His fingers tightened. He inquired curiously, "Is there something wrong with me that I should know about? You're beginning to make me feel like an actor in a commercial for mouthwash!"

In spite of herself Gemma giggled at his remark, pleasantly astonished that he had a sense of humor. In her experience, most men didn't. She suggested lightly, "Maybe you just use the wrong brand of after-shave lotion."

She felt Jordan quiver with laughter. "Minx," he murmured. After a moment Franco asked what was so funny, and Jordan translated the joke into rapid Italian. The boy looked puzzled but smiled obligingly.

It was into this congenial scene that Beatrice di Mario suddenly intruded. She halted abruptly halfway down the short flight of steps descending from the upper level, and she stared at the trio in the living room with a disgruntled expression that reminded Gemma of a teacher stepping into a classroom of rowdy students. When Jordan noticed her, he frowned at the scowl that formed when she saw him touching Gemma. Slowly he gave Gemma's shoulder a squeeze and turned to confront his mother, his own face coolly challenging.

"Giordano, what's going on here?" she demanded in Italian.

Jordan shrugged. *"Non importa, mamma."*

"But, Giordano—"

"Mother, I said, never mind." His voice remained low, deceptively languid, but to Gemma his words had the cutting force of a whip. She could not help being intrigued by the relationship between the sculptor and his mother. They were both strong characters, each preferring to dominate, but Jordan was clearly the head of his family. He obviously loved and respected Beatrice, treated her with a great deal of tolerant affection, but any time she trespassed into his personal sphere of influence, he let her know at once that she was going too far. Gemma wondered curiously if Jordan's mother always meddled as awkwardly as she had been doing these past few days. She did not strike Gemma as a basically clumsy person.

With a tact Gemma would not have credited him with, Franco broke the taut silence by asking, "Signora di Mario, tell me, please, how is Caroline?"

Beatrice relaxed, and she stepped down into the living room and crossed to the boy, her worn face gently reassuring. "She is doing fine, Franco. She's just a little tired now. You'll have to come to see her again tomorrow after she's rested."

"*Grazie, signora*. I would like that." As Franco spoke, Gemma reflected with humor on the resilience of the adolescent heart. No one listening to the boy now would credit that only a few days before, he had dismissed the girl as a "child" and had instead been avidly pursuing Gemma. Gemma supposed she ought to be piqued that she had been so easily supplanted in Franco's affections, but all she felt was relief. She had enough problems without fighting off a lovesick teenager.

Beatrice turned to her son and said, "Caroline seems like a sweet girl. She reminds me a little of Sylvia at that age, don't you think so, Giordano?"

Jordan puzzled. "Like Sylvia? I don't know. Sylvia's a lot taller. That long brown hair, perhaps...." He glanced at Gemma. "My younger sister used to have the most beautiful hair, down to her waist, a gleaming golden brown. I did several paintings of her before I specialized in sculpture. Then when Sylvia started college, she suddenly decided she no longer liked her hair the way it was, and without telling us, she had it all chopped off, leaving only a... a stubble, something suitable for a schoolboy, with no sheen, no movement.'' His dark eyes glared accusingly at Gemma's short no-nonsense crop. He said flatly, ''I have never been able to understand why any woman with beautiful hair would want to disfigure herself by cutting it short.''

Gemma's eyes closed. For just a second in the depths of her memory she could hear the metallic rasp of the nail scissors as she had hacked at her long tresses, Sister Katharine's anguished cry.... She stammered hoarsely, ''Well, long hair d-does take a tremendous amount of...of care.''

Jordan declared, ''For beauty, any amount of effort is justified,'' and Gemma felt as if he had struck her.

''Francesca,'' Beatrice interjected with an air of smug triumph, ''Francesca says that caring for her looks is a full-time occupation. Of course, in her case, all that work is certainly worthwhile.'' She paused before adding brightly, ''Giordano, since we seem to be forming sort of a house party, why don't you telephone Francesca in Florence and invite her to come stay with us for a week or so? After the way she has been caring for her father so devotedly, I'm sure she would enjoy a change of scenery.''

Gemma's heart sank at the thought of sharing the villa with the elegant Francesca. One spiteful sarcastic woman was already about as much as she could handle. While she quickly tried to think of a plausible excuse for returning to the *pensione* with Franco, one of Jordan's brows quirked sharply as he inquired, ''You think Francesca is anxious to trade one sickroom for another?''

Beatrice flushed and said, "Well, I'm sure our other... guests... would not expect her to...."

Jordan stated flatly, "No, mother, I don't want Francesca—or anyone else, for that matter—staying with us while Miss Somerville convalesces. The excitement would not be good for the girl. Besides, Francesca has gone to New York."

Gemma's surreptitious sigh of relief was effectively masked by Signora di Mario's startled gasp. "New York! But, why? When? She didn't mention—"

Jordan shrugged. "She told me several days ago, the day of the accident, in fact. A spur-of-the-moment offer. Another model fell ill, and in her place Francesca has been offered a part in a big advertising campaign—some new perfume, I think. If it catches on, she may finally get that break she's always dreamed of."

Beatrice looked confused. "But, Giordano, what about the Madonna? Francesca is the model. Won't you need her to—?"

"Mamma," Jordan said gently, ironically, "do you really believe that after all these years I can't sketch Francesca from memory?" When his mother seemed inclined to pursue the point further, Jordan added brusquely, "That's enough of that. Now Gemma and I need to get back to Sergio's workshop. We'll take Franco to his home on the way. *Addio!*"

Although the rented Alfa Romeo Jordan drove was somewhat larger than Gemma's ill-fated Fiat had been, it was rather cramped for three people, but even so, Gemma felt freer in it than in the echoing expanse of Villa Sogno Dolce, where Signora di Mario's baleful presence seemed to overwhelm her. However, the car was obviously still much too small for a man of Jordan's height. Gemma watched his restricted movements as he backed skillfully out of the Riccis' driveway after dropping off Franco, and she noted conversationally, "I expect you'll be glad when your new Ferrari is ready. Do you think it will be available soon?"

Jordan said, "Yesterday I had a telephone call from the dealership in Pisa. I'll be able to pick up my car in a couple of days, just as soon as the insurance paperwork is taken care of. I was wondering if you would like to come with me when I run down there?"

Gemma frowned. "All the way to Pisa?"

"It's only about thirty-five kilometers—a little over twenty miles."

Gemma shook her head in wonder. "I will never get used to European distances!" she exclaimed. "Everything is so close together. All my life I've heard of the great city-states of the Renaissance— Pisa, Florence, oh, so many others—and I always envisioned them as great fortresses existing independently in the vastness of Italy. Now that I'm here, I find that these cities are practically suburbs of each other!"

"If you recall that most of my country was settled literally thousands of years ago," Jordan said, "when the only means of transportation was by foot, you'll realize that twenty miles of moderately rugged terrain can be quite as daunting a distance as several hundred are today."

Gemma sat half-turned in her seat, watching Jordan as he drove. Behind her sunglasses her gray blue eyes were intent on his face, and a little smile hovered around her mouth. Jordan looked at her curiously, thoughtfully. When his gaze could not penetrate the barrier of her smoked lenses, he seemed to note instead the inquisitive tilt of her head, her short hair shining in the sunlight, and his eyes wandered down to appreciate the way her small breasts strained against the fabric of her shirt when she leaned one elbow on the back of her car seat. Just as Gemma began to feel uncomfortable under his appraisal, he returned his attention to the road—they were entering the narrow twisting streets of Pietrasanta—and he asked casually, "So what are you thinking?"

Gemma pulled off her sunglasses. "Why do you ask that?"

He shrugged. "Oh, you were sitting there smiling like a modern-day Mona Lisa, and I've always been curious as to what goes on behind a smile like that."

Gemma's lips twitched, and suddenly conscious of his eyes on her mouth, she shielded it from his gaze with her hand. "Darn," she giggled, "now I won't be able to move a muscle without thinking you're watching me."

"I like watching you," he said blandly. "Now tell me what you were thinking, or else I'm liable to come up with some wildly improbable—and lascivious— explanation of my own."

Gemma took a deep breath. After a second she said, "I was just thinking about the way you said 'my country' so casually. I liked the sound of it. Most Americans wouldn't use an expression like that unless they were making a specifically political statement."

Jordan grinned engagingly. "I guess that's something I picked up from my father. You know, of course, that since the fall of the Roman Empire, the Italian peninsula has been invaded by one conquerer after another, even as late as the Second World War. Part of this vulnerability derives from the historic division among the people, the tendency to think of oneself as a Neapolitan or Venetian or Roman, rather than an Italian. My father was very much a nationalist, and he always taught Sylvia and me to think of Italy as *our* country, and that way, he said, we would fight to keep it our own if we had to.''

"Didn't you say your father was in the Resistance during the war?''

Jordan nodded. "Yes, he and Sebastian Buscaglia, Francesca's father, led one group. The next time I go to Florence I'll have to take you with me to meet Sebastian. I think you'll like him. He's quite a character.''

"Thank you, I'd like that—if I'm still here,'' Gemma said politely, but inside she cringed at the prospect. If she remembered correctly, Signora di Mario had said that Francesca's father had been ill, and Gemma did not relish the thought of playing nursemaid to an elderly invalid while Jordan was entertained by the beautiful model. She fell silent as Jordan searched for a parking place in the crowded streets, and she gasped in surprise when he suddenly downshifted and with a squeal of tires wheeled the little car into a narrow space between two vans, just nosing ahead of a Lancia that had been aiming for the same spot. The other driver called out something highly anatomical and made a rude gesture before driving away in a huff.

Jordan switched off the ignition and looked up to see Gemma regarding him dubiously. He chuckled dryly, "Don't judge my driving by American standards, *carissima*. Here the only right of way is that which you make for yourself. If I had let him take the parking space, he would have lost all respect for me as a driver."

"And we can't have that, can we?" Gemma muttered.

He smiled with infuriating benignancy. "No, we can't. I'm glad you're beginning to understand."

As they strolled along the sidewalk toward the Carcione studio, Gemma ventured hesitantly, "Your mother said you're doing a new statue of Francesca—a Madonna, I think she mentioned."

Jordan halted in the middle of the pavement, heedless of the flow of people moving around them. His expression was inscrutable as he gazed down at Gemma. He said repressively, "Yes, that's right. I'm doing a Madonna. What about it?"

Strain made Gemma's voice even huskier than usual. Gaudy color painted her wide cheekbones as she wondered where she had found the nerve to bring up the subject in the first place. Gulping hard, she stammered, "Well, I...I was just curious as to...to why I haven't seen it. Y-you've been so...generous with everything else, showing me your sketchbooks, your maquettes, I...I couldn't help wondering if there was some special reason why you keep this piece hidden from me." Her head drooped, and she stared resolutely at his shoes.

He didn't reply at once. In the middle of the hot dusty street she began to shiver as if in a snowstorm, certain that she had angered him far beyond any hope of reconciliation. Damn, why couldn't she keep her mouth shut! She had no right to ask him to show her anything. She was not his equal. He was an artist, and she was only a half-assed drawing teacher. When he caught her chin in his rough fingertips and tilted her head back so that she had to meet his gaze, she blinked hard, fighting back tears. But to her amazement, his dark eyes were regarding her not with anger at her insolence, but with uncertainty, hesitation, even—no, it was impossible—embarrassment as he said quietly, "Yes, Gemma, there is a good reason why I haven't shown you the Madonna. It's quite simple really." His thumb moved over her parted lips, stilling their trembling. He sighed and explained, "You see, my dear, I'm very much afraid you won't like it."

IN THE AIRY DARKNESS of her bedroom that night, Gemma thought about Jordan's words.

After showering and washing the marble dust from her hair, she had changed into a cool cotton nightdress of almost monastic plainness, a slim tube of white challis that draped softly over her breasts and fell straight to the floor, barely touching her narrow hips. Gemma had looked in on Caroline and had found the girl sleeping peacefully, but when she returned to her own room, she had made sure the communicating doors of the joint bathroom were ajar so that she could hear Caroline if she called out during the night. Now Gemma stood in front of her window, heavy wooden shutters opened wide, and she brushed her silky hair dry as the freshening breeze played through it, lifting the silver gold strands and fluttering them like moth wings. She gazed out over the shadowy landscape, and one part of her mind noted and appreciated the wavering gleam of moonlight on wind-kissed grapevines, but all her thoughts were centered on the stuffy noisy studio of Sergio Carcione, where in the din and the flying dust she had at last breached the deceptively anonymous partition into the inner room, the sanctum sanctorum, to view Jordan's latest project.

She wasn't sure what she had expected. What could anyone tell from a work that was only half-finished? She had seen a massive block of white Cararra marble, higher than a man, marked with grease pencils and gouged by pneumatic hammers. Only to an active imagination did it yet bear any resemblance to the seated figure of a woman. The pile of chips cluttering its base gave evidence of the many hours of labor that had already gone into its creation, hours when Carcione's crew had struggled to scale up Jordan's two-foot-high maquette into a statue that would eventually stand larger than life size. On a rough workbench beside the pallet on which the marble rested, weighted down by a heavy pair of calipers, there had lain a handful of smudged sketches, working studies for the Madonna, and next to the drawings had stood the original model itself. Gemma had stared at Francesca's stunning face recreated in clay. Even as she admired the artistry and impeccable skill with which Jordan had given the appearance of motion and softness to the veil draped across the woman's flawless cheek, Gemma had felt disappointment, dismay.

Beside her, Jordan had murmured, "Well, Gemma, what do you think of it?"

All she could think to say was: "Francesca is very beautiful."

Jordan had waved away her words impatiently. "Of course she is," he snapped, "but that's not what I'm asking, and you know it." But when he pressed Gemma further, she would only shrug helplessly.

As she brushed her hair in the moonlight, she wondered just what he had expected her to say, what she, a rank amateur, *could* say. She knew she could never voice her first thought, that for anyone else it might have been a masterpiece, but for Jordan di Mario it was hackneyed and lifeless and insincere. Her second thought had been bewilderment that he had been given such a commission at all. Sergio had mentioned that the Madonna was destined for a small Florentine chapel, which was all fine and well, except that surely the patron who had sponsored the work must have realized that Jordan's forte was representing the sensual, the sexual, not innocence and spirituality.

Jordan himself seemed to have recognized his limitations, for the sketches lying around the studio indicated that he had changed his mind repeatedly about the design, and the carving that had already been done varied markedly from the original concept.

Gemma wondered suddenly if Jordan's problems stemmed from his emotional involvement with his model. The woman was incredibly lovely, of course, with a face Botticelli would have wept for, but after all these years Jordan must surely know her too intimately to envision her as the embodiment of purity.

When he looked at Francesca, he would not see the Virgin; he would see instead a woman whose head had lain beside his on a pillow, her cheeks still flushed in the aftermath of....

Gemma's hairbrush suddenly slipped out of her fingers and bounced onto the floor, clattering on the terrazzo. Surprised at her clumsiness, she squinted into the shadow by her feet, and when she spotted the faint reflection of moonlight on the brush handle, she stooped to retrieve it. When she straightened up again, Jordan was standing just inside her bedroom, quietly closing the hallway door behind him.

She stared across the room at him, his dark outline limned against the slightly lighter shadow that was the pale stucco wall. He stood immobile, gazing intently at her, and she frowned in confusion until she noticed the rectangle of moonlight shining on the floor, the silhouette of her slender body only faintly obscured by her thin cotton gown. Quickly she stepped out of the light, and as she did, Jordan reached over and switched on the lamp.

Gemma blinked against the brightness, her gray eyes taking in every detail of his long lean body. He was still dressed as he had been earlier in the day, in his usual casual attire, but his blue knit body shirt was unbuttoned almost to the waist, and Gemma could see the gold religious medal glinting in the fine black hair on his chest that grew downward over the flat plane of his stomach until it was hidden by the belt of his tight low-slung jeans. She felt a peculiar stirring deep inside her, then she dropped her lashes in embarrassment, blushing at the hot glow in his eyes. The obvious question—"What do you want?"—trembled on her lips and died away, squelched by the equally obvious answer.

He did not speak. Instead he watched her with silent purpose more eloquent than words, and at last she managed to whisper huskily, "Jordan, you shouldn't be here."

His hard mouth curved upward in a mocking smile. "No, Gemma? Weren't you expecting me?"

"Of. . . of course not," she stammered, aware even as she spoke that she was lying. She had known he would come to her; she had always known what he would expect if she moved into his house. From the beginning he had made his intentions plain. What she did not understand was why he should desire her when he already had Francesca for a mistress. Nor could Gemma understand why she allowed herself to be put in a position where he might reasonably assume that he could have her.

Her fingers clenched the handle of her brush. "Jordan, I. . . I think you'd better go, please." She turned away and applied herself to vigorously brushing her hair again.

He crossed the room in two long strides, halting so close to her that she could feel his breath warm against her nape. He caught her wrist in a powerful grasp and pulled the hairbrush out of her hand and tossed it onto the dresser. "You don't need that anymore," he said. "You'll give yourself a head-ache, banging on your scalp that way, or else you'll pull out what little hair you have left." As he spoke he began to sleeken her silky tresses with his fingers, smoothing them into a shining cap that hugged the outline of her well-shaped head, leaving her neck bare and vulnerable. His rough thumbs stroked across her exposed nape, and Gemma shivered. "You have such beautiful hair," he murmured, "like living moonlight. How can you bear to cut it?" As he spoke, he bent his dark head and caressed her sensitive skin with his lips.

Gemma jerked as if touched by an electrode. He was affecting her in a way totally outside her experience, and the impact of his closeness alarmed her. In an effort to hide how he was making her feel, she tittered nervously. "My hair used t-to be l-long. When I was a. . .a girl, I could sit on. . . ." Her voice died out in a strangled gulp as his hands slid under her arms and cupped her small breasts through the thin nightgown, pulling her back against the hard length of his body. His mouth moved along the length of her neck, scorching her, and to her dismay she felt her breasts swelling and firming under his probing fingers, matching his growing excitement. She began to panic. She arched away from him and sobbed, "Jordan, please don't—"

Against her shoulder he growled, "*Dio*, you're so goddamned stubborn." He twirled her around in his arms and scooped her off her feet, flinging her onto the chaste handwoven coverlet of her bed. Even as she tumbled onto the mattress, he fell across her, and her cry of protest was smothered by the possessing force of his mouth.

CHAPTER SIX

THE WEIGHT OF HIS BODY on hers was strangely seductive, his long denim-clad thigh rough against the smoothness of her legs where her nightdress had bunched around her hips. His skin had a subtle tangy male scent that made her dizzy, and his black curls tickled her chin when he buried his face in the curve of her throat. Later she thought that if only his fingers hadn't clamped around her wrists like shackles, piningoning them against the bed on either side of her head, if only he had not kissed her so fiercely, bruising her lips....

Gemma panicked.

"Don't *grab* me!" she wailed, and she flailed wildly, her slender body bucking and thrashing beneath him. When she tried to jerk up her knee in the classic defense her brothers had taught her years before, Jordan quickly released her and rolled away to the other side of the bed. A deep flush painted his high cheekbones, and he was panting hard as, leaning on one elbow, he stared grimly at her.

His dark eyes raked her, noting her pallor, the rapid rise and fall of her breasts under the flimsy fabric of her gown. She glanced sidelong at him with fear-filled eyes and retreated further, hugging the edge of the mattress. He jeered, "All right, I get the message. There's no need to throw yourself off the bed.''

With an effort she regained control of her composure. As her breathing became less ragged, she pushed herself upright and started to smooth her gown down over her legs, coloring hotly when she realized just how much of her body had been bared in her struggle. With trembling fingers she pulled the hem of the nightdress down to her ankles, then she swiveled her legs around so that she sat on the edge of the bed with her back to him. Straightening her shoulders, she said, ''Jordan, I want you to leave this room at once.''

She stared down at her toes dangling just above the terrazzo, and she waited for the mattress to give under his shifting weight. He did not move. After a moment she heard him ask curiously, ''Did I really frighten you so much?'' His voice became raw, and he taunted, ''Or do you just like to tease?'' Gemma listened in amazement. Her panic ebbed away, only to be replaced instantly by a wave of blinding anger. She was about to lash out at him, when suddenly she realized she could not. She shuddered with the effort to keep quiet. She must never let him see how he affected her; she must remain cool, calm. In reserve there was strength; emotions were weak, feminine. He was a man: naturally he could intimidate her physically. But if he ever suspected he could touch her spirit. . . . Jordan took her prolonged silence for an answer, and he muttered, ''I'll bet you put that fiancé of yours through hell.''

Gemma shivered again, and this time she could not entirely suppress her reaction. She looked back over her shoulder and regarded Jordan with baleful eyes. "How perceptive you men are," she said bitterly. "You don't need to tell me I put Dave through hell; he kindly informed me of that point already. According to him, I deliberately kept him on a string for nearly seven years, then when I finally gave in to his...demands...I pigheadedly wouldn't...." Her voice cracked.

Jordan's mouth thinned, and he sat up beside her, his long legs just brushing against hers. He asked darkly, "What in God's name did Blanchard do to you?"

Gemma shrugged. She was disturbed by Jordan's nearness; yet somehow his concern seemed comforting, soothing. She began to relax. Jordan repeated, "What did he do to you, Gemma? Did he hurt you?"

Slowly she shook her head. "No. I'm not being fair to Dave. He was always good to me, he tried to be...considerate. In the end he just became frustrated because I never—" She stared down at her hands, at the strip of white at the base of her ring finger. "He didn't understand. He kept telling me it would be better after we were married."

Jordan caught her hands in his and gently pried apart her curled fingers. "And would it have been better?" he asked softly, stroking her palm.

Gemma didn't answer. She watched the rhythmic motion of his thumbs. When she glanced up at him, her wide gray eyes meeting his narrowed black ones, deep-set in the harsh arresting planes of his long face, she wondered curiously what there was about him that could induce her to tell him the intimate details of her relationship with another man.

Jordan asked suddenly, "Are you still in love with Blanchard?"

Gemma's lashes fluttered, and she lifted her chin to gaze pointedly at the Picasso lithograph, masking her dismay as she realized that, although she had just vowed not to let Jordan breach her defenses, intrude upon her emotions, already she had let down her guard enough to permit him to inquire about her most personal feelings. Her eyes followed the stark tangle of lines, vivid primary colors, so deceptively simple, so bewildering. The heart was like that. She had thought of a hundred obvious reasons why she should love Dave, and the harder she had tried, the more tortured she had felt. She said stiffly, "It doesn't matter what I feel about Dave because I broke the engagement after the incident at the school."

"What incident?" he persisted.

Gemma muttered, "You don't know when to give up, do you?" Her mouth curved upward in mirthless irony because she was echoing the remark Jordan had made to her. She took a deep breath, and suppressing the deep-seated revulsion she still felt whenever she thought of that awful afternoon and its equally harrowing aftermath, she said tonelessly, "It's not much of a story; it happens all the time these days. At school one Friday a couple of weeks after Easter, I stayed late as usual to mix paints, check supplies and make sure the students hadn't left any messes that would set over the weekend. I always did this, and sometimes a few of the kids would help me. I was alone that particular Friday, but when this boy showed up just as I was getting ready to leave, I didn't think much about it.'' She hesitated, power-less to halt the quaver in her words. When she continued again, her husky voice was vitriolic. She spat, "Why should I have been suspicious? After all, he was one of my students, his father was the director of the school, and he was only sixteen.''

"Madonna," Jordan choked, "are you telling me that he—that you were—"

She shook her head roughly. "No," she said with grim satisfaction. "For once I discovered that there are certain advantages to having grown up with three big brothers. My bruises faded in a couple of weeks. His—some of his, at any rate—probably took a little longer.''

"What happened then?"

Gemma's face was rigid with tension. "What happened? Exactly what I should have known would happen: the male establishment closed ranks against me. The boy claimed I had...invited him, and since he was a juvenile, he ended up with a couple of months' suspended probation. I was regretfully informed that my teaching contract would not be renewed for the coming school year."

Jordan stared at her. "Where the hell was your faithful fiancé when all this was going on? Why didn't he and those three older brothers of yours beat the kid to a pulp?"

Gemma took a deep breath and pulled her hands loose from Jordan's. She said, "Don't blame Dave or my family. I was the one who insisted on filing charges against the boy, and for once they did as I wanted.''

Jordan scowled, and the dark aspect of his face

was totally Latin, showing a primitive anger untempered by any trace of his American heritage. He stated flatly, "They were fools to listen to you. No woman can think clearly in those circumstances. If someone assaulted my sister Sylvia or any of my women, regardless of what she thought ought to be done, I would make sure that he sang soprano the rest of his life!"

Gemma looked at him askance. "Then I'm awfully glad I'm not one of your women," she said.

Something flared in his eyes, and he inquired quietly, "Are you, Gemma? Are you really?" One large hand reached up to cup her defenseless nape, turning her face toward his, and the fingers of his other hand gently brushed back the tendrils of flossy silver hair that had fallen over her eyes. His gaze caressed her face, lingering momentarily on her lips, and her pulse quickened. One long finger stroked the curve of her cheek, feathering down over her jaw and throat, marking a burning trail that continued lower until it hesitated at the modest gathered neckline of her nightgown. He studied her face questioningly, and Gemma bit her lip. Unable to look at him, she closed her eyes. Her long lashes vibrated delicately against the faint blush of her cheek, a blush that deepened dramatically when she felt him tug at the drawstring and slip his hand inside her gown. His hand was warm, so warm, against her cool breast, like the kiss of the sun on an opening flower, but its gentle languorous heat was surpassed by the fever his mouth aroused when it began to follow the trail marked by his seeking fingers. Her eyes still closed; she felt him ease her down onto the bed again; and when his long hard body lay beside her, she snuggled against him, welcoming his exploration, lost in an erotic fantasy in which there was no haste, no threat—until he murmured huskily, "You'll see how good it can be, Gemma, when you belong to me."

At his words Gemma recoiled instantly and instinctively, the spell broken. Her lashes flew up, revealing gray blue eyes that had a gunmetal sheen as she glared at him. "Damn you," she growled deep in her throat, "I won't belong to you. I will not be a chattel!" And before she could ponder the wisdom of her action, one of her hands snaked out and slapped him hard across the face.

Even as he reeled, he caught her wrists with workhardened hands and pinned her to the mattress. His long legs straddled her body, his breath coming hard and fast, and the gold religious medal he wore swung in a hypnotic arc as it dangled before Gemma's eyes. His face was still shadowed with the lingering shreds of his desire as he stared down at her, and across one cheek was the distinct imprint of her fingers. "You crazy wildcat," he hissed, "what the *hell* is wrong with you?"

He was crushing her breath from her, but she met his gaze unswervingly. "I...I belong to...to myself," she gasped defiantly. "No man has a claim on me, and I won't let you use me or order me around."

For endless seconds he looked down at her, his expression unreadable. Then, amazingly he shook his head slowly and smiled. He released her hands and sat back on his haunches as he murmured, "You little fool, you haven't the faintest idea what you're talking about."

As she struggled to free herself, her fingers became entangled in the flapping lapels of his shirt and the crisp hair that ran in a narrow swath over his flat stomach. She was distracted by the texture of his skin, the powerful muscles rippling beneath it. A tremor of awareness shook her, and Jordan grinned openly.

His condescension infuriated her further. "Don't be so damned *smug*!" she railed, pressing her palms flat against the taut denim stretched over his flexed knees and trying to lever herself out from beneath him. But before Jordan could respond, they were interrupted by a gasp of horror and outrage. In unison their heads jerked around to see Beatrice di Mario standing frozen in the communicating door of the bathroom, gaping at them.

Her homely face was ashen against the splendor of the fashionable lilac-toned dressing gown she wore, but as she stared at the couple entwined provocatively on the bed, her sallow complexion became suffused with hot indignant color. "Giordano," she choked in Italian, "what in God's name are you doing?"

Gemma felt a sudden urgent longing for a dark hole she could crawl into, and she tried to roll onto her side, away from the pale accusing eyes of Jordan's mother, but the weight of Jordan's heavy body held her captive. He seemed curiously unmoved by Beatrice's presence. He drawled lightly, "Really, *mamma*, you really shouldn't have come in here."

His unruffled calm seemed to startle her. She blinked and stammered, "I . . . I was just checking on the . . . the girl, and through the door I heard— noises."

Apparently unconcerned by the flagrantly compromising posture his mother had discovered him in, and still in that same cool voice he said, "I would have thought you had better sense than to intrude on something that obviously doesn't concern you."

Beatrice snapped, "And I would have thought you had more respect than to consort with a—a woman like that under your mother's roof!"

Gemma flinched violently. Jordan, feeling her shudder, quickly eased his weight off of her, swinging his lean torso away from the bed. Freed of him, Gemma covered her face with her hands and groaned sickly. As he stood up, he patted her arm reassuringly, then he confronted his mother. His voice was edged with cold steel as he stated flatly, "All right, you've said quite enough."

"But, Giordano," she persisted, "how can you permit a little—you dishonor me when you—"

"*Basta!*" he bellowed, drowning out her furious protest. His voice quieted, and he smiled with sardonic humor. "Really, *mamma*, have you forgotten so soon what it's like to be young and in love? Do I have to remind you that I was born four months after you married my father?"

The silence that followed was so sudden and so total that Gemma forgot her own humiliation long enough to take her fingers away from her eyes and peek at the two people squared off in the center of the room. The tall ungainly woman was staring up at her still-taller son with a face bleached so white that her light blue eyes seemed dark by contrast. She was visibly trembling. Her mouth worked mutely for several seconds as she struggled to force out the words. At last she grated, "How could you, Giordano? *Infamia, che infamia*, that you should speak thus to your mother!"

Jordan seemed unmoved by her denunciation. Cocking his head slightly to one side, he crossed his arms over his broad chest and observed coolly, "You know I love and respect you, and I would never have said anything if you hadn't forced me to." His thin lips curled up in a gently mocking grin as he drawled, "Honestly, mother, *'infamia, che infamia!'* A line like that might have worked for Anna Magnani, but don't you think it's a bit extreme for a girl from Memphis? Anyway, my statement was true, wasn't it?"

When Beatrice spoke again, she bit off the words. "Of course it's true. You know it is—and you know why." Her eyes flicked scathingly over Gemma's slim figure still lying supine on the coverlet, then they returned to rest once again on her son's face. With an air of bitter triumph she added acidly, "At least your father and I got married!"

Jordan received this last thrust in silence. After a moment he blinked and nodded in acknowledgement of her hit. Then he smiled blandly. He said, "Well, then, *mamma*, if that is your only concern, you need trouble yourself no further. You see, Gemma and I also are going to be married—just as soon as it can be arranged."

GEMMA DID NOT SPEAK to Jordan again until his mother had left the room. He stepped out into the hallway with her, murmuring reassurances in low urgent tones, and Gemma heard the woman ask in anguish, "But what about Francesca?" Gemma did not wait for Jordan's answer. While the di Marios talked outside the door, she leaped up from the bed and went into the bathroom, where she raked her shining hair into some semblance of order and donned a bathrobe of well-worn navy blue serge, tightening the cloth belt about her narrow waist. She moved about aimlessly, puttering with her toilet articles, refusing to think about Jordan's outrageous statement. She glanced through the other door into Caroline's room and saw that she was slumbering peacefully. She wondered what Beatrice had given the girl to enable her to sleep through all the uproar.

When at last reluctantly she returned to her own room, Jordan was waiting for her. He regarded her silently, dismissing her uncompromisingly modest robe with a snort. He said, "That looks like something left over from your convent school."

Gemma shrugged, her eyes downcast. Splaying her fingers over the dark fabric she said lightly, "As a matter of fact, it is. It's wool, guaranteed to last forever, and I've never seen any point in replacing it."

"Very thrifty," Jordan commented dryly. "But if you don't mind, when we buy your trousseau, I'd prefer you to get something a little less . . . nunlike."

Gemma's eyes flew to his face, and the expression she saw there left her unaccountably shaken. "L-look," she ventured uneasily, "it was very . . . noble of you to . . . to spring to my defense as you did, but don't you think the gesture was really a . . . a bit much? After all, it's quickly going to become obvious that you didn't mean what you said—"

"But I did mean what I said, Gemma. You and I are going to be married."

She stared at him, her gray eyes wide and stormy. He stood resolute, his powerful body as unyielding and immovable as the statues he carved. "You're out of your mind," she said.

He chuckled mirthlessly. "You keep telling me that, and yet I think you are the only one who doesn't know her own mind. From the moment I met you I've known exactly what I wanted." With infuriating thoroughness his gaze began to move languidly over her body, his black eyes probing through the blue robe to caress the swell of her breasts, the curve of her slender waist, the long line of her thighs.

Gemma felt herself blushing under his scrutiny, the rosy tint of her cheeks deepening further when she realized that beneath the modest layers of her nightclothes, her treacherous body was beginning to react to his appraisal. She gulped, "That's all very fine and well, but it's not what I want. I have no intention of marrying anybody."

Jordan scowled. "You were all set to marry Blanchard," he pointed out.

Gemma nodded reluctantly. "Yes, well...that was a mistake. I...wanted children, and I thought.... Now I realize that I have no business marrying anyone. It will be better for all concerned if I forget about having my own children and henceforth just devote myself to teaching."

Jordan's expression was thoughtful. After a pause one corner of his hard mouth quirked upward, and he mocked, "As you said, very noble. But you're going to have to rethink that decision yet another time.

The only vocation you are going to devote yourself to is your art, and you *are* going to marry me—whether you like it or not.''

Gemma was too flabbergasted to feel anything other than mild curiosity. ''And just how do you think you're going to enforce this...proposal, if that's what it is?''

Jordan shrugged. ''Oh, it's definitely a proposal, and I hope your good sense will make you see the advantages of my offer without my having to, as you say, enforce anything. But if not—'' he tilted his head toward the door to Caroline's room ''—just remember that on the other side of that bathroom sleeps an injured child, one who, as you have constantly pointed out to me, is your responsibility. Bluntly, her continued recovery depends on my good will, and it is not yet too late to have her charged with drunken driving.''

Now Gemma was afraid. She felt the blood seep from her body, draining into some deep bottomless cavity where her stomach once had been. She began to tremble. ''You...you can't mean that,'' she stammered.

He appeared unmoved by her distress. ''Do you know me well enough to say for sure that I don't mean it?''

''I don't know you at *all*!'' she sobbed. ''That's the whole point!'' She was suddenly torn between terror and exasperation, but she was determined to hide her reaction from him. ''For God's sake, Jordan,'' she said in as flippant a tone as she could manage, not daring to look at him, ''what is the point of this? Why are you being coy? If you really...want me as badly as you claim, you know damned well I couldn't fight you off if you.... There's no reason to mention any nonsense about marriage.''

There was a prolonged silence, and when Jordan spoke, his voice was expressionless. ''Then that's all you think this is about—satisfying my unbridled lust?''

''Well, what else?''

''If I told you I fell in love with you the first moment I saw you, would you believe me?''

Gemma's scorn was blistering. ''You mean like something from a romantic novel? No, of course I don't believe that.''

Again Jordan hesitated. ''I see,'' he said at last. His tone was dry and mocking. ''Of course, how could I be in love with you? You are stubborn and sarcastic and completely blind to your own femininity. It is utterly unreasonable that I should be aroused by the charms you hide with such determination, but strangely enough, I am. You have an air of fragility about you that—'' He broke off his words impatiently. ''Forget about that. Suffice it to say that I do want you. I flatter myself that, given the time, I could make you want me in return, but unfortunately you insist on going back to Colorado as quickly as possible to waste your incredible talents pursuing a teaching career for which you are plainly unsuited. I can't let you do that, Gemma. For your sake, as well as my own, I must keep you with me. And I see no way to do that except by marrying you.''

She regarded him steadily. ''I still don't believe you,'' she said.

His expression hardened, and he shoved his hands deep into the pockets of his jeans. "No? What will it take to convince you? Must I telephone the *commissariato di polizia* and tell whoever answers that I've just recalled that the other driver seemed intoxicated, perhaps strung out on drugs—"

"No!" Gemma squealed. She flung herself at him, clutching the lapels of his shirt, pinching star-shaped creases into the fabric as she stared up into his stern implacable face. "You can't do that to Caroline. She's never hurt you!"

Jordan shrugged. "She caused the destruction of an automobile that I was very fond of, one that cost me more than fifty million lire. That's not a loss to be taken lightly, you know."

Gemma blanched as she mentally converted lire to dollars. Even in U.S. currency the figure was impressive. "My God," she muttered, trying to back away from him. He pulled his hands out of his pockets and caught her shoulders in a light but inescapable grip. As always, his nearness seemed to have a disturbing effect on her composure, and she tittered nervously. "That's how much, about sixty thousand dollars? Maybe I...I should be flattered. I imagine even Francesca would hesitate to value her...her favors that high."

"Leave Francesca out of this," he ordered grimly, his fingers biting through the dull fabric of her robe. "You're the one I'm interested in now."

Gemma winced at his strength. "And having decided that you want me, in typical male fashion it follows automatically that you must have me?" She gestured angrily toward the bed whose coverlet still bore the imprint of their bodies. "All right, Jordan," she snarled, "there it is and here I am. Why don't you just get it over with and then leave Caroline and me in peace?"

His dark eyes flamed, and his voice was heavy with suppressed rage as he ground out, "*Cristo*, Gemma, you refuse to even try to comprehend what I am saying! There is more at stake here than mere sex. I am not interested in rape or a one-night stand, nor do I want an affair from which you could walk away the instant the girl is well enough to leave the country."

Gemma interjected, "Even if we were married, there's no guarantee that I would stay here once Caroline was safely out of your reach."

Jordan sighed, and his hold loosened. "Maybe not. But if you were my wife, you would have at your disposal every resource necessary to develop your talent as a sculptor: unlimited materials, the finest instructors.... I think you are too much of an artist to abandon all that, even if staying means the loss of a little of your personal pride."

Again Gemma tried to pull out of his arms, and this time he let her go. She stepped backward and slumped wearily on the edge of the bed, her clasped hands dangling in front of her knees. "If you were my wife..." he had said, and she had to admit that the words had a certain tantalizing appeal. To be the wife of Jordan di Mario, to work beside him in Carcione's studio, to watch each new masterpiece take shape under his skillful and gifted fingers—through her lashes she eyed him appreciatively—to sleep in his arms each night.... It might be sheer bliss—for as long as she did what *he* wanted. Gemma had no illu-

sions about which of them would come out the winner
in any contest of wills. She took a deep breath and
brushed a strand of shining hair out of her eyes. She
lifted her head to look up at Jordan, who towered over
her, watching her intently. She pleaded softly, "Jordan, I beg of you, don't make me do this. It would be
hell for both of us." She gulped hard, trying to clear
the hoarseness that was excessive even for her naturally husky alto voice. Somehow she had to make him
understand. She continued reluctantly, "I left Colorado for a lot of reasons, but mainly it was to get
away from a man who, although he loved me, thought
he knew the best way to run my life. I know damn well
you don't love me, and you're a hundred times more
ruthless than Dave could ever be. If you force me to
marry you, I'll...I'll hate it. I'll hate you."

Jordan nodded slowly. "Yes, I know you'll hate
me," he murmured. "You already despise men. But I
hope to—"

Gemma's head jerked up, and her gray eyes
stretched wide. *I do not despise men,* she wanted to
protest indignantly. *I'm just tired of having to fight all
the time.* She looked away again without speaking.

Jordan's expression deepened as he gazed thoughtfully at her, and when he spoke again, his deep voice
was tinged with sadness. "No, perhaps I was wrong.
What you really hate is...being a woman. I'll have
to see if I can change that—after we're married."

GEMMA STARED OUT HER WINDOW, watching the
dawn. Shafts of sunlight, rising behind the hill on
which Villa Sogno Dolce was situated, first gilded the
crowns of the tall pine trees, then picked out seams of

marble shining through the thin soil on the hillsides and made them glow. As the sun climbed higher in the sky, Gemma could see the endless rows of wine-heavy grapevines come to life, wide dusty leaves buzzing with bees and moths while errant green tendrils waved above them as if groping for the light. The faint breeze that wafted in, carrying with it the sweet rich bouquet of the fruit, was already sultry; the day was going to be hot. But inside, behind the shelter of the thick walls of the villa, the air was deceptively cool—as deceptive as the silence that echoed through the empty corridors.

Gemma turned away from the window. She was exhausted; she had not slept all night, too over-wrought to relax after that bewildering scene with Jordan. She still could not believe that he meant to go through with this absurd marriage, but she admitted that she did not yet know how she could stop him if he did. She wished she could calm herself enough to think clearly. This was Jordan's house, his town, his country. She was a stranger in a strange land, without friends or family to help her. Gemma's jaw tightened. Her family and friends had been of little help when she charged that boy with assault, but despite their disapproval she had found the courage to pursue the course she thought was right. Somehow she would garner the strength to defy Jordan. She just needed some rest and time to think. Alone she could have balked him with relative ease by simply refusing to cooperate with his outrageous plans; she could have fled to the American consulate at the first opportunity. But there was Caroline to think of now. Whatever Gemma ultimately decided to do, she

could not take a chance on Jordan's venting his anger
on the girl.

Certain that brooding would accomplish nothing,
she laid out her usual jeans and cotton shirt on the
bed and went in to take a shower. The cool water
revived her somewhat physically, but it did nothing
to lighten the foreboding that weighed on her mind.
After she had dried off, she donned her blue robe
and glanced through the door into Caroline's room.
The girl was awake.

Gemma forced her mouth into a smile and crossed
to her friend's bed. "Good morning, Caro," she
greeted with arch enthusiasm. "How are you feeling?"

Caroline lifted a limp hand in greeting. Her color
seemed a little less pasty, and her voice was stronger,
but when she spoke, her expression was troubled. She
said, "I'm better, thank you. I guess I really just
needed some rest, as Mrs. di Mario said."

"Are you hungry? Shall I get you something?"

Caroline shook her head, and her dark brown curls
fluffed about her face. "No, not yet. Thanks, anyway." She hesitated, choosing her words. "Gemma," she ventured, "is...is it really all right for us
to be here? Aren't we...imposing?"

Gemma blinked, but her smile never wavered as
she hastened to reassure the girl. "No, of course not,
dear. This is a huge house, with lots of room, and
Jordan's mother said you were more than welcome to
stay till you're back on your feet."

Caroline persisted, "Yes, Mrs. di Mario has been
very nice to me, but...." Her voice dropped to a
whisper, and she glanced around uneasily. "Gemma,

last night I heard *yelling*. At first I thought I was dreaming, but after a while I realized I couldn't be because mostly it was in Italian, and I couldn't dream in *Italian*, could I? I can hardly understand it when I'm awake.''

"Perhaps you just overheard a television program or something," Gemma improvised wildly.

"But I heard someone say my name!" Suddenly she appeared close to tears. "They don't want us here, do they, Gemma? We're being pests, and it's all my fault. Nobody ever wants me." She sniffed inelegantly. "I know I've been unbearable the whole time we've been on this trip, and I'm sorry, truly I am, Gemma, but sometimes I feel.... Mama said she needed some time to herself, and my father's new wife doesn't want me around at all, and...and nobody asked me to the graduation dance."

From the hallway door a deep voice interjected, "What? Feeling sorry for yourself this early in the morning? We can't have that!" Jordan stepped into the room, bearing a tray with a pitcher of orange juice and hot fragrant rolls and some bright blue pills. Gemma stepped aside, and he smiled engagingly at Caroline as he set the tray on the nightstand. At the sight of him her wan expression vanished instantly.

"Good morning, Jordan," she said shyly. "Uh...I mean, *buon giorno.*"

"Buon giorno, graziosa signorina," he replied, catching her plump fingers in his and kissing them lightly. "My mother is...running behind schedule this morning, so I have brought you a little something to tide you over until she comes in. No doubt

your drooping spirits are due to your having eaten so
little yesterday." He poured some juice into a glass
and handed it to her with her medication, which she
took without demur. Jordan nodded his approval
and said, "Good. You'll feel much better after
you've breakfasted. We can't have you looking
depressed when Franco calls on you."

"Is he coming today?" Caroline asked eagerly.

"Of course he is," Jordan said. "What hot-
blooded Italian male could resist the opportunity to
visit a pretty girl, especially in her bedroom?"

Caroline blushed becomingly, preening her long
hair with her fingertips. As Gemma watched the
byplay between Jordan and her friend, she had to admit that he employed his undeniable Latin charm
very skillfully, teasing and flirting just enough to
bring the ailing girl out of her doldrums, without en-
couraging her to attach her interest to him personally. Gemma knew it couldn't be any great pleasure for
a man like Jordan to have to make small talk with a
vapid teenager. She might have been impressed with
his kindness had he not made threats against Caroline only hours before.

Gemma's skepticism must have showed in her
face, for Jordan glanced sharply at her and then
asked Caroline, "Has Gemma told you yet that she
and I will be going away for a few days?"

Gemma blanched, and Caroline looked startled.
"A few days? But where? Why?"

As Gemma held her breath, Jordan said casually,
"We have to go to Pisa to pick up my new Ferrari."

"And that will take several days?" Caroline asked.

Jordan shrugged. "There is a lot to see in Pisa,

some really fine Romanesque art and architecture. Old churches." Caroline's face expressively portrayed her opinion of Romanesque art and architecture. Jordan added with a grin, "By the time we get back, you ought to be well enough to get out a little, so if you like, I promise I'll give you the first ride in the new Ferrari."

"That would be wonderful," Caroline said, "but while you're gone, what am I—?"

"You're going to get better, that's what you're going to do," Jordan said firmly. "Don't worry. My mother will take excellent care of you. In fact, I know she'll enjoy having a chance to pamper you. She told me that you remind her of my sister, the daughter she hasn't seen in several years. It will make her happy to have you here."

"Well, if you're sure. . . ."

"Of course I am." Jordan stood up and said with mock sternness, "Now quit your chatter and eat your breakfast—*presto!*" Out of the corner of his eye he glanced at Gemma. He murmured, "I want to talk to you privately."

Gemma nodded reluctantly. "Yes, of course. Just a moment, please."

As soon as Jordan had disappeared through the door that communicated with the bathroom and Gemma's bedroom, Caroline demanded in an urgent whisper, "Gemma, are you really going away with him?"

Gemma clenched her fists in the folds of her robe. "I—I'm not sure, Caro."

The girl picked up the note of apprehension in Gemma's voice. "Is something wrong? Do you *want* to. . .to be alone with him?"

Gemma shrugged with affected insouciance, realizing that she could not involve Caroline in her private struggle with Jordan. She drawled, "Caro, my dear, you've seen him. Could you blame any woman for wanting to be with Jordan?"

Caroline remained unconvinced. "Well, he is very handsome," she conceded, "but he's...he's kind of...overwhelming, too. And anyway, it just doesn't seem like you to...." She frowned, wrinkling the colorful bruise on her forehead. After a brief hesitation she said meekly, "Gemma, I know I've been more trouble than I'm worth on this trip, but...but I want you to know, if you need help with...with anything, I'll do whatever I can."

Moved by her friend's concern, Gemma swooped down and hugged her hard. As her cheek touched Caroline's, Gemma said fiercely, "Don't worry, I'm going to be all right. You just concentrate on getting better, and don't bother about anything else. Promise me." Before the girl could reply, Gemma fled to her own room.

She found Jordan standing beside the bed, staring down at the pants and top she had laid out. "Do you have some kind of a dress with you?" he asked tersely, not looking at her.

Gemma started. "Well, yes, one, but it—"

"Then you'd better put it on. I'd prefer my bride not to wear jeans at the wedding."

She backed away, clutching at her blue robe as if to shelter herself. *No, no,* she thought wildly, *not like this;* she needed time to *think.* "My God," she choked, "you can't mean...surely not *today!*"

He lifted his head, and when his dark eyes met

hers, his expression was grim. "Yes, today. I've already been on the phone tending to the arrangements." He took a deep breath before inquiring, "When you told me you attended a convent school, did that mean you are a Roman Catholic?"

"More or less," Gemma answered, puzzled. "Why?"

"Good," he said. "It's much simpler that way. If a priest marries us, the wedding will automatically be registered. With any other denomination, we would have to go through a civil ceremony, as well, to make it legal."

"I don't want to be married in a church," Gemma said.

Jordan regarded her obliquely. "May I ask why?"

She began to shiver violently, but her voice betrayed little of her agitation as she said, "I should have thought that was obvious. What you're doing to me is bad enough without. . . . I may not be the most devout person in the world, but I will not commit blasphemy by standing before the altar and vowing— I won't do it, Jordan."

"I see," he said expressionlessly, noting after the briefest of pauses, "and, of course, a purely civil marriage would be easier for you to terminate if you walk out, as you have threatened."

Gemma met his gaze squarely. "Yes, there's always that to be considered."

He said, "I am Italian, Gemma, and I find the idea of a marriage unblessed by the Church—distasteful. What if I insist?"

"I pray you won't."

Slowly one dark eyebrow lifted. "Very well, it

shall be as you wish. However, I still want you to wear a dress.'' He glanced around the room. ''You'll have to bring your passport for identification, of course, but apart from that, I don't think you'll need anything except possibly your toothbrush. In Pisa we will buy you enough clothes to tide you over until we can get to Florence, to one of the better fashion houses—''

''I have clothes,'' Gemma interrupted.

Jordan smiled cynically. ''You mean you have a few garments adequate to cover your nakedness. I would hesitate to classify that sexless garb you affect as clothing, and certainly I do not consider it appropriate for the wife of Jordan di Mario. It is not in the guise of a scrawny boy that you interest me, Gemma.''

She felt herself quiver with suppressed rage at his arrogance. ''You mean to change everything about me, don't you?'' she demanded.

''If I have to,'' he said. ''Now hurry up and get dressed. We have a long day ahead of us.''

When she went into the dressing room, she was still trembling. She removed her blue cotton shirtwaist dress from the hanger and stared at it, noting the serviceable fabric and unimaginative design. Her wedding gown? Even in her agitation she could not help chuckling at the irony of the notion. She had never quite got around to purchasing the dress she would wear when she married Dave, always finding some excuse to delay just a little longer, but he had hinted broadly that he wanted her to come to him bedecked traditionally in white satin and lace, with crinolines and possibly a train; he had not realized that she found such a garment offensive, the awkward weight and length of it symbolically recreating in Gemma's mind the hobbling ankle chains brides had once worn as they were given over to the possession of their husbands.

Slowly she donned the dress and cinched a white leather belt around her narrow waist. She slipped medium-heeled white sandals onto her bare feet, thankful that her slim legs were tan enough to dispense with panty hose in the humid Italian heat. In the bathroom she flipped a brush through her short tousled hair and then, as an afterthought, she smeared a little pink lipstick onto her small mouth. Against her pallor it seemed to glare, so she rubbed it off again with a tissue. She stared ruefully at her reflection. Even in a dress she looked wan and uninteresting. True, the deep blue of the fabric seemed to pick up and emphasize the sky-colored flecks in her gray eyes, and her hair clung smoothly to her head like a helmet of electrum, but... she looked like what she was, nondescript, an American tourist, certainly not the would-be bride of a famous Italian artist. People carried their identity around with them regardless of the clothes they wore. She remembered one of the teachers at the convent school, a vivacious woman who had entered the Order fairly late in life after a successful career as a swimming coach. Even in her habit she had always looked as if instead of a cross she ought to be wearing a gym whistle around her neck.

Gemma wondered what would become of her own identity if she let Jordan force her into this outlandish marriage. Either she could fight his efforts to

change her and become so exhausted trying to com-
bat his superior physical and mental strength that she
eventually lost the ability to fight him at all, or else
she could conserve her energy by submitting
meekly—and still lose. In either case, Jordan would
take control of her, and soon she would be his
creature; there would be no Gemma left. Oh, God,
she didn't think she could stand it! If only there were
someone who could help her, tell her what to do. She
wondered about Signora di Mario and quickly discarded that notion. Although the woman was obviously bitterly opposed to an alliance between her
son and Gemma, Gemma had already seen that
Beatrice was no more able to oppose his will than she
herself was.

Suddenly she thought of Dave.

She wanted to laugh at the paradox of it, that those
attributes that she had deplored in her fiancé, his
stolidity, his humorless practicality, were the very
qualities she needed now to work her way out of an
absurd and asinine situation. If only she had not
discouraged him from coming to Italy.... She
brightened. Even at a distance of several thousand
miles, Dave would be able to help her. She admitted
that she was not thinking clearly, her mind clouded
by fatigue and anxiety and her bewildering physical
response to Jordan, but if she explained to Dave
exactly what had happened, his down-to-earth mind
would instantly spot the loophole through which she
could escape Jordan's coercion. If she could just get
to a telephone....

She supposed there were extension telephones
throughout the villa, but the only one she knew of for

certain was the one in the kitchen, almost at the opposite end of the house. Quickly Gemma slipped into the hallway, looking both ways. She saw no one, and as quietly as possible she made her way along the corridor toward the lower level, wincing each time her sandals clicked on the hard terrazzo. She descended the short flight of steps and wended her way through the low sleek furniture in the living room, sternly ordering herself not to be distracted by Jordan's marvelous art collection. When she saw the door to the kitchen, she sighed with relief, almost convinced that she was safe, but the instant she stepped inside, she came face-to-face with Beatrice di Mario.

The woman looked up from the sink and glared at Gemma balefully. Her pale eyes surveyed the trim figure in the blue dress, and her languid drawl was almost drowned by the venom in her voice as she observed bitingly, "Well, at least you look like a woman for a change."

Gemma refused to react to her baiting. "Please, *signora*," she said urgently, "I have to use the telephone."

Beatrice gestured toward the wall phone, and Gemma went to it at once. "Bragging to your American friends already?" she inquired sarcastically.

Reaching for the receiver, Gemma was distracted enough to glance back over her shoulder and ask curiously, "Why do you always say 'American' the same way you'd say 'Martian'? You're an American."

"Correction," Beatrice said, "I *was* an American. When I married Giordano's father, I became Italian, just as you will if you persist in this mad scheme to

ensnare my son. That's something you ought to consider carefully. Divided loyalties can be painful—
which is one reason I want him to marry one of his
own countrywomen.''

"You mean Francesca?"

"Of course I mean Francesca. She is beautiful and
accomplished and rich; they have known each other
since they were children, and she is also Italian. She
understands the society Giordano must live and work
in. She would be the perfect wife for him."

As Gemma lifted the receiver to her ear and began
the frustrating wait for the dial tone, she couldn't
resist noting, "Jordan certainly doesn't seem to have
been in any great hurry to marry her."

"I told you," Beatrice flared, "Francesca had her
own career to pursue. Now that she is back, it is only
a matter of time—or it would have been, had you not
come along! Although what he sees in an oppor-
tunistic little nobody like you...."

Gemma looked at the woman steadily, a little sadly, hearing behind her insults the bewildered fears of
a possessive mother. She said softly, "You may not
believe this, *signora*, but I don't want to marry
Jordan."

Beatrice stared back, patently skeptical. "Then
why did you allow him to say—" She tossed her head
and snorted eloquently. "Don't think you can play
me for a fool, young woman, because I won't have it.
Naturally you want to marry my son. I've seen it all
before. Do you suppose you are the first little
sculpture groupie to try to trap him into some kind of
commitment? They come here every summer, a
horde of dirty greedy pot-smoking tourists, all eager

to play at being 'great artists' for a few months. There are some few who are serious about their work, but in general their lack of talent is surpassed only by their lack of morals. Half the men would play the gigolo to get a 'patron' of either sex, and the women.... Did you truly think that in the midst of such chaos, a shining prize like Giordano di Mario would go unnoticed?''

"But I'm not like that," Gemma said, tapping on the button of the telephone in an attempt to summon up the dial tone.

Behind her, Beatrice said coldly, "Of course you are like that. The wonder is that for some reason, Giordano doesn't see it." She stalked away.

When the woman left the kitchen, Gemma sagged with relief. Although she knew that Beatrice's contempt was unwarranted, still her scornful words had cut deeply, unwelcome echoes of the charges made against Gemma when she tried to prosecute the boy who had assaulted her. She wasn't sure how much more of this sort of thing her already mangled self-respect could take. She pressed the lever again, and this time she was rewarded by the slow dash-dash-dash sound of the dial tone. "Thank God," she whispered fervently, and she began to dial the number for the intercontinental operator. "Oh, please, Dave, be home," she murmured as she flicked the "one" and then made the longer circuit for the "seven." But just as she inserted her fingertip into the hole that dialed the "zero," her ear was suddenly filled with a loud dissonant beeping that made her jerk away from the receiver. She stared at it in confusion, startled and bewildered, trying to recall what Jordan had told her a dot-dot-dot sound meant on an Italian telephone.

Before she could remember, long scarred fingers reached around her and pulled the receiver out of her unresisting hand. Jordan listened for a second, nodded and hung up the telephone. He said lightly, "The central computer is jammed again. There's no telling how long it will be before the lines are clear."

Gemma stared mutely at him, fear in her face. He said, "When I went back to your room and found that you had left it, I knew at once where you were. I could hear you arguing with my mother." She remained silent, and his eyes narrowed. "Who were you trying to call, Gemma," he demanded harshly, "your erstwhile lover?" Still she couldn't answer. He caught her shoulders in a bruising grip from which she knew there would be no escape. She felt only a sensation of utter hopelessness as he spat out, "Forget about Blanchard, Gemma. Forget about everyone, and concentrate on being my wife. From this moment on, you belong to me."

CHAPTER SEVEN

THE HOTEL SUITE overlooked the ramparts of the Quadrilateral of Pisa, and from her vantage point at the window Gemma had a clear view of the ancient cathedral and baptistery and tilting bell tower, illuminated in the night by a green spotlight. During the course of that endless bewildering day Jordan had hustled her past the famous landmark, allowing her to pause just long enough to admire the delicacy of the architecture, the succeeding rows of narrow arched columns—which unfortunately were at the moment plastered with tattered political posters—but they had not braved the crowds of tourists waiting to go inside; Jordan had promised to take her back in a day or two. Now, as Gemma stared out the window at the vast enclosure only just visible in the moonlight, she thought with amusement that no amount of photographs could ever really have prepared her for the vertiginous impact of standing in the shadow of the Leaning Tower, that giddy, irrational and overwhelming certainty that, although the structure had maintained its awkward angle quite stably for more than eight hundred years, any moment now it would fall, crushing and destroying her.

As she lifted her hand to pull the draperies shut, the muted light from the lamp beside the long couch flashed on the plain wide gold band now encircling her wedding finger. She chuckled sardonically.

On the other side of the room Jordan looked up to ask, "What's so funny?"

Gemma turned to face him, her expression carefully impassive despite the fact that she trembled as she looked at him. He wore a summer-weight business suit of impeccable, rather British cut, the conservative tailoring at odds with the pale cream fabric that owed more to the Via Condotti than to Savile Row. Before that day she had not seen him dressed in anything other than the most casual of work clothes, and if his lean hard body had been impressive in denim, garbed in gabardine and silk it exuded a sexual aura that was damned near overpowering. With forced lightness she said, "I was just thinking that you and the Leaning Tower have a lot in common."

He wrinkled his brow. "How so?"

Gemma shrugged. "Well...you're both tall and Italian."

He glanced at her suspiciously, but before he could pursue the matter, they heard a sharp knock at the door. "That will be our dinner," Jordan said. His dark eyes flicked over the rumpled blue dress she was still wearing, and he suggested coolly, "Why don't you go on into the other room and change into something more...comfortable while I take care of this? You'll find a box on the bed. I'd like you to try on what's in it."

Gemma hesitated. She wondered if Jordan wanted to get her out of the way while the waiter was in the room, lest she bolt the instant the door opened. The rapping was repeated more forcefully, and Jordan urged, "Please, Gemma. I want to see how you like your present."

"Of course," she replied, and she ducked into the bedroom. Closing the door firmly behind her, she leaned back against it, breathing hard, her eyes tightly shut. From the sitting room the rattle of the dinner cart filtered through the wood paneling, and she could hear the low unctuous tones of the waiter, followed by a gasp of surprise and a fervent, *"Grazie, mille grazie, signore!"* as, she presumed, Jordan tipped the man lavishly. She could almost envision him genuflecting as he retreated from the suite.

Slowly Gemma lifted her lashes and surveyed the bedroom, which she had studiously avoided since they checked in three-quarters of an hour earlier. From the swiftness with which they had been escorted to their lavish suite, Gemma realized that Jordan must have made their reservation before leaving Pietrasanta, and now, as she stared with wide gray eyes at the *letto matrimoniale*, the vast bed draped with a vivid velvet spread, resting in stately splendor on a dais under an ornamented ceiling, she felt a surging sense of resentment that he had been so confident she would go through with the wedding.

And yet...and yet, Gemma admitted with a sigh, she had not fought him as she might have done had she been thinking more clearly. Even without help from outside sources this was not the Middle Ages; Jordan was not some bandit chieftain abducting her to his mountain lair, and today, even in a country as traditionally male-dominated as Italy, a man could not compel a woman to marry him unless she acquiesced. And she had certainly acquiesced....

As if in a trance, she had sat silently beside him as he swiftly guided the Alfa Romeo out of the winding hills and onto the *autostrada* that led southward to Pisa. Without a word of protest she had stood before a bewildering succession of clerks, produced her passport and signed her name to official-looking documents. Finally, when she and Jordan faced the harried registrar seated behind a cluttered desk, the man had barked out a couple of sentences in Italian that she could only half understand. Jordan had made his responses quietly but firmly, she'd heard herself mumble *si*, and the official had nodded tersely, scrawling his name at the bottom of the license and stamping it. When he rose to extend his hand for a perfunctory handshake, suddenly Gemma had awakened to the enormity of what she had just done, that she had actually married Jordan di Mario.

She had looked up at him then with something like fear in her eyes, and he had smiled complacently as he murmured, "*Moglie mia*—my wife," and bent his head to hers. But before he could kiss her, a crowd of laughing people had burst into the little office, and Jordan and Gemma had been pushed aside to make way for a couple in wedding dress, the very young groom beaming tenderly at his even younger bride, a plump, pretty girl with a wreath of jasmine in her hair.

Later there had been an excursion into a jeweler's shop to buy the rings there had been no time to purchase earlier. Gemma had listened in silence as Jordan and the proprietor argued over what kind of stone would best suit her creamy skin and fair hair; the jeweler seemed to favor sapphires, but Jordan decreed that his wife should have opals, "to match her eyes." With an expressive gesture the other man admitted reluctantly that although he did carry a few fine pieces—naturally far better than anything one could get from those *ladroni*, his competitors—he had no opal rings of a quality to do justice to the flashing eyes of the *bionda signora*, for whom an indulgent bridegroom would of course require the very best. . The magnificent opal, the *signore* would understand, was an unusual stone, not much in demand, appreciated only by the most discriminating. But if the *signore* would care to look at some. . . . Sensing that the man was about to embark upon another oration, Gemma had spoken up for the first time, stating impatiently that she didn't want any kind of jewels. For a long moment Jordan had regarded her steadily, his expression inscrutable, before at last he waved away the tray of engagement rings and pointed instead to a selection of simple gold bands.

After leaving the jewelry store, Jordan had taken Gemma to a restaurant a few doors down the street. While she picked glumly at her *pesce fritto*, Jordan had suddenly excused himself for a moment, and the waiter was trying to tempt her appetite with *castagnaccio*, a pastry made of chestnut flour, when Jordan finally returned. After lunch they had gone to a boutique where, again ignoring Gemma, Jordan and the saleslady had selected the dresses, lingerie and beautifully made Italian leather shoes that he seemed to think might suffice until such time as he could take Gemma to Florence to buy "real" clothes. As if he were dressing a doll, she had thought indignantly, and she wondered if Jordan was really all that interested in what she wore, or if this was simply his none-too-subtle way of reinforcing his ownership.

The salesclerk had been able to supply elegant leather suitcases—a far cry from Gemma's plaid soft-sided luggage—to hold her new wardrobe, and the bellmen who escorted her and Jordan to their hotel suite had carried all the bags into the spacious dressing room, but now, as Gemma looked about her, trying unsuccessfully to ignore the significance of that vast bed, she noted one long box emblazoned with the name of the boutique, lying on the heavily quilted coverlet.

Her fingers shook a little as she opened the box and folded back the tissue paper, and when she saw what lay inside, she caught her breath. It was the most beautiful nightgown she had ever seen, a long sleek fall of heavy smoke-colored silk, its stark simplicity relieved only by an intricate pattern of fern leaves embroidered around the plunging neckline in pearly silk floss. As Gemma gazed at the gown, admiring its unusual color and design, she realized with surprise and pleasure that Jordan had gauged her taste perfectly; with the insight of an artist he had guessed that she would have loathed pastels and lace. With a gurgle of feminine delight Gemma lifted the gown from its nest of tissue paper, and when she did, something fell out of the folds and bounced back into the box. Fishing around for a second, she retrieved the item, and as she held it up, she gasped.

Again Jordan had surprised her. Dangling from her fingers on a long platinum chain was a magnificent teardrop-shaped opal, white with a sparkling luster that reminded her a little of uncut marble, and deep within it bits of blue fire flashed like the flecks of blue in her eyes.

A gift for a lover, Gemma thought awefully, and then she quickly dismissed the notion. Jordan didn't love her. Railroading an unwilling woman into marriage was hardly an act of love. He had married her because as a sculptor he had been offended by the idea of her wasting her talent. And yet... and yet, might not such careful attention to her taste, as evidenced by his gifts, be interpreted as an expression of consideration, even... even tenderness? Or was it simply that his artistic sensitivity was too strong to allow him to give her something patently unsuited to her person and life-style? She had no idea. She didn't understand Jordan any more than she understood why she had married him, why she hadn't put up a stronger fight. All she knew was that she *had* married him, she had promised to live with him as his wife in every way, and now the time had come to fulfill that promise.

When with considerable trepidation Gemma opened the bedroom door and stepped hesitantly into the sitting room, the somber fabric of her gown swirling sinuously around her legs, Jordan was standing beside the small dining table, lighting candles. He had discarded his coat and tie, and his brown silk shirt was unbuttoned about halfway. One of the small flames would not stay lighted, and in the flickering light the gold medallion he always wore flashed against the tangled mat of black hair on his chest. Concentrating on the candle, he did not notice Gemma right away. For endless seconds she gazed silently at him, appreciating the shadowed planes of that hard arresting face, the lithe grace of his powerful body. Soon, soon she would touch that face, that body.... Deep inside her a knot of awareness twisted spasmodically, making her skin prickle, her breasts lift and tauten. She thought in amazement, *I want him, I really want him,* and along with that knowledge came the equally stunning realization that in all her twenty-four years she had never wanted anyone else.

He glanced up from the candles. When he spotted her standing in the doorway, his eyes widened, and he stared at her. He did not come closer. Instead he stood riveted beside the table, his intent gaze moving over her slowly, appreciation obvious even at a distance, stroking her hair, her face, her bare shoulders. Every flicker of those all-seeing eyes sent shock waves through her as if he had touched her. This profound awareness was a new and alarming sensation to Gemma, and she found herself nervously fingering the opal pendant that lay cool against her heated flesh in the hollow between her small breasts. The jerky motion of her fingers attracted his attention to the neckline of the gown, which plunged almost to her waist. Gemma flushed, hoping he would not notice the outline of her nipples already pressing against the clinging fabric, evidence of her increasing arousal. But when he caught his breath sharply, she knew her hope had been in vain. She wondered if he would mock her after the way she had so assiduously denied any interest in him as a man. Anxiously she waited for him to say something, anything, but instead he stood mute, letting his eyes speak for him as they wandered over her slender body with eloquent purpose.

Just when she thought she would scream if the tension were not broken, Jordan said huskily, "The gown suits you, Gemma."

She smiled faintly, spreading her fingers over the front of the gown, smoothing the silk. "Th-thank you, Jordan. It's very beautiful. The... the necklace, too. I don't know when I've ever seen anything so lovely. Thank you for both my presents. I... I like them very much."

"*Prego,*" Jordan murmured.

Gemma said sheepishly, "I'm sorry I didn't get you anything." The notion of gifts hadn't even occurred to her, and now, in the face of Jordan's largesse, she felt rude and boorish.

Jordan shrugged away her apology. "Well, there was hardly time, was there?" he drawled. Before Gemma could protest again, he forestalled her by pulling a large bottle of champagne out of the ice bucket where it had been cooling. "Wine?" he asked, the question obviously rhetorical since he was already unwinding the foil and twists of wire that held the cork in place.

Gemma crossed the room to watch him wrap a linen napkin carefully around the bottle. She wondered cynically if there was something inherent in the male, some inborn love of ceremony, that required them to make a ritual of opening a champagne bottle. She could still remember the elaborate pains her father had taken, when she and Dave announced.... She caught herself sharply. She was not going to think of Dave, or her father, or anyone. This was her wedding night. She wasn't going to let any unwelcome memories spoil it. Aloud, with an effort at lightness, she teased, "Is that a good American vintage, or is it just domestic?"

From beneath furrowed brows Jordan glanced at her, his expression indicating that he had picked up some hint of her troubled thoughts. When she smiled faintly, he grinned and popped the cork. "Actually," he said, pouring the pale golden liquid into tulip-shaped goblets, "it's French. I'm a great believer in drinking the local brew, but for celebrations, Italy simply does not produce anything to compare with French champagne." He handed her a glass, and Gemma gazed as if mesmerized at the tiny bubbles that sparkled and popped fragrantly under her nose. Jordan commented, "I'm glad you're relaxing enough to make a little joke, Gemma. I've never met anyone who lives in such a constant state of tension as you do. *Salute, Gemma mia.*"

"*Salute,*" she echoed, and they touched glasses, the fragile crystal clinking like temple bells.

Jordan said, "They've brought us what looks like an excellent supper. Would you care to eat something? I know you scarcely touched your lunch."

Gemma surveyed the dinner cart, and despite the appetizing aromas wafting from beneath the silver covers, she shook her fair head. "I'm sorry. I'm really too tired to eat."

Jordan studied her wan features. He asked seriously, "Did you get any sleep at all last night?" When she shook her head again, he sighed. "I'm sorry, Gemma. After everything that's happened in the past twenty-four hours, you must feel as if you've been hit by a locomotive.''

"You do tend to have that effect on people," she admitted.

He said gently, ''I assure you, I don't mean to. Would you care for more wine?'' When she said no, he continued, ''Then here, come sit with me.'' He took her empty wineglass away from her and set it beside the sweating ice bucket. Catching her wrist, he led her toward the couch, but she held back, suddenly nervous. He scowled. ''We'll just talk—for now,'' he said, and after a moment she followed him meekly.

He settled her beside him on the soft cushions of the sofa, and she leaned her head back wearily, staring upward so that all she could see were the gilded cornices crowning the walls, and the highly colored ceiling. The bright colors used in Italian architecture and decoration had startled her at first, but the longer she remained, the more she realized that the vivid hues that at first glance had seemed gaudy were in fact only a pale reflection of the country itself, where the earth, the sky, the very light were all more vibrant, more intense, than in anyplace else she had ever seen. Perhaps, she thought, that was why the Italian people themselves were so vibrant, striking in feature and effervescent in personality, because anything more subdued would be overpowered by the landscape.

As Gemma herself had been overpowered.

She turned her head to one side and looked at Jordan, studying his features in profile as he sipped his second glass of champagne. From the widow's peak topping his high forehead, the velvety eyes deep-set above pronounced cheekbones, to that long straight nose and determined chin, he had extraordinarily attractive features, all evidence of his strength. Did he have any idea how very overwhelming he was, she wondered. He was not a typical Italian, he was not a typical anything, his brilliance setting him high above the common herd. His tastes inclined toward elegant simplicity, his personality and attitudes were less volatile and more cosmopolitan than those of his countrymen, obviously a heritage from his mother, although that perhaps was ironic, since for some reason Beatrice di Mario chose to deny her American birth. And in looks.... He had charisma, Gemma decided, hesitating to use a word that had been debased by casual application to everyone from politicians to pop singers; he had an intense personal charm. He had everything. Now he even had Gemma.

When Jordan lifted his head suddenly and discovered Gemma studying him, she blushed and looked away, her long lashes drooping silkily over her heated cheeks. She waited nervously for him to say something, and she was surprised when instead of speaking, he caught her left hand in his and began stroking her slim fingers. For a moment he toyed silently with the wide gold band, then he noted nonchalantly, "I do intend to buy you an engagement ring."

Gemma said, "I'd rather you didn't. Actually I don't care much for rings. They get in my way when I'm working."

Jordan's expression hardened. "You wore one for what's-his-name, you'll wear one for me."

Annoyed by his proprietary air, she frowned at him and asked acidly, "But why? We couldn't have been engaged more than twelve hours."

His scowl faded, replaced by a wry smile. "Yes, it was rather a whirlwind courtship, wasn't it?" he murmured. He rested his large hand palm upward on his thigh and lay her hand over it, measuring her fingers against his. Her skin looked pale and smooth against his scored work-hardened palm, and her fingertips barely reached the last knuckle of his. As she gazed down at their joined hands, he said suddenly, "Have you ever thought about what a miracle of creation the human hand is, how infinitely complex? Over a quarter of all the bones in the body are in the two hands, each one is operated by twenty-eight muscles, and on the fingertips the nerves are more closely concentrated than anywhere except in the brain. The result is an engineering marvel that can soothe a baby or detonate a bomb, thread a needle or beat a hunk of rock into a semblance of human form." He began to trace her lifeline with his blunt nails. "It has always seemed to me that form is the essence of life. I suppose that's why I knew from the beginning that I had to be a sculptor, rather than, say, a painter. We live in a three-dimensional world, and without that third dimension, even the most sublime ideas, presented by the greatest artist, are still somehow...removed from us."

His voice deepened, and he began to talk about his work, his goals, the passions that had driven him from a very early age, and Gemma listened with growing enchantment, lulled by the deep soothing tones of his voice, the gentle stroking motion of his fingers moving caressingly along her bare arms. As she relaxed, her eyes slowly closed, and her head slipped sideways, somehow coming to rest on Jordan's broad shoulder. She was tired, so very tired; she needed to rest, she needed to quit fighting. She smiled as she drifted, disarmed by a vision of a very small boy playing in the soft rich earth of his father's vineyard, his chubby fingers earnestly shaping the damp soil into models of puppies and geese and even his baby sister, risking a scolding because he was supposed to be helping his father prune the grapevines.

"Gemma," he murmured, his lips brushing her ear, feathering tendrils of flossy hair against her cheek. His breath was sweet with the aroma of the wine. Mumbling an incoherent protest, she snuggled closer, eyes still closed. She thought she heard a dry chuckle, but perhaps that was just part of her deepening dream, like the strong arms that lifted her with seductive and irresistible strength and carried her, floating over the bright Italian countryside, until at last they laid her down tenderly on the velvet grass. When they released her, she felt a momentary unease, a sense of loss, but soon they wrapped about her again, warm and protective, and even in her sleep she knew now that she was safe.

SHE AWOKE sometime in the very early hours of the morning, when the approaching dawn was only a sheen of pearl overlaying the darkness. At first, blinded by the night, she could not remember where she was, and she jerked with alarm, but a deep voice whispered in her ear, "Easy now, *carina*—quiet, my pretty one," and Jordan's muscular arms enfolded her gently and pulled her close against him, her head resting on his shoulder, and her slim body curling instinctively into the warmth of his hard contours. With a sigh she shut her eyes again and relaxed, nuzzling her face into the crisp hair on his chest, her nostrils filled with the musky male scent of him.

She felt his lips move lightly across her temple, her cheekbone, and the arm beneath her shifted so that he could splay his rough fingers over the back of her nightgown, pressing her still closer. His free hand brushed along her side, stroking hip, waist, breast with exquisite casualness through the smoke-colored silk, never lingering, until the knuckles encountered her small but firm chin and, almost by accident, tilted her face upward so that his seeking mouth could find hers.

His touch was so delicate, weightless as cobwebs, that Gemma wondered if she still dreamed, if the lips urging hers to part were of a kind with the spectral arms that had borne her aloft over the bright landscape, the fields passing beneath her view like patches on a crazy quilt—or had it been the coverlet on the vast bed? Suddenly confused, she gave a little moan, and her mouth opened to the tender invasion of his kiss.

He was an unhurried lover, learning each zone of her face, her body, with great thoroughness before moving on. His sensitive fingers shaped her bones and studied the texture of her skin, fondling and caressing until she began to think he must know her very structure as intimately as if he had sculpted her of clay over an armature. When he lifted himself away from her and brushed the narrow straps of her nightgown from her shoulders, pushing it down past her waist to bunch at her hips, Gemma shivered at the cool air on her bare heated flesh, but she did not resist. She opened her eyes to stare up at him, his large body looming over her, features only just outlined in the predawn darkness, and although she was sure he could not see her curving mouth, she smiled in welcome.

"You're so beautiful," she heard him murmur.

Slowly she shook her head. "You make me beautiful," she whispered huskily, and she wondered if he knew how literally true that breathless statement was. She had never been beautiful, she had never been alive before this moment. She was inert material waiting for the master's touch to endow her with form and motion, Galatea longing for Pygmalion to free her from the marble. *Figure of a Newborn Woman by Jordan di Mario,* she thought dreamily, marveling at the way her breasts responded to his touch, as if it were indeed his deft fingertips that made her nipples so firm and erect, and not the strange fire pulsing through her veins. His hands traveled further, parting, probing, intent on knowing every part of her. *"Diletta mia,"* she heard him murmur thickly. When he lowered his head, and his mouth followed the course of his fingers, she gasped, not certain she could endure the sensations he was arousing in her, the burning ache, the dizziness. She caught at his hair, thinking to steady herself, thinking to push him away, but when his springy curls wrapped around her own fingers, and she felt the shape of his noble head, Gemma suddenly remembered that she, too, was a sculptor.

The first caressing motion of her palms across his broad shoulders seemed to startle him, and he looked up quickly, peering at her intently in the rising light, a question in his eyes. Afraid she might have displeased him, she stammered nervously, "Do...do you mind if...if I touch you, too?"

Jordan gasped in disbelief, "Do I *mind*? *Santo Dio*, if you had any idea...." He pulled her to him in a crushing embrace, his mouth scorching hers, then he released her and rolled onto his side, leaning on one elbow, one knee slightly flexed, and as Gemma surveyed his powerful body—muscular chest, flat stomach, strong loins, absurdly long legs—she realized with a blush what the darkness had hid from her, but what she ought to have realized from the beginning, that Jordan was entirely and unashamedly nude—except, a small flash of light revealed, for that gold medallion.

Tearing her eyes away from the compelling sight of him, Gemma instead reached out an exploratory finger to tap the medal with her fingernail. "Who is this?" she asked curiously.

He glanced down at the tangle of hair on his chest. "Saint Luke, of course," he muttered with a distracted air, "patron saint of artists."

"But isn't he for physicians?"

Jordan shrugged. "Both, I think. He must have been a busy man." He caught her wrist and pulled her hand against his chest as he drawled, "Darling, I thought you said you...wanted to touch me?"

Her eyes widened, then closed again, and slowly,

almost fearfully, she began to move her fingertips over his skin, smooth and dry in the early morning coolness, but with a deep subtle radiance like that of earth overlaying a dormant volcano. As pleasure began to build up in her, her tentative touch became firmer, surer, both hands stroking, massaging, exploring with ever growing urgency. Her breath quickened. But as she fondled him, she suddenly wondered if the fire pulsing inside her was indeed communicating itself to him through her fingers. He seemed unmoved. She glanced up at Jordan's face and was dismayed to find him staring back at her with eyes like obsidian, impenetrable, a hard flush of red streaking each cheekbone.

Her hands dropped away, and she retreated from him, humiliated. She cursed herself for a fool. The sensations that felt so extraordinary and novel to her were nothing new to him. He was eleven years older than she was. While she had still been a girl, he was investigating the limits of his sexuality with women like Francesca, pliant, knowledgeable, *skilled* women, in comparison to whom she must seem clumsy and utterly naive. She stammered in a low hoarse voice, "I'm sorry, Jordan. I don't...I really don't know much about...about pleasing you. If you expected—if because what I told you about my relationship with.... I'm sorry."

She turned her head to keep from seeing the scorn in his eyes, but he caught her chin firmly and forced her to look at him. The harsh planes of his face had softened into a smile of curious tenderness, and his dark eyes were no longer opaque as he beamed at her. "Oh, Gemma," he sighed wryly, rubbing his roughened thumb delicately across her lips, "if you only knew what you do to me! Don't you understand? I've been...holding back...deliberately—and nearly going mad in the process—because I wanted to be absolutely certain that you were...ready." His fingers tightened, and he groaned, "But, God help me, I can't wait any longer!" His arms slid around her slender body, and he propelled her backward against the cool linen sheets.

She knew then that he was out of control, and just for a second as his weight crushed her into the yielding mattress, she panicked, crying out her instinctive fear of the dominant male. But his lips stopped her cry, moving quickly, soothingly over her face, and he whispered urgently, "Don't think about the past, Gemma. Let this be the first time."

But how can I forget, when you won't, the part of her mind still capable of thought questioned dazedly even as her heated blood began to respond to the beat of his desire as ringing and insistent as mallets on stone. Then she was beyond question, as was he. They were plastic, twisting and weaving and molding, shaped by that pulsing beat into new life forms, Gemma and Jordan. Then there was only one form, one life, GemmaJordan, moaning out the pangs of its creation with one voice.

THE SECOND TIME SHE AWOKE, the sun was high in the sky, and coins of light worked their way between the fluttering draperies and sprinkled the carpet. The air was already sultry, thick with the promise of heat, but even warmer was the arm flung heavily across her waist, pulling her back into the curve of his body.

One long thigh effectively pinned her legs beneath him, his dark, hair-roughened skin contrasting sharply with her creamy flesh, and his fingers cupped possessively around a small breast. When Gemma tried to ease herself away from him, his body wrapped more tightly about hers, and his lips nuzzled her nape, making her shiver involuntarily with delight.

As Gemma lay helpless in Jordan's arms, that spasm of pleasure faded, only to be replaced instantly by nagging resentment that he had so much power over her that he could enforce her response even in his sleep. Again she tried to wriggle out of his grip, and this time he released her, rolling onto his back with a muffled groan. For several seconds Gemma waited breathlessly to see if he would waken. When he did not, she relaxed and slid carefully off the bed, her toes encountering a wad of dark gray silk as they touched the floor. With trembling fingers she picked up the gown and laid it carefully across a chair, smoothing out the wrinkles, thinking as she did that of all the clothes Jordan had purchased so casually the day before, the beautiful nightgown was the one garment that really seemed to belong to her.

She frowned as she surveyed the contents of her wardrobe. Certainly those bright, almost aggressively feminine dresses and frilly lingerie had little connection with the Gemma Culver she knew. Gemma di Mario, she corrected herself; she had to remember that she was Jordan's wife now—not that there could be much doubt after the night the two of them had just shared. Her wary glance shot over to the dark figure slumbering contentedly on the wide bed, and at the sight of him she felt her bare skin tingle with remembered response. She caught her breath sharply. She had to get out of there, she had to think, and she knew Jordan's nearness made intelligent thought impossible. He had only to awaken and stretch out his hand to her to. . . .

Quickly selecting the items that seemed least offensive to her, she donned a crisp tailored sun dress of lemon-yellow cotton and slipped on slim hand-made walking shoes that, she had to admit, were every bit as beautiful as they were comfortable. After running a comb through her pale hair, she grabbed her new handbag, checking for wallet and sunglasses, and quietly left the suite.

When Gemma passed through the lobby of the hotel, she noticed with astonishment that the dining room was already being set up for lunch; she had had no idea it was so late. Outside, the noonday light was almost blinding, and she slipped on her big round-lensed sunglasses, blinking with relief. All around her the sidewalk bustled with tourists surging toward the Porta Nuova, the entrance to the Quadrilateral enclosing Pisa's most famous landmarks, and after a momentary pause Gemma allowed herself to be carried along with the crowd, aiming instinctively for the Leaning Tower. At home in Colorado, in moments of personal stress, Gemma had always driven up into the Rockies to think things out, hoping that the elevation would literally give her a new perspective on her problems. She had fled to the hills when Dave asked her to marry him; a year later it had been atop Lookout Mountain that she had finally admitted to herself she could not go through with the marriage.

Now, ironically, she needed to find someplace where she could decide how to cope with her marriage to Jordan, and although the town of Pisa was in fact surrounded by hills, the upper terrace of the Leaning Tower was the highest and despite the crowds—or perhaps because of them—the loneliest spot she could think of.

She kept her mind steadfastly blank as she slowly wended her way up the long spiraling staircase, glancing instead at the vista revealed through the narrow doorways opening out onto each level. Behind her a middle-aged woman in Bermuda shorts grumbled irritably to her camera-laden husband, "Two hundred and ninety-four steps! Believe me, Harry, the view had better be worth it!" By the time Gemma reached the eighth and uppermost level, Harry and his impatient wife had dropped back, as had most of the crowd, and she was more literally alone than she had expected, sharing the magnificent panorama with only three couples and a solitary young man who looked like a college student, toting a backpack.

The windy terrace slanted just enough to make Gemma dizzy, especially when she glanced straight down and saw only empty air between her and the earth far below. The grounds directly under the overhang had been fenced off, she noticed, probably to prevent sightseers from dropping things on the waiting crowds. To regain her equilibrium, she clutched at the rail and inched her way around to the upper edge of the terrace, where she gazed out over the trees and red-tiled roofs, spotting grand *palazzi* and cemeteries, unsuspected little squares lost in a maze of narrow ancient streets, a sharp contrast to the broader thoroughfares built since the Second World War, when half the town had been destroyed in bombing raids. *"My country,"* Jordan had said with pride, and Gemma was beginning to understand that pride. Italy was a beautiful country, with a beautiful people—but it was Jordan's home, not Gemma's. There was no way she could turn herself into an ersatz Italian the way his mother had done, and if he expected her to do so, well.... That was yet another reason for her to escape him as quickly as possible, although, she frowned curiously, flight suddenly did not seem as desirable as it had.

A wooden clatter broke into her thoughts suddenly, and she looked down to see a pencil rolling along the incline, past her feet. The student with the backpack dropped a notebook he had been holding and made a grab for the runaway pencil, but his load hampered him, and he missed it. Gemma caught it easily and returned it to him with a polite smile. He mumbled, *"Merci, mademoiselle."*

Automatically she replied, *"Pas de quoi."*

He looked at her with more interest. *"Pardon, mais parlez-vous français?"* he asked, with an air of great relief as if he had been searching desperately for someone he could talk to.

Gemma hesitated, wondering if he was just making conversation, or if this was the prelude to a pickup. Her gray eyes quickly counted the tourists on the terrace, whose numbers had been increased by two nuns and an English couple who took turns peering through binoculars while the other read aloud from a guidebook. The crowd seemed large enough to prevent the young man from becoming a nuisance, so, on the off chance that he might really need help with something, Gemma dug back into her memory for a few scraps of high-school French and answered slowly, her voice huskier than usual because of her unfamiliarity with the language, *"Je ne parle qu'un peu de français*—I speak only a little French."

Obviously encouraged by her response, the student's smile broadened into a grin, and his gaze began to travel over her slowly and appreciatively, noting the way the hot breeze whipped her skirts around her slim legs and ruffled her silvery hair. Gemma's spirits sank as she interpreted the familiar look in his eyes. Damn, she ought to have ignored him, let the blasted pencil roll right over the edge. She wasn't afraid; there were too many people close at hand for that. But from past experience she guessed that the young man was probably going to prove tiresome and annoying at a time when she wanted more than anything just to be left alone. Assuming what she hoped was a quelling expression, Gemma reached up with her left hand to push her sunglasses back into position on her nose, and as she did, the sunlight flashed brightly on her shiny new wedding ring. The young man noticed it, and his smile faded with almost comical speed. "You are married?" he asked in dismay.

Gemma nodded. *"Oui,"* she said casually, and he began to back away at once.

"Je vous en prie, madame!" he murmured. *"Je pensais. . . excusez-moi—"*

Chuckling with quiet amusement at his discomfiture, Gemma turned away as he made his retreat. She stared out over the railing again, dismissing him from her mind, and as she did, the thought suddenly occurred to her that this was the first time since she was fourteen years old that someone had made advances toward her that had not filled her with fear and loathing. She had been able to view the student's mild pass objectively, seeing him not as a threat, but merely as a silly boy attracted to her slender figure and gleaming hair the way a raven was attracted to glittering objects.

Instinctively her hand traveled up to toy with a strand of her short silky hair as she went back in her mind to the days when her silver gilt mane had been so long she could sit on it. Despite the constant care it required, she had loved her hair. That boy had liked it, too. . . . That boy. Gemma smiled ironically. She really ought to remember the name of someone who had played such a pivotal role in her life, but after ten years he was just "that boy," a fellow student in her ninth-grade algebra class who came home with her one afternoon to study together. They had sprawled in front of the fireplace and puzzled over coefficients and quadratic equations until, her attention diverted for a second, he had pulled the pick out of her wide leather barrette, and her hair had flooded loose over her shoulders, glowing in the firelight. With an indignant squeal she had lunged at him, pummeling him with her fists as if he were one of her brothers, and soon they were giggling and wrestling on the hearth rug, their schoolbooks forgotten. Gemma fought well, but eventually the boy pinned her shoulders to the floor. She gasped, "All right, you win" and waited for him to release her. Instead he had leaned over her, breathing hard as he stared at her flowing hair and her blouse that had come askew over her heaving breasts. His flushed features twisted into a new and puzzling expression. "Hey," she had laughed uneasily, "what's the—" But before she could finish her question, he lowered his body over hers and kissed her, his lips moving tentatively on hers. And before Gemma could react to that first hesitant kiss, her father had walked in on them.

Gemma's fingers clutched the railing to stop her shaking. Across a span of a decade and a distance of five thousand miles, those memories still made her wince. She could recall every vile name her ranting father had called her, even though half of them had been meaningless at the time. Her soul still carried bruises from his rage. Although she was mature enough now to understand that many fathers had great difficulty accepting their daughters' awakening sexuality, she did not think she could ever forgive him for calling her a "little slut" and packing her off to the convent, abandoning her for three years, during which her young bewildered mind had decided that, for a woman at least, sex meant grief and shame and loss. As an adult she realized that if she had ever voiced any of those feelings to her teachers, they might have been able to offer the guidance she need-ed, but she had always been a very self-contained girl, and as a result, for ten years she had lived with the idea that her sexual feelings were degrading, that what passed for love between men and women was a grim joyless experience that had to be endured if she wanted children. That attitude had colored, perhaps actually destroyed, her relationship with Dave, and even now, if Jordan hadn't been so persistent, so tender, so *giving*....

Gemma closed her eyes and smiled gently, thinking with rapture of the night before. Despite Jordan's incredible high-handedness, he had shown her ecstasy such as she had never dreamed possible. No matter how strongly she resented the way he had taken over her life, no matter what the outcome of this trumped-up marriage might ultimately be, she would always be grateful to him for ridding her of those childish fears, for at last showing her the great pleasure of being a woman.

She was tingling with the memory of every caress they had shared, her nerves re-creating the delicate skill with which Jordan's hands had moved over her languid body, when suddenly her erotic reverie was shattered by those same hands clamping brutally over her thin shoulders as he whirled her around to face him.

"Jordan!" she cried in astonishment, the lingering delight in her voice vanishing instantly when she saw the fury marring his handsome features.

He was panting with exertion, giving her the startling notion that he had sprinted all the way up the long spiral staircase, as he demanded, "What the hell are you doing here? I've been going out of my mind, looking everywhere for you!" He shook her hard. "Why did you run out on me like that?"

Gemma winced at the bruising strength of his fingers digging into her soft flesh through the thin fabric of the yellow sun dress, but when she gazed up at him, she saw with surprise that behind his mask of rage his face was pallid with fear. She said urgently, "But, Jordan, I didn't run out on you. I...I just wanted to...to be alone so that I could do some thinking. I was coming back."

His expression did not alter. He grated, "How was I supposed to know that? You left no message, nothing. *Cristo*, do you have any conception of how I felt when I woke up, and you weren't there? For one crazy moment I thought—" He shook his head fiercely, muttering, "No, forget that." He seemed to become aware of the pain he was inflicting, and his grip eased slightly. He said, "I might still be searching for you, were it not for the fact that that hair of yours reflects the sunlight like a beacon. When I looked up to the top of the tower, I recognized you at once. What made you come here?"

Gemma shrugged with feigned nonchalance. "I told you, I wanted to...to think."

He glanced around, noting the wind and the ever shifting crowd. "You came *here* to think?" he questioned.

She said lightly, "It seemed as good a place as any."

"I see." He paused, studying her face intently. "And what was it that you had to think about so deeply that you left your marriage bed to do so?"

Gemma colored faintly, uncomfortably aware of the numerous people standing nearby. She stammered, "I...I had to think about us, what's to become of...of us."

"I see," Jordan said again, his deep tones darkening and drawling. "Funny, but I thought we answered all those questions satisfactorily last night."

Gemma reddened more, her embarrassment changing to annoyance at the amused and proprietary note in his voice, but she forced herself to meet his gaze. "Last night didn't change a thing," she said.

"It made our marriage an irrevocable fact," he observed blandly.

She shivered with suppressed anger, suddenly despising herself for the incipient tenderness she had been feeling, for letting her very real concerns be overcome by Jordan's prowess as a lover. She snapped, "Sleeping with you can't alter the fact that you blackmailed me into this marriage, that you're trying to take over my life; it just makes it worse! You forced me to make love with you, so ultimately what happened between us proves nothing—no matter how good it was."

Jordan stared at her, and his face grew steadily grimmer as she spoke. "At least you do admit that it was good," he murmured after a moment; "I suppose I ought to be grateful for that small concession." His hands dropped away from her shoulders, and he turned to peer out over the countryside, squinting against the bright light. Gemma stood beside him, her gray eyes following the direction of his gaze from behind her dark sunglasses, and she had to strain to hear his words over the noise of the wind and the other tourists. In a light, almost conversational tone he said, "You know, Gemma, I've never met a woman as stubborn as you—except possibly my mother, and even she occasionally has the grace to admit defeat. But you, you never give up, even when you're dead wrong and you know it. And you'd better believe you're wrong about us. I didn't make you marry me. Granted, my proposal was a trifle unorthodox, but you're far too intelligent to believe that I could really have forced you into marriage had you not *chosen* to do so."

Humiliated that he could so echo her own thoughts of the previous day, Gemma interjected bitterly, "Isn't that the old alibi men used to use, that no woman could be raped unless she acquiesced, so whatever happened was really her fault, even if he had been holding a knife to her throat?"

He spun around and grabbed her arms, his dark eyes aglow with a white-hot rage that seemed to bore through the smoked lenses of her glasses, scorching her brain. "You little bitch," he rasped, "I ought to beat you for that! How you can even *dare* to compare what we—goddamn it, Gemma, you know you wanted it, you know it meant something to you. You couldn't have responded the way you did if it hadn't!"

She tried to pull away, frightened not only by his fury but also by the astonishing wave of desire that flooded through her the instant his fingers closed around her bare arms, making her skin prickle with awareness. Behind the shelter of her sunglasses she glanced up at him, at his harsh face and powerful body rigid with anger, obdurate as the stone he carved, and she tried not to remember that only hours before he had been hard and unyielding with another kind of passion.

He growled, "Gemma, admit you wanted me."

She lowered her lashes, afraid to look at him again, afraid that even now he might see the hunger in her eyes and, seeing it, would know he owned her. She searched her mind frantically for some plausible excuse, and then at last she hit upon the one lie that he as a sculptor would be bound to believe. Wincing at the effort her words cost, she gulped and slowly shook her head. "N-no," she stammered, "no, it wasn't you I wanted." She forced a chuckle through her constricted throat. "D-don't you know? I've been in love with your... self-portrait ever since I saw *Privilege* seven years ago. Of course I didn't realize then.... It's your own f-fault for being such a good artist. When I touched you, it was as if at long last I was making love with the... the statue."

The lie having been uttered, Gemma looked up at him warily. She did not know what reaction to expect, anger or disgust or even ridicule, but she was surprised by his apparent lack of response. For endless seconds he gazed down at her, his face impassive, masklike. At last he murmured pensively, "So I served as surrogate for my own likeness? That's a... piquant situation, a new one for me, but I suppose it's not unlike what happens to actors when their fans develop mad crushes on the characters they play, and not the men themselves."

One hand released her arm and slid upward, stroking lightly over breast and throat until it captured her small chin and held her face immobile. He studied her flushed defiant features, then he bent his head and brushed his lips across hers. "Perhaps I should thank you for being so honest with me," he whispered into her ear, his warm breath teasing the hair at her temple. "In return I shall be equally honest with you and tell you my plans for the day." Suddenly his low voice was a silken threat. He said quietly, "We're going to have some lunch, you and I, and after that we'll do a little sight-seeing. Maybe I'll show you the fresco that inspired Liszt's *Dance of Death*. By then it will be siesta time, and we shall return to our hotel room, and there, my little groupie, I am going to make love to you—how I want, when I want, for as long as I want—until at last you admit that it is me you want, not some statue, not some phantom from an old love affair, but me, Jordan di Mario, your husband, the man you belong to."

CHAPTER EIGHT

By THE TIME THEY RETURNED to Pietrasanta three days later, Gemma was subdued and resentful, cowed by Jordan's perplexing swings in mood. During the daylight hours he had been a charming and congenial companion. He had escorted her all around Pisa, mingling with the crowds of sightseers and pointing out details of art and architecture with the polished aplomb of a tour guide. Gemma had viewed everything with appropriate appreciation, but curiously, the sight that had given her the most pleasure had been the dingy little antique shop just off the Borgo Stretto, where, Jordan told her, he discovered the lovely bronze statuette that now graced his private art collection. Eagerly Gemma had plunged into the morass of old newspapers, shabby furniture and dirty unidentifiable objects piled in the storage room, calling out to Jordan that she intended to find a piece for herself. He had watched her benignly, and when at last she came back to him, disappointed and a little bedraggled, he handed her a thin dusty book and said, "Here, I found something for you. This isn't art, but I'm sure you'll find it interesting."

Gemma's forehead had wrinkled as she gazed at the faded gilt letters on the cover, pronouncing the title with care. "*Codice cavalleresco italiano.* I can't translate any of that except the last word."

"It's *The Italian Gentleman's Guide to Chivalry,*" Jordan explained, "a Victorian book of rules for conducting a duel. A hundred years ago, no proper household would have been without one. Even now, very occasionally—well, not all that long ago a Roman journalist was challenged to a duel by the editor of a Communist newspaper. The journalist declined, on the grounds that a Communist was not a gentleman." Gemma had joined in her husband's laughter, just then feeling closer to him than at any other time during that brief bewildering honeymoon.

For no matter how they spent the days, each night was the same: Jordan made love to her with stunning skill, his hands and mouth arousing her deliberately until, vanquished, she begged for release. Then, after he had carried her with him to a devastating climax, she would lie in his arms, shaking, breathless— bereft. The tenderness that had so disarmed her on their wedding night was gone now, wiped out by her own rash words. Left in its place was—not brutality, but what was perhaps worse—suave insolence. Jordan disregarded her wishes and subjected her to his own will, using her ruthlessly, forcing her to admit her reluctant need of him and then rewarding her defeat with a satisfaction in which there was no fulfillment. Each night when she submitted to his potent caresses, she swore it would be the last time— and each morning she found herself looking with anguished longing toward the night to come.

As he whipped the new Ferrari, a duplicate of the one that had been wrecked, around the curves of the road leading up to his villa, Jordan glanced over at Gemma's white face and asked dryly, "Am I going too fast for you?"

She closed her eyes and leaned back, almost horizontal in the low-slung seat. Shaking her head, she murmured, "No, you obviously know how to handle the car at speed. I think what bothers me most is being so close to the ground. I keep expecting to scrape bottom."

"You'll get used to it," he said, shrugging. "Anyway, we're almost home." He downshifted, slowing the sleek red automobile as he approached the final steep grade up to the house.

Gemma did not open her eyes. *Home,* she repeated silently, the word echoing in her troubled mind, *from now on I have to think of the villa as my home....* She thought of her apartment in Colorado, small but furnished exactly to her own taste with items she had collected one at a time over the past few years, mostly well-designed pieces of golden oak that were not quite old enough to qualify as antiques. She wondered wistfully what would happen to her furniture and other belongings if she stayed in Italy. Like Jordan, she, too, had an art collection, some of her own work and a couple of paintings she had purchased from especially promising students. Those pictures had given her great pleasure, but now she supposed they would have to be stored away. She could hardly expect Jordan to let her display them next to his Rembrandts and Picassos.

Jordan's deep voice cut into her thoughts. "We appear to have visitors," he noted as he swung the Ferrari into the driveway.

Lifting her head, Gemma blinked against the bright light and looked around curiously. In front of the main entry to the villa a dark green taxi stood idle, its driver perusing a newspaper. Jordan switched off the ignition of his car, his long fingers tapping out a code number on the buttons of the computerized security locking system while Gemma was still struggling to unfasten her shoulder harness. "Can't you get that undone?" he asked impatiently, then without awaiting an answer he reached across her and released the catch, his arm inadvertently brushing her breasts as he did. Gemma quivered. Her gray eyes flicked up toward his, then she glanced away quickly, dismayed by her instant arousal. She knew he had noticed her reaction, and when he straightened up in his seat, he touched her again, quite deliberately this time, silently fondling her until through the fabric of her fashionably simple day dress he could feel her breasts lift and tauten against his hand. Almost against her will Gemma arched her back to deepen the caress. She heard Jordan catch his breath, and she licked her lips, waiting for him to kiss her.

Instead, he dropped his hand and said briskly, "Hurry up with your seat belt, *cara*. I'm going to see who's here." He opened his door and got out of the car.

With a disgruntled sigh Gemma watched him stride across the driveway to the waiting taxi, where he bent down and spoke briefly to the driver. By the time Gemma joined him, he was at the front door, smiling. "Good news, my dear," he said in answer to the unspoken question. "It appears that word finally got through to Caroline's mother. She just arrived."

"Marsha's here? Thank God!" Gemma exclaimed fervently. She felt suddenly as if a tremendous burden had been lifted from her. "I must see her at once. If you only knew how worried I've been," she said, reaching eagerly for the doorknob, only to have Jordan stop her by catching her wrist. She looked up at him, puzzled.

He murmured, "Don't be in such a hurry. The traditions must be observed." And before she could guess his intention, he swept her up into his arms.

Startled by his blatantly romantic gesture, and aware of the taxi driver who had laid aside his paper to watch them with open amusement, Gemma giggled uneasily, "You idiot, you don't have to carry me across the threshold."

"Yes, I do," he said, his voice rich and silky. "It's a fine old Roman custom, to protect the bride from any evil spirits that might be lurking around the doorway—and believe me, my darling, you're hard enough to handle without evil spirits getting into the act!" He bent his dark head and kissed her lingeringly. The instant his mouth touched hers, Gemma was engulfed once again by the wild driving hunger he aroused in her, and, closing her eyes, she flung her arms around his neck and kissed him back, dizzy with desire. She forgot about the driver who watched them, Marsha and Beatrice who waited inside the villa. For endless seconds there was no one except her and Jordan, no reality except her lips moving beneath his, her fingers weaving into his thick hair. She could feel him shudder. Against her mouth he groaned, "Gemma, Gemma, why do you fight me? Don't you know that as long as we can share this, nothing else matters?" Still kissing her, he reached awkwardly for the door handle and pushed it open.

After the torrid heat out-of-doors, the still air in the villa's marble entryway seemed almost too cool, and Gemma shivered and snuggled closer in Jordan's arms, relishing the warmth of his hard powerful body. When slowly and reluctantly he broke off the kiss and eased her onto her feet, which seemed strangely unstable, she slid her thin arms around his waist and, eyes still closed, leaned her head against his chest. She could hear his heart pounding under her ear, and she thought with wonder how very soothing that firm steady rhythm could be, lulling away all her fears and anxieties. She felt his lips brush across her hair, and he murmured, "Welcome home, Signora di—" He broke off his words abruptly, and his arms clenched about her in a cruel embrace, crushing her against him.

Gemma gasped painfully, her gray eyes wide with astonishment at his sudden shift of mood. He was not looking at her; he seemed almost unaware of her presence. His intent gaze was directed over her head, rooted to a point somewhere behind her, and the cold grim light in his eyes chilled her. His grip did not loosen, and with great difficulty Gemma squirmed far enough away from him to enable her to twist around in his arms. When she saw what Jordan was gaping at, she wished with sickened shock that she had not looked.

Three people clustered in the living room; three pairs of eyes stared back with varying expressions at the man and woman clinging together by the front door. Beatrice di Mario's aggressively plain features were made even less attractive by a hard humorless smile of almost smug triumph. Marsha Somerville frowned with frank puzzlement. But it was the third face that tore at Gemma's heart, the face of the stocky man who stood beside Caroline's willowy red-haired mother. Beneath his sandy hair his features were deathly pale, bleached of all color, except for the hazel eyes that were stricken with horror, anguish, disbelief.

"*Dave!*" Gemma choked.

Before Dave could react, Marsha broke the strained silence. "Oh, Gemma," she exclaimed remorsefully, taking a step forward, "I'm so glad to see you! What you must think of me, going away like that without—I was only just up at Ouray for a couple of weeks, and like a fool, it never even occurred to me that—" Her voice cracked.

Gemma tore herself away from Jordan, who stood as if petrified, and she caught Marsha in a fierce comforting hug. "Don't worry," she ordered her friend sternly, "Caroline's going to be all right. Have you seen her yet?"

Marsha nodded. "Yes, but she was asleep, and Mrs. di Mario said it would be better not to wake her. But, Gemma, she was so *pale*—"

"That's just because she's been indoors. I tell you, she'll be fine." Gemma looked questioningly at Jordan's mother. "She was all right while we were gone, wasn't she?"

"Yes," the older woman said matter-of-factly, addressing Marsha, "Caroline is recovering rapidly. I've had her out of bed every day since...since Giordano and...Gemma left for Pisa." Only a faint stiffness at the corners of her mouth hinted at the effort it had cost Beatrice to refer to that trip so calmly.

Gemma was impressed by the way Jordan's mother never let her personal feelings interfere with her duties as a nurse, and she said sincerely, "Marsha, even if you'd been here, you couldn't possibly have given Caroline better care than Signora di Mario did."

She glanced again at the older woman, searching for some softening in her manner, but before Beatrice could reply, Dave found his voice again and demanded harshly, "Gemma, what's going on here?" His color had returned, too, and beneath his sandy hair his features were flushed, his eyes angry and contemptuous as they flicked between Gemma and Jordan. "What the hell have you been up to?" When she didn't answer, he grabbed her arm as if to shake her.

Jordan said quietly, "Keep your hands off my wife."

Dave's fingers bit into Gemma's soft skin as he gaped at Jordan. "What did you say?"

Jordan grated, "I said, take your goddamned hands off my wife before I break your arm."

"Wife!" Dave roared, and he looked at Gemma's hand, noticing for the first time the wide gold band that graced her ring finger. "But how? When? Gemma, your father didn't say anything about—"

Jordan drawled, "I'm afraid we didn't get around to wiring the news to Gemma's family until this morning, just before we left Pisa. Of course, we should have told them right away, but you know how it is with honeymoons."

Dave's eyes widened, and he flung Gemma away from him as if she were unclean. "No," he said hollowly, "it's not possible. How could she—Gemma's mine. I love her. She and I—we even.... She's going to marry *me*!" He glared at Jordan belligerently.

Jordan shook his head. "Too late, Blanchard. You had your chance and you blew it. She belongs to me now."

Aghast and furious, Gemma listened to this exchange with mounting indignation. She fumed as the two men squared off as if any second now they might come to blows, and when Dave insisted, "But for seven years her father and I—" Gemma exploded.

"Damn it, *shut up*!" she bellowed. Everyone stopped, stunned, and stared at her. "How dare you?" she hissed at the combatants, biting off the words. "How *dare* you talk about me as if I weren't here, as if I were a...a bone two dogs were fighting over? What do you think I am? Who do you think you are? I don't belong to either one of you, I belong to myself...and as far as I'm concerned, you can both go to hell!"

She glanced back at the two women who were unwilling spectators to this little scene. Beatrice di Mario's expression was unreadable, but Marsha looked embarrassed and troubled, and Gemma felt a wave of compunction that her friend should have been exposed to an ugly shouting match when she already had enough to worry about. When Marsha murmured a confused protest, Gemma touched her hand lightly and said, "Don't bother yourself about me. I'll explain everything later. Right now, you just concentrate on Caroline; she's the one who needs you." As she checked her handbag to make sure that she had her wallet, Gemma added, "I really am glad you're here, Marsha." And she stalked toward the front door.

When she passed him, Jordan caught her arm and demanded, "And where do you think you're going?"

She gazed accusingly at Jordan's hand, his long fingers marking her skin alongside the row of bruises already formed by Dave's merciless grip. Gemma shook him off. "Don't grab me, Jordan," she said coldly. "I've told you before, I can't stand being manhandled."

"But where—?"

She shrugged, and her voice grew hoarse with bitterness. "I don't know where I'm going, but wherever it is, you needn't be concerned. I'll be back—" She met his eyes squarely. Beneath her long lashes her expression was glacial. "Of course I'll be back. After all, you've made damn sure I have nowhere else to go, haven't you?"

THE TAXI DROPPED GEMMA OFF in front of Sergio Carcione's studio, but when she tried to go inside, she discovered that the door was locked. As she knocked, she glanced at her watch, realizing with dismay that the workmen all must have left for the long afternoon lunch-and-siesta break. She turned away without expecting an answer, but before she had walked more than a couple of steps, the door suddenly opened behind her. "Fräulein Culver!" a heavily accented male voice called, and Gemma looked back to see Dieter Stahl standing framed in the doorway.

She greeted him with pleasure and relief, suddenly aware of how relaxing it was to meet someone unconnected with the tense situation at the villa. He ushered her inside, and she glanced around the cluttered studio, noting the hollow echo in the large room that was usually drowned out by the deafening racket of the air hammers. Statues in various stages of completion stood silent, their exalted beauty incongruous against the prosaic background of roughly framed walls and abandoned tools strewed about their bases.

Gemma studied them intently, hoping to divert her troubled mind from the emotional scene she had witnessed at the villa, the pain she had seen in Dave's eyes. She did not want to have to think about whether or not she had wronged a man who loved her. Instead she gazed enthralled at the statues in the main workroom, analyzing each design, each cut, and after a while the consummate skill of the work began to soothe her, as if the marble were imparting its coolness to her heart. Slowly Gemma relaxed.

She debated whether she ought to go through the partition into the room where Jordan labored on his statue of Francesca. Perhaps now, in the silence, without distractions, she could look at the Madonna and figure out what was wrong with it, why it did not live up to the promise of Jordan's earlier projects. Perhaps she could decide why it hurt her to look at it.

Resolutely she returned her attention to the pieces Sergio and his crew were currently working on, including the one destined for the new convention center in Oslo. Jordan's involvement in the enlarging process was unusual, Gemma knew. To the best of her knowledge, the Norwegian artist who created the Oslo statue had never set foot in Pietrasanta, preferring instead to let Carcione work solely from a small preliminary model. The thought occurred to Gemma that the carvers would have to be far more than merely skilled craftsmen. They would have to possess a great deal of artistic insight of their own, if, using only miniature models in the confined quarters of the studio, they could carve statues of a size to grace spacious parks or large buildings. When she was a student, Gemma had been a little dubious about the practice of having workmen "scale up" a statue from a small maquette, even though the technique was a common one, used by everyone from Rodin to Henry Moore. It had seemed to her that a sculptor ought to carve his work directly, that employing intermediaries somehow detracted from his achievement. Now that she had seen what a slow painstaking process carving was, requiring months of intense effort even to complete one piece—and always with the threat of a single slip of the chisel obliterating those months of work—she realized that the sheer physical limitations of the medium would severely hamper the output of any artist who tried to work solely on his own. Now she began to understand that the sculptor modeling his maquettes was analogous to the composer writing a symphony; neither one was any less a genius because he required the assistance of other people, workmen or musicians, to present his creation to the world.

With the sensitivity of an artist, Dieter had remained silent while Gemma prowled around the studio. Now she smiled at him and asked, "Are you all alone, or is Claretta here with you?"

The German shook his head, brushing a lock of his blond hair out of his eyes, which suddenly had a bleak look. "No," he sighed, "Claretta is not here."

Gemma frowned. Something was troubling Dieter, she could tell, and she wished she knew him well enough to offer to help. For all his rather ponderous formality, she liked the young sculptor; during the time she had studied alongside him, she had realized that he had the makings of a talented and very dedicated artist. He listened to Sergio's and Jordan's words as if they had been delivered from Mount Sinai, and he went about his business with an air of grim determination that seemed to soften only in the presence of his ebullient Italian girl friend. Gemma hoped they hadn't had a fight.

She sat down beside Dieter at a long table that was littered with half-finished sketches and crumpled sheets of drawing paper. Several were recognizable portraits of Claretta. "Working on a new idea?" she asked lightly.

He shrugged. "I was trying to, but inspiration seems to elude me." He surveyed Gemma's fashionable dress. With an effort at gallantry he noted dryly, "And may I inquire what brings you here today, *Fräulein*? That frock, while extremely attractive, is hardly suitable for work, and besides, Carcione said he did not expect you back in the studio again before the beginning of next week."

At Dieter's casual reference to her absence from the studio, all the confused emotions that Gemma had tried so hard to suppress flooded back into her. To disguise the trembling of her fingers, Gemma picked up a pencil and began doodling on a scrap of paper. She said offhandedly, "I suppose I...I just wanted to get away from the villa for a while."

Dieter nodded, watching the point of her pencil slash across the paper in quick vitriolic lines. Her wedding ring flashed as her hands moved. Dieter commented mildly, "So you did indeed marry Herr di Mario? I could hardly believe it when Carcione told me that was what you were planning. It must have been a most precipitous courtship."

"Yes," Gemma muttered, concentrating on her drawing.

After an uneasy silence, Dieter reached over and tapped her hand, stilling it. Gemma looked at him in surprise. With a touch of sadness he said obscurely, "Try not to blame your husband, *Fräulein*—I mean, Frau di Mario. He is a true artist, a genius, and he does not see things as we do. He looks for the essence of things, searching out emotional shortcuts, while you and I must plod along over the same well-worn paths. You must forgive him if sometimes he seems— impatient."

Gemma said, "I'm not sure I understand what you mean. Are you saying that you believe that genius excuses everything?"

Dieter shook his head. "No, not everything. But a great deal."

While Gemma puzzled over the exact meaning of that esoteric statement, Dieter studied her sketch. She had been only half-aware of what she was drawing, letting the images flow unconsciously through her fingers, and when he set it in front of her again, she saw that with a few rough lines she had described a high stone wall, the edges of each block sharp and threatening. Only just visible over the top of the wall was a woman's slim hand with broken bleeding nails, flailing in the air as it felt for a handhold, its search hampered by the weight of the massive metal band on the wedding finger.

Gemma stared at it for a long moment, then she glanced up at Dieter, who watched her with lifted brows. He smiled ironically and said, "Not bad. The symbolism is perhaps a trifle obvious, but I do envy your ability to put so much emotion into a few hasty lines." He paused, then he turned away, murmuring as he did so, "But just for the record, *gnädige Frau*, I think I ought to remind you that women are not the only ones who can feel trapped by marriage."

After that, Gemma changed the subject, and she and Dieter were conversing quietly about art, disagreeing good-naturedly over the merits of a couple of nineteenth-century expressionists, when they heard an imperative knock on the front door. Dieter went to see who it was, and a deep familiar voice ground out Gemma's name. Quickly she crushed the drawing into a shapeless wad. A second later Jordan stalked into the workroom. Behind him she saw Dieter, who took one quick glance at the man looming over Gemma and quickly and discreetly disappeared into another part of the studio.

Jordan said flatly, "I've come to take you home."

Gemma's gray eyes flashed at his tone, but she shrugged and said mildly, "I was planning to take a taxi back. There was no need for you to waste time searching for me."

Jordan said, "It didn't take much searching. Once I realized you were not at the Riccis' *pensione*, I assumed you must be here."

"You went all the way to the Riccis' house? It's clear on the other side of town. Why didn't you just call?"

"Franco and his mother don't have a telephone, remember?" Jordan pointed out, watching Gemma closely as he added, "Besides, I had to take Blanchard there, to see if they could accommodate him for a few days."

Gemma grimaced, trying to imagine the two men boxed together in the close confines of the Ferrari. That must have been a memorable drive. She asked, "What about Marsha?"

"She will stay at the villa, of course, until her daughter is well enough to travel. My mother has put her in the room you were using." Gemma did not say anything, but her eyes traveled to Jordan's face, which seemed curiously flushed. He snapped, "Of course, there would have been more than enough space for Blanchard, as well, but, damn it, Gemma, I will not have your old lover in my home!"

"I...I didn't expect you to," Gemma mumbled, turning away, her own cheeks pink now as she thought in amazement, *jealous, my God, Jordan di Mario is jealous of Dave Blanchard?* In her mind she compared the two men: Jordan, so handsome, volatile and brilliantly talented; Dave, with his mediocre good looks and conservative personality. She would have laughed at the absurdity of any rivalry between them, except that she was afraid Jordan would assume she was laughing at him, and already his mood seemed dangerous enough, without fueling his anger with wounded vanity. But for him to be jealous of Dave—it made no sense. A different kind of woman might have been flattered, might have interpreted Jordan's possessive attitude as indicating a personal interest in her, but Gemma refused to believe that, no matter how appealing the notion seemed. She knew better. Her husband didn't care about her; to him she was just a thing, something he owned. But perhaps that was it, Gemma decided suddenly, with a sinking feeling. Jordan wasn't jealous; he was simply resentful, angered that she had come to him—less than intact, as angry as if a piece he acquired for his art collection had proved to be flawed.

Jordan said sternly, "Let's go, Gemma. We have to return to the villa. Mrs. Somerville has a great many questions to ask you. You were incredibly rude to leave her so abruptly."

Gemma bowed her head in submission. "Yes, you're right," she admitted with a sigh. "I...I'm sorry. I wouldn't hurt Marsha for the world, but I just had to get away from—for a while. I'm not usually such a coward, running off like that."

"No?" Jordan murmured, regarding her enigmatically. "I would have said that you've been running away for years."

As they once again drove into the hills, Gemma sat silent, watching Jordan's long deft fingers curled around the steering wheel, guiding the sleek car with polished skill. He had such finesse, she thought with wistful envy; it showed in everything he did, whether driving, or creating some new artwork, or making love.... For just a second she allowed her thoughts to dwell pleasurably on the nights they had shared, but when her body began to react to those heated memories, she recalled herself to the present with an effort and began to make polite conversation. She said, "I enjoyed talking to Dieter today. He's an interesting man. When we're working, unfortunately, we rarely have time to exchange more than a few words.''

Jordan shot a quick glance at Gemma, then turned his attention back to the road, swerving to avoid a hay cart. "So just what did you and Stahl find to talk about?" he asked curiously as he straightened the wheel.

Gemma shrugged and leaned back in her seat, closing her eyes. The day had been a long one, and overly eventful—she had trouble remembering that only hours before, she had awakened in Jordan's arms in their honeymoon suite in Pisa—and now she was beginning to feel very tired. She said, "I don't suppose we chatted about much of anything except art. I got the impression that Dieter was rather depressed. I think he and Claretta must have quarreled."

"I'm not surprised," Jordan noted dryly. When Gemma lifted her lashes long enough to frown at him, he continued, "Didn't Stahl tell you?"

"Tell me what?"

Jordan chuckled sardonically. "Obviously he didn't. Well, Gemma *mia*, when I drove Blanchard to the *pensione*, I discovered that he is not the only new guest the Riccis have taken in recently. It seems that while you and I were away, another visitor arrived from West Germany, one Gretchen Stahl— Dieter's wife."

Gemma jerked upright and blinked in amazement. "His *wife*? I didn't know Dieter was married!"

"Nor did anyone else," Jordan said, "especially not, I'm sure, his pretty girl friend from the post office."

Gemma shook her head. "Poor Claretta," she murmured.

Jordan mocked, "You mean, poor Dieter. Having met his wife, I can't say that I blame him for pretending she doesn't exist."

Recalling Dieter's bitter little aside about marriage being a trap, Gemma asked, "Is she so very awful?"

Jordan shrugged. "To be fair, I suppose it's a matter of definition. Frau Stahl is attractive enough, in a very tailored sort of way, a blonde who wears her hair severely braided into a coronet, and despite the fact that she appears to be very young, the style suits her. I suspect that she is frighteningly efficient in everything she does. When Franco introduced us, she thanked me politely for taking an interest in her husband, then added that it was time he quit indulging his artistic foolishness and returned with her to Düsseldorf, where a good position was open for him in her father's plumbing-supply company."

"Ouch," Gemma winced. "What did you say?"

"Very little. There didn't seem to be much I could say." Jordan glanced at Gemma oddly. "You know, I rather expected you to sympathize with the woman—in light of your professed desire to go back to Colorado to teach. Does this mean you're beginning to realize that I was right?"

Gemma stiffened. "The two situations are not at all comparable," she said coolly. After a moment she asked, "Do you think he'll go?"

Jordan snorted. "Who knows? Naturally I would prefer Dieter to stay here and continue his studies—he's not a brilliant artist, but he shows much promise—but I would be very reluctant to make bets on a contest of wills between him and young Gretchen.''

"What about Claretta?''

Staring out at the road ahead, Jordan scowled. He said slowly, "She may accept her disappointment gracefully. Local people often form attachments with tourists, but no one really expects them to last past the end of summer.''

Gemma looked at him questioningly, wondering. Did he honestly think Claretta felt that way about Dieter, or was Jordan subtly telling Gemma that he did not expect their own relationship to persist into autumn? Despite his insistence that Gemma "belonged" to him, could Jordan be putting a time limit on his ownership? The thought was strangely chilling. She turned away, aware that although she had hated being ensnared in this marriage, some perverse twist in her nature did not want Jordan to be the one to release her. She frowned pensively, deeply disturbed. Why wasn't she thrilled at the possibility of escape? Was her pride so overweening that it would accept freedom only on her own terms? She was silent during all the rest of the drive back to the villa.

Gemma spent an hour with Marsha and Caroline, marveling at the improvement in the girl now that her mother had arrived. Between the two Somervilles there was obviously a deep and abiding affection, and Gemma envied them the closeness of their relationship; she wondered if she would have been as close to her own mother, had she lived.

Relieved that her daughter's injuries were mending so well, Marsha relaxed enough to explain with lighthearted detail the pains Dave had taken to locate her, making his accomplishment sound like something from a spy thriller. Each time she mentioned Dave's name, Marsha looked sharply at Gemma, and Gemma knew she was dying to ask questions. Caroline seemed to have taken the news of Jordan and Gemma's sudden marriage philosophically, far more interested in her mother's trip to Ouray, a popular resort high in the Colorado Rockies.

The Somervilles joined Gemma and Jordan and Beatrice for dinner, Caroline still dressed in her yellow bathrobe, but much steadier on her feet than she had been. Conversation was pleasant and undemanding, consisting mostly of discussions about what sights were indispensable to anyone touring Italy, and it wasn't until after Marsha had taken Caroline back to her room that Signora di Mario looked at her son and announced, "I've moved all my things into the housekeeper's apartment."

Jordan stared at her blankly. "You've what?"

Beatrice repeated her statement, adding goadingly, "If you had married an Italian girl, I would have continued in my proper role as your hostess, but since you did not, I assume my position in this house will be somewhat...reduced. Also, I imagine your...wife will be wanting my room now. Next to your own, it is, of course, the largest in the house."

Jordan took a deep breath. Gemma, who was too stunned by the woman's blatant provocation to react at once, watched him warily, noting the line of white that suddenly appeared around his hard mouth, evidence of his tension. She could tell by the unnatural rigidity of his body that he was furious, and she waited for him to explode. Instead, to her amazed admiration, after a moment he said quietly, his deep voice harsh but controlled, "You must suit yourself, mother. You know this grandiose gesture of rejection was entirely uncalled-for. I love and respect you, and my marriage does not change that. However, if it makes you feel better to pretend that you have been turned into a servant in your own home, that is your privilege." He paused before continuing dryly, in a creditable imitation of his mother's languid drawl, "But really, *mamma mia*, you ought to know me well enough to know that there is no way on God's good earth that my wife and I are going to have separate bedrooms." He stood up and held out his hand imperiously to Gemma.

IN THE MORNING Gemma sent Jordan on to Carcione's studio without her. He was anxious to get back to work, and she promised that she would take a taxi into town after she had visited with Marsha and Caroline for a while. Accepting her decision without demur, he left her with a light peck on the cheek that was utterly divorced from the demanding passion he had shown her the night before in the privacy of their shared bedroom, when he had made love to her fiercely, feverishly, as if he were staking his claim.

As soon as Gemma was alone with the Somervilles, Marsha turned on her and accused, "Gemma, I don't know how you can even hold up your head after treating Dave the way you have. To jilt him like that—"

Surprised by Marsha's attack, Gemma interrupted quietly, "I didn't jilt him. The engagement was over.

I gave him back his ring before Caroline and I left Golden.''

"Well, Dave didn't see it that way," Marsha said heatedly. "He told me you had had an argument, but when you called him from Italy, he assumed you had got over it. Then he came halfway around the world, only to find you married to someone else—"

Gemma did not answer, thinking that if Dave could interpret that strained long-distance conversation as some kind of reconciliation, he must have been the victim of as great a self-delusion as Gemma had been when she had considered marrying him in the first place. But then, Dave had never taken her seriously. Jordan did. He might consider her irritating, misguided and pigheaded, but at least he afforded her the courtesy of believing she meant what she said.

When Gemma did not speak, Caroline broke the silence to say eagerly, "Mama, it was the most romantic thing you ever saw: Jordan took one look at Gemma and just swept her off her feet. It was like something out of a movie—"

Marsha shook her red hair impatiently as she looked at her daughter. "Life is not a movie, Caroline, and the sooner you learn that, the better off you'll be." She turned to Gemma again, her expression reproachful. "Dave Blanchard is a fine man," she declared, "and any woman ought to be proud and honored to be loved by him. You've hurt him badly, Gemma. You used him and then discarded him, and he didn't deserve that. I know you've been through an awful lot lately, but I never would have believed that you could be so cruel."

Quelled by the other woman's vehemence, Gemma

looked at her oddly, surprised by the notion that suddenly came to her. Did Marsha want Dave? She was older than he was, but through Gemma they had known each other for years. It had never occurred to Gemma that Marsha might regard Dave as anything other than a friend of a friend. Gemma admitted to herself that she had given little consideration to whether Caroline's divorced mother was really content with her lot, whether a life that revolved around her pottery shop and her daughter was enough for her. The indignation with which Marsha decried Gemma's supposedly callous treatment of her former fiancé made Gemma wonder curiously if the older woman had envied her her engagement, if she would have liked a much more personal relationship with Dave herself.

Marsha said urgently, "You've got to talk to him, Gemma. You owe him an explanation. Your...your husband whisked Dave away from here last night before he could even open his mouth, and while I guess I can understand why he doesn't want him around, you can't just leave Dave vegetating in some boardinghouse in town, not after all the trouble he's gone through to get here."

Gemma flushed, wondering why Marsha's words made her feel so unaccountably guilty. She had terminated her engagement weeks ago; she was under no obligation to offer explanations to Dave. She owed him nothing—except, she conceded, the common courtesy due to a friend of seven years' standing. She took a deep breath and said, "Of course, you're right, Marsha. I'll go to the Riccis' house at once."

A LITTLE LATER, when Gemma telephoned for a taxi, Beatrice di Mario overheard her and asked bluntly, an eager light in her pale eyes, "You are going to meet that man who came here yesterday?"

"Yes," Gemma answered. She met her mother-in-law's gaze squarely, refusing to be intimidated by the *signora*'s obvious interpretation of her action. "I am going to the *pensione* to see Dave. If Jordan should call to find out why I'm delayed, tell him I'll be along to the studio presently."

Beatrice said, "I shall make certain Giordano gets your message."

Gemma brushed a silvery strand of hair from her forehead and smiled cynically. "I'm quite sure you will," she murmured.

She crossed the Riccis' gravel driveway slowly, her sandaled feet crunching on the pebbles, uncertain of the welcome she would receive after the way she had left the *pensione* so unexpectedly. But Signora Ricci bustled out of the kitchen and greeted Gemma like a long-lost daughter, hugging her to a bosom redolent with oregano and fennel. Without pausing for air, she congratulated Gemma on her fortunate marriage—*il signore di Mario, che premio*—complimented her on the stylish pantsuit she was wearing and vowed by the soul of her late sainted husband never again to rent rooms to Germans, although she ought to have known better after the way the Germans had tried to corrupt her innocent babe, Franco. . . . Gemma listened to all this with tolerant amusement, rather pleased at the ease with which she followed the *signora*'s involuted sentences, but that last remark about Germans puzzled her until the woman's tongue stilled long enough for her to take a deep breath, and Gemma could hear the quarrel going on upstairs in one of the bedrooms.

Gemma recognized Dieter's voice at once, but his violence surprised and shocked her; she had never heard him speak with anything other than punctilious formality. Repeatedly interrupting his harangue were the lighter tones of a woman, clear and cold and precise, and Gemma assumed that the speaker was Dieter's wife, Gretchen. Gemma looked at Signora Ricci meaningly.

The Italian woman shrugged. "They have been at each other's throats ever since that woman arrived. Day and night the arguments continue until at last he storms out. She waits here, making a nuisance of herself, poking in my kitchen, and when he returns, it begins all over again. If she yelled at him, perhaps it would be better; he could hit her. But she never raises her voice, that one; she is more like water dripping on a stone. I do not trust women who hold their emotions in all the time. Such composure is not honest. I think I would feel sorry for him, were it not for the shabby way he has treated Claretta."

Gemma asked, "Yes, what has become of Claretta?" But before Signora Ricci could answer, their conversation was interrupted.

"Gemma," Dave said hoarsely, and she turned to see him standing at the top of the staircase, his hazel eyes roving over her hungrily as he gazed down at her.

"Dave!" Gemma exclaimed with forced cheerfulness, watching him descend. Aware of Signora Ricci's suddenly disapproving frown, she wondered if Jordan had ordered the woman to keep his wife from talking to the new guest. Gemma said reassuringly, "Mr. Blanchard is an old friend of my family, *signora*, and he's brought me news of my father and brothers. If we could just use your parlor...." Her voice trailed off suggestively, and after a moment Signora Ricci nodded toward the *salotto*. When Gemma and Dave trooped silently into the little room and seated themselves on the old-fashioned sofa, their manner as stiff and uncomfortable as the horsehair upholstery, Gemma glanced back and noticed that the other woman had apparently felt a sudden pressing need to dust the furniture in the hallway, just in view of the two Americans.

Dave saw her, too, and under his breath he muttered explosively, "Damn it, is it asking too much for a person to want a little privacy around here?"

Gemma shrugged lightly. "Italians tend to be very gregarious. They don't value privacy the same way we do."

Dave looked at Gemma sharply. "Then I don't see why you wanted to marry an Italian. You were always the most private person I ever knew." Gemma did not reply, instead toying nervously with her wedding ring. Goaded by her silence, Dave cried, his heavy features flushed, "For God's sake, Gemma, why did you do it? I don't understand any of this. How could you forget all we shared and and jump into bed with the first—"

With careful emphasis, Gemma cut in, "It was over between you and me, Dave. I told you that weeks ago. If you refused to accept it, then I'm afraid that's your problem."

"But... but what about our plans... all those times we—your father—"

"Leave my father out of this!" Gemma snapped, her temper rising in spite of herself. "He's caused enough trouble already." She sank back against the arm of the sofa. Her gray eyes traveled warily toward the archway opening into the hall, and she saw that Signora Ricci stood clutching her long-handled duster like a weapon, ready to fly to Gemma's aid should Dave make a threatening gesture. Gemma forced herself to smile reassuringly. With all the violent arguments going on under her roof, the poor woman was probably beginning to feel like a referee at a boxing match.

When she looked at Dave again, he was staring at her oddly, his expression unreadable. After a moment he demanded, "Is that where I went wrong? All these years I've tried so hard to be careful, and you can't forgive me for liking your father? Is that why you married di Mario, a foreigner and an *artist*—" he almost spat the word "—because you knew your father would hate it? This ridiculous marriage is some sort of crazy revenge for whatever wrongs you've imagined your—"

"Don't be absurd," Gemma interrupted more calmly than she felt, her heart pounding as she wondered if there was a grain of truth in what Dave said. Ignoring his uncharacteristically blatant prejudice because she could hear the bewildered pain driving him, she averred, "My father has nothing whatsoever to do with it. But just for the record, I think even he might be able to tolerate an artist who's as successful as Jordan is."

Dave's eyes narrowed, "You mean you married him for his money?" he asked contemptuously.

Gemma jumped to her feet, her face white. "There's no point in continuing this discussion," she said through clenched teeth. "Marsha seemed to think I owed you some kind of explanation, but I can see right now that you're more than capable of making up your own."

She turned to storm out of the room, but Dave caught her wrist. "Don't get high-and-mighty with me, Gemma Culver," he growled, yanking her against him. Out of the corner of her eye, Gemma could see Signora Ricci poised to rush in, and she waved her back, fearing the older woman might get hurt. Dave was out of control. His hands pawed at Gemma, bruising and humiliating her. She tried to push him away, and her resistance only inflamed him. He dug his hands into her shining hair and held her head immobile as he ravaged her mouth. Knowing she was lost to him, against her lips he rasped, "My God, when I think of all those years I held back, treating you as if you were made of glass, putting up with your whims, and then you go and sell yourself to a perfect stranger—"

"I *didn't*!" Gemma cried.

"Of course you did. Why else did you marry him? Don't try to tell me you fell madly in love with di Mario because I won't believe you. I know you, Gemma, I know what a frigid little bitch you really are—"

Gemma wrenched one hand free and slapped Dave as hard as she could. The force of the blow sent him reeling, and as he staggered backward, he released her. She fled from the *salotto*, running into the hallway, where Signora Ricci gathered her into her

comforting embrace. Gemma leaned heavily against
the woman's shoulder, shaking uncontrollably. She
was only marginally aware of Dieter and a young
woman with braided hair who hovered in the middle
of the flight of stairs, or of Franco, laden with
groceries, halting in surprise in the front door.

"Gemma, please, I'm—" she heard Dave choke in
an altered voice behind her, but Signora Ricci waved
her duster at him like a spear, and Dieter stepped forward menacingly. Gemma felt rather than saw Dave's
retreat. Rapping out orders, Franco's mother passed
Gemma over to her son, and quickly he led her outside. As soon as they stepped onto the gravel driveway, crossing to Franco's ramshackle Fiat, Gemma
could hear a commotion start up inside the house, the
signora's voice rising eloquently above all the rest.
Despite her distress Gemma had to suppress a giggle as
she wondered how Italians managed to sound so musical, even when they were telling someone off. By the
time Franco had pulled his car out into the road, Gemma's giggles had turned into strangled sobs.

At Gemma's request Franco drove her around until she had regained her composure. When they finally reached Carcione's studio, he offered to go inside
with her, but she thanked him politely for his concern
and assured him she would be all right. The spasm of
remorse that had racked her so violently was over,
finished, and she would not lose control again. She
dug a small mirror from her handbag and surveyed
her reflection critically. There was little she could do
about her reddened eyes, but she combed her hair
and tried to disguise her bruised lips with a pale pink
lipstick. Against her pallor the makeup looked

clownlike, and she wiped it off again with a sodden handkerchief. With one final sniff, Gemma smiled at Franco and slid out of the Fiat. She watched him pull away from the curb, then straightening her thin shoulders, she marched into the studio.

The racket was deafening as usual, the air filled with flying dust, and the workmen glanced up from their pneumatic hammers just long enough to nod a greeting to her before returning to their tasks. Gemma waved casually and crossed to the partition that separated the main room from the cubicle where Jordan's Madonna was housed. When she stepped inside the doorway, she saw Jordan and Sergio conferring heatedly, too engrossed in their discussion to notice her at once. For a long moment Gemma gazed at her husband's back. He stood with one foot resting on the edge of the low pallet holding the partially carved block of marble, and his dark hair stood up in spikes, as if he had been running his hands through it. His sleeves were rolled back to reveal his powerful arms, and he leaned one elbow on a denim-covered thigh, while his other hand gesticulated earnestly as if drawing sketches in the air. His spine and the muscles of his broad back pressed against the taut fabric of his shirt, and Gemma quivered, remembering the feel of those muscles under her stroking fingertips as she clung to him in the night.

She shook her head, her mouth curving in painful irony. "Frigid," Dave had called her, and the injustice of his accusation hurt less than the thought of all those years the two of them had wasted, trying to build a relationship that was obviously doomed from the start. Even if she had married Dave, even if they had lived in intimacy the rest of their lives, Gemma knew now that he never would have been aware of even a fraction of the passion Jordan had discovered in her almost at once.

Jordan's deep voice broke into her thoughts. "Gemma," he said, and she glanced up at him, her gray eyes murky. He had left Carcione and was towering in front of her, studying her pale features intently. "Gemma," he repeated, his dark brows coming together sharply at the traces of fierce emotion still marking her face, "where have you been?"

She shrugged. "Oh. . . just around."

His eyes narrowed as he looked at her mouth. He said carefully, "My mother called to tell me you were going to see Blanchard."

Gemma's tender mood vanished instantly. She glared up at Jordan, but aware of Carcione openly monitoring their conversation when she spoke, she kept her voice quiet and rigidly controlled. "Yes, I saw Dave. Did you really think I wouldn't?"

Jordan's expression became thunderous. "Gemma," he gritted, stepping menacingly toward her, "she telephoned hours ago. What the hell have the pair of you been doing all this time?"

Gemma took a deep furious breath to bolster herself. Two jealous overbearing men were more than she could handle in one day. With a trace of a sneer she suggested acidly, "Tell you what, Jordan, why don't you just ask your mother? I'm sure she has some ideas on the subject!" And she spun on her heel and stalked out of the studio.

CHAPTER NINE

SEVERAL DAYS LATER, after Caroline's doctor pronounced the girl fit to travel, she and her mother and Dave left Pietrasanta. Despite the summer crowds Jordan had managed to procure first-class reservations for them on the train to Florence, where they would transfer to the new ultrafast *direttissima* that would speed them southward to Rome. Caroline said she wanted to throw a coin in the Trevi Fountain, as she had seen some actress do in an old movie on television, and Marsha expressed a desire to find a piece of real Capo di Monte porcelain. Dave said almost nothing.

They stood on the platform with Gemma and Jordan, waiting in awkward silence for the train to pull into the station. Beatrice had already told Caroline goodbye at the villa, embracing the girl as if she were her own daughter, and when the woman turned away abruptly and fled to her room, Gemma thought she had spotted tears in her pale blue eyes. In the train station, after Jordan had kissed Caroline's hand with the overblown gallantry she seemed to enjoy so much, Gemma hugged her convulsively. Confused by the unexpected depth of the emotions tearing at her, with mock sternness she ordered her to make good use of her time in Rome. "You must go to the

Vatican," Gemma said firmly. "It houses the greatest art collection in the world, and of course, you can't miss the Sistine Chapel or Michelangelo's *Pieta*—"

"Or the altar canopy by Bernini," Caroline chimed in. When Gemma looked astonished, the girl teased, grinning, "Well, I just didn't want you to think I'd forgotten *everything* you drummed into us in art class!"

Gemma laughed, then, growing serious, said, "I really am glad you're feeling better, Caroline. I hope the rest of your vacation is more enjoyable than the first part was."

Caroline nodded, her expression equally somber. "I think it will be now that my mother's here. Not that there was anything wrong with you, but...." She hesitated, then murmured in an undertone, "I don't pretend to understand what's going on between you and Jordan, Gemma—when I asked mama, she told me I should mind my own business—but I can see that something isn't right. I'll write, I promise, and I want you to promise me that you'll tell me if you need help, okay?"

"Okay, Caro," Gemma agreed, touched by her concern. Sniffling inelegantly, she hugged her again and said roughly, "I'll be expecting a postcard every—"

"Oh, look, there's Franco!" Caroline squealed suddenly, spotting the boy who lingered on the edge of the crowd, yet another food basket in his hands. She pulled away from Gemma and started to dash to him, but just in time she remembered her dignity and progressed across the platform with affected casualness. Gemma chuckled and turned back to the adults.

Jordan was just releasing Marsha's hand, and the faint blush washing her white skin indicated that she was nót as immune to his undeniable charm as she would have liked Gemma to believe. Then, rather to Gemma's surprise, Jordan turned to Dave and extended his hand to him. He said stiffly, "Blanchard, I'd like to thank you for your efforts in finding Mrs. Somerville and escorting her to us. I know these past few days have been trying ones, and I'm sure your presence has made the trip easier for her."

Dave's mouth hardened. Gemma watched anxiously, afraid he was about to make some cutting retort, but to her immense relief he merely nodded and with rigid formality accepted Jordan's salute. Then his hazel eyes flicked warily to Gemma at her husband's side, and all at once, with the air of one burning his bridges, Dave swooped her into his arms and kissed her hard. "Oh, God, Gemma," he groaned hungrily, "how I wish—"

Before Gemma, stunned, could react, Jordan's arm snaked out, and he caught her wrist, yanking her away from Dave. Through clenched teeth he said curtly, "Goodbye, Blanchard." He nodded to Marsha and turned to stalk away, slicing a path through the milling crowd as he dragged Gemma behind him.

In the parked Ferrari, Jordan stared at Gemma's tearstained face and growled, "If you must cry over another man, at least have the decency to wait until I can't see you."

Gemma shook her head fiercely. "Damn you, Jordan di Mario, I'm crying because you hurt me!" She flexed her aching wrist, where bright red ovals marked the spots where his powerful fingers had dug into her soft skin. "Do you have any idea how strong you are?" she asked indignantly. "Every time you touch me, I get bruised. You're the most... the most *physical* person I ever met."

One dark brow arched as Jordan's expression altered subtly. "Am I?" he murmured. He caught her hand once more, this time with studied gentleness. Lifting her wrist to his face, he caressed the marks with his lips, trailing the tip of his tongue across the pulse point. She quivered, helpless to deny the sensations quaking through her. "Poor Gemma," Jordan mocked dryly as he watched her through hooded eyes, "what sensitive skin you have... and how you love me to touch it."

Blushing furiously, Gemma tried to tug loose. "N-no," she stammered unconvincingly, "no, you're wr-wrong. I... I don't like—"

"Don't lie," Jordan interrupted sharply, releasing her and shifting around in the low bucket seat so that he could switch on the ignition. "Don't ever try to deceive me about that because I know you far better than you realize. You may bitterly resent the fact that I am your husband, but there's no way you can deny that the only time you really come alive is when—" He was interrupted by the deafening blare of a diesel horn, and huge wheels slid to a halt with a piercing metallic squeal that made Gemma's teeth shiver. She wanted to turn around to watch the train's arrival, but she was afraid Jordan would think she was trying to get one last look at Dave. Jordan squinted at the rearview mirror, watching the activity on the railway platform behind them. After a second he let out his breath, as if he had been holding it, and muttered, "*Bene*. Your friends seem to be boarding without difficulty. Now that that's taken care of, let's get out of here and go to Sergio's. We have work to do."

THAT EVENING, while Gemma was showering away the grime of the day's activities, she heard the extension telephone ring in the room at the uppermost level of the villa, Jordan's private studio. She wondered sometimes what secrets were hidden at the other end of that short flight of stairs, but, remembering his vehemence when she had innocently asked to see the studio the first day she met him, she had never dared inquire again, and he had not invited her. Since that room was off limits to Jordan's mother and the women who came in daily to clean, Gemma assumed his wife would be unwelcome, as well.

She stepped out of the shower into the steamy bathroom, accepting the large towel Jordan proffered her with an impersonal nod. She began to dry herself, and Jordan returned to combing his thick hair, which was still damp from his own shower. As she rubbed her slender body, making her creamy skin glow, Gemma acknowledged wryly that self-consciousness did not survive long when you lived with someone. Despite the difficulties attendant to their marriage, in a very short time she had become as matter-of-fact about the more prosaic intimacies of daily life as if she and Jordan had been husband and wife for years. She heard the telephone ring again, and then it broke off abruptly, indicating that someone had answered it elsewhere in the house. After a moment Beatrice's voice floated into the room, carried along the echoing corridors by the peculiar acoustic quality of the stone floors and bare walls. "Giordano, it's for you," she called in Italian, and Jordan muttered an apology to Gemma and loped out of the bathroom, mounting the steps to his studio two at a time.

He did not return right away, and when Gemma wrapped the towel around her, securing it over her breast, and crossed the bedroom to her dresser to get fresh underwear, through the open door she could hear the rumble of Jordan's deep voice as he spoke in rapid Italian to someone. At one point a shout of laughter rang out, and Gemma found herself thinking wistfully how pleasant it must be to be on such easy terms with her husband, to talk and joke with him without the constant tension that made their relationship so wearing.

By the time he came back to the bedroom, Gemma had dressed in a slim shift of hydrangea blue, and Jordan regarded her approvingly. "That's fine for a quiet evening at home, but tomorrow you'd better plan on pulling out all the stops if you don't want to be outshone. That was Francesca on the phone. She's just got back from New York, and I've invited her to dinner."

Gemma gaped at him, blanching. "You...you've invited her *here*?" she choked. "Why?"

Jordan frowned. "What do you mean, why? I asked her because I wanted to. She always comes back from one of these trips full of gossip and funny stories."

"Did...did you tell her about us getting married?" Gemma queried nervously.

"No," Jordan admitted. "I thought it would be better to break the news to her in person."

"She isn't going to like it. She might not have wanted to come if she knew."

Jordan shrugged. "I think you worry far too much. I can't see how my being married will affect Francesca one way or the other. Besides, she wants to see how the Madonna is coming along. While I wish I could report that we were making better progress, since she is the model for the statue, and her father is paying for it, I can't very well refuse to show it to her."

Gemma said blankly, "I didn't know Francesca's father was the one who commissioned the Madonna. I thought it was for some church."

"It is. Sebastian is making a gift of it as a memorial for Francesca's mother. Usually I don't take commissions, but he has been after me for years to do this for him, and finally he—" Jordan glanced sidelong at Gemma and grinned roguishly "—he made me an offer I couldn't refuse."

She stared. "You mean he's a...a...?"

Jordan chuckled. "You shouldn't take everything so literally, *cara*. Let's just say that it isn't always tactful to question Sebastian Buscaglia about where he got his money." He fell silent, the subject obviously one of little importance to him.

As Jordan's dark eyes roved over Gemma's slender figure, they suddenly took fire. Spanning his large hands around her narrow waist, he pulled her close to him, the tips of her breasts just brushing his shirt. Gemma caught her breath. The fresh tang of soap and after-shave lotion mingled with the clean male scent of his body, and Gemma could feel the warmth of him through the barrier of their clothing. Silky lashes drooping over her pale cheeks, she leaned her forehead against his chest, despising herself for that conscious gesture of submission, yet knowing she had no defense against the sexual aura Jordan radiated. She did not understand why his attraction was so devastating, why he could arouse her as no other man had ever been able to do, but she knew that whenever he touched her, she lost all desire to fight him; in fact, she welcomed his caresses. The only trouble was, Jordan knew it, too.

His lips began teasing the sensitive skin behind her ear, each tiny movement setting up shock waves that amplified as they traveled along her spinal column and spread to her extremities. Groaning, she slid her hands up over his broad chest and shoulders and dug her fingers into the damp hair brushing the back of his collar. As he turned his face to hers once more, she felt him shudder triumphantly. When his mouth locked over hers, she was lost, seduced by the sweet heady taste of him, his tongue and teeth rubbing intimately against hers. She was not even aware that he had begun to slowly nudge her across the room until her calves struck the edge of the bed, and she lost her balance, falling backward across the silk coverlet and pulling him down on top of her.

SOON, FAR TOO SOON, he lifted himself away from her, and Gemma blinked hazily, not yet ready to break out of the sensual dream he had woven around them. She raised her fingers to stroke the hard line of his mouth, then her hand slid downward along the strong column of his neck, slipping inside his shirt that had somehow come unbuttoned, weaving into the coarse hair on his chest until it found his heart, pounding raggedly under her palm. She gazed up at him in frustrated wonder, tense with the curious notion that she had been on the brink of some momentous discovery, that only a few seconds more and she would have known. . . .

Beatrice's voice echoed through the hallway once more, and Jordan said wryly, "I think dinner is ready."

Gemma sat up, disgruntled. "We'd better go, then," she muttered. "We wouldn't want your mother charging in to find out why we're late."

"Oh, I imagine she knows why we're late," Jordan drawled. "Here, if you'll turn around, I'll fasten your dress for you." As he tugged the long zipper into place, he suggested, "Why don't you plan on wearing the rose chiffon tomorrow night? I like that color on you."

"Tomorrow night?" Gemma asked blankly, all memory of their previous conversation wiped out by the heated passion they had just shared.

Jordan said, "Of course, for when our guest comes. I know you don't care much about fashion, but I did think women preferred to be well dressed in the presence of other women, especially one like Francesca, who always looks stunning."

Gemma stared down at her hands as she toyed with her wedding ring. "I. . . I still wish you hadn't invited her," she mumbled in an undertone.

Jordan lifted her chin so that she had to look at him. He studied her face, frowning. After a moment he said, "I explained all that to you before, Gemma. I can't really see why you are making such a fuss. Anyone would think you were jealous."

"Jealous!" Gemma exclaimed indignantly, blushing. "Why should I be jealous?"

Jordan regarded her silently, his dark eyes shuttered. When at last he spoke, he said, "That's a good question, my dear. Perhaps you'd like to answer it?"

She stared at him, sensing a trap. He seemed to be waiting expectantly for her reply, waiting for her to make some admission, say something that would reinforce his dominance. She jerked out of his grasp and shook her head fiercely. "There is no answer, because I am not jealous of Francesca. I don't care what you—" She halted abruptly, suddenly aware that she was lying through her teeth. She did care what Jordan did; she did want his fidelity. He had become necessary to her, physically if not emotionally. The thought of him touching his mistress the way he had just touched her made her sick.

Jordan was still watching her intently, so Gemma finished with lame insistence, "I just don't want Francesca here because... because I hate scenes. I'm not sure I could take another argument like the one that happened when Dave...."

Jordan rocked back, scowling. His expression seemed almost disappointed. He said, "There will be no scene, Gemma. Francesca will accept our marriage with good grace—perhaps better than you have done." He rose from the bed, towering over Gemma as he rebuttoned his shirt and adjusted his belt. "*Andiamo,*" he said brusquely.

"Married?" Francesca repeated blankly, pronouncing the word as if she had never heard it before. The beautiful brunette posed languidly against the back of one of the low sofas in the living room. Gorgeous as usual, this time in ruffled tiers of crimson silk, her heavy perfume wafting upward toward the vaulted ceiling, she appeared relaxed, but as Gemma faced her, she noted that Francesca's hands were clenched, and her clawlike nails were digging viciously into the upholstery of the sofa. Her remarkable features crinkled into an expression of frank bewilderment as she gazed up at the tall man standing next to Gemma. "Giordano, this is—you are making some kind of a joke, *non è vero?*"

He shook his head. "No, Francesca, it's quite true, I assure you. Gemma and I were married in Pisa weeks ago." With an affectionate gesture he slid his arm around Gemma's rigid waist and pulled her close against him, hugging her.

For the first time Francesca looked directly at the slim blond girl at Jordan's side. Her fine dark eyes raked Gemma's slight figure, now draped in floating pink chiffon that added color to her cheeks and disguised the boyish contours of her body, and she puzzled aloud, "Have we met, *signorina?*"

"Signora di Mario," Jordan corrected quietly.

"Of course," Francesca amended with a sickly chuckle, "forgive me, I meant Signora di Mario. How strange that sounds—" she glanced at Jordan's mother, who stood apart, watching the confrontation, her face carefully blank "—strange, except when applied to you, dear Beatrice." She looked at Gemma again, frowning. "But we have met, have we not? I seem to remember...." Her expression became accusing. "I know," she declared. "It was the day Giordano's lovely Ferrari was wrecked. You were intoxicated and ran into him."

Gemma blinked. "That was a friend of mine, actually," she murmured.

Francesca shrugged. "Whether it was you or your friend, a very valuable car was—"

Jordan cut in smoothly, "There was fault on both sides, and no lasting damage to anyone, so let's forget it, all right?"

"Of course," Francesca said silkily, her musical voice suggestive. "But I can't help thinking what a...unique way it was to meet one's future husband, almost as if it were fated. Or perhaps, considering what has developed from that encounter, one might even say, almost as if it were...arranged."

Gemma felt her temper rise at the insinuation, but as she searched her mind for a properly scathing retort, Jordan said repressively, "Enough, Francesca. I can fight my own battles. What I hope now is that you, as one of my oldest and dearest friends, will give Gemma and me your best wishes for our marriage."

Gemma glanced up at Jordan, alarmed by the harsh note in his deep voice. His jaw was set, and the intent light in his narrowed eyes made it clear he would brook no refusal. Francesca obviously interpreted his expression the same way Gemma did, for after the briefest of hesitations she murmured, "*Naturalmente*, Giordano *caro*, you know I have never wanted anything but your happiness." Pushing Gemma aside, she flung her arms around his neck and plastered her voluptuous body against the hard length of him and kissed him passionately.

When Jordan's hands lifted automatically to catch Francesca by the waist, Gemma turned away, feeling faintly queasy. Her gray eyes happened to meet Beatrice's, and she was shaken by the smug, almost gloating look distorting the woman's plain features.

Gemma saw that same look again later on Francesca's beautiful face when she escorted the model to the guest room she would occupy. She had been startled when, over dessert, Beatrice mentioned casually that Francesca would be staying the night. When Gemma indicated her surprise, Jordan said sternly, "Surely you didn't expect Francesca to have to drive all the way back to Florence tonight, did you?"

Blushing at her implied ungraciousness, Gemma had stammered uncomfortably, "But no, it's just that—I mean, no one told me...." Her voice trailed off in a hoarse whisper as the others scowled at her condemningly. Later, although as she was decidedly reluctant to be alone with Francesca, she tried to make up for her lapse by helping her settle in for the evening. Optimistically she had hoped that Francesca would take Jordan's defection with at least surface good grace, but the instant the door closed, shutting the two of them inside the bedroom that was far more luxurious than the one in which Gemma had been housed when she first came to the villa, Gemma's hopes died. Francesca turned on her in a rage.

"*Donnaccia*—bitch!" she spat, her needlelike nails raking the air as if she wished it were Gemma's face. She glared venomously. "Who do you think you are, a skinny little nobody like you, to try to take him away from me?''

Gemma had half expected this attack, and she watched cautiously, furious that Jordan would allow her to be put in this position. It was just another example of his disregard for her rights as a person, she thought indignantly. He was far too intelligent to really believe that Francesca would accept his marriage without a fight, and it did not seem to bother him in the least that Gemma was the one who would have to bear the brunt of the woman's anger. Thinking, *damn it, he can take the blame himself for once,* Gemma said flatly, ''I know you're upset, Francesca, but I'm afraid you have it all wrong. It was Jordan's idea that we get married. I didn't want to.''

For just a second, Francesca looked as if the air had been punched out of her, then she snorted contemptuously. ''I don't believe you. You must have forced his hand somehow, otherwise he never would have consented to such a...an asinine match. What did you do, lure him into bed and then cry 'rape'? Better men than Giordano have been caught that way.'' Gemma was silent. Francesca stared at her in wonder and muttered, ''What I can't understand is how you managed to seduce him in the first place. You're colorless, and you have no figure.'' She shook her head, and her blue black curls swirled lustrously around her shoulders. ''There is no understanding the ways of men,'' she said with philosophic scorn after a moment. ''In any event, it makes no difference why Giordano bedded you. He is still mine, he's always been mine, I tell you. We have been lovers since we were children.... I was his first,'' she added triumphantly.

Despite her efforts to remain unmoved, Gemma winced at those last words. She had always known that the woman had been her husband's mistress, but this talk of being his first lover made it seem—real, somehow, threatening. Gemma did not want to think of Jordan as he would have been years before, a handsome youth meeting the younger, but already breathtaking girl, both of them vibrant with budding sensuality. Noting that Francesca was watching her reactions closely, Gemma schooled her features and said quietly, "Yes, I knew you were his mistress."

Gemma's calm response to her provocation seemed to surprise Francesca, and she hesitated, her eyes sharp and shrewd as she debated how to continue. After a moment she corrected, "I was his *fidanzata*. We were to be married."

"Then why weren't you?" Gemma asked.

Francesca shrugged, framing her reply. "We argued," she said. "Giordano was too possessive, too jealous. When he was just beginning his career, I posed for him often, but as his work became known, and my face with it, I began to receive many offers of modeling jobs from other artists and photographers, opportunities for travel, a screen test, even marriage proposals from men who knew only my beauty...." She smiled with fond satisfaction at her memories, and Gemma, seeing that wistful expression, thought dryly that Francesca's total self-absorption would have been amusing were the woman not so deadly serious about it. Francesca continued, "I had less time for him as it became clear that I could have a career of my own—and Giordano did not like that so much. He thought I ought to devote my entire life to helping his work, saving myself only for him. When I refused, he became like a wild man. He had just completed *Privilege*, and he threatened to smash it to bits if I did not marry him right away—''

Gemma's lashes flew up, and her mood with them, as she thought with sudden conviction, *liar, he would never do that. No artist would, not for you, not for anyone.*

Unaware of Gemma's skepticism, Francesca went on blithely, ''I just laughed and told him he would be better off to use that energy to find some little mouse of a wife who would tend to his needs and put up with his tantrums.''

She paused, staring at Gemma. ''Some little mouse—'' she repeated, her face lighting, then she laughed cynically. ''Of course, that would explain it! The day Giordano met you, we had had yet another argument about marriage. I had been in Florence for several weeks, caring for my father, and Giordano thought that at last I was ready to give up modeling and become his wife. When I told him I had to go to New York on an assignment, he flung off in a huff, and that was when he had the wreck with his Ferrari.''

Gemma's spirits sank as quickly as they had risen. She conceded in a monotone, ''Yes, he did mention something about being upset because of a quarrel.''

Francesca nodded. ''Of course. I rejected him yet again, and while he was still reeling, he met you, a meek little nobody who would obviously be delighted to give up everything to nurture his career, grateful for any crumbs of affection.''

At this, Gemma felt it necessary to protest aloud. ''I'm an artist, too, you know,'' she pointed out.

Francesca's beautiful mouth curled up into a sardonic smile. "An artist? You dare to call yourself that in the same breath that you speak of Giordano di Mario? Do you really believe that?" Gemma sat very still. No, she had never believed that, and seeing the uncertainty in her eyes, Francesca probed deeper. "Of course, you know it is not true. I heard what Giordano said at dinner tonight, but knowing him the way I do, I can tell you, he is merely using this talk of your 'great talent' to bind you more closely to him. In the end, his needs are the only ones that will count for anything."

She paused again, noting Gemma's growing pallor, and this time when she spoke, her expression was syrupy with pity. "Poor deluded American girl," she condoled. "You came to Italy looking for romance, and you have given him your heart, a man who cares only for the marble, who has never given a damn about any woman made of flesh and blood—except me. I think I almost find it in myself to feel sorry for you. After all, I know that your presence will make no difference at all to my relationship with Giordano. Why, he might even come to me tonight." Gemma's stricken disgust at that remark was palpable, and Francesca, seeing it, rushed in for the kill. She cooed, "For your own sake I hope you will not become too...comfortable in this marriage you have made so rashly, because someday, when I grow weary of the glamorous life of a fashion model, I shall return to Giordano and tell him that at long last I am ready to settle down. And in his rush to reach me, you will be kicked aside like a worn-out footstool."

Gemma left Francesca without saying another

word. As she made her way back to the room she shared with Jordan, she appeared outwardly calm, her face a bland mask, but in fact she felt dizzy, her temples pounded like timpani, and deep inside her there was a dark cold void where once her stomach had been. Her brain did not seem to be functioning properly, either, and she had to deliberately think out each movement of the muscles that manipulated her legs, with great effort urging her body along the corridor toward the master bedroom. Once or twice she stumbled. She was in shock—a reaction not to Francesca's taunting claims that she would steal Gemma's husband, but rather to the uncanny accuracy of half a dozen words that Francesca had thrown in so casually that she might not even remember uttering them: "You have given him your heart...."

Oh, my God, Gemma thought with a groan, praying she would reach the privacy of her room before she collapsed from the pain of that revelation, *she's right, I've fallen in love with him!*

She ought to have known, she admitted as she kicked off her shoes and fell across the bed, heedless of the pink chiffon settling over her slender body like mist at sunset. When she had asked herself repeatedly why Jordan was able to arouse her sexually as no one else had ever done, she ought to have been intelligent enough to complete the equation, to understand that his physical attraction was so intense because it derived from an ever stronger emotional one. But no, she had tried to pass off those strange new feelings as having to do with her respect for him as an artist. She had spent so many years denying that love was possible between a man and a woman that when she finally did fall in love, she couldn't even recognize what had happened to her.

Not that it changed anything. She loved Jordan, but he loved only.... Suddenly she thought of the moment such a short time before—it seemed like aeons now—when she had sat beside the highway with Franco and Caroline, and she had compared their frustrated pursuit with the figures on a Greek vase, Caroline chasing Franco chasing Gemma. She had thought that only one figure was lacking to complete the circuit, someone she herself chased after. Well, now at last she knew the identity of that shadowy figure, but ironically the vase was proving larger than she had expected, and the design did not end with her pursuit of Jordan.

Where was he, she wondered, glancing at her very functional-looking digital wristwatch. When they had sat in the living room, sipping their after-dinner liqueurs, Francesca and Beatrice had chatted with an intimacy that deliberately excluded Gemma from the conversation. Jordan had seemed slightly tense, and he had said something about going for a stroll before he retired. But that had been hours ago, and still there was no sign of him. He ought to come to bed; he needed the rest. He had been working hard, and he had promised Sergio Carcione that they would make an early start in the morning to try to put the Madonna back on schedule. Why was he still out walking, or was that so-called walk merely an excuse....

Clutching a pillow, Gemma closed her eyes tightly against the pain that threatened her. She breathed deeply, and she realized that the pillow slip was im-

printed with the indefinable combination of odors—
soap, body oils, cologne—that meant her husband's
head rested there at night. She burrowed her face into
the comforting softness, and as she did, she wondered with anguish if the linens on Francesca's bed
would be marked with that scent by morning.

"OH, HELL," she heard Jordan growl, his deep voice
echoing in the silence of the near-empty studio. Carcione's crew had laid aside their tools and departed
for lunch, and when in disgust Jordan flung his chisel
onto the chip-covered floor, the metal blade rang out
with the dissonant clang of a cracked bell. He
stepped down off the pallet, declaring, "There's
something wrong with this piece of marble, Sergio.
The grain isn't right."

Gemma glanced up from her workbench just in
time to see Carcione's black shoe-button eyes flick
between her and Francesca, who lounged on the one
comfortable chair in the room, carefully brushing
away bits of marble dust with a silk scarf. Gemma
rubbed one hand across her face, smearing a streak
of gray clay on her chin. The heat was oppressive,
and already she was tired after her restless night, but
when Jordan elected to work through the hours of
siesta, she had not dared to leave, knowing that
Francesca would remain. Carcione looked at Gemma
again, and his wizened features were stolid. He
squatted down to retrieve the chisel, and as he stood
up again, testing the edge with his thumb, he said
quietly, "The problem is not with the stone, Giordano."

Jordan stared at him, and a faint flush appeared

on his high cheekbones. "Damn it," he snapped forcefully, "I tell you there's a flaw somewhere. The deeper I cut, the more convinced I am of it."

Carcione shrugged. "Okay, okay, so the quarrymen and my crew are all idiots and don't know how to choose a sound block of marble. That means it's up to you to save us from our incompetence, all the more reason you should keep your mind on what you are doing and not allow distractions—" he paused significantly "—to interfere with your work. If you don't start trying, this piece is going to be a disaster, Giordano."

"Well, *I* think it is going to be beautiful," Francesca cut in languidly, stretching so that her voluptuous figure was outlined to advantage in the clinging sun dress she wore. "Papa will love it."

"Grazie," Jordan murmured, nodding gallantly in her direction. "Of course, with you for a model, it could hardly be other than exquisite."

Sergio, who, Gemma knew, had no use for Francesca, ignored that little exchange, and Gemma, taking her cue from him, turned her attention once more to the model on which she was laboring. As she concentrated on building up the shape with tiny pellets of clay, a shadow fell across her bench, and she could sense Jordan towering behind her. Hot prickles rose along her spine at his nearness, making her hands unsteady, and contrarily she wished he would go away.

Just before sleep and emotional upset had overwhelmed her the night before, she had stripped off her chiffon dress and slid naked between the cool sheets on her side of their king-size bed, trying not to be aware of Jordan's continuing absence. When she awakened in the morning, she had found the linens on his side mussed, indicating that he must have come to bed sometime during the night, but she did not know when, and she was certain that he had never crossed the pristine and undisturbed center of the bed to touch her.

With a determined effort, Gemma collected herself and continued modeling. She was making a new, larger version of her "nun" figure, incorporating changes into the design that would be necessary if the maquette was to be scaled up in marble. Sergio had offered several grudging suggestions whose insight had surprised Gemma when she used them, and once she had seen him nodding approvingly when he thought she wasn't watching. She was beginning to realize that the man's persistent pessimism was simply his manner, a habit ingrained in him by his peasant forebears as a way of combating the evil eye. Under Sergio's tutelage Gemma could already see improvement in her work, and Jordan, too, although he was careful not to impress his own ideas on her, seemed pleased with what she was doing. Before he became so engrossed in his struggles with the Madonna, there had been moments when he had studied one of her sketches or modeling exercises and then had turned his dark eyes to her. When she met his gaze, for a fraction of a heartbeat there had been a line between them direct from his mind to hers, a fleeting instant of harmony when they had communicated not as lovers, but as artists.

Thus she was unprepared for the ridicule in Jordan's voice when he leaned over her shoulder and jeered, "Is this what you've been wasting your time with today? What kind of bungling, inept—"

Gemma swiveled around on her stool, gasping at the attack, her eyes wide and stormy. She swallowed twice, trying to find her voice, but before she could speak, unexpectedly Sergio Carcione came to her defense. He charged, "Giordano, what's the matter with you? Have you gone blind? Any fool can see that your wife is learning rapidly, already showing remarkable improvement."

Jordan waved one large hand toward the model threateningly, as if he would have liked to crush the soft clay. He snorted, "Oh, I'll grant you she's getting better technically, but in the process she's losing all the creativity she once had. Just look at that; it's insipid!"

Gemma jumped to her feet, crowding her thin body between Jordan and the maquette on the workbench, a mother tigress protecting her cub. Out of the corner of her eye she noticed that Francesca was listening with rapt attention. Gemma choked, "What do you mean, Jordan? What's wrong with it?"

He backed off slightly, breathing hard, but his voice was still heavy with scorn. "If you can't tell what's wrong with it, Gemma, then you're not the artist I thought you were. Those sketches you showed me when we met were wonderful, full of fire and passion, and the first model was incredibly sensitive despite the crudeness of execution. I truly thought...." He gestured toward the bench again. "But just look at that, it's slick and cold and lifeless, with about as much artistic worth as a picture on a Christmas card!"

Gemma stared at him, blanching, sickness burning in her throat like acid. She thought with anguish of all the tiring painstaking hours she had devoted to that new model, spurred on only by the conviction that when she was finished, she would have created something really good. She protested, "But I'm trying, I'm learning, I'm—"

"All you're learning is to be dishonest, to hide what you had," Jordan declared flatly. "You're using a superficially glossy technique to cover up your feelings—" He stopped abruptly, his dark eyes narrowing. "Or perhaps you do it on purpose," he suggested with a bitter chuckle. "I told you once that your work revealed the real you, and you can't stand that; you can't bear the thought that someone might get close to that cold little heart of yours."

"Giordano," Sergio reproved sharply, "just because you're having trouble with your own work is no reason to—"

Gemma said, "Thanks, Sergio, but I can handle this myself." She stepped closer to Jordan, her slight body taut with challenge. As she stared up at him, all memory of her love was overwhelmed by her rage at the injustice of his attack on her work. Hoarsely she shouted, "Dishonest, am I? Well, if I'm hiding my feelings, at least I'm truthful enough to admit what I'm doing! It's better than that damned Madonna of yours! I'm not spending a fortune carving a hunk of sentimental schlock and then trying to palm it off to myself and the world as a piece of great art!"

Just for a moment Gemma thought Jordan would hit her. She could see him go rigid with fury, his fists clenched, and involuntarily she backed away until she was brought up short by the low bench. Suddenly his ragged breathing seemed to fill the cramped space of the private workroom, and as he leaned closer,

Sergio hissed through his teeth, *"Per l'amore di Dio, Giordano!"* Jordan turned his head slowly to peer with blank obsidian eyes at the older man. Sergio said, "There's no need to lose your temper, boy. You've had critics who said worse."

Jordan faltered, then nodded reluctantly. He blinked, life returning to his dark eyes, and when he spoke, his voice was even. "Thank you, Sergio," he said. "I'm glad I can always count on you to keep my artistic temperament in check." He glanced at Gemma, noting the apprehensive line of her body, as if she were poised for flight. He said, "Forgive me if I alarmed you, my dear. I would not have—I'd never.... I think it was a mistake to work through lunch—we're both rather tired and hungry—so you go on now and get yourself something to eat."

Gazing up at him, Gemma saw the genuine contrition marking his graven features, and she relaxed. The instant she had uttered her rash words, she regretted them, not necessarily because they weren't true but because they were, well, certainly not tactful. As an artist, she knew how painful it could be when inspiration proved elusive, and she ought to have sympathized with Jordan's difficulties. She was impressed by his apology, one she frankly doubted she would have had the grace to make, and wiping her clay-stained fingers on a grimy cloth, she reached out to touch his hand. She asked tentatively, "Why don't you come with me, Jordan? I know I'm not dressed for anywhere fancier than a *tavola calda*, but perhaps—"

With a harsh laugh Francesca interrupted, "I do hope you aren't expecting me to eat at a snack bar,

Giordano.'' She ran crimson-tipped fingers over the sleek fabric of her sun dress. "It's bound to be so crowded we couldn't get a table, and even if we didn't have to stand up to eat, the grubby tourists who frequent those places would almost certainly soil my new frock.''

Gemma froze. Jordan hesitated, his gaze shifting from Gemma to the beautiful model, then back to Gemma again. He said, "Gemma, I told you once that Pietrasanta's dress standards are fairly lenient. I'm sure we can find a restaurant where—''

Gemma had a brief but acutely unpleasant vision of herself in her stained denims and chambray shirt, sharing a table with Jordan and the ever elegant Francesca. She'd be as out of place as a paper plate in a collection of Wedgwood, and for once her usually dormant feminine pride was too strong to allow herself to be put in that unenviable position, even if it meant she must leave her husband alone with his mistress—as if he didn't already spend enough time alone with her. Shaking her head at the irony of the situation, Gemma said with a briskness that belied her pain, "No, Jordan, I don't want more than a sandwich, so if you don't mind, I think I'll just go on without you.''

Frowning, he shrugged. "As you will. It happens that I have a few more things to do here before I leave. I'd like to test the stone a little more thoroughly just to make sure I'm not imagining a possible flaw. It may be rather late by the time we get back home. We'll see you then. *Ciao.*''

Gemma drooped, the significance of that "we" not lost on her: Francesca would be staying yet another night. Perhaps yet another night when Gemma would lie sleepless for hours, waiting for her husband at last to come to bed—her bed, at any rate. She peeked up through her lashes, gazing at Jordan with a frustrated longing that tore at her vitals. Her gray eyes lingered on the hard line of his mouth, remembering all the times—so many, so few—when those lips had touched hers. Would there be more? With Francesca at hand, he had no need for anyone else. The thought that he might never kiss her again was almost more than Gemma could bear, and with an awkward attempt at flirtation she smiled and stammered, tripping clumsily over the words, "Well, if you won't eat with me, won't you at least...at least k-kiss m-me goodbye...." Her voice trailed off as his expression hardened, his astonishment obvious. When he did not speak, Gemma blushed furiously, stung and humiliated by his blatant rejection. She glanced at Francesca, whose classic features were glowing with a fierce triumphant elation, like some avenging goddess watching the downfall of a presumptuous mortal. With a choked, "I'll see you later," Gemma grabbed her handbag and fled from the studio.

SHE ORDERED A SALAMI SANDWICH at the first *tavola calda*—a "hot table" or Italian snack bar—she found open, but as soon as she had paid for it, she realized she didn't want it. Wrapping the thickly stuffed hard roll in a paper napkin, she tucked it into her purse and walked away, ignoring the halfhearted importunings of a young man in overalls. Inside her purse she had noticed a long envelope addressed to

Colorado, a letter to her father that she had spent days writing and more days raising the courage to mail. Since Dave and Marsha would no doubt relay their own impressions of her hasty marriage back to her family, Gemma knew she could no longer delay sending the letter. She headed for the post office.

With practiced impersonal movements the dark-haired woman behind the counter weighed the letter, stamped it and murmured, *"Ottocento lire, per favore,"* before she glanced up at Gemma.

"Claretta!" Gemma exclaimed, smiling with recognition. "It's good to see you again." Even as she spoke, she noticed that the girl looked unwell. Her bright smile was missing completely, and even her usually bouncy curls seemed to mirror her depression, dangling limply over her shadowed eyes. As she slid a thousand-lire note across the counter, Gemma asked quietly, "How goes it with you these days?"

"I...I think you already know how it is with me," Claretta mumbled forlornly after a brief hesitation.

"Is there anything I can do to help?"

"If we could just talk," Claretta said. "I need advice. My family wants me to go to Zia Anna in Milano, but I—" The man in line behind Gemma coughed impatiently. Claretta blushed and checked her watch. She whispered urgently, "Gemma, in a few moments the post office will close for the day, and as soon as I have put everything away, I will be able to leave. Will you wait for me outside?"

"Of course," she said, pocketing her change, "I'll be in the park across the street. *Arrivederci.*"

Gemma found a shady park bench and sat down to eat her sandwich, alternately nibbling the spicy meat and scattering crumbs to the gray-and-white pigeons that flocked about her feet, their contented cooing a soothing background to her troubled thoughts. Every few seconds she glanced toward the post office, and after a brief interval she saw the final customers leave, and the *aperto* sign in the door was reversed. Soon Claretta would be coming out. Gemma sighed and tossed the remains of her lunch to the greedy birds. She wasn't sure she was overly qualified to give advice on romantic problems, although she had always had enough sense not to become involved with a married man. Apparently the girl's parents wanted to pack her off to some relative, at least until Dieter was safely out of the way, and Gemma wasn't sure that might not be the best idea. She just hoped Claretta wasn't pregnant.

The click of light quick footsteps caught Gemma's attention, and she looked up just in time to see a small blond woman stride briskly to the post-office door and rattle the handle, obviously indignant when it would not open. As the woman turned away in disgust, she peered off into space, squinting against the bright sunlight, and Gemma frowned, certain she had seen her somewhere before. Then the woman's gaze drifted in Gemma's direction, and when she saw her, she brightened visibly. As Gemma watched her march across the street toward the park, with a sinking feeling she recognized her as Gretchen Stahl, Dieter's wife.

The pigeons scattered as Gretchen approached the bench. She planted herself in front of Gemma and said in heavily accented English, "Good afternoon, Frau di Mario. We have not been properly introduced, but I believe you are a friend of my husband." Gemma nodded, and the woman extended her hand stiffly. "*Sehr gut*. Then perhaps you can assist me. I wish to mail letters, but for some reason the post-office doors were locked. There was some kind of sign, but I do not read Italian."

Shaking her head, Gemma said, "*Chiuso* means 'closed,' Frau Stahl."

The woman scowled. "At only two o'clock. That seems most inefficient." Her expression was eloquently scornful, and Gemma felt a sudden rush of dislike as Gretchen sat down beside her on the bench.

Gemma glanced uneasily across the street, alarmed that Claretta might not spot the German woman before she came over to the park. Gemma said brightly, "If you only want to mail your letters, there are mailboxes all over the place. You can't miss them, they're bright red. If you need stamps, there is a *tabaccaio*, a tobacco shop, down the street there, where you can purchase stamps. Just ask for *francobolli*, and they'll know what you want."

Gretchen shook her head. "*Nein*, I shall wait until morning—although I don't know why I bother, since it is likely that we shall be home in Düsseldorf again long before the letters arrive there." She turned to study Gemma indifferently. "My husband tells me you are a sculptor," she said.

"Yes," Gemma answered, beginning to understand why Jordan had taken such an instant aversion to the woman. Despite her obvious youth—she appeared to be younger than Gemma—Gretchen Stahl oozed smug complacency. She reminded Gemma of a staid and disapproving dowager, so certain of her own superiority that anything that varied even slightly from her notion of rightness was immediately and irrevocably dismissed as beneath her notice. Gemma said, "I've enjoyed working with Dieter. He's very talented."

Gretchen clicked her teeth. "Yes," she acknowledged magnanimously, "I suppose he does have a certain flair for sketching or whatever, and I was willing enough to let him indulge that talent for a while. But now it is time for him to return home and get back to his proper work."

"Manufacturing toilets?" Gemma asked, hoping she didn't sound as waspish as she felt.

Apparently she didn't succeed. Gretchen's expression hardened as she regarded Gemma narrowly. "Yes, manufacturing toilets," she echoed, her voice harsh and guttural, "also pipes and sinks and bathtubs, a most practical and profitable and necessary line of work. But perhaps you wouldn't understand that, living in a town where being dusty and dirty seems to be a mark of—"

Gemma wasn't listening. Her gray eyes were fixed on a point across the street, where Claretta stood at the post-office door, her face stricken as she gaped back at Gemma and the woman behind her. Jumping up, Gemma interrupted hastily, "Frau Stahl, I must—" But the woman detained her, catching her wrist in a grip of surprising strength.

Gemma stared at her. Gretchen declared, "I am telling you this so you can relay it to your...your artist friends. Dieter is my husband. He was a good husband, with a responsible position in my father's firm, until he was seduced by this notion of becoming a sculptor.'' Her blue eyes took on a fanatic gleam. "I am not unreasonable, I am not devoid of sensitivity. I know that the best of men get these... these impulses occasionally, and I gave him three months to work it out of his system. But the time is up, and now he must go home with me. It is his duty. And one way or another, he *will* go home, no matter what I have to do to make him do so.''

Gemma tugged on her hand again, and this time Gretchen released her. Murmuring a hasty goodbye, Gemma dashed across the street, only just avoiding being run down by a speeding pickup truck laden with squawking chickens in wire cages. The shaken driver yelled and waved his fist at her, and incensed at the delay, Gemma responded by shouting something she had heard Sergio call one of his workmen who broke a pneumatic hammer. She was unsure of the exact meaning of that phrase, Jordan having refused to translate it for her, but the truck driver blanched and looked startled. He nodded respectfully to Gemma and drove away at a sedate pace. Instantly forgetting him, Gemma sprinted the rest of the way to the post office, but by the time she got there, Claretta had disappeared. Frantically Gemma looked in both directions, her short silvery hair flying as she whirled her head back and forth. There was no sign of the girl.

Upset and depressed, Gemma debated trying to call Claretta, then realized that the Fiore family was unlikely to have a telephone. At last she hailed a cruising taxi and returned to the villa. After informing her obviously delighted mother-in-law that Jordan was still in town with Francesca, Gemma fled to her bedroom, where she flung herself across the bed, exhausted and drained. She felt faintly queasy, the result, she supposed, of nerves topped by a salami sandwich. She was just beginning to relax when she heard Jordan's Ferrari roar up the hill to the villa.

The sound of Francesca's and Beatrice's chatter was drowned out by the reverberation of Jordan's heavy footsteps as he stormed up the long corridors, mounting the steps to each successive level two at a time. When he burst into the bedroom, Gemma lay quiet on the bed, watching him through her lashes, so still that he thought she was asleep. He glanced sharply at her motionless figure, then he turned away, the erect line of his body suddenly drooping with fatigue. He leaned limply against the inside of the door, his long legs sagging, and his head lolled forward into his hands as he rubbed his eyes wearily. His fingers stretched around to massage his nape. Watching him, Gemma sensed a great wave of frustration, almost of despair, washing over him, and the love she felt for him welled up inside her, canceling out her own tiredness. She opened her eyes and sat up on the bed. "Jordan," she said, her husky voice gentle, "what's wrong?"

He jerked upright and scowled blankly. "You're awake."

"Yes, of course," she said. "Now, tell me what's wrong. What's happened? Why are you upset?"

He raked his fingers through his black hair, making it stand up in spikes. "If you hadn't run out on me like that, you'd know what's wrong—although, of course, considering your opinion of my work, you may think it's good news."

Gemma stared, wondering if he could possibly have forgotten already that he ordered her to leave the studio. "What on earth are you talking about?"

He snorted, "The statue, of course, the Madonna. I was right, we did find a deep flaw in the marble, running right through the stone at the point where the face is supposed to be. If I can't work out a new design for the head, the entire project will have to be scrapped."

"Oh, Jordan, I'm so sorry," Gemma cried contritely, anguished by the thought of all the work he had devoted to the statue.

Jordan smiled sardonically and said, "Spare me your condolences, Gemma. At least, if I do have to begin again, it will give me a chance to make my next effort rise above the level of—what did you call it—'sentimental schlock.'" Gemma winced, but before she could say anything, Jordan continued curtly, "Now you'd better get busy packing. We're driving to Florence tonight. We have to see Francesca's father."

CHAPTER TEN

"Tonto capellone!" Sebastian Buscaglia shouted indignantly, waving his cane at the long-haired youth who had just run a red light on his motorcycle, almost knocking down Gemma and the old man as they crossed the street. The cyclist revved his bike and sped away without looking back. "Crazy hippie," Sebastian muttered again, readjusting his white Panama hat that had come askew when he and Gemma jumped out of the way.

Gemma touched Sebastian's arm. "Are you all right?" she asked anxiously, her low voice husky with fright.

"Of course, *cara*," Sebastian laughed, patting her hand reassuringly, but as Gemma studied his seamed face, she wasn't so sure he was telling the truth. For days now Francesca's father had been showing Gemma the sights of Florence, heedless of the crowds and the sweltering heat as he guided her, dazzled, through palaces and churches where every door seemed to open onto vistas of unimaginable splendor, every room was filled with paintings and sculpture she had only previously known through art books. Names sounded in her head like the bells in the tall Campanile: da Vinci, Botticelli, Giotto, Michelangelo.... With the overstimulated confusion of a child at

Christmastime, Gemma had hesitated in front of each new discovery, longing to absorb all the beauty the work had to offer, yet eager to see what would come next. Sebastian had let her set the pace as he viewed her delight with indulgent pleasure, but now Gemma wondered if the effort had been too much for him. He looked very weary.

As they stepped out of the roadway onto the safety of the bustling sidewalk, Gemma, suspecting that Sebastian's masculine vanity would be offended by any hint that he was too old to escort her, said lightly, "Oh, please, I can't keep up with the pace you set! Do you think we could find a café where we could sit down for a while until I catch my breath?"

Sebastian's relief was palpable. He answered gallantly, "Of course, my dear," and directed her toward a crowded café just down the road.

The restaurant appeared packed, but Gemma noticed that a table was somehow found immediately for her and Sebastian, just as she had already noticed that his presence seemed magically to open doors to galleries and shops that were closed to the general public. The frail old man with his dark indomitable eyes had only to hint at some desire, and people fell all over themselves in their rush to do his bidding. Sebastian was in fact what Franco Ricci had once called Jordan in jest—a man whose wealth, power and influence made him an object of fear or at least respect, a *uomo rispettato*.

And yet Gemma liked him. She had not thought she would. As she and Jordan had sped toward Florence on the sweeping *autostrada*, Jordan had told her a little about Francesca's father, about his evolution from grammar-school teacher to Resistance leader to powerful industrialist, with a little dabbling in the black market and organized crime on the side. He had acquired polish and a modicum of respectability by marrying the spinster daughter of a penniless Florentine aristocrat; Jordan suspected that the baron's decaying *palazzo* just off the Via dei Tosinghi had interested Sebastian more than the bride did. When his wife died giving birth to a daughter of remarkable beauty, Sebastian had become a doting father, and for the sake of his child he abandoned his more nefarious activities, although when strikes and ruinous taxation threatened his factories, he did follow the quasi-legal practice of many other large Italian companies and began to contract work out to small groups of craftsmen in remote villages beyond the spidery reach of government control, where people did not mind laboring under sweatshop conditions as long as the pay was steady.

"And thus," Jordan had concluded, "Sebastian prospers—except for his health. In spirit he is as vigorous as ever, but a series of heart attacks in recent years has left him physically weakened, and frankly, I do not think he will survive another." Jordan sighed. "I will be very sorry if Sebastian dies. I've known him all my life. My father was a sentimental idealist, and Sebastian was always a cynical pragmatist, but they were the best of friends, and papa used to say that there was no man better at resolving an impossible situation than Sebastian Buscaglia."

Glancing up from her Campari and soda, Gemma watched Sebastian through her long lashes and thought, *here's an impossible situation for you to resolve: your daughter and I both love the same man—and the fact that he's my husband doesn't seem to make any difference.*

Sebastian toyed with the stem of his wineglass, the last drops of Chianti swirling in the bowl like the tail of a ruby-colored kite. He said, "I thank you for these past few days, Gemma. You have awakened me once more to the beauties of my city." When Gemma looked puzzled, he continued with a wry smile, "I know that most people think of Firenze as sort of an open-air museum, but to those of us who live here, it is a modern city with traffic congestion and industry and all the trappings of contemporary life. We grow bored and blind to the very things that give us stature in the eyes of the rest of the world—it must be twenty years since I last went to the Galleria dell'Accademia to look at the *David*! What a pleasure it has been to see it all anew, and in the company of a young beautiful woman." He paused, watching Gemma closely, then without warning he asked, "Does it bother you to leave Francesca and Giordano alone together, working on new sketches, while the two of us go on our little tours?"

Gemma was unable to control the fiery blush that swept over her face and throat, scorching her with its heat. Remembering her thoughts of only a few seconds before, she wondered if Sebastian could read her mind. Certainly he seemed to have no difficulty interpreting her stricken expression. She choked unconvincingly, "I...I have n-no fear that—"

"Then you ought to have," Sebastian interrupted

shortly. "My lovely but spoiled daughter means to have your husband."

Gemma stared at him. "B-but, if you already knew that, then why did you insist—"

"Because getting the Madonna finished is more important to me than your marriage," he said bluntly, "or my daughter's morals, for that matter. Nothing must interfere with the completion of that statue. Giordano needs to make more sketches, work out a new placement for the head that will avoid the flaw in the marble. The easiest way for him to do this is with Francesca modeling for him. If throwing them together this way creates temptation, rekindles old flames—well, then, Gemma, for your sake I am truly sorry, but you must understand, there is no time to handle things differently."

Gemma stared at him, flabbergasted. "Doesn't it...doesn't it bother you that your daughter is...is pursuing a married man?"

Sebastian shrugged elaborately. "Francesca is a grown woman. She knows the score, as you Americans say, and what that score adds up to is that Giordano is your husband, not hers. She should have married him years ago when she had the chance. But she didn't, and now the best she can hope for is another affair, such as they had when they were adolescents."

His words stabbed at Gemma. "And y-you d-don't mind?" she stammered, flinching.

"Of course I mind!" Sebastian raged, banging his cane on the table with such force that their glasses bounced. His querulous voice rang out over the roar of traffic. "That any child of mine should—" His withered face darkened, and he began to assail Francesca eloquently, his vocabulary surpassing even that of Sergio Carcione. People at adjoining tables turned to stare with frank curiosity, and Gemma wanted to crawl into a dim corner somewhere. Then, just as quickly, Sebastian's fury calmed, and he smiled ironically. "But who am I to condemn her? She is, after all, my daughter. Forgive me, Gemma," he said contritely, noting her feverish cheeks. "You are a bride of only a few weeks, and it must be difficult for you to watch another woman making eyes at your husband."

Gemma paled. His casual attitude baffled her, his bland acceptance of a liaison between Jordan and Francesca as bewildering as it was painful. "Are you suggesting that it would be easier if we had been married longer?" she asked in amazement.

Sebastian shook his head. "No," he agreed wryly, "probably it would not be. Italian men like to pretend that their wives understand about these little...lapses, that they will accept anything so long as the husband returns to home and hearth, but I know that Francesca's mother, may the Blessed Virgin watch over her, never really...." His voice trailed off, and for a fleeting moment his features were furrowed with a sadness that made Gemma wonder if Sebastian had been fonder of his late wife than Jordan had implied. Then just as quickly his expression altered, his dark eyes taking on a ruthless gleam that reminded Gemma forcibly of other stories Jordan had told her about the man. Sebastian said, "I like you, Gemma, and I regret that you may be hurt. But I want the Madonna finished now, and if the cost of its completion is an affair between my daughter and your husband, then we will pay that cost. The statue must come first."

"But why?" Gemma asked urgently, still trying hard to understand. "Why are you in such a hurry that you won't even let Jordan start again with a sound piece of stone? Don't you know that by making him alter his original design, anything he produces will be a compromise, only second-best?"

"Second-best from Giordano di Mario is better than first-best from anyone else," Sebastian intoned piously. He watched Gemma in silence for several minutes. Finally he said gently, "You want a reason, my child? All right, I will give you one. I am an old man, older in health than I am in years, and in spirit, ancient. Soon I will die. When I was younger, I faced death fearlessly, but now I...I am afraid. I think of the good things I have done, and they are so few, especially when weighed against all the other not so good things. I need something to help balance the scales."

His voice grew hoarse, as if he were pleading for her understanding. "When I was convalescing from my second heart attack, I had a lot of time to think about what I could do. Of course, I could give money to charity, but money has no meaning, and as quickly as it is given, it vanishes. I needed something that would last, something of real value. So I thought of my old *compagno d'armi* di Mario, and the time we were ambushed by a German patrol as we led a downed pilot back to the American lines. My friend was gravely wounded. He told me to leave him behind, but instead I carried him for miles slung over

my shoulders—oh, to be so strong again. That was
one of my few good deeds, saving his life so that he
could survive the war and father a son who would
grow up to become a great artist. Then I said to
myself, 'Of course, I will ask Giordano to carve a
Madonna, like the masters who went before him.' At
first he said he did not want to. 'Religious subjects
are not my style' is the way he phrased it, if I remember correctly. But I reminded him of his father
and the war, and at last he gave in, as I knew he
would.''

An offer he couldn't refuse, Gemma recalled suddenly. She had thought Jordan was talking about
money.

Sebastian concluded, ''Now for me he makes a
statue of great reverence and beauty, with my lovely
Francesca as the model, and before I die I will give it
to a church so that people will admire it long after I
am gone.''

Gemma nodded silently, but she was deeply troubled. She could sympathize with Sebastian's desire to
buy his way into heaven, even if she didn't agree with
his motives or his theology. Since the beginning of
time, men had tried to propitiate the gods with lavish
gifts, and she knew that many of the most revered
works of art in Florence had nothing to do with
piety, but only with the vanity of the artist's patron.
Like those wealthy men in centuries past, Sebastian
had on a whim demanded that Jordan carve him a
Madonna, and Jordan had agreed reluctantly, co-
erced not by money but by a debt of much longer
standing, the fact that once Sebastian had saved Jordan's father's life. But Jordan had proceeded with

difficulty, acutely aware that his talents were no more suited to the subject of the Holy Mother than Francesca was an appropriate model, and now Sebastian was compounding the problem by insisting that Jordan finish the statue haphazardly.

Seeing her anxious expression, Sebastian queried, "You do understand, don't you, Gemma? I can't afford to wait the months it would take to complete a new statue. The Madonna must be finished soon, because. . . because I haven't much time left."

Gemma forced a smile as she reached across the table to pat the man's gnarled hand. "I hope you live forever, Sebastian," she said huskily.

"With Giordano's help, perhaps I shall," he sighed, and his obvious sincerity made Gemma feel jaded and cynical.

"I. . .I THINK I'LL GO on to bed now," Gemma ventured.

Jordan glanced up from his conversation with Sebastian and Francesca and frowned at Gemma, his black eyes surveying her curiously, observing the weary slump of her slender body in her long blue dress. "Isn't it a little early to be retiring?"

"I really am tired, Jordan," she said quietly. "I think the heat must be getting to me." Either the heat, she added silently, or the sight of her husband sitting beside Francesca on the florid velvet settee, thighs touching, their dark heads bent toward each other, two vital passionate creatures, so incredibly handsome, so *right* together.

Scowling, Jordan nodded. "Yes, you do look rather washed-out."

"Young people—no stamina!" Sebastian chuckled, adding kindly, "I can tell that I've been too much for you. Get some rest, and I promise that tomorrow we will set a slower pace. *Buona notte, cara.*"

"Good night," Gemma murmured, and she turned to mount the sweeping gilt-carved staircase that led to the second floor of the old *palazzo*.

Just as she reached the halfway point, Francesca suddenly jumped up from the sofa and cried archly, "Oh, forgive me, I am forgetting my duties as a hostess! I will come with you, Gemma, and see that you are settled."

With a sinking feeling Gemma waited as the other woman hurried up the steps. Even the flowing lines of her hostess gown could not disguise the provocative sway of her voluptuous body. Out of the corner of her eye Gemma noticed that Jordan seemed to be watching Francesca's progress, as well. Just for an instant she wistfully envisioned the model tripping and landing at the foot of the stairs on that round bottom of hers, but, Gemma had to admit, the odds were against such a grimly satisfying accident taking place. Francesca moved with a natural agility heightened by all the years she had spent prancing on runways or posing in front of cameras. When she reached Gemma, she caught her arm and gushed, "I know I have neglected you these past few days, but Giordano and I have been so busy. You must tell me if there is anything you need."

"Everything is fine," Gemma said stiffly. "Your home is lovely." In point of fact, Gemma found Palazzo Buscaglia atrocious and rather decadent.

After the spare understated elegance of Villa Sogno Dolce, the lush interior of the Florentine mansion, with its ornamented ceilings and overabundant mirrors, seemed to Gemma to epitomize the very worst of rococo architecture and decoration, all gilt and flourish. At best she might call the house "interesting," but privately she thought it looked like an eighteenth-century brothel.

Francesca guided Gemma into the vast bedroom she and Jordan shared, a room noteworthy for its two large—but very separate—beds. Noting the way Francesca's eyes flicked over the pristine coverlets, Gemma wondered suddenly if the obsequious chambermaid had been filing daily reports about which beds had rumpled sheets; she found a certain smug pleasure in the fact that to date only the bed nearest the bathroom had been used at all, even if since coming to Florence, she and Jordan had done no more each night than kiss casually and fall asleep back to back. Aloud, Gemma said, "It was kind of you to see me to my room, Francesca, but if you don't mind, I'd like to be alone now. I'll take a couple of aspirins and—"

Francesca shook her head, and a long strand of blue black hair toppled into her eyes. As she brushed it aside she said, "No, I can't go yet. There's something I...I want to show you." From out of a hidden pocket in her long hostess gown Francesca pulled a crumpled sheet of drawing paper and offered it to Gemma. Gemma did not move. Francesca shook the paper slightly. "Here," she insisted, "you must look at this. It's time you found out what goes on between Giordano and me when we are alone."

She caught one of Gemma's suddenly icy hands and pressed the paper into her fingers.

Noting Francesca's heightened color, Gemma steeled herself as she slowly unfolded the smudged drawing, but even so, she was unprepared for the shocking impact of the drawing. She stared numbly at it for endless seconds, her blood cold, her brain only partially functional. At one level her mind remarked the way Jordan's extraordinary talent shone even in what had obviously been merely a quick sketch, how with but a few lines of sepia ink he had delineated the naked entwined bodies in all the heat of their coupling, a moment of passion captured in amber. As Gemma mentally saluted the artistry of the drawing, at another level she cringed, aware of Francesca's dark eyes watching expectantly, avidly for her pained response. Gemma knew she would die rather than give the other woman any satisfaction. With quiet resolution she refolded the paper into a neat square and handed it back. She said huskily, "I have seen erotic drawings before, you know. Most great artists do at least a few of them."

Francesca blinked, obviously surprised by Gemma's apparent lack of reaction, but after a moment she persisted heavily, "But have you ever before seen such a picture of your husband with another woman?"

My dear, you have about as much finesse as a bludgeon, Gemma judged acidly, and that thought helped keep her voice steady as she admitted, "No, that was a first."

She fell silent again, her face blank behind a pasted-on smile, and her composure seemed to rattle the other woman. Francesca's manicured hands began to semaphore her bafflement. "How can you be so calm?" she demanded. "What kind of woman are you? Have you no pride? If you know that while you and my father play tourist, Giordano and I are—how can you let him climb into your bed at night, after...after—"

Gemma said stiffly, "What happens between Jordan and me is none of your business, Francesca. I'm not about to discuss it with you or anyone else. Now, please, if you don't mind, I am very tired."

She nodded toward the door, and after a second Francesca turned to leave. Just as she touched the doorknob, she glanced back, her sleek black hair flowing over her shoulder. Scowling, she muttered, "I do not understand you at all, Gemma. If Giordano were my husband—"

"But he's not your husband," Gemma said quietly. "He's mine." She stood tall and unassailable, armored by her pride, until Francesca departed.

The instant the door closed, Gemma's self-possession vanished, and she collapsed against the bedpost, her knees suddenly rubbery. With great care she settled herself onto the edge of the bed, still clutching at the heavily carved upright, sure that if she released her convulsive grip, her limp body would slide off the silky coverlet, and she would land in a sad little heap on the floor. She closed her eyes slowly, then quickly opened them again, unable to face the image seared into the gray blankness behind her lids, that explicit sketch of Jordan and Francesca.... Oh, damn him, damn him, how could he *dare* to draw such a thing, commit his most intimate secrets to paper that way, where they could be seen by the world, by his wife? And to do it at the same time he was supposed to be working on.... Gemma flung herself across the bed and began to sob.

Her face pressed deep into a pillow, her ears filled with her own muffled anguish, Gemma did not hear the hall door open again, nor was she aware of Jordan's presence in the room until he strode to the bed and dropped onto the mattress beside her, gathering her into his strong arms. "For God's sake, Gemma," he exclaimed with evident concern, turning up her face so that he could study her tearstained features intently, "what's wrong?" She stared at him with wide pain-filled eyes. She wondered how he managed to look so worried about her, when only hours before, he and Francesca.... When she did not answer, he asked urgently, "Are you ill?"

She shook her head unconvincingly and stammered, "I'm...I'm all right. It's just that I feel...I feel...." Choking weakly on her own tears, she couldn't continue.

Jordan scowled, still intent on her health. Fingering the fragile bones of her shoulder, he said flatly, "No, you're not all right. You're very pale, and I think you've lost weight, something you can hardly afford to do. It must be a reaction to the heat. I'm sure it can't be this hot or this humid in Colorado, and you haven't yet learned to pace yourself. Heat exhaustion can be insidious. You may need a doctor."

Gemma shook her head again. "No, I...I just need some rest." Even the humiliating knowledge of his betrayal could not prevent the instant response his touch always aroused in her, and she was hotly ashamed of the way her body was reacting, curving against him with unwitting invitation.

Solicitously Jordan drew her closer, reaching around to unzip her dress. His fingers traced along her spine, brushing aside the loosened fabric of her gown, and wherever they touched her naked skin, she began to tingle. He slid the dress down over her arms, baring her to the waist, except for the wispy scrap of lace that passed for a bra, and his clever hands quickly disposed of that, too. Tensing, Gemma shivered.

"Relax, darling," Jordan murmured against her shoulder, his lips starting to tease the sensitive hollows of her throat. He lay down beside her and moved still closer, one long leg flung across her to trap her beneath him.

"Jordan, don't," Gemma gasped, her voice thin and unconvincing as she tried not to react to the tickling caress of his warm breath, the seductive weight of his body. To her dismay she felt her breasts lifting and firming, and she knew he was as aware of her increasing arousal as she was of his. "Please don't," she repeated in quavering tones, certain she would despise herself if she let him take her now after what Francesca had told her.

He raised his head to stare at her, and his eyes were so black that the line of gold rimming the irises gleamed like the corona surrounding a total eclipse. He said thickly, "Gemma, it's been ages."

"And whose fault is that?" she couldn't help crying.

He lifted himself up on one elbow and surveyed her stricken features, frowning. After a moment he sighed, "My fault, I suppose. It wasn't personal, I assure you. It's just that when I get involved in a project, I tend to forget about everyone and everything except my work."

Liar, she thought with bitter anguish as she gazed upward into his handsome face, wanting him, loving him, hating him.... *You never forgot about Francesca!* Aloud, she demanded, "Am I supposed to be flattered that after ignoring me—'for ages,' you said—you finally happened to remember that you have a wife?"

"What do you mean?" he asked warily.

By now Gemma was too overwrought to care what she said or how she said it. Blinking hard, she accused, "You're the most fickle man I've ever known. This is just a game to you. I rejected you, so you made me marry you, you made me want you. Oh, yes, I admit that I want you, just the way you told me I would. And now that I'm no longer a challenge, you've gone back to your old—interests. All these past nights, you on your side of the bed, me on mine, and you never reached out, you never—" She choked on the lump rising in her throat as she remembered the drawing, proof that his days had not been spent so chastely. With an effort she forced out the last vitriolic words. "I don't know why you've suddenly decided you want to sleep with me now; I would have thought Francesca was more than willing. But if she's not, that's just too bad. I will not let you use me, Jordan. I will not let you take me for no better reason than that your mistress has turned coy!"

He stared at her, his face a dark impenetrable mask. His eyes raked over her slender figure from her shining hair to her toes, lingering for the merest fraction of a second at her bared torso or the blue dress bunched around her hips. He closed his eyes, and Gemma saw a tremor of some painful emotion shake him visibly. When he lifted his almost effeminately long lashes again, his expression was grim, but when he spoke, his tone was dry, conversational. "'Use,' 'take'? Those are harsh words, Gemma. Do they really describe what happens when I touch you? Do you honestly believe I regard you as an object, some kind of plaything I stroke and fondle when there's nothing better to do?" A large hand reached out to close over her left breast, and he began to toy absently with the nipple, making it come hard and alive under his caressing fingertips. Gemma caught her breath, trying unsuccessfully to control her reaction, and she could feel hot mortifying color flood over her. Jordan watched the progress of that blush with impersonal curiosity. After a moment he continued, "Well, perhaps you're right: I do 'take' you—but only because you never *give* anything. You could have reached across the bed as readily as I, taken me into your arms, but that idea never occurred to you, did it? No, of course not, that would have meant sacrificing a little of that overweening pride of yours, and you would never do that, would you, Gemma?" He paused again, gazing down at the hand that cupped her small breast, swarthy against the creamy whiteness of her skin. He said, "I can feel your heartbeat. Right now it's pounding, in fact, and to feel it, you'd think it was made of warm vital human tissue—but it's not. Your heart is stone, virgin stone, untouched by anyone, and frankly, *cara mia*—" here he pulled his hand away from her and with one lithe sweeping movement sat up on the bed "—no matter how much you grudgingly admit that you may want me, from now on I think your body can stay untouched, as well."

And before the force of his rejection, uttered in a quiet controlled voice, could penetrate Gemma's confused mind, Jordan swung his long legs around so that his feet touched the floor. She watched helplessly as he stalked across the room to the pristine shelter of the other empty bed.

BY THE TIME THEY RETURNED to Pietrasanta, Gemma knew that their relationship had deteriorated completely. No longer bound even by the tenuous thread of physical desire, the marriage had fallen to shreds. In the presence of other people, Jordan treated Gemma with careful civility, but alone in their room, he ignored her. She found herself actually looking forward to seeing Villa Sogno Dolce and her mother-in-law again. Beatrice's candid dislike at least had the virtue of being personal.

When they finally left Florence, Gemma discovered rather to her surprise that what she missed most was Sebastian. The city's beauty was forever tainted in her mind as the setting for the breakup of her marriage—when Jordan abandoned her bed, she knew beyond any doubt that Francesca had won— but the old man had been a friend. Despite his admittedly shady past, she found him a sort of primitive innocent who harked back to a less complicated era, one untroubled by degrees of morality. A few centuries earlier, Sebastian would have been one of those

feudal barons who climbed to power over the bodies
of his enemies, advancing himself and his family by
whatever means were necessary, and in the end seeking atonement for any incidental sins by giving lavish
gifts to the Church. Sebastian was selfish, pragmatic
and expedient, but unlike his daughter, he was not
spiteful or devious, and Gemma liked him. She
thought that in other circumstances, if he had not
been so obsessed with the Madonna, he would have
been someone she could have turned to for help.

As it was, Gemma did not confide in Sebastian,
and she wondered if he was aware of the estrange-
ment between her and Jordan. More than once as
they had sat together in the salon of the *palazzo*,
physically close and yet light-years apart, she had
noticed the old man watching them with a puzzled
frown. Francesca knew, of course. Her sharp eyes
had picked up the signals at once. Gemma couldn't
bring herself to believe that Jordan would actually
tell his mistress that he was no longer sleeping with
his wife, but the chambermaid had most likely reported that both beds in the guest suite were now being used each night. At any rate, whenever Francesca
looked at Gemma, her beautiful face was filled with
smug supercilious triumph, and sometimes Gemma
thought that it was only her regard for Sebastian that
kept her from clawing the woman's eyes out during
the final days in Florence.

When the Ferrari was at last speeding toward
Pietrasanta again, Gemma, in no mood for scenery,
had leaned her silvery head back against the cush-
ioned headrest, her eyes closed wearily as she
occupied her time by wondering what new sleeping

arrangements, if any, would be made when she and Jordan reached his home. She hoped that he didn't intend for them to continue to share the king-size bed in the master suite. His desire for her had apparently vanished so completely that it would not trouble him to lie chastely alongside her each night, but Gemma, who still ached with longing whenever she looked at him, thought she would shrivel up and die if exposed to such a blatant display of his indifference. Maybe she ought to offer to move into the bedroom that Beatrice had vacated. She could just hear what her mother-in-law would have to say on that subject.

More to ease her mind than to break the silence, Gemma leaned over and switched on the stereo car radio. A punk-rock group blared out, filling the interior of the Ferrari with its dissonance, and she quickly pressed the tuning buttons until she found a news broadcast, the radio announcer's voice bland and reassuring. Gemma began to relax. Then the announcer casually mentioned the date, and suddenly all petty concerns were wiped out of Gemma's mind. With grave foreboding she counted back mentally over the past weeks to that frantic honeymoon in Pisa, when Jordan's sexual mastery had blinded her to consideration of anything but the unprecedented sensations he aroused in her. She counted the days again, and yet again, but each time they added up to the same answer. With a groan of dismay Gemma realized that she must be pregnant.

Jordan heard the sound and glanced at her sharply. "Are you all right?" he asked, scowling.

"Yes, of course," Gemma murmured automatically, and with a shrug he returned his attention to the road. Surreptitiously she watched him, his long frame folded behind the steering wheel, his dark features grimly intent as he guided the sleek red sports car around the steeply banked curves of the *autostrada*. Gemma shivered. She could almost feel the wall of icy reserve between them. Jordan was a stranger, aloof and brooding, utterly divorced from the ruthless passionate lover who had swept her along in the whirlwind of his desire since their marriage; even less did he remind her of the man who had touched her with such tenderness and consideration on their wedding night—the one whom she had driven away with her ill-chosen words. Gemma shivered again, clutching her thin arms across her abdomen in an unconsciously protective gesture, as if she were warding off a blow. A child grew inside her, offspring of this cold stranger, and she didn't know what she was going to do about it.

SHE FELT EVEN MORE UNCERTAIN the following day after she had seen a doctor. During the afternoon siesta, while Jordan went over his new sketches with Sergio, Gemma quietly excused herself and walked to the hospital, where she consulted the physician who had attended Caroline. After reproving Gemma for her poor color and the weight she had lost since he last saw her, the man quickly confirmed her suspicions: her baby was due late the following April—assuming, he added bluntly, that she was able to carry it full term. "You are too high-strung, *signora*," he said with weary impatience, "like an overbred race horse, all nerve and no stamina. Add to that your rather fragile build, especially those narrow hips, and the odds against your having this child increase dramatically.'' Gemma said nothing, but her expression was eloquent. The doctor added quickly, ''I assure you I am not saying that it will be *impossible* for you to have your baby, *signora*, you must understand that. Many women in much poorer condition give birth to healthy infants. What I am telling you is that you must *want* your child—''

''I do,'' Gemma insisted huskily with absolute certainty. Out of all the chaotic thoughts that had tumbled around in her mind for the past twenty-four hours, this one fact had emerged: she wanted this baby. When the end of this farcical marriage came, as she knew it soon must, when Jordan finally recovered from the temporary madness that had made him want to possess her, at least she would have his child, a living reminder of those fleeting halcyon days when she had loved and—after a fashion—been loved in return. She repeated, ''More than anything in the world, I want to have this baby.''

''Bene,'' the doctor said, ''I'm glad to hear that. Nowadays....'' After chiding her for the foolish way she had let her nerves deplete her strength, he began to outline a strict regimen of diet and vitamins. ''And rest,'' he continued. ''You must not tax yourself in any way. Your work at the studio must cease immediately.''

Gemma winced at the thought of Jordan's likely reaction if she told him she could no longer study with Sergio. The art lessons were the only mutual interest they had left. She said, ''I'm still just using clay. That's hardly strenuous.''

The doctor nodded wryly. ''Yes, but it has been

my experience with you artists that when you are working, you tend to forget all about meals and rest and any consideration of your own well-being.''

"I promise I'll be careful," Gemma said.

The doctor sighed. "Very well... but just stay away from the air hammers!''

"Of course," Gemma said, smiling. Then her smile faded quickly as she forced herself to ask one last question. "*Dottore*, what about travel? There is a... possibility... that I might go back to America to... to see my family.''

"I wouldn't advise it," the doctor said sternly. "Even plane travel can be extremely tiring. You would be far better off to wait until afterward when you can show your *bambino* to his proud grandparents.'' He saw the stricken look on Gemma's face, and his tone softened. He said gently, "Of course, I understand, this is your first child, and it is natural that you want to be with your mother. Perhaps in the second trimester, if everything goes well....''

"I see," Gemma said, rising to leave. "*Grazie, dottore*, you've been very kind.''

As she reached the door, the doctor called out, "*Signora*, one last thing." Gemma halted, puzzled. He said with a grimace, "This is something I sincerely regret having to tell a new bride, but I think, for both your sake and that of the child, that it would be better if, during the next few weeks, you and your husband refrained from—''

"That won't be a problem," Gemma muttered, blushing at the doctor's astonished expression, and before he could pursue the point, she ducked out of the room.

WHEN SHE RETURNED to the studio, she found that Jordan and Sergio had put aside their work and were sitting at a rough table, eating massive slabs of garlic sausage between slices of coarse chewy bread. Sergio offered a sandwich to Gemma, and she declined with a wan smile, hoping she wouldn't be sick. Jordan frowned at her. "Where have you been?" he asked.

Gemma did not dare look at him, sure he could read her secret in her face. Didn't people always say you were able to tell by a woman's eyes? And just what would Jordan think if he found out, she wondered. He'd be... he'd be *surprised*, she knew, the corners of her mouth curling at the ironic inadequacy of the word. The prospect of children had never figured in this peculiar marriage of convenience that he had forced upon her. Perhaps he would be angry; he might even blame her for failing to take adequate precautions—and that would be downright unfair, she thought resentfully, considering the way he had swooped her off to Pisa. During the first days following their wedding she had had no time to even think about the possible consequences of the driving passion he had shown her.

But... but maybe she had it all wrong, Gemma thought suddenly, with a glimmer of hope. Maybe Jordan wouldn't be angry at all. Italians were supposed to like children. Gemma had heard that Italian marriages were so stable not just because divorce was difficult, but also because even the most flagrant playboys still honored the mother of their children. If she gave Jordan a child, perhaps she would stand a chance against Francesca. It wasn't exactly the way she would prefer to hold him, but if he loved her baby, maybe in time he would learn to love her, as well.

Jordan asked again, "Gemma, where have you been?"

She looked up at him through her lashes. She wanted to tell him, but not here, not in front of Sergio. She would do it tonight in their bedroom before he had a chance to disappear into the secret refuge of his private studio as he had done the evening before. She stammered, "I...I just went for a walk. I wanted some fresh air." He seemed to note the quaver in her voice, the flush on her cheeks, and he regarded her suspiciously. Quickly Gemma turned to Sergio and asked with elaborate unconcern, "Where's Dieter? I haven't seen him all day."

The older man gulped the dregs of the harsh red wine he drank and wiped his mouth with the back of his hand. "That's right, I guess you two don't know yet: while you were in Firenze, Stahl went back to Germany."

"What?" Gemma exclaimed, staring. A picture formed instantly in her mind: Dieter and Claretta kissing passionately in the hallway of the *pensione*. Gretchen Stahl had said she meant to get her husband back, but Gemma couldn't believe he would have left Italy willingly. "Why did he go?" she asked helplessly. "He was happy here."

Raising his palms as if in supplication to the heavens, Sergio said, "His wife told him she was pregnant."

Gemma whitened. Jordan did not seem aware of her sudden loss of color. As he pulled the wine bottle across the table to him, he quirked one dark eyebrow. "That's quick work," he muttered skeptically, "or are we supposed to believe that she's been carrying around this little surprise since before he left Germany in the first place?"

Sergio shrugged. "What we believe isn't important. The only thing that matters is that young Gretchen has managed to convince her husband she's telling the truth, and as a result he has left his studies and returned to Düsseldorf to her papa's company. Presumably he'll make a steady income selling toilets and bidets. He thinks it's his duty."

"Duty?" Jordan snorted indignantly, banging his glass on the table. He swore violently. "Dieter's duty was to his art! The man has *talent*!"

Gemma interjected weakly, "But, Jordan, if Gretchen really is expecting a—"

Jordan growled, "So what if his stupid wife is pregnant? Any bitch can have pups. It's artists who are rare!"

With a sinking heart Gemma subsided into her chair, clinging to the edge of the hard seat to keep from sliding limply onto the chip-covered floor. She knew now that she could never tell Jordan about the baby.

CHAPTER ELEVEN

"JUST A MOMENT, GEMMA," Claretta said as Gemma slipped her stamps and wallet back into her shoulder bag, "I spotted a letter for you in this morning's mail. If I can just find it. . . ." She rummaged behind the counter and after a few seconds produced a vivid pink envelope decorated with bright flowers.

Gemma glanced at it in surprise, noting the childishly round back-slanted handwriting and the Roman postmark. She exclaimed with pleasure, "It must be from Caroline. I didn't expect her to have time to write." She looked up again and smiled at Claretta. "You met Caroline, didn't you?"

The girl did not return the smile. Her usually ebullient features were subdued and shuttered as she murmured quietly, "*Si*. The day the two of you arrived at the *pensione*, I was there with. . .with. . . ." Her voice died away in a sigh of deep depression.

Gemma watched compassionately, regretting her unthinking words. Claretta's pain was palpable, and she certainly needed no tactless reminders of Dieter. With real concern Gemma asked, "Claretta, do you know what you will do now?"

The girl glanced back over her shoulder to make sure that her supervisor was not listening, then, shrugging, she said tonelessly, "My family still want me to go to my aunt's home in Milano. There is a young man there, a nephew of Zia Anna, and they would like us to meet.''

Gemma frowned, aware that in Italy such an arranged meeting was tantamount to an engagement. "Is this what you want?" she persisted.

Suddenly Claretta's head was bent so that only her black curls were visible, shimmering as if she trembled with fierce emotion. She stammered brokenly, "Gemma, *per favore*, don't...don't.... If I had listened to my parents in the first place.... My family knows his, and he has a good job at the Alfa Romeo factory." When she lifted her chin again, her dark eyes gleamed with unshed tears. "Please," she pleaded huskily, "I...I can't talk. My boss is watching." She straightened her shoulders in abrupt dismissal and, sniffing, flashed a bleary smile at the patron who stood in line behind Gemma.

Gemma left the post office deeply troubled, regretfully aware that she had not helped Claretta at all; by her well-meaning nosiness she might, in fact, have increased the girl's suffering. Impatiently she asked herself why the hell she thought she of all people was qualified to give advice to the lovelorn.

She trudged along the sidewalk, winding her way back toward Sergio's place. Part of her mind observed absently that the narrow streets were much less crowded than they had been only weeks ago, and as she passed the cubbyhole-sized studios, the din of air hammers was less pronounced. Singly and in groups the summer artists were leaving Pietrasanta to return to the "real" world. Gemma wondered with a pang how soon it would be before she joined the migration. For almost a month now she had delayed making a decision. She had denied the need for hurry, falling back on the excuse of her art studies, when, in fact, she knew that the only reason she clung so abjectly to a failed marriage was because hell with Jordan was still somehow preferable to hell without him. But time was running out. If she did not want Jordan to know about the baby, she could not wait much longer; already she had noticed Beatrice looking at her with a thoughtful expression, and it had suddenly occurred to Gemma that her husband's mother, with her medical training, would probably spot the signs of pregnancy long before Jordan did. And, she realized with a shudder, while Beatrice had never pretended to like Gemma, it was entirely possible that she would try to prevent her unborn grandchild from being taken to the United States, especially since she had never seen her other grandchildren who already lived there. Gemma had no idea of the finer points of law in this case, but she was afraid that because she was the wife of an Italian national, the di Marios might be able to have her visa canceled.

And there was another, even more important consideration now. That morning, although Gemma had used the post office as an excuse to leave work for a few minutes, her real destination had been the hospital, for a checkup. There the doctor had been scathingly direct, with a bluntness that made her cringe: the pregnancy was not progressing normally, and unless Gemma took better care of herself, she was going to lose her baby. Even Gemma's insistence that she had been taking her vitamins religiously and had avoided strenuous activity did not placate the doctor. He said, "All the medication in the world will not make up for a troubled spirit, *signora*. Look at you, thin as a rake! You are consuming yourself with nervousness, and that cannot continue. Now, more than at any other time in your life, you ought to be calm and serene, filled with the wonder of the miracle of what is happening inside your body."

Serene, Gemma thought wildly, *how can I be serene when my husband flaunts his mistress openly, and his mother despises me?* Aloud she said, "Such peace of mind is not always possible, *dottore*."

The man regarded her sadly, with tired eyes that had long ago lost all illusions. "As bad as that?" he asked quietly.

Gemma nodded. "I'm afraid so." While the man clucked his tongue regretfully, she framed her next question. *"Dottore,"* she ventured, "some time ago I mentioned that I...I might want to leave Italy to...to see my family. Will you give me permission to do so now?"

Grimacing, he folded his hands together into a church and mashed his nose against the steeple, lost in thought. At last he let his breath out with a hiss and said, "Ordinarily, *signora*, I would say no without hesitation, but in this case.... I am not a priest, I do not make moral judgments; my only concern is your health and that of your child. And since Pietrasanta obviously does not agree with you, I think there is probably less risk in your going back to America than there would be if you stayed here."

"I see," Gemma murmured. She tucked her new prescriptions into her handbag and stood up. She was aware that a momentous decision had just been made for her, but strangely she felt nothing, neither joy nor sadness, relief nor distress. She was numb. Conscious of the doctor's intense scrutiny, she shaped her small mouth into a smile and said, "*Grazie*, you've been very understanding, very kind. I...I'll be in touch with you again before I go."

"Good. If you like, *signora*, I can write up a report for you to give to your physician in—where did you say you came from?"

"Colorado."

The doctor puzzled a second, then brightened. With an air of accomplishment, he exclaimed, "Ah, yes, Colorado. Yellowstone Park, right?"

Thinking of the national monument in Wyoming, Gemma started to correct him, then she halted. "Right," she said, "it will be good to see it again. *Addio, dottore.*" With a wave of her hand, she left the office.

WHEN SHE RETURNED to the studio, Jordan was alone. Sergio and his crew had departed en masse for a near-by bar to celebrate Italy's victory over Belgium in the soccer finals, and Jordan sat in silence in the private workroom, drinking strong bitter coffee. He was leaning far back in a straight wooden chair, balancing on two legs, his feet propped on the edge of the pallet that supported the marble Madonna. From the doorway Gemma watched him in silence for a moment, seeing with a pang all the aching discontent that scored his tired face as he stared at the near-finished statue. She heard him murmur plaintively in Italian, "Why can't I make it work the way it does in my mind?"

The artist in Gemma longed to reach out to him to soothe his distress, but the woman in her knew that she could not. Her decision was already made. Jordan did not want her or her baby; any overtures from her now would only serve to embarrass him. Nor could they delay the moment when she had to leave. Better to remain aloof and keep what little dignity she had left. "Jordan," she called quietly, coolly.

He jerked his dark head around in surprise, eyeing her intently, but when he spoke, his deep voice was polite and impersonal. "Oh, hello," he said as he scraped back his chair and stood up. "You were gone a long time. Anything of interest at the post office?"

"There was a letter from Caroline," Gemma said. "I haven't had a chance to read it yet." She unfolded the flowery stationery and scanned the contents of the note: Caroline was fine, Rome was dreamy, and she was having a wonderful time with mama and Dave. She hated the fact that in a few days she would have to leave Italy to go back home to get ready for— ugh—school again. Mama and Dave said she ought to at least give college a try before she made up her mind to quit altogether. She sent her love to Gemma and Jordan, and if they should happen to run into Franco, they should tell him she said *ciao*. Mama and Dave sent their regards, too.

Watching Gemma, Jordan inquired, "So how is our patient doing these days?"

"Very well, apparently. She says she got pinched at the Trevi Fountain."

"The ultimate compliment from an Italian male," Jordan drawled as Gemma passed the letter to him. "I hope she appreciated it." As he read the note, he glanced at Gemma with hooded eyes, his expression guarded. "I get the impression," he commented casually, "that Blanchard and Mrs. Somerville are embarking on a beautiful friendship."

Gemma agreed, "Yes, that's what I thought, too, from the way Caroline keeps coupling their names."

"Are you going to follow them?" Jordan demanded harshly.

Baffled, Gemma stared at him. "What do you mean?"

Jordan grated, "Ever since we married, you have held over me the threat that you would leave Italy the instant Caroline was 'safely' out of my reach. *Cristo*, that you could actually think I would hurt that silly child." He rattled the pages like a saber. "Well, by now the girl and her mother and your erstwhile fiancé are no doubt back in the United States once more, so I'm asking you bluntly, Gemma: Do you plan to go, also?"

Gemma sank weakly into a chair. She dropped her purse and plaited her slim fingers into a knot of anxiety. As she gazed at them, she wondered why she wasn't laughing hysterically at the irony of the situation. For weeks she had been wondering how she could leave Jordan without arousing suspicion about the baby, what excuse she could use—and here he was, telling her that all along he had expected her to go! To Gemma, Jordan's implied blackmail and her own frenzied resistance to their marriage now seemed like fragments of some bizarre and half-forgotten fantasy, memories without substance when compared to the painful reality of her unrequited love for her husband.

At her silence Jordan repeated irritably, "Gemma, I refuse to live any longer like Damocles with a sword over my head, so I want you to tell me now: Do you intend to return to Colorado?"

His persistence puzzled her. She wondered why he was suddenly forcing the issue. Then she realized with a sinking heart that Francesca must be pressuring him to make an end to this sham of a marriage. For the past month the model had been steaming into Pietrasanta with the regularity of a commuter train on the flimsiest of excuses, ostensibly to help the progress of the statue "in any possible way," but actually, Gemma was sure, because she wanted to make certain there was no attempted reconciliation between her lover and his wife. As if there had been any chance of that.

For a fraction of a second Gemma knew a flash of anger and resentment; Jordan was the one who wanted out of the marriage, and she didn't see why she should have to be the one to leave, to make it easy for him. Then just as quickly, she acknowledged that she had too much pride to stay where she was obviously not wanted. Besides, there was the baby to be considered. She looked up at Jordan again, the longing in her gray eyes veiled by her thick lashes. Oh, God, she loved him so much, and to him she had never been more than a convenient body, desirable only because he happened to consider her a promising art student. When Gemma spoke, her husky voice was quiet, and each word stabbed her like a chisel gouging out the stone heart Jordan had once accused her of having. She said, "I . . . I do think it will be better for everyone if I go home soon."

"I see," he murmured heavily, nodding, his expression inscrutable. Gemma watched his tense powerful body slump with—with what, relief—as he leaned back against the statue. He flexed his long scarred fingers as if they ached, and when he discovered a new nick in his dark skin, he sucked on it absently. After a moment he inquired in neutral tones, "I suppose you'll want to leave as soon as possible?"

Like a hotel clerk hinting he wants the room keys back, Gemma thought indignantly, but she forced herself to sound as unconcerned as Jordan. "If. . . if I may," she agreed. He nodded again before lapsing into a strained silence, and she gazed at him, her thoughts ironic and uncomfortable. In another life they had married, made love and started a child together. Funny to think that the only reason she had considered marrying Dave Blanchard, whom she had known for years, was because she wanted children, but it had been this taciturn stranger who gave her her baby, and now she had to hide it from him.

Suddenly on the other side of the partition, the main room of the studio was filled with noise and male bantering as Carcione's work crew returned from their break. Gemma could hear Sergio's voice grow louder as he approached. Jordan heard him, too, pausing on the other side of the door to give instructions to one of the men, and before Sergio could enter the smaller room, Jordan asked quickly, "Gemma, I know you're in a hurry to. . .to leave Pietrasanta, but would you do me one favor?" The tentative uncertainty in his voice bewildered her, and she waited curiously for him to continue. He asked huskily, "Will you please stay until the Madonna is completed? It shouldn't be much longer now, and since you've seen the work almost from its inception, I'd...I'd like you to be able to observe the final steps."

"You want me to stay because of the statue?" Gemma echoed, gasping at his callousness.

"Yes," Jordan said. "And of course, Sebastian will be very disappointed if you miss the dedication."

She turned away, all hope crushed. She thought wryly, wistfully, that she would have done almost anything at all to stay with Jordan. She would have sold her soul if in exchange her husband had turned to her suddenly and begged her to stay because he needed her at his side. But apparently the market for bruised and battered souls was in a recession. When Jordan asked her to linger awhile longer in Italy, it was as always only his art that concerned him, that and courtesy to Francesca's father, and somehow she didn't think Sebastian's daughter would appreciate that act of politeness.

Although she admitted with bitter humor that spiting Francesca might almost justify the pain of living with Jordan's indifference, still her amusement faded before a sardonic chuckle could force its way through her constricted throat. She couldn't stay longer, no matter how appealing the idea of confounding the flashy model might be. There was something at stake far more important than Gemma's wounded pride. Life with Jordan had turned into an emotional time bomb, and every day increased the risk to her child. Taking a deep ragged breath, Gemma said hoarsely, "I'm sorry, Jordan, but there's no way I can remain here for the dedication.''

Jordan scowled at her with consternation. ''Sebastian's going to be very hurt. I thought you liked him.''

''I do, but—'' Gemma heard Sergio turning the door handle. She said quickly, ''I'm sorry, Jordan, but I just can't wait that long. There are reasons why I must go home to Colorado as soon as possible.''

Jordan stared at her, his dark eyes clouded with contempt. ''I see,'' he said grimly. ''Very well, if that's the way it must be.'' Abruptly he turned away from her, and over his broad shoulder she heard him growl, ''No matter what your objections, Gemma, I do insist that you stay here until the final carving on the Madonna is completed, which should be very soon. I promise I'll get it finished somehow. After that you'll be free to dash back to America and your lover. I won't let Marsha snatch Dave from you!''

''THANK GOD THAT'S DONE!'' Jordan said fervently, and he stepped back and tossed the fine-bladed detail chisel onto the workbench with a clatter. Around the pallet Sergio's crew gazed at the statue in critical silence for several seconds, appraising the completed Madonna. Despite the curious angle of her head as she regarded the Child, giving the viewer the impression that she was a trifle nearsighted, the combination of Jordan's skill and Francesca's face had somehow overcome the hackneyed treatment and made the figure a beautiful piece of work. Spontaneously the men burst into applause.

From her perch halfway up the tall wobbly ladder

where she had observed the final steps in the carving, Gemma watched them crowd around her husband, pounding him jovially on the back, clasping his callused hands in their even rougher ones. Jordan's expression—and the way his dark eyes blinked rapidly—made Gemma suspect that this moment of masculine camaraderie, when he received the accolade of his peers, was a very personal and deeply moving one to him. She would not have intruded on it for the world.

Francesca obviously felt no such compunction. For the past hour she had been sitting with studied impatience beside Sergio on the sidelines—probably resentful, Gemma thought waspishly, because she was not the center of attention. As Jordan slowly and meticulously made the last tiny cuts, Francesca had frowned restlessly. When he ran his sensitive fingertips over the features of the Madonna, reassuring himself that each detail was exactly as he wanted it, Gemma had noticed Francesca's hand rise to stroke her own face, as if to remind any viewers just whose face that really was. Now Francesca jumped to her feet and squealed, "Giordano, darling, it's wonderful!" as she elbowed her way through the cluster of men to launch herself into Jordan's arms.

Flustered, the workmen retreated, opening a space that enabled Gemma to watch, stricken, from her vantage point as the voluptuous model plastered her body seductively against Jordan's lean hardness, murmuring, "Well, *caro*, didn't I tell you we make a good team?" Automatically he caught her by the waist, and when Gemma saw his hands clasp Francesca, she choked as if those constricting fingers had closed around her own throat. The hoarse strangled sound she made attracted the attention of the other men, and they all turned at once to glance up at her ashen face. Then, even more quickly, they all looked away again, uncomfortable, suddenly evincing extreme interest in the walls or the marble chips on the floor. Gemma alone watched as Francesca's long nails wove into Jordan's black curls, and she pulled his head down to kiss him.

The embrace seemed to go on forever, Francesca's mouth moving greedily over Jordan's. As Gemma watched, her gray eyes bleak and tortured, something deep inside her twisted. She gulped, dizzy and disoriented, and clutched at the old ladder as if to a lifeline. It swayed slightly. Jordan and Francesca continued kissing. Sergio glanced at Gemma, his small sharp eyes eloquent, then he turned to his crew and barked, "All right, you worthless *pelandroni*, it's time to quit gawking and get back to work! Giordano here may have finished his part of the job, but yours is just beginning. I want this mess cleaned up *immediatamente*, every last chip and piece of gravel, then I want you to make Our Lady here shine like glass! Do you hear me, you lazy...."

As if grateful for the distraction, the men scurried to do Sergio's bidding. In the midst of the bustle Jordan and Francesca at last pulled slightly apart, their arms still linked. Francesca's cheeks were flushed, but Jordan, breathing hard, appeared pale under his tan, and his expression as he looked up at Gemma was oddly defiant. Their eyes met, and she stared silently down at him, her torment raw and exposed to his scornful gaze. Then the dizziness swept over her again, and she screwed her eyelids shut. Clinging to the worn risers to keep from falling, she began to inch her way down the ladder.

She felt divorced from the activity around her, separated as if trapped inside a glass cage. No one seemed aware of her struggle. Weighted with nausea and despair, her creeping descent stretched endlessly. She prodded with her toe for the next rung, and with a sigh of relief she at last located the step and began to lower her insubstantial weight onto it. Just a few more seconds and she would be safe....

One of the workmen brushed past her carelessly, carrying an electric buffer and a can of emery powder. Gemma lost her footing. With a yelp of surprise she slid the rest of the way to the floor, banging her shins, flailing her arms to keep her balance. Her elbow struck hard against one of the uprights of the unsteady ladder, and the intense jarring pain momentarily robbed her of breath and motion, even when she saw that the force of the blow had lifted the ladder onto two legs. Intent on their own work, the others did not seem to notice what was happening until it was too late. As Gemma watched, gasping, the ladder teetered precariously for a fraction of a second, swayed, and then with the slow-motion grace of a felled giraffe, toppled over, only just missing Jordan and Francesca as it collapsed onto the Madonna and snapped off the nose.

The reverberation of the impact rolled around the tiny room like a thunderclap, passing over the suddenly petrified figures of the people there until it faded into turbid silence. Gemma stared dizzily at the Madonna, at the grotesquely disfigured face. Somehow the odd angle of the head made the statue look as if it were peering cross-eyed at the jagged stump that had been its nose, and the aspect was so unexpectedly comic that Gemma tittered nervously. All at once Francesca shrieked stridently, "She did it on purpose, Giordano! Goddamn the little bitch. She's jealous of me, and she wrecked my statue on purpose!" Gemma blanched, aghast. "I tell you, she did it to spite me!" Francesca screeched again, clutching at Jordan's arm as she pointed a clawlike finger in accusation.

Gemma gaped at her husband. His graven features were livid as he gazed at the devastated ruin of the statue he had struggled so painfully to create. When he looked directly at Gemma again, his eyes grew opaque with rage. "J-Jordan," she stammered, "it...it was...." He shook Francesca off of him and took a long deliberate step toward Gemma. Instinctively she retreated. Out of the corner of her eye she noticed the other men were backing toward the walls, well out of Jordan's path.

Only Sergio stood his ground. He grated, "*Basta*, Giordano—that's enough!" But Jordan ignored him as, fists clenched, he stalked silently and inexorably toward his quailing wife.

"For God's sake, Jordan, you can't really believe—" Gemma pleaded, even in that last instant hoping to find in his face some lingering trace of the man she had married, the tender and sensitive lover she had known in Pisa.... Suddenly her words blurred and faded. Her gray eyes clouded as her vision turned inward toward a new pain, a deeper pain, a nagging ache that twisted and raked at her with tiny claws. She closed her lids with a moan and crumpled into a disjointed heap at Jordan's feet.

She could hear the shuffle of hard-soled shoes as the workmen rushed toward her, and even with her eyes closed she could sense Jordan towering over her, gazing down at her anxiously. Her fall seemed to have loosened him from the fury that had gripped him, and she heard him rasp, "*Nel nome di Dio*, Gemma!" His deep voice was anguished and remorseful. He knelt beside her, and she felt strong, achingly familiar hands slide under her limp body and start to lift her.

Gemma raised her long lashes, blinking dazedly. Behind Jordan she could see Sergio and the rest of the crew staring down at her, and she blushed, flustered. "Please, I . . . I can stand," she said shakily. Jordan nodded doubtfully, and she tried to push herself upright, only to find that the dizziness had become overwhelming. She looked pleadingly at Jordan, and with infinite care he pulled her to her feet.

The instant she stood up she groaned, and Jordan caught her fragile shoulders and demanded, "Are you all right?"

Gemma shook her head absently. "N-no," she said slowly, "I—I don't—" She gasped.

He asked again, "Darling, are you all right?"

Gemma looked up at him, stricken. She knew now the source of the pain, the bewildering faintness that had seized her. "My baby," she whispered desolately.

"What?" Jordan asked, his brows coming together sharply.

"My baby," Gemma repeated huskily.

Jordan stared at her, stupefied, his hard jaw drooping. "Oh, my God," he croaked. "You mean you...you're—"

From somewhere behind the gathered workmen Francesca's voice rose. "Giordano, what's going on?" she demanded irritably. "What is all this fuss about?"

Gemma winced at the coarse sound of the other woman's voice, once more remembering all that she had forgotten in this moment of supreme loss. She gazed helplessly at her husband, agony in her face. She saw that his own features were now bleached of all color—except for a streak of Francesca's vivid scarlet lipstick smeared beside his mouth.

Suddenly Gemma doubled over, groaning. Jordan cried hoarsely, "For God's sake, Gemma, don't— here, let me—" He tried to draw her back into the shelter of his arms.

She shook her head fiercely. "No," she moaned, pushing impotently at his chest with what was left of her waning strength. "Don't touch me! I...I...." Her words were dying out in a gurgle as she succumbed to the pain. With great effort she whispered, "I hate you." And then she fainted.

"*SIGNORA*, YOU HAVE A VISITOR," the nurse said.

Gemma peered irritably over the top edge of her book, stifling a retort. The woman was Suora Letizia, the nun who had reassured her so kindly when Caroline was first brought into the hospital, and because of that, Gemma forced herself to reply courteously. "Thank you for telling me, Sister, but I still don't want to see anyone."

The nun looked reproachful. Gemma's continued refusal to have visitors had distressed her, especially when Gemma made it clear that even "Signore Giordano" was unwelcome at her bedside. It had taken a directive from the physician to curtail Suora Letizia's well-meaning meddling, saying that it impeded Gemma's recovery, but now that she was about to be released from the hospital, the hints had begun again. "*Signora*, surely you—"

From the corridor a familiar and unwelcome voice cut in firmly, "I think my daughter-in-law will see me now." And before Gemma could protest, Beatrice strode into the room, a sheaf of yellow gladioli in her arms.

Gemma blinked in astonishment. Jordan's mother was the last person she had expected to visit her, and as she looked up at the woman, her surprise rapidly turned to suspicion. The instant Suora Letizia had left the room in search of a vase for the flowers, Gemma asked bluntly, "What are you doing here, Beatrice?"

Beatrice switched to English, and as always, her lilting drawl startled Gemma. "I'm here because I thought you might need someone."

"I don't need anyone," Gemma said with deliberate rudeness. "I suppose I ought to thank you for your gracious gesture in coming here, but it was quite unnecessary. When I'm discharged, I'll make my own arrangements."

Beatrice's expression was enigmatic. "You really can't stand me, can you?" she murmured.

Gemma shrugged. Apparently this was the time to get everything out in the open. Brushing a strand of silvery hair out of her eyes, she said, "You must admit you haven't been exactly forthcoming with offers of friendship yourself. That's why I think this sudden concern for my well-being rings a bit false."

Beatrice stared down at her, shaking her head sadly. She said roughly, "Honey, give me credit for a little compassion. I'm sorry you lost your baby. I'm sorry you've been ill. The fact that I didn't want you to marry my son does not make me some kind of monster."

Gemma's eyes widened. "No," she agreed wryly, "considering the way things turned out, it just shows that you're a woman of intelligence and foresight." She motioned to the straight wooden chair beside the bed. "Won't you please sit down?" As Beatrice settled herself, smoothing her fashionable dress over her scrawny lap, Gemma asked warily, but with a hopeful note she could not entirely repress, "So Jordan didn't send you?"

Beatrice's pale blue eyes met hers. "Giordano is in Florence now," she answered quietly.

"I. . . I see," Gemma whispered, hoarsely, slumping weakly against her pillow. "I guess that. . . that's it, then." She blinked hard, wondering why her lashes suddenly felt damp.

Beatrice studied her with professional concern. "You don't look well at all," she judged, frowning. "Are you sure you're ready to be released?"

Gemma said, "I expect I'll convalesce for a while once I'm home in Colorado. Right now I just want to get out of Italy as quickly as possible."

"You hate this country so much?"

"I don't hate the country at all. Italy is very

beautiful. I...I just haven't been very happy here, that's all."

Beatrice smiled wryly. "That's funny. All the happiness I've ever known has been in Italy." Her pale eyes darkened as she stared blankly at the wall, lost in memory. Her face softened with reminiscent tenderness. "I grew up in the shadow of two big sisters, both lovely Southern belles, and next to them I was always the homely one, the wallflower—I think the best compliment I ever got as a child was that I looked 'tidy.' When the war came, they both promptly married officers in the Air Corps, and I began nurse's training. I figured if I couldn't be desirable, I'd be diligent, and that's the way it continued for several years, until one night in Italy I was checking the wards. A new patient had been brought in since my last shift, and when I went to take his pulse, suddenly I found myself looking at the handsomest man I've ever seen."

"Jordan's father?" Gemma asked.

"Giordano's father," Beatrice sighed, nodding. "My son is a remarkably attractive man, but compared to his father—well, in my mind there simply is no comparison."

Her eyes closed for a second, and suddenly her plain features seemed illuminated and exalted. *The face of love,* Gemma thought awefully as she watched her. Oh, God, if Jordan had ever looked at her that way....

Beatrice opened her eyes again. When she looked at Gemma, her expression hardened. She said briskly, "For the first time in my life I was in love, and perhaps even more miraculously, he was in love with me, too. Foolishly I thought that my family would rejoice with me when I wrote them the news.''

"But they didn't?"

Beatrice shook her head. "No. I suppose I was naive. At a time when many Americans were upset over the number of war brides soldiers were bringing back from Europe, some, like my parents, found it even more appalling that an American woman would wish to marry a European man. 'Protecting our womenfolk' has always been one of the primary duties of the Southern male; in that respect they are not unlike Italians. When my mother answered my letter, she hinted that she and her friends would find me a nice husband, if only I'd come home. My father was blunter: he asked, 'What's the matter? Aren't Americans good enough for you?' When I read that, I thought for a while, remembering all the snubs and rejection I had suffered as a girl, and I compared them with the passion and consideration and tenderness shown me by the man I loved. Finally I answered my father, 'No, they're not good enough for me.' I said that if my family was not prepared to accept him, I would become an Italian—"

" 'Thy people shall be my people'?" Gemma interjected.

"Exactly," Beatrice said. "I won't pretend it was easy, abandoning the culture I was born in, but I made my decision and I've always abided by it.... I never heard from my parents again."

Gemma shook her head, wondering with bitter irony if there was ever an end to conflict between parent and child. Each generation seemed as possessive and narrow-minded as the one before. If she had suggested to Beatrice that in her own way, with her disdain of her former compatriots, she had become as prejudiced as her parents had been, she doubted the woman would have understood her. Gemma asked, "So you and Jordan's father just went ahead and got married?"

"No, it wasn't quite as simple as that," Beatrice answered with a sardonic smile. "I was, after all, a lieutenant in the army, and I needed my commanding-officer's permission to marry. It turned out my father had written to him, too. In the end I was forced to take drastic measures. I deliberately became pregnant in order to force the army to discharge me."

As Gemma listened to the almost flippant way Beatrice tossed out that last sentence, she suddenly remembered the anguish and mortification that had been evident in the woman's voice the night Jordan had tauntingly reminded her of his "premature" birth. She wondered if Jordan had any notion at all of the humiliation his mother must have suffered so that she could be allowed to marry his father. Gemma ventured slowly, "It...it must have been hard for you."

"Hard?" Beatrice echoed harshly. "You don't know the half of it, the shame, the scorn of people I had called my friends. I had been a good nurse, a good officer, and they—but that doesn't matter anymore. I would have endured anything for the man I loved." She paused, staring pointedly at Gemma. After a moment she muttered, "Of course I've known for weeks that you were pregnant. At first I thought that you would use the child to try to bind yourself to Giordano when he came to his senses and overcame this obsession he had for you. I admit I was...surprised that you did not."

"I would never manipulate someone that way," Gemma said flatly, suddenly weary. Since the double loss of her husband and her child, she had been conscious of a spiritual lassitude, a numbness that enveloped her whenever she tried to think about that hellish scene in the studio. She supposed her subconscious was trying to protect her shattered emotions, but it seemed to have robbed her of physical strength, as well.

Beatrice's mouth curled cynically. "No? It's a time-honored ploy. Women do it all the time. Look at Dieter Stahl's wife. Look at me—"

All at once Suora Letizia bustled into the room, bearing the bouquet of yellow gladioli that Beatrice had brought, now beautifully arranged in a large vase. "You must forgive me for taking so long with these lovely flowers," she chirped as she set the vase on Gemma's nightstand. The nun was obviously gratified to see her sullen taciturn patient speaking to her mother-in-law. "A slight emergency in pediatrics— all is well now, *grazie a Dio*—delayed me, but I am sure the two of you had much to talk about."

She beamed pointedly at Gemma, and Gemma murmured politely, "Yes, the flowers are lovely. Thank you so much, Beatrice. It was...good of you to come see me."

Beatrice recognized the note of curt dismissal in Gemma's tired voice, even if the nurse did not. With a sigh she stood up, smoothing the skirt of her dress. She gazed down at Gemma, the expression in her pale blue eyes unreadable. One brow arched slightly. As Gemma returned the gaze silently, she realized for the first time that while Jordan obviously had inherited his extraordinary good looks from his father, his expressions, the movement of his facial muscles, had come from his mother. Ignoring the presence of Suora Letizia, who smiled benignly, her grasp of the English language limited, Beatrice said softly, "You know, Gemma, you're not at all what I assumed you were when we first met. I think perhaps that under different circumstances—" At Gemma's frankly skeptical snort, the woman halted. Taking a deep breath she said briskly, "No, you're right. This is no time to start being sanctimonious. But I hope you'll believe me when I say I am truly sorry that you've been ill, and if there's anything I can do for you..."

Gemma said, "Yes, there is one thing, if you will. My clothes at the villa—I mean the jeans and things I brought with me, I don't want the new stuff Jordan bought—if you would have someone pack them for me and take them to the Riccis' *pensione*, I'll probably be staying there for a day or two until I can get my flight arranged."

Something flickered in Beatrice's eyes, but her face remained impassive. "Your clothes," she repeated, as if mentally ticking off items on a list. "Anything else?"

Gemma nodded. "In the top middle drawer of our dresser—" she winced as she thought just how short a time they had actually shared that dresser, that room "—in that drawer you'll find a jewelry case. Inside there's an opal pendant necklace. It's rather valuable, and I'd be grateful if you'd make certain

Jordan gets it back safely...." Her voice was just dying away as a gleam of gold caught her eye, reminding her with tortured insistence that she had one last item to return to her husband. Gritting her teeth, Gemma wrenched her wedding ring from her slim finger and held it out to Beatrice. "Here," she choked huskily, ignoring Suora Letizia's gasp of horror, "you'd better give this back to Jordan, too." When Beatrice hesitated, Gemma poked the ring at her. The comforting numbness was passing, and she did not know how much longer she could retain her faltering composure. "Damn you, take it!" she cried, and as soon as the woman's fingers had closed around the little gold circlet, Gemma collapsed back against her pillow and turned her face to the wall.

Behind her she heard the nun protest importunately in Italian. Beatrice murmured something in the same language, and after a moment the swish of a long habit brushing through the door told Gemma that Suora Letizia had left the room. There was another awkward pause, then Gemma heard her mother-in-law say, "Well, I reckon that's it, then. *Addio*, Gemma."

Gemma whispered, "Goodbye, Beatrice," and as soon as she heard the door swing shut a second time, she began to cry.

BY THE TIME she left the hospital, her tears had all dried. At the *pensione* she sat alone by the window in the little bedroom she had shared with Caroline. Squinting at the bright sunlight reflecting off the gravel in the courtyard below, she waited impatiently for someone to bring her luggage from the villa. She had left the hospital dressed in the same jeans and work shirt she had been wearing at the studio the day she fell off the ladder, and she was anxious to change. While Signora Ricci had laundered the garments with such care that they looked almost new, leaving no trace of that tragic accident, Gemma knew that as soon as she was safely home again, she was going to burn them.

She thought with longing of the apartment waiting for her in Colorado, where she would recuperate among her beloved golden-oak furniture and the handful of paintings she had collected. Despite the fact that since losing her job at the school, the rent had seriously depleted Gemma's savings, doggedly she had continued to make the payments, even after she and Jordan were married. When Jordan discovered that she had made arrangements for the money to be transferred from her bank account each month, he had made one of his incomprehensible sarcastic remarks about Gemma retaining the apartment just so she could keep an eye on Dave. She had snapped back that Dave wasn't the one who needed watching. She supposed she had known all along that soon she would need a refuge, a place to run to when the marriage failed. Now, in a very short time, she would be on her way back to Colorado, back to the beloved surroundings of her childhood, the healing remoteness of the mountains. In the morning Franco was going to drive her northward to Genoa, where she would catch her plane. In less than forty-eight hours from now, Gemma would be home.

Gemma sighed, glancing at her handbag. She had her passport in hand, and her ticket reservation had

been confirmed by telegram. All she needed now was
the rest of her luggage.

Her thoughts were interrupted by the approaching
purr of a well-tuned and powerful engine, and as she
looked on, puzzled, a sleek crimson Ferrari pulled
into the courtyard. From her second-story vantage
point he could not see the driver, and she wondered
who would have the audacity to take Jordan's car.

The door on the driver's side sprang open, and as
Gemma watched, her astonishment turned to dismay
when she saw her husband unfold his long lithe frame
from behind the steering wheel. Gemma gasped. She
had not expected Jordan to be the one who brought
her things to her. He was supposed to be in Florence.
When he glanced toward the upper windows of the
house, Gemma jumped up from her chair and quickly drew back away from the window, afraid he might
see her. Surreptitiously she peeked through the ruffled curtains, following his movements hungrily as he
opened the trunk of the car and pulled out the elegant
leather suitcases he had purchased for her on their
wedding day. The foreshortened angle prevented
Gemma from seeing Jordan's expression, but the
controlled force with which he banged the lid shut
warned her that he was angry. She watched him heft
the bags as if they were weightless, then he stalked
across the crunchy gravel toward the front door of
the *pensione*. When he reached the porch, the
overhanging eaves hid him from Gemma's view, but
she could hear his imperative knock. Seconds later
a muffled conversation floated up the staircase toward her, and Gemma began to smooth her hair and
straighten her clothes, mentally girding herself for

the call that should come any moment now, when she
would have to descend the steps to confront her husband for the last time. . . .

Her hand stilled in mid stroke, her fingertips
resting lightly on her silver gilt tresses. *The last time,*
she thought with a stab of pain. Flinching, she was
suddenly blind, the narrow confines of her bedroom
dissolving to a shimmering blackness that quickly
brightened again as she turned her vision inward to
the memory of the first time she had ever seen Jordan. She pictured the clearing beside the highway,
lambent and sultry on that summer afternoon such a
pathetically short time before. She heard again the
distant whistle from the marble quarry, smelled the
dust in the air. She lifted her head as if she were
glancing up from the devastated Fiat, and she saw . . .
she saw. . . .

"Gemma," a deep, achingly familiar voice murmured from the doorway.

She blinked hard, returning with a jolt to the present. The hand that had been touching her hair
dropped to her side, and she squared her shoulders
and forced her small mouth into a semblance of a
smile. Swallowing hard, she turned to face the man
whose large frame filled the doorway. The last time
she saw him he had been stalking toward her. . . .
With an elaborate attempt at casualness Gemma
croaked, "J-Jordan, how unexp-p—" Jordan's dark
eyes widened in astonishment, and Gemma broke off
abruptly. His nearness was rattling her far more than
she had anticipated. She cleared her throat again,
and this time when she spoke, her voice came out in
something approaching her normal husky alto. "Jor-

dan," she said, pronouncing each word deliberately, "I'm surprised you're here. I thought you were in Florence with Francesca."

"I drove to Florence to see Sebastian," Jordan corrected quietly. "He had to be consulted about the statue, naturally, and after you refused to see me, I decided to get that over with. I just got back this morning."

"I understand," Gemma said with lame apology. She wondered if Beatrice had misled her on purpose, or if all the misunderstanding had been in her own mind. "I . . . I suppose Sebastian is very upset about the Madonna?" she asked. "It meant so much to him—"

"He's more concerned about you," Jordan cut in sharply, "as are we all. You shouldn't be out of the hospital yet. You look dreadful."

"Thanks a lot," Gemma muttered dryly.

"I'm only telling you what anyone with half an eye can see." He rammed his hands deep in the pockets of his denim trousers and stared at the toes of his shoes. For just a second, something about his attitude reminded Gemma of a sulky little boy. She thought with remorse, *if we had had a son. . . .* Jordan glanced up at her, his dark eyes veiled. "Has the doctor really given you permission to leave the country?"

With affected nonchalance Gemma shrugged. "He's accepted the fact that nothing will keep me here a moment longer than necessary."

Jordan flinched visibly. He gestured toward the beautiful luggage. "Well, if you're really determined to go. . . . My mother packed your things—*all* your things."

"I told her I didn't—"

"Damn it, I know what you told her!" Jordan snapped. "And I don't care what you said. I gave the clothes and the jewelry to you, and I want you to take them with you. After you get back to Colorado, you can give it all to charity, if that's the way you want it, but you're taking everything with you. I insist."

Gemma shook her head stubbornly. "No, I won't. If for no other reason, the duty on the pendant alone would...." Her voice trailed off in embarrassment. They were squabbling like children, and she had so hoped their last few moments together would be graced with a little dignity. She turned away with a sigh.

Jordan frowned. "Do you need money?" he asked. "I'm sorry. I didn't think. I've been meaning to give you—"

"Oh, Jordan, please don't," she cried, her voice tortured. "Don't reduce it to that level."

She fell silent again, and for half a heartbeat Jordan hesitated. Then with a groan he demanded, "Gemma, for God's sake, why didn't you tell me about the baby?"

She couldn't answer. The loss of her child was too new, the wound too raw, and she could not speak of it yet. She wondered if she'd ever be able to talk about it.

Jordan continued huskily, his bewilderment obvious, "I've tried so hard to understand. I want to understand—and the only possible explanation I can think of.... Was it Blanchard's child? Is that why you were afraid to tell me, because you knew I wasn't the father?"

The words hung heavily between them. Gemma turned her gray blue eyes toward her husband and regarded his beloved features impassively, the bafflement that sat so awkwardly in his sharp intelligent face. She wondered if he even realized how insulting he was being, she wondered why she wasn't screaming. She supposed that maybe after all that had happened to her lately, she was becoming inured to pain. With an odd little smile she asked curiously, "Is that what you think of me? Can you truly believe I would have married you, knowing I was carrying another man's child?"

Jordan shook his dark head helplessly. "I didn't think it was possible, but it did seem plausible: the man was your lover, and—" He broke off, swearing under his breath. "Oh, how the hell should I know?" he snapped. "I've never understood the way your mind works!"

"You never tried," Gemma said softly. "From the beginning you forced me to do things your way, and whenever I protested, you either laughed at me or got angry—or hauled me off to bed." She took a deep breath. "If it will set your mind at rest, Jordan, then let me reassure you, the baby was yours. Ours. And I would have told you, only you made it clear that you didn't want it."

His astonishment was patent. "What the hell are you talking about?"

She regarded him wearily. "Don't you even remember? You said it yourself: 'Any bitch can have pups. It's artists who are rare.'"

Hot color flooded Jordan's face, turning his graven features into a mask carved of mahogany. He stepped toward her, catching her thin shoulders in his strong fingers, and when he spoke, his deep voice was hoarse with guilty torment. "*Gesu Cristo*, Gemma," he choked urgently, "I wasn't talking about *you*. You couldn't have thought—you misunderstood—"

His touch was torture to her frayed nerves, and with great effort Gemma twisted away from him. She sighed and turned away. "Did I? Well, perhaps that's to be expected: the two of us were always misunderstanding each other. I suppose it has to do with the differences in our cultures. Your mother certainly knew what she was talking about when she said it wasn't easy to adapt." Gemma forced an ironic chuckle through her constricted throat. "It doesn't really matter anymore, you know. Tomorrow I'm leaving, and you can—"

With unexpected humility, Jordan pleaded, "Gemma, don't. . .don't—" and reached out a hand to her. When she ignored it, he drew himself up rigidly to his full height and said with the air of an attentive host, "At least let me take you to Genoa, to make sure that you get safely on your plane."

Gemma shook her head firmly. She was in control of herself now. She would be able to make her farewells, say what had to be said without losing her composure again. Her coolness matching his own, she said, "There's no need for you to make chivalrous gestures at this late date, Jordan. All the arrangements have already been made. Franco Ricci will transport me to the airport tomorrow, and I'll be out of your life for good. You'll be free to resume things with Francesca without a wife to interfere." She blinked hard. When she met his gaze, his magnetic eyes were opaque with an expression she could not interpret. She continued stiffly in a tone unnaturally high for her, "I . . . I do hope that you and Francesca will be happy together, Jordan, but I'm not sure that she's the woman for you, any more than I am. She can be very demanding, and I don't think you're prepared to give her the attention she requires. Please think about that before you make any permanent commitments. Women, even one as beautiful as Francesca, are really nothing but a convenience for you, you know." Gemma swallowed, and when she spoke again, her voice was thick. "The only thing you've ever loved is your art, Jordan. I just hope and pray that in the end it turns out to be enough for you." She turned away resolutely, and she did not move again until she heard the bedroom door close softly behind him.

CHAPTER TWELVE

"*TEEEA-CHER*," THE LITTLE GIRL WAILED, her six-year-old voice shrill with indignation, "Martin yanked my hat off!"

With a sigh Gemma turned away from the blackboard. She quickly surveyed the rowdy row of children impatiently lining up to go out into the play yard. Her gaze settled on the accused culprit, a little boy in a hooded parka adorned with a big Denver Broncos patch. He met her gaze with suspiciously angelic green eyes, his hands behind him. By now his victim seemed on the verge of tears. "I can't go outside without my hat," she sobbed, her lower lip quivering. "My mother *said*!"

The classroom was situated at the end of the corridor, adjacent to the large glass doors that opened out onto the playground, and every time someone opened the classroom door, a frigid blast of air blew in. As Gemma signaled the other children to go on outside, she reminded them not to forget to shut the doors behind them. They scrambled away, and she called after them, "We mustn't waste energy!" She was hoping to touch their incipient ecological awareness, if not their sense of common courtesy. The door remained ajar. With a wry sigh Gemma stepped over to close it, then she turned back to the two children still standing beside her desk. She said quietly but sternly, "Martin, give Amy back her hat now."

The boy stared down at the scuffed toes of his rubber rain boots as from behind his back he reluctantly produced a cap knit of white yarn with a bright pink pom-pom. "I was gonna give her old hat back, Miss Culver," he mumbled sullenly, drooping his head so that his tousled sun-streaked locks dangled over his face. "It was only a joke."

"I know," Gemma said, brushing his hair back out of his eyes and drawing the hood up over his head. "But you mustn't pull off anyone's hat, even for a joke, when it's so cold outside. We don't want anyone to get sick." She patted his head and added, "Now, tell Amy you're sorry, then go on and play."

"Sorry, Amy," Martin muttered perfunctorily as he dashed out of the room, heedless of Gemma's call to walk not run. Trying to ignore the bone-chilling draft that blew in through the door that had once again been left open, Gemma busied herself with soothing the offended sensibilities of her other charge. She squatted down so that her face was on a level with the girl's, and she began to arrange the cap over her blond curls. "This is a pretty hat, Amy," she said, shivering, as she pulled it down to cover her ears. "Did your mother make it for you?"

"My grandma did," Amy answered, squirming, her eyes focused on the game of hopscotch that was being organized on the frosty blacktop beneath the window. Little balloons of steam hung around the children's mouths as they breathed, comically giving them the look of cartoon characters. Amy said,

"My hat was a Christmas present. Can I go now?"

"Sure, sweetheart," Gemma murmured, "but be sure to close the—" Amy was already rocketing after Martin, squealing, "Hey, I want to play, too!"

The door banged shut behind her, and Gemma relaxed with a sigh of relief, smiling at the volatility of children. She leaned wearily against the side of her desk. Her first-glade class were all adorable, of course, but she was not ungrateful that for the next fifteen minutes they would be the responsibility of the yard monitor, not her, and she could catch her breath. She scraped back the heavy wooden "teacher's" chair—thick oak, unpadded, with a contoured seat and slatted back. She wondered sometimes if there was an eleventh Commandment that said all schools must come equipped with that particular model. She plopped into it, massaging her legs, happy to be off her feet for a little while. The long suede boots she wore were as pretty as they were expensive, their dove color exactly matching the gray in the plaid of her calf-length skirt and the fringed scarf that held back her shoulder-length hair. But their stylishly high heels were utterly impractical for standing for hours in front of a classroom. She ought to have bought shoes with sturdy crepe soles and good arch supports, ugly but comfortable. Gemma gazed at her boots with ironic appreciation. One unexpected benefit she had gained from her brief sojourn in Italy was an increased awareness of fashion, of the way she looked and dressed. Considering the ache in her calves right now, she wasn't so sure that was a good thing.

She leaned over and pulled open the bottom desk

drawer to retrieve her thermos of coffee. She poured a cup of the steaming brew, nestling it in her hands to warm them. She was so cold. She had been cold for months, ever since she came back from Europe, in fact, as if the time she had spent in that sultry clime had somehow altered her body's chemistry. The wild mountain winters she had weathered easily all her life now seemed almost unendurable.

She set down her coffee cup and hugged her thin arms through the thickness of her amber-colored sweater. She knew she was evading the issue. The chill permeating her had nothing to do with her physical environment; it was the result of spiritual emptiness, the emotional void she had existed in ever since returning to Colorado. For months now she had lived superficially, going through the motions of her daily routine, conversing with simulated interest, smiling when other people smiled, but beneath it all she was conscious of a numbness, a profound depression. Without Jordan, nothing seemed to matter very much, not even her art. She hadn't picked up a drawing pencil in months.

Her family had noticed her mood, of course. She had not expected to resume her old life without being subjected to a barrage of probing questions from her baffled relatives, and when she first returned, she did not visit any of them; she simply telephoned to let them know she was back. After a few days of silence Gemma had not been surprised when suddenly her oldest brother's wife asked her over for Sunday dinner. When she got to Bob's house, she found that her father and her other brothers and their wives had been invited, too, all looking at her askance. Gemma had always been aware that the rest of her family considered her "peculiar," a changeling, but by their standards, her latest escapade surpassed all her previous ones, even that awful time when she had dragged the Culver name through the mud by publicly accusing that boy. Before long the inquisition had begun. Gemma had answered them as calmly as she could, refusing to react to their tacit reproach. Yes, she really had married an Italian artist after a whirlwind courtship. No, she hadn't ditched Dave in order to do so; their engagement had been terminated before she left the States. And, finally, yes, the marriage was already finished, and she assumed her husband would be seeking a divorce soon; she had no plans to do so because she had no intention of ever marrying again. . . .

The one thing she did not tell them about was the baby.

When one of her sisters-in-law, the wife of her middle brother, Tom, irritably demanded to know whether Gemma realized that her irresponsible actions had broken up a lifelong friendship between her husband and Dave Blanchard, the look of mute despair scoring Gemma's pale face had suddenly become so pronounced that Tom ordered his wife to shut up. Everyone fell uncomfortably silent, and later her third brother, Chris, had hugged her solemnly.

And her father. . . . When they had confronted each other in the hallway as they fetched their coats, Gemma stiff and reserved, her father troubled, he had stared at her ravaged face and said awkwardly, "Honey, I . . . I know maybe we haven't always . . . talked the way we should, especially since your mother died, but you must believe that I've only ever wanted what was best for you.''

Gemma had looked at him with dawning compassion. Her father had harmed her in many ways he would never comprehend, but that didn't make him some kind of inhuman tyrant. He was just a man, as much a victim of his prejudices as she was, and probably he had never really recovered from the loss of his wife. Gemma greatly resembled her mother; perhaps it had hurt to have her around, to remind him.... Standing on tiptoe to kiss his cheek, Gemma had murmured thickly, "I love you, daddy." Then she ran out the door.

In her classroom Gemma gazed pensively across the neat rows of undersized desks. Her eyes rested on the brightly crayoned drawings displayed on the far wall above the shelf laden with metal lunch boxes ornamented with pictures of superheroes and television actors. The thought occurred to her that in this classroom she had found more contentment than anywhere else she could remember. Because she had returned to Colorado too late to get a full-time job for that school year, she had been commuting daily from Golden to Denver, filling in as a substitute teacher. In some ways the work was unsettling and frustrating, never knowing what school or grade level she would be dealing with next, but at the same time it had offered her a challenge that kept her mind occupied so that she wouldn't waste her time brooding over things that couldn't be changed. For that reason she had been oddly reluctant to accept the more permanent position that had become available in the new year when a first-grade teacher broke her leg in a skiing accident at Aspen and had to spend several weeks in traction. Gemma had considered declining the job on the grounds that she had no experience with very young children, but she finally accepted, recognizing that it was time she quit feeling sorry for herself and put her life back together.

Perhaps the funniest part of it all, she thought now, was that she had discovered that she loved teaching the elementary grades, something she had once thought would never appeal to her. The children charmed her with their innocence, their naive wonder at the world they were just discovering, their vivid imaginations that were as yet unfettered by convention. Her artistic spirit delighted whenever one of them presented her with a drawing of orange sky and purple grass, dotted with birds and animals that could exist only in a six-year-old mind. Of course, her little pupils weren't angels. They could be cranky and noisy and rebellious, and every now and then she prayed for permission—please, God, just this once—to smack a few bottoms, but on the whole she was enjoying her work with the children. She had about decided that she was going to take some graduate courses in primary education, and then she would try to get a permanent job as an elementary-school teacher.

Suddenly Gemma's ruminations were interrupted by an authoritative rap on the hall door, and she glanced up curiously. "Come in," she called, and she was surprised when the school secretary stepped inside. "Hi," Gemma murmured automatically. "May I help you with something?"

The secretary shivered and clutched her red wool

blazer tighter around her chunky shoulders as she exclaimed, "Lord, it's cold in this room, I don't see how you stand it! Are you sure the heat is coming through all right?"

"I think it is," Gemma answered, shrugging. "It's just that every time someone opens the door—"

"Well, maybe I'd better have the custodian make certain the ducts aren't clogged, okay? Is that coffee?" she added hopefully. "We finished off the pot in the office during lunch, and no one has made fresh."

"Help yourself." Gemma fished in her desk drawer for a second Styrofoam cup, then, as the secretary poured out the last of the thermos's contents, Gemma waited for her to continue. When she did not, Gemma asked again, "Was there something you needed?"

Momentarily the woman looked blank, then she said, "Oh, of course, I'm sorry. The principal wants you in her office right away. You have a visitor."

"A visitor? I wasn't expecting anyone. Why didn't she just direct whomever it is to me here?"

"Well," the secretary said as she savored the fragrant liquid, "the principal was feeling a bit flustered, I think. She didn't know quite what to make of him. It's some Italian gentleman—"

"Who?" Gemma choked, blanching, her hand at her throat.

"Some Ital—" the secretary started to repeat. But she spoke to an empty room.

Gemma ran down the corridor toward the principal's office, ignoring the startled exclamation of the hall monitor as she dashed past him. All she could think was that Jordan was here, Jordan had come for her.

"Sebastian?" she gasped in dismay when she saw the old man who sat beside the principal on the short couch. He was bundled in a black overcoat and muffler, his hands jammed deep into his pockets, and his hat pulled low over his eyes at a sinister angle. Coupled with his thickly accented English, his appearance seemed to alarm the principal, and Gemma might have been amused by the woman's reaction, were she not so desperately disappointed. "Sebastian?" she said again, forcing her mouth into a semblance of a polite smile. "What on earth are you doing here?"

"Oh, Miss Culver," the principal sighed, standing up, her relief palpable. "Then this...this gentleman is a friend of yours?"

"Yes, of course," Gemma murmured. She held out her hands to Sebastian, and when she spoke, she automatically switched to Italian. "How goes it with you, *amico*?"

He withdrew his hands from his pockets and caught her fingers in his own. Sadly Gemma noticed that his skin looked translucent, blue veins clearly visible. Whatever the reason that had brought him here, his health was obviously failing. But despite his evident frailty, he swept his hat from his head and exclaimed with polished gallantry, "Ah, *cara* Gemma, you grow more beautiful each time I see you." He hesitated before adding heavily, "Forgive me for not standing, but this cold weather does not seem to agree with my arthritis."

Quickly Gemma sat down beside him. "It doesn't

matter. Tell me, please, what brings you here?'' She studied his seamed face anxiously. During the past months she had thought frequently of Sebastian, remembering him fondly despite his obsession with the ill-fated Madonna, and she had wondered how he fared. More than once she had considered writing to him, as she had thought about writing to Claretta, assuming she hadn't married the young man who worked in the Alfa Romeo factory, or the Riccis. Then she had decided that it would be better for her to make a clean break with everyone she had known in Italy. A chilling thought struck her. "My God," Gemma choked, "nothing has happened to Jordan, has it? You haven't come to tell me that. . .that—"

Before Sebastian could reply, the principal interrupted sternly, "Miss Culver, I must remind you that you have a class to teach. I really can't permit your personal visitors to interfere with—"

The old man turned to the woman and regarded her balefully, and when he spoke, even the thickness of his accent could not disguise his quelling tone. "Madam," he said, "I have journeyed a great distance to bring this young woman news of her husband. Be so kind as not to disturb me."

"Husband?" the woman echoed. "Miss Culver, I—"

"Please," Gemma said urgently, "it's. . .it's a complicated situation. If I could only have a few minutes. . . ."

Glancing warily at Sebastian again, the principal yielded. "Oh, all right. There's just an hour left until dismissal time, I'll have my secretary keep an eye on your class for the rest of the day. You run along. But if something like this happens again, I'll have to report it to the district office.''

"Yes, yes, I understand," Gemma exclaimed, leaping to her feet. "I'll run back to the room and get my things." She raced out the door.

When she returned to the office a few minutes later, she saw that Sebastian had struggled to his feet and was leaning painfully on a cane as he made his farewells to the principal. Watching his labored movements, Gemma began to realize the tremendous strain it must have been for him to fly halfway around the world to find her. Whatever his mission, Sebastian obviously considered it of life-or-death importance.

At his request, they found a restaurant where they could talk undisturbed. In the overheated atmosphere Sebastian seemed more comfortable, and at last he shed his overcoat and hat, revealing the nattily dressed man Gemma had known in Florence. But he had aged greatly, she saw with regret. Only his dark eyes were as sharp and knowing as ever.

She waited until Sebastian was staring dubiously at the plate of lasagna that had been set in front of him before she said quietly, "All right, why don't we just come to the point? Why are you here? Obviously it has something to do with Jordan, and I don't think it can be that he's ill or hurt, or you would have told me right away. So what is it?" An ominous thought occurred to her. "Is it—did he—did Jordan send you to ask me for a divorce?"

The old man bridled, and Gemma knew that she had offended him. "*No one* 'sends' Sebastian Buscaglia anywhere, to do anything!" he said huffily. "I came as a friend."

"I'm sorry," Gemma sighed. "It's just that—"

Sebastian waved a hand to silence her. "Forget it, *piccola*. I know what you meant. If it will make you feel better, I will tell you this: Giordano does not know I am with you right now."

Gemma's long lashes veiled her eyes. "I see," she said slowly. "Then suppose you tell me. . . ."

"I want you to come back to Firenze with me," Sebastian said.

Gemma looked up, startled. "Florence? Why?"

Sebastian shrugged eloquently. "Well, if for no other reason, you promised me once that you would stay for the dedication of my Madonna."

"The Madonna?" Gemma gasped. Even now, whenever she thought of the havoc she had wrought, she felt like blushing. "You mean it was able to be repaired?"

Sebastian shook his head. "Giordano has carved another one," he said quietly. "Since the accident he has been working like a madman, and now at last the new statue is ready to be set up in the chapel. It's a masterpiece, Gemma, the best thing he's ever done. I want you to be there."

You want me to be there to see still further evidence of Jordan's love for Francesca, Gemma thought in bewilderment. *Sebastian, how can you be so cruel?* Silently she shook her head.

As if reading her mind, Sebastian said, "Gemma, my daughter won't be there. She has gone back to Paris."

Gemma stared. "Paris? But what about the—I don't understand," she said helplessly.

Sebastian sighed. "What's to understand? I sent

her away. After the shameful way she interfered in your marriage, I refused to have her in my home any longer.''

Now Gemma was completely baffled. "But when we were in Florence, you told me—"

"I told you I could have stomached a discreet affair between her and Giordano if that was the price of completing my statue. An affair is temporary, of no importance. But to come between you and Giordano the way she did, to...to gloat when you lost your child...." Sebastian stretched his hand across the table in supplication. "Forgive me my blindness, Gemma. I have talked to the head of the studio in Pietrasanta, and he told me frankly of Francesca's actions, her taunts. I did not know. I could have controlled her, but I did not, and because of that:..."

He winced, and when he spoke again, his voice was harsh with remembered pain. "Francesca's dear mother died when my daughter was born, did you know that? You remind me of her in many ways. Not in looks, of course—she was a brunette, typically Italian—but in constitution: she was also frail and high-strung. When Giordano came to me and told me that you were so ill, that you had lost your child, it was as if...as if...." His voice died away, and he stared blindly at the tablecloth, rheumy eyes blinking hard. Gemma patted his hand helplessly. After a few moments he regained his composure. He said, "I ask you again, Gemma: Come with me to Firenze. Don't...don't spoil my last chance to do something that will carry weight with the Recording Angel."

Gemma shook her head. "No, thank you, Sebastian. I'm truly sorry to disappoint you, but I can't go back to Italy."

Sebastian scowled, pursing his lips, as he looked at her slyly. "You are stubborn," he observed, "and that is not a trait that I admire in women. But no matter, I am even more so. How else have I managed to live long past the time my doctors allotted me if not because I am too stubborn to die?" He paused, then he asked, "Does your refusal have something to do with this American man I have heard about, the one who came looking for you?"

Her relationship with Dave was so much a thing of the past that Gemma had to think for a moment before she realized whom Sebastian was talking about. She sighed ironically. "The last time I heard, Dave was living with my best friend—or at least, someone who used to be my best friend. A lot of things have changed recently...."

"What about your father? Perhaps if you talked to him—"

Sebastian's persistence was beginning to annoy Gemma. "My father," she interrupted coldly, "would probably be the first person to tell me to go back to Italy. 'A woman's place is with her husband,' he'd be bound to say. But the point is, my father's opinions have little or no bearing in my life anymore—and besides, my husband doesn't want me! Before I left Pietrasanta, Jordan put on a very touching show of concern for my welfare, but since then he hasn't contacted me even once."

"Giordano has been working very hard, Gemma," Sebastian said quietly.

"I'm sure he has. His work has always been the one thing that could get his undivided attention!" She sniffed, aware that she was perilously close to tears. "And if that's the way he wants it, that's the way he...he—'' She bit her lip to stifle the sob that threatened. She couldn't break down, not now, not here in a public restaurant. "Please, Sebastian," she begged huskily. "Don't do this to me, don't make me remember. I was getting over it. I was—"

"Then prove it's all over," Sebastian snapped. "Come back to Firenze with me for the dedication. Show the world that you're not afraid." He inhaled deeply, his eyes taking on a speculative gleam as he studied her set features. Suddenly Gemma had an intimation of what his business associates must have felt whenever he confronted them across a conference table. Sebastian said quietly, "If it will make you feel better, I'll tell you right now that Giordano will not be at the dedication. Once a piece is finished, he informs me, he never looks at it again; otherwise he would keep seeing things he wished he had done differently. So if you really don't want to see him, you won't have to. Also, Gemma, before we leave, I promise I will give you the return half of your airline ticket. That way you will know that you are free to come back to the United States whenever you want."

Gemma relaxed in her chair, brushing back a strand of her long blond hair that had escaped from the gold-and-gray plaid scarf that held it in place. She smiled wryly, admitting defeat. "You really are a cunning old devil, aren't you, Sebastian?" she murmured. "You'll say anything to get what you want."

His eyes gleamed. *"Cara,"* he drawled, "in the kind of life I've lived you don't survive any other way." Chuckling with satisfaction, he picked up a fork and attacked his cooling lasagna with renewed gusto.

THE CHAPEL was small and dark and beautiful, hung with crackled oil paintings and lighted by hundreds of flickering votive candles. From her seat in the rear pew, Gemma surveyed it curiously. She thought she could still detect in the discolored masonry lingering traces of the catastrophic floods that had devastated Florence in 1966, wiping out art treasures of inestimable value despite heroic efforts to save them. She glanced at the massive draped object standing in a flower-bedecked alcove toward the front of the church. Those things that had survived the flood were more precious than ever, and Gemma felt a shiver of pride, perhaps inexplicable under the circumstances, that a piece of Jordan's work was about to be cataloged with them.

The waiting congregation was sparse. Besides Sebastian and the two priests who conversed in hushed tones, Gemma counted six nuns, three tourists, and an old woman in a shabby cloth coat who fingered her rosary beads and droned in a monotone during the entire service. Gemma hoped wryly that Sebastian really was doing all this for the greater glory of God, because earthly publicity seemed to be a trifle light. Then, just as she chided herself for her irreverence, the chapel door banged open and two men strode in noisily, their eyes directed purposefully toward the swathed statue. Several heads turned to regard them reproachfully, and the men belatedly seemed to remember that they were in a church and lowered their voices. They took a seat in the pew opposite Gemma's, and as she watched, one produced a small notebook and began to write in it. After a few seconds she recognized him as a well-known New York art critic. The bulky zippered bag his associate carried identified him as a photographer. Gemma smiled ironically. Sebastian had obviously been at work again.

Of Jordan there was no sign. Gemma's spirits flagged, and she pulled her black lace mantilla, a present from Sebastian, forward over her fair hair. She closed her eyes and tried without success to meditate. She had thought Jordan would be there. Despite her assertions that she did not want to see him, despite Sebastian's promise that she would not have to see him, Gemma knew in her heart that Jordan was the only reason she had agreed to return to Italy. When the jet had touched down at Fiumicino, on the coast just outside Rome, Gemma had glanced around with breathless anticipation, hoping to spot her husband's dark head towering over the crowds in Leonardo da Vinci Airport. In Florence, when Gemma and Sebastian had disembarked from their first-class carriage on the *direttissima*, she had looked again, but it had been Sebastian's chauffeur who greeted them and drove them to Palazzo Buscaglia. At every turn Gemma was disappointed, and she was beginning to fear that unless she sought out Jordan herself, she would have to return to Colorado again without ever having seen him at all.

She wondered what he would say if she suddenly appeared on the steps of Villa Sogno Dolce—or what his mother would say. She had a hideously painful foreboding of the likely dialogue: "Hi, I'm back!"—"So what?" And the door would slam in her face.... And even if they did greet her civilly, what possible excuse could she use for her presence: "I just happened to be in the country and thought I'd drop by"? The only valid reason she had to see her husband again—apart from the irrelevant fact that she could not go on living without him—was to talk about their divorce, and Gemma did not think she could bear to seek out Jordan just so they could arrange to part permanently.

Voices emanating from the front of the church distracted Gemma from her brooding, and she lifted her head again, brushing the mantilla away from her face. The old scarf was very beautiful, and Gemma knew that the intricate black lace contrasted attractively with her sleek pale hair that had grown almost down to her shoulders, but it was at Sebastian's insistence that she wore it. "It belonged to my wife," he had explained simply, and after that she had not argued, although privately she doubted she would be able to do the mantilla justice. Somehow its graceful folds made her feel clumsy, and she suspected that only a Latin woman would have the innate panache to handle it properly. A woman like Sebastian's late wife—or Francesca. Gemma straightened her shoulders. The service was beginning. She knew the next few moments were going to be difficult for her, especially when the statue was unveiled and she had to look upon Jordan's newest creation, evidence of his continuing devotion to his beautiful mistress.

Gemma wondered what it would be like. The outline under the drape did not seem to resemble the statue that had been destroyed. That had been rather pyramidal, a traditional seated Madonna with the veiled head at the apex. The line of this one appeared longer and lower, suggesting a reclining figure, an unusual stance for this particular subject. Remembering the intense frustration Jordan had suffered when his first statue did not go well, forcing him to resort to a rather hackneyed treatment, Gemma thought with a sense of profound relief, *perhaps at last he has found his inspiration.* . . .

When Gemma heard one of the priests mention Jordan's name, she started, her head pounding as she glanced around quickly to see if he had suddenly appeared. But still there was no sign of Jordan. The priest was extolling the virtues of the famous sculptor, who, under the patronage of the renowned philanthropist Sebastian Buscaglia, had labored to create this magnificent work of art, a gift whose generosity would be remembered through the ages.

He pulled a cord, and the drape fell away, and Gemma and the other onlookers saw for the first time *Nostra Signora nella paglia*, the "Straw" Madonna.

A gasp of surprise went up from the congregation, followed by tender delighted sighs. For from the snowy purity of the finest Carrara marble Jordan had carved not a regal Queen of Heaven, but a very poignant and touching portrait of a young girl looking on her Child for the first time. She lay on a cloak spread over a pile of straw, weariness evident in the way she half raised herself on one elbow to get a better view of the baby nestled beside her. But even in stone her heart-shaped face seemed to glow with elation, and wonder and awe showed in the finger that stretched out tentatively to stroke a tiny cheek.

Profoundly moved, Gemma stared until she felt tears beading her lashes. As she brushed them away, she thought that Sebastian had been right, after all.

Even across the distance of the chapel, she could tell that the Madonna was the finest piece Jordan had ever done, surpassing even *Privilege*. Where before his work had been coolly sensual, now it was warm and sensitive. Gemma didn't know who the model was, but she most definitely wasn't Francesca, and she had inspired Jordan to heights he had never reached before.

The service continued for a while longer, but Gemma, gazing raptly at the statue, was only marginally aware of what was going on. She did notice the art critic scribbling madly in his little book, and when the photographer's camera flashed, she blinked. It was not until Sebastian tapped her lightly on the shoulder and murmured, "Gemma, my dear, it's all over now," that she realized the other people were filing out.

She looked up, her gray eyes wide, and said hesitantly, "Please, Sebastian, I'd really like to get a better look at it, if I may."

The old man smiled benignly. "Of course, *cara*. Take all the time you want. I'll wait out front." He shuffled away, his weight bearing heavily on his cane.

In the silence of the chapel Gemma approached the statue. The wavering candlelight gilded the cool surface of the marble, giving it warmth and movement. Gemma almost felt that she could reach out and touch living flesh.... As she studied the Madonna, she was humbled by the depth of Jordan's talent. He was a genius, a master artist, one of those whose gifts transcended the normal range of human capabilities. Surely a man who created beauty such as this could not be expected to adhere to the petty conventions of marriage, fidelity.

She frowned slightly, puzzled by a tantalizing familiarity about the face of the Madonna. She wondered again who the woman was—and why Jordan had not used Francesca. Had they argued? When Francesca went back to Paris, at her father's order, had Jordan been so angry that he had deliberately chosen another model just to spite her? Gemma bit her lip. No, there had to be another explanation. Work such as this did not derive from petty emotions like spite and jealousy. Whoever the model was, Jordan had been deeply, intensely involved with her; it showed in every line, every delicate cut of the chisel. There was something about those wide cheekbones and narrow jaw, the fine straight hair that flowed like silk.. . .

Gemma froze. "Oh, my God," she whispered hoarsely, clutching the mantilla under her chin with thin nervous fingers, too stunned at first to think or to hear the door of the chapel opening and quietly closing again. She blinked and stared, her heart pounding. She was afraid to believe the evidence of her eyes, fearful that it was her own fevered longing that was shaping the Madonna's face into her image, making her see in the Child's infant features a mixture of hers and Jordan's, the baby they did not have. She repeated softly, "Oh, dear God in—"

Behind her a deep voice murmured, "Gemma."

She whirled around, her face pale and startled as she stared up into Jordan's face. She could not read his expression. As she scanned his features hungrily, she noted that he looked taller, if that were possible, and thinner, too, and around his eyes and mouth weary lines were etched that had not been there when she left six months before. Her smooth brow wrinkled as she observed with surprise that a faint hint of gray was beginning to frost his wavy black hair at the temples.

"Gemma?" he murmured again when she did not reply.

The desire to fling herself into his arms was making it difficult for her to think properly, and she stammered stupidly, "But. . . but Sebastian told me that I wouldn't. . . wouldn't see you at the dedication."

Jordan's hard mouth curved up in a dry smile, making her heart race. "Well, you didn't see me, did you?" His voice was dark honey flowing over her raw nerves. He drawled, "Surely you must realize by now that Sebastian is more than willing to bend the truth if he thinks it necessary."

"But why should he think it so necessary to bring me here?"

"Because I asked him to," Jordan answered simply. "I had to make sure that you saw the statue." He hesitated, waiting for Gemma to speak. When she did not, he asked heavily, "So what do you think of it?"

She was so lost in the wonder of seeing him again, hearing him, that for a second she could not remember what he was talking about. "The. . . the statue," she choked, frowning. Reluctantly she half twisted to gaze at the exquisite work of art once more, and when at last she spoke, her voice was thick with emotion. "What can I say? What do you want me to say? It's beautiful. It's inspired. It's the best thing you've ever done." She took a deep breath and turned to look at him again. "But, Jordan," she said, confusion in her face, "I don't know what it means. Why did you use my face, and not... and not...?"

He regarded her with black eyes full of pain. One scarred hand lifted as if in supplication, then fell resolutely back to his side. He seemed determined to make her understand what he was trying to tell her before he touched her. "When you were in the hospital after your... accident," he began stiffly, each word an effort, "I would come at night and sit beside you while you slept." One brow arched at her obvious bewilderment. "You didn't know that, did you? Suora Letizia sneaked me in." His expression grew grave again. "For hours I'd just sit there and watch you. You looked so ill, so utterly unhappy, even in your sleep, and I kept thinking that if I hadn't been impatient, if only I hadn't been such a jealous, egotistical fool.... I promised myself I'd make it up to you. But whenever you were awake, you flatly refused to see me, and when we finally did meet, at the Riccis' house, it was the same old arguments and recriminations all over again. I knew then that there was no way I could ever make you believe the *words*. There was only one way to show you that I loved you."

Gemma stared. The flickering light of the votive candles shadowed the harsh planes of his face, hiding the expression in his deep-set eyes. "L-love me?" she stuttered, wondering if she was hearing things, if her frustrated longing for him was making her hallucinate. "B-but you don't...."

"I have loved you," he said, "since the evening of the first day we met, from the moment I stepped out of the hospital and saw you curled up on the edge of a marble fountain, weeping, with starlight in your hair. Even in your jeans you were so lovely, and so unaware, rather like the bronze dancing girl I discovered in that shop in Pisa. I wanted to be the one to discover *you*. I wanted to comfort you and caress you, and wrap your beauty around me like a cloak." He paused, his thin mouth twisting mirthlessly. He said, "I was so intent on what I wanted that I never paused to consider that you had a life of your own, with plans and ambitions—and loves—that had nothing at all to do with me."

Gemma watched him silently, warily, half-seduced by the enchantment of his words, yet afraid to believe him. She dug her fingers into the lace of her shawl to keep from reaching out to him, and Jordan noted dryly, "You're going to strangle yourself with that, if you're not careful." He caught her hands in his and gently pried them loose from the mantilla, holding them so that she could not prevent the black lace from sliding down to her shoulders, revealing the silken fall of her tresses, gleaming like satin in the candlelight. Jordan gasped, his grip tightening. "You've let your hair grow," he murmured in wonder, and he released one of her hands to lift reverent fingers to capture a silvery strand. "I always knew it would be...*bellissima*." Gemma shivered as his palm brushed against her temple, and Jordan's eyes narrowed. Both hands dropped away, leaving her bereft, and he asked with a sigh, "Do you believe anything I've told you?"

Gemma's small white teeth bit deeply into her lower lip. "I...I'd like to believe you," she admitted quietly, frank gray eyes trained on him, "but I...I don't see how I can, when...when Francesca...." Her voice faded, and she shrugged helplessly.

Jordan winced. "Are you going to blame me for

the past? Francesca and I had an affair a long time ago, I've never denied it. It meant very little to either of us—"

"But it must have meant something," Gemma interrupted, confused. "She told me she was your... your first lover."

Jordan's brows lifted in amused surprise. "Francesca said that?" he drawled ironically. "She always did underestimate me." His face darkened, and he grew serious again. "Yes, she and I were lovers when we were very young," he said candidly. "The whys and wherefores aren't important. From the time we were children, our parents hoped we would get married, but Francesca wanted to try a modeling career, and even then I could see beneath her beauty a...a certain hardness that troubled me. We parted by mutual consent. I haven't touched her since."

Gemma shook her head in bewilderment. "But... but she showed me a picture—"

"What picture?" Jordan demanded harshly.

"The...the one...." Cheeks flaming, Gemma haltingly described the erotic drawing.

Jordan clapped his hand to his forehead. "Oh, God," he groaned in disgust, "I had no idea she still had any of those."

He caught Gemma's thin shoulders and shook her lightly. "You idiot, couldn't you tell how old the picture was? I did a few of them years ago, but I thought they had all been destroyed. You must understand, the drawings were only an exercise in schoolboy vanity, like using myself for the male figure in *Privilege*." He looked at her searchingly. "I don't suppose you ever went into my private studio, did you?"

"No. You told me not to."

"And of course, once you were told to stay out, you never let your feminine curiosity—what an unusual woman you are, Gemma!" he declared, shaking his head. "I ought to know that by now." He sighed heavily. "I wish you had gone into the studio, just once. You would have seen the pictures I've drawn of you."

"Me?" Gemma exclaimed in disbelief.

"Yes, you. Hundreds of them, I think. From the day I met you, you have been my favorite subject. I've drawn you laughing, crying, working—making love.... Whenever we argued, whenever you accused me of treating you like an object rather than a person, I would fling off to my studio and attempt to put into pictures all the things I couldn't tell you in words."

She stared up at him, trying desperately to understand. "But why couldn't you tell me?"

He shrugged eloquently, his dark face wry. "Pride, I suppose—or jealousy. I loved you so much, and you were involved with Blanchard. No matter how much you pretended it was all over between the two of you, you insisted on seeing him privately, and it was to him that you turned when you needed help. Faced with competition like that, it was easier for me to stay quiet and let you think I was seeing Francesca because I wanted to, not because Sebastian asked me to use her as the model for the first statue."

Gemma looked down at the floor, her narrow shoulders slumping. So much pain, so many misunderstandings.... She muttered, "If you were only using Francesca as a...a red herring, then you weren't being very fair to me. She wants you back, you know.''

Jordan nodded grimly. ''Yes, I do know, but you needn't waste your sympathy on her. Francesca has never cared for anyone but herself, and her interest in me is strictly mercenary. Her career has been in a decline for several years—by the ridiculous standards of the fashion world, a woman in her thirties is long past her prime—and she has apparently decided that it would be prudent to settle down, preferably with me. My own mother hasn't helped matters any by making it clear that she concurs with Francesca's plans.''

The mention of Beatrice chilled Gemma, reminding her that the beautiful model was not the only obstacle to a reconciliation with Jordan. ''Your... your mother does like Francesca a lot,'' Gemma ventured.

''She's dazzled by her,'' Jordan said with a shrug. ''For one thing, Francesca has always been on her best behavior around my mother. For another—you have to understand, Gemma, *mamma* has always been very self-conscious about her appearance, her so-called homeliness. To her, Francesca's beauty makes her everything she ever wanted in a daughter-in-law, everything she felt she herself could not be. And of course, like so many mothers, having once picked what she considers to be the most appropriate candidate for my wife, *mamma* refuses to admit that I might have other plans entirely....'' He hesitated before adding quietly, ''If you're worried about encountering my mother again, Gemma, you needn't be. She isn't here, she isn't even in Italy now. I sent her to Connecticut on an extended visit, to see Sylvia and her family.''

Gemma looked puzzled. "I thought she swore she'd never go back?"

"She did. But after a great deal of...discussion, I convinced her that it was high time she quit brooding about something that happened over thirty-five years ago. She needs to renew her acquaintance with the country she abandoned, and with her grandchildren."

At the mention of children, Gemma's eyes were drawn irresistibly to the figure of the Madonna and Child, and she felt rueful tears well up in her eyes. She wondered if Jordan, so carefully explaining away the twin problems of Francesca and his mother, had any notion of her true feelings, the core of her pain. Could he even begin to imagine how she felt each time she remembered that if only things had happened differently, if only she had not had the accident, she might at this very moment be gazing at her own baby for the first time. As she gnawed at her knuckle, a deep rasping sob forced its way through her constricted throat.

Suddenly his arms were around her, strong and familiar, clasping her tightly against the hard length of his body. Even in her anguish she felt herself being seduced by his comforting familiar warmth, and her thin arms crept around his waist, under his coat. She could feel the tension in him as she clung to him, the muscles of his back rigid under her stroking fingertips, her cries muffled by the lapels of his jacket. As his hands began to move restlessly over her, she felt him tremble, and he buried his face in his bright hair. "Don't cry," he groaned. "Gemma, there can be more babies—if you want. There can be more of everything—if only you want."

It had been so very long since he touched her, and she was swiftly losing herself in his nearness, responding with the force of needs and desires too long denied, tempted to push all nagging doubts aside and give herself up to the ecstasy of his embrace. Surely it was enough that he claimed he loved her. She ached with the effort to pull away from him, but she knew there were still things that had to be said, issues that had to be faced before she could succumb to the sensual dream he was weaving around them. Blinking away the moisture beading her lashes, she stammered, "Jordan, please, I . . . I can't think when you . . . ."

"Don't think," he murmured. "Just listen." One large hand captured her chin and tilted her head so that she had to gaze directly into his dark eyes. In the uncertain light of the chapel the gold rim around his black irises seemed to glow with inner fire. "Listen to me," he whispered again, more softly, his breath hot on her cheeks. "I'm asking—not ordering or demanding, but *asking*—you to forgive me my pigheaded selfishness and come back to me."

With amazement she heard his pleading words, the words that had tormented her dreams nightly during the endless months since she had left him: "Come back to me. . . ." Oh, God, if only he had known how much she had suffered, thinking he did not want her! When she tried to speak, to tell him, he placed one long finger across her lips, hushing her. He said, "No, don't say anything. I know you're afraid. When we met before, you were so elusive, like a butterfly, and I was a greedy boy, grabbing at you and crushing you between my hands when you tried to fly away. You think that if you stay with me, it will all happen again, that I'll try to take over your life, your career. I can't prove to you that I've changed; I can only promise that from now on, how you choose to use your artistic talent will be entirely your decision, whether I agree with it or not.''

He hesitated once more, and this time when he spoke again, the humility in his deep voice shook her. Jordan said, ''Gemma, I know that despite this physical attraction we have between us, you don't love me—and indeed, why should you? All I've ever done is hurt you. I don't know if there is any way I can nurture that attraction so that someday you might learn to feel about me the way I feel for you, but that's a chance I must take if I am to survive.'' His voice thickened, and aware that he was deliberately revealing his vulnerability to her, at last Gemma truly believed that he meant what he was saying. He choked, ''You have to come back to me, Gemma, because without you, the career of Jordan di Mario is at an end. Without you, my darling, for me there will never be any inspiration, any art, any beauty in anything, ever again.''

Gemma stared, her gray eyes wide and gleaming. In the wavering candlelight her pale face began to glow. ''How,'' she mused huskily, her low-pitched voice warm and consciously provocative, ''can any man be so artistically sensitive and insightful and still be so incredibly blind? Oh, Jordan, haven't you figured out yet why I go up in flames whenever you touch me? I love you. I've loved you since—I don't know when, but for such a long, long time.''

He studied her face with eyes filled with yearning

uncertainty. "Gemma?" he grated hoarsely. "Are you sure?"

For the first time in their relationship, Gemma felt in control. "Yes, darling, I'm sure," she laughed, reaching up to pull his head down to hers, "and don't you think we've talked long enough?"

After that there was no need for words, and they were lost in the wonder of rediscovering each other. Twining together, they kissed hungrily, their mouths probing and biting, as if only by devouring one another could they satisfy the feverish craving that engulfed them both. Jordan molded her slender body against his, making her hotly aware of his need of her, and she gloried in the brush of his long fingers against her breast, her hip. Only when she felt him fumbling with her zipper did she remember where they were. With a sheepish smile, Gemma pulled away. Jordan tried to draw her back into his embrace. "Don't tease me," he groaned distractedly. "If you only knew how much I've needed you, the hell it's been without you all these long lonely months...."

"Oh, my love," Gemma mumbled breathlessly, her lips wet and swollen, "for me, too. I thought I'd die of wanting you...." She hesitated. "But...but, darling, a church isn't exactly the proper place for...."

Jordan lifted his head and glanced around the dark interior of the chapel with eyes still half-glazed with passion. "No," he agreed wryly, shaking his head as if to clear it, "you're right. It's definitely time for us to get out of here. Let's go home."

Gemma puzzled. "Home? You mean Palazzo—"

"No," he said gently. "Sebastian doesn't expect us to stay with him. I mean home, the villa in Pietrasanta."

Dizzy with desire, all she could think about was the endless drive from Florence to the little town near the coast, the hours before she and Jordan could be alone at last and free to love each other. "But that's such a long way away..." she wailed in frustration.

At the disappointment evident in her flushed face, Jordan smiled tenderly. "I know, *carina*. How I'm going to be able to drive, when all I want is to lie with you naked in my arms.... But don't worry, we'll be there faster than you can imagine." With tantalizing delicacy he brushed his lips across hers and curled his long fingers around her slim wrist. He grinned slyly as he murmured, "The Ferrari I have now has an even more powerful engine than the one that was wrecked. Just watch me set a new speed record." For a second their fingers wove tightly, intimately, forming a bond as unbreakable as the silent vow that passed between them. Then with a mutual sigh they turned, and hand in hand they strode out of the chapel.